Daireen-Complete

by

Frank Frankfort Moore

Double 9
BOOKS

Daireen-Complete

by Frank Frankfort Moore

ISBN: 978-93-60461-56-0

Published by

DOUBLE 9 BOOKS

2/13-B, Ansari Road
Daryaganj, New Delhi – 110002
info@double9books.com
www.double9books.com
Tel. 011-40042856

ABOUT THE AUTHOR

Frank Frankfort Moore was an Irish writer, journalist, and playwright who lived from 1855 to 1931. He was a Protestant from Belfast and a unionist. But during the years of Home Rule protests, his historical fiction did not shy away from themes of Irish Catholics being pushed out of their homes. Moore was born in Limerick but grew up in Belfast. He remembers seeing religious rioters being chased by dragoons with sabers drawn in the street below his nursery window as his oldest memory. It was a pretty well-off family; Moore's father was a successful clockmaker and jeweler, and French and German were spoken. But because the older Moore was a member of the very strict Open Brethren sect, he wanted his kids to only read religious and educational books. The preacher Michael Paget Baxter often went there. He said that Emperor Napoleon III was the Beast from the Book of Revelation. Moore went to school at the Royal Belfast Academical Institution and quickly learned to take a step back from his father's views. He remembered that some slanderous lines called "Mr. Baxter and the Beast" were going around, "proving" that Baxter was the Antichrist.

CONTENTS

CHAPTER I

A king
Upon whose property...
A damn'd defeat was made.

A king
Of shreds and patches.
The very conveyances of his lands will hardly lie in this box; and must the inheritor himself have no more? *Hamlet.*

MY son," said The Macnamara with an air of grandeur, "my son, you've forgotten what's due" — he pronounced it "jew" — "to yourself, what's due to your father, what's due to your forefathers that bled," and The Macnamara waved his hand gracefully; then, taking advantage of its proximity to the edge of the table, he made a powerful but ineffectual attempt to pull himself to his feet. Finding himself baffled by the peculiar formation of his chair, and not having a reserve of breath to draw upon for another exertion, he concealed his defeat under a pretence of feeling indifferent on the matter of rising, and continued fingering the table-edge as if endeavouring to read the initials which had been carved pretty deeply upon the oak by a humorous guest just where his hand rested. "Yes, my son, you've forgotten the blood of your ancient sires. You forget, my son, that you're the offspring of the Macnamaras and the O'Dermots, kings of Munster in the days when there were kings, and when the Geralds were walking about in blue paint in the woods of the adjacent barbarous island of Britain" — The Macnamara said "barbarious."

"The Geralds have been at Suanmara for four hundred years," said Standish quickly, and in the tone of one resenting an aspersion.

"Four hundred years!" cried The Macnamara scornfully. "Four hundred years! What's four hundred years in the existence of a family?" He felt that this was the exact instant for him to rise grandly to his feet, so once more he made the essay, but without a satisfactory result. As a matter of fact, it is almost impossible to release oneself from the embrace of a heavy oak chair when the seat has been formed of light cane, and this cane has become tattered.

"I don't care about the kings of Munster—no, not a bit," said Standish, taking a mean advantage of the involuntary captivity of his father to insult him.

"I'm dead sick hearing about them. They never did anything for me."

The Macnamara threw back his head, clasped his hands over his bosom, and gazed up to the cobwebs of the oak ceiling. "My sires—shades of the Macnamaras and the O'Dermots, visit not the iniquity of the children upon the fathers," he exclaimed. And then there came a solemn pause which the hereditary monarch felt should impress his son deeply; but the son was not deceived into fancying that his father was overcome with emotion; he knew very well that his father was only thinking how with dignity he could extricate himself from his awkward chair, and so he was not deeply affected. "My boy, my boy," the father murmured in a weak voice, after his apostrophe to the shades of the ceiling, "what do you mean to do? Keep nothing secret from me, Standish; I'll stand by you to the last."

"I don't mean to do anything. There is nothing to be done—at least—yet."

"What's that you say? Nothing to be done? You don't mean to say you've been thrifling with the young-woman's affection? Never shall a son of mine, and the offspring of The Macnamaras and the——"

"How can you put such a question to me?" said the young man indignantly. "I throw back the insinuation in your teeth, though you are my father. I would scorn to trifle with the feelings of any lady, not to speak of Miss Gerald, who is purer than the lily that blooms——"

"In the valley of Shanganagh—that's what you said in the poem, my boy; and it's true, I'm sure."

"But because you find a scrap of poetry in my writing you fancy that I forget my—my duty—my——"

"Mighty sires, Standish; say the word at once, man. Well, maybe I was too hasty, my boy; and if you tell me that you don't love her now, I'll forgive all."

"Never," cried the young man, with the vehemence of a mediaeval burning martyr. "I swear that I love her, and that it would be impossible for me ever to think of any one else."

"This is cruel—cruel!" murmured The Macnamara, still thinking how he could extricate himself from his uneasy seat. "It is cruel for a father, but it must be borne—it must be borne. If our ancient house is to degenerate to a Saxon's level, I'm not to blame. Standish, my boy, I forgive you. Take your father's hand."

He stretched out his hand, and the young man took it. The grasp of The Macnamara was fervent—it did not relax until he had accomplished the end he had in view, and had pulled himself to his feet. Standish was about to leave the room, when his father, turning his eyes away from the tattered cane-work of the chair, that now closely resembled the star-trap in a pantomime, cried:

"Don't go yet, sir. This isn't to end here. Didn't you tell me that your affection was set upon this daughter of the Geralds?"

"What is the use of continuing such questions?" cried the young man impatiently. The reiteration by his father of this theme—the most sacred to Standish's ears—was exasperating.

"No son of mine will be let sneak out of an affair like this," said the hereditary monarch. "We may be poor, sir, poor as a bogtrotter's dog——"

"And we are," interposed Standish bitterly.

"But we have still the memories of the grand old times to live upon, and the name of Macnamara was never joined with anything but honour. You love that daughter of the Geralds—you've confessed it; and though the family she belongs to is one of these mushroom growths that's springing up around us in three or four hundred years—ay, in spite of the upstart family she belongs to, I'll give my consent to your happiness. We mustn't be proud in these days, my son, though the blood of kings—eh, where do ye mean to be going before I've done?"

"I thought you had finished."

"Did you? well, you're mistaken. You don't stir from here until you've promised me to make all the amends in your power to this daughter of the Geralds."

"Amends? I don't understand you."

"Don't you tell me you love her?"

The refrain which was so delightful to the young man's ears when he uttered it alone by night under the pure stars, sounded terrible when reiterated by his father. But what could he do—his father was now upon his feet?

"What is the use of profaning her name in this fashion?" cried Standish. "If I said I loved her, it was only when you accused me of it and threatened to turn me out of the house."

"And out of the house you'll go if you don't give me a straightforward answer."

"I don't care," cried Standish doggedly. "What is there here that should make me afraid of your threat? I want to be turned out. I'm sick of this place."

"Heavens! what has come over the boy that he has taken to speaking like this? Are ye demented, my son?"

"No such thing," said Standish. "Only I have been thinking for the past few days over my position here, and I have come to the conclusion that I couldn't be worse off."

"You've been thinking, have you?" asked The Macnamara contemptuously. "You depart so far from the traditions of your family? Well, well," he continued in an altered tone, after a pause, "maybe I've been a bad father to you, Standish, maybe I've neglected my duty; maybe— —" here The Macnamara felt for his pocket-handkerchief, and having found it, he waved it spasmodically, and was about to throw himself into his chair when he recollected its defects and refrained, even though he was well aware that he was thereby sacrificing much of the dramatic effect up to which he had been working.

"No, father; I don't want to say that you have been anything but good to me, only— —"

"But I say it, my son," said The Macnamara, mopping his brows earnestly with his handkerchief. "I've been a selfish old man, haven't I, now?"

"No, no, anything but that. You have only been too good. You have given me all I ever wanted—except— —"

"Except what? Ah, I know what you mean—except money. Ah, your reproach is bitter—bitter; but I deserve it all, I do."

"No, father: I did not say that at all."

"But I'll show you, my boy, that your father can be generous once of a time. You love her, don't you, Standish?"

His father had laid his hand upon his shoulder now, and spoke the words in a sentimental whisper, so that they did not sound so profane as before.

"I worship the ground she treads on," his son answered, tremulous with eagerness, a girlish blush suffusing his cheeks and invading the curls upon his forehead, as he turned his head away.

"Then I'll show you that I can be generous. You shall have her, Standish Macnamara; I'll give her to you, though she is one of the new families. Put on your hat, my boy, and come out with me."

"Are you going out?" said Standish.

"I am, so order round the car, if the spring is mended. It should be, for I gave Eugene the cord for it yesterday."

Standish made a slight pause at the door as if about to put another question to his father; after a moment of thoughtfulness, however, he passed out in silence.

When the door had closed—or, at least, moved upon its hinges, for the shifting some years previously of a portion of the framework made its closing an impossibility—The Macnamara put his hands deep into his pockets, jingling the copper coins and the iron keys that each receptacle contained. It is wonderful what suggestions of wealth may be given by the judicious handling of a few coppers and a bunch of keys, and the imagination of The Macnamara being particularly sanguine, he felt that the most scrupulous moneylender would have offered him at that moment, on the security of his personal appearance and the sounds of his jingling metal, any sum of money he might have named. He rather wished that such a moneylender would drop in. But soon his thoughts changed. The jingling in his pockets became modified, resembling in tone an unsound peal of muffled bells; he shook his head several times.

"Macnamara, my lad, you were too weak," he muttered to himself. "You yielded too soon; you should have stood out for a while; but how could I stand out when I was sitting in that trap?"

He turned round glaring at the chair which he blamed as the cause of his premature relaxation. He seemed measuring its probable capacities of resistance; and then he raised his right foot and scrutinised the boot that covered it. It was not a trustworthy boot, he knew. Once more he glanced towards the chair, then with a sigh he put his foot down and walked to the window.

Past the window at this instant the car was moving, drawn by a humble-minded horse, which in its turn was drawn by a boy in a faded and dilapidated livery that had evidently been originally made for a remarkably tall man. The length of the garment, though undeniably embarrassing in the region of the sleeves, had still its advantages, not the least of which was the concealment of a large portion of the bare legs of the wearer; it was obvious too that when he should mount his seat, the boy's bare feet would be effectually hidden, and from a livery-wearing standpoint this would certainly be worth consideration.

The Macnamara gave a critical glance through the single transparent pane of the window—the pane had been honoured above its fellows by a polishing about six weeks before—and saw that the defective spring of the vehicle had been repaired. Coarse twine had been employed for this purpose; but as this material, though undoubtedly excellent in its way, and of very general utility, is hardly the most suitable for restoring a steel spring to its original condition of elasticity, there was a good deal of jerkiness apparent in the motion of the car, especially when the wheels turned into the numerous ruts of the drive. The boy at the horse's head was, however, skilful in avoiding the deeper depths, and the animal was also most considerate in its gait, checking within itself any unseemly outburst of spirit and restraining every propensity to break into a trot.

"Now, father, I'm ready," said Standish, entering with his hat on.

"Has Eugene brushed my hat?" asked The Macnamara.

"My black hat, I mean?"

"I didn't know you were going to wear it today, when you were only taking a drive," said Standish with some astonishment.

"Yes, my boy, I'll wear the black hat, please God, so get it brushed; and tell him that if he uses the blacking-brush this time I'll have his life." Standish went out to deliver these messages; but The Mac-namara stood in the centre of the big room pondering over some weighty question.

"I will," he muttered, as though a better impulse of his nature were in the act of overcoming an unworthy suggestion. "Yes, I will; when I'm wearing the black hat things should be levelled up to that standard; yes, I will."

Standish entered in a few minutes with his father's hat—a tall, old-fashioned silk hat that had at one time, pretty far remote, been black. The Macnamara put it on carefully, after he had just touched the edges with his coat-cuff to remove the least suspicion of dust; then he strode out followed by his son.

The car was standing at the hall door, and Eugene the driver was beside it, giving a last look to the cordage of the spring. When The Macnamara, however, appeared, he sprang up and touched his forehead, with a smile of remarkable breadth. The Macnamara stood impassive, and in dignified silence, looking first at the horse, then at the car, and finally at the boy Eugene, while Standish remained at the other side. Eugene bore the gaze of the hereditary monarch pretty well on the whole, conscious of the abundance of his own coat. The scrutiny of The Macnamara passed gradually down the somewhat irregular row of buttons until it rested on the protruding bare feet of the boy. Then after another moment of impressive silence, he waved one hand gracefully towards the door, saying:

"Eugene, get on your boots."

CHAPTER II

Let the world take note
You are the most immediate to our throne;
And with no less nobility of love
Than that which dearest father bears his son
Do I impart toward you.

How is it that the clouds still hang on you?

Affection! pooh! you speak like a green girl.
Hamlet.

WHEN the head of a community has, after due deliberation, resolved upon the carrying out of any bold social step, he may expect to meet with the opposition that invariably obstructs the reformer's advance; so that one is tempted—nay, modern statesmanship compels one—to believe that secrecy until a projected design is fully matured is a wise, or at least an effective, policy. The military stratagem of a surprise is frequently attended with good results in dealing with an enemy, and as a friendly policy why should it not succeed?

This was, beyond a question, the course of thought pursued by The Macnamara before he uttered those words to Eugene. He had not given the order without careful deliberation, but when he had come to the conclusion that circumstances demanded the taking of so bold a step, he had not hesitated in his utterance.

Eugene was indeed surprised, and so also was Standish. The driver took off his hat and passed his fingers through his hair, looking down to his bare feet, for he was in the habit of getting a few weeks of warning before a similar order to that just uttered by his master was given to him.

"Do you hear, or are you going to wait till the horse has frozen to the sod?" inquired The Macnamara; and this brought the mind of the boy out of the labyrinth of wonder into which it had strayed. He threw down the whip and the reins, and, tucking up the voluminous skirts of his coat, ran round the house, commenting briefly as he went along on the remarkable aspect things were assuming.

Entering the kitchen from the rear, where an old man and two old women were sitting with short pipes alight, he cried, "What's the world comin' to at all? I've got to put on me boots."

"Holy Saint Bridget," cried a pious old woman, "he's to put on his brogues! An' is it The Mac has bid ye, Eugene?"

"Sorra a sowl ilse. So just shake a coal in iviry fut to thaw thim a bit, alana."

While the old woman was performing this operation over the turf fire, there was some discussion as to what was the nature of the circumstances that demanded such an unusual proceeding on the part of The Macnamara.

"It's only The Mac himsilf that sames to know—. knock the ashes well about the hale, ma'am—for Masther Standish was as much put out as mesilf whin The Mac says—nivir moind the toes, ma'am, me fut'll nivir go more nor halfways up the sowl—says he, 'Git on yer boots;' as if it was the ordinarist thing in the world;—now I'll thry an' squaze me fut in." And he took the immense boot so soon as the fiery ashes had been emptied from its cavity.

"The Mac's pride'll have a fall," remarked the old man in the corner sagaciously.

"I shouldn't wondher," said Eugene, pulling on one of the boots. "The spring is patched with hemp, but it's as loikely to give way as not—holy Biddy, ye've left a hot coal just at the instep that's made its way to me bone!" But in spite of this catastrophe, the boy trudged off to the car, his coat's tails flapping like the foresail of a yacht brought up to the wind. Then he cautiously mounted his seat in front of the car, letting a boot protrude effectively on each side of the narrow board. The Macnamara and his son, who had exchanged no word during the short absence of Eugene in the kitchen, then took their places, the horse was aroused from its slumber, and they all passed down the long dilapidated avenue and through the broad entrance between the great mouldering pillars overclung with ivy and strange tangled weeds, where a gate had once been, but where now only a rough pole was drawn across to prevent the trespass of strange animals.

Truly pitiful it was to see such signs of dilapidation everywhere around this demesne of Innishdermot. The house itself was an immense, irregularly built, rambling castle. Three-quarters of it was in utter ruin, but it had needed the combined efforts of eight hundred years of time and a thousand of Cromwell's soldiers to reduce the walls to the condition in which they were at present. The five rooms of the building that were habitable belonged to a comparatively new wing, which was supported on the eastern side by the gable of a small chapel, and on the western by the wall of a great round tower which stood like a demolished sugar-loaf high above all the ruins, and lodged a select number of immense owls whose eyesight was so extremely sensitive, it required an unusual amount of darkness for its preservation.

This was the habitation of The Macnamaras, hereditary kings of Munster, and here it was that the existing representative of the royal family lived with his only son, Standish O'Dermot Macnamara. In front of the pile stretched a park, or rather what had once been a park, but which was now wild and tangled as any wood. It straggled down to the coastway of the lough, which, with as many windings as a Norwegian fjord, brought the green waves of the Atlantic for twenty miles between coasts a thousand feet in height—coasts which were black and precipitous and pierced with a hundred mighty caves about the headlands of the entrance, but which became wooded and more gentle of slope towards the narrow termination of the basin. The entire of one coastway, from the cliffs that broke the wild buffet of the ocean rollers, to the little island that lay at the narrowing of the waters, was the property of The Macnamara. This was all that had been left to the house which had once held sway over two hundred miles of coastway, from the kingdom of Kerry to Achill Island, and a hundred miles of riverway. Pasturages the richest of the world, lake-lands the most beautiful, mountains the grandest, woods and moors—all had been ruled over by The Macnamaras, and of all, only a strip of coastway and a ruined castle remained to the representative of the ancient house, who was now passing on a jaunting-car between the dilapidated pillars at the entrance to his desolate demesne.

On a small hill that came in sight so soon as the car had passed from under the gaunt fantastic branches that threw themselves over the wall at the roadside, as if making a scrambling clutch at something indefinite in the air, a ruined tower stood out in relief against the blue sky of this August day. Seeing the ruin in this land of ruins The Macnamara sighed heavily— too heavily to allow of any one fancying that his emotion was natural.

"Ah, my son, the times have changed," he said. "Only a few years have passed—six hundred or so—since young Brian Macnamara left that very castle to ask the daughter of the great Desmond of the Lake in marriage. How did he go out, my boy?"

"You don't mean that we are now——"

"How did he go out?" again asked The Macnamara, interrupting his son's words of astonishment. "He went out of that castle with three hundred and sixty-five knights—for he had as many knights as there are days in the year."—Here Eugene, who only caught the phonetic sense of this remarkable fact regarding young Brian Macnamara, gave a grin, which his master detected and chastised by a blow from his stick upon the mighty livery coat.

"But, father," said Standish, after the trifling excitement occasioned by this episode had died away—"but, father, we are surely not going——"

"Hush, my son. The young Brian and his retinue went out one August day like this; and with him was the hundred harpers, the fifty pipers, and the thirteen noble chiefs of the Lakes, all mounted on the finest of steeds, and the morning sun glittering on their gems and jewels as if they had been drops of dew. And so they rode to the castle of Desmond, and when he shut the gates in the face of the noble retinue and sent out a haughty message that, because the young Prince Brian had slain The Desmond's two sons, he would not admit him as a suitor to his daughter, the noble young prince burnt The Desmond's tower to the ground and carried off the daughter, who, as the bards all agree, was the loveliest of her sex. Ah, that was a wooing worthy of The Mac-namaras. These are the degenerate days when a prince of The Macnamaras goes on a broken-down car to ask the hand of a daughter of the Geralds." Here a low whistle escaped from Eugene, and he looked down at his boots just as The Macnamara delivered another rebuke to him of the same nature as the former.

"But we're not going to—to—Suanmara!" cried Standish in dismay.

"Then where are we going, maybe you'll tell me?" said his father.

"Not there—not there; you never said you were going there. Why should we go there?"

"Just for the same reason that your noble forefather Brian Macnamara went to the tower of The Desmond," said the father, leaving it to Standish to determine which of the noble acts of the somewhat impetuous young prince their present excursion was designed to emulate.

"Do you mean to say, father, that—that—oh, no one could think of such a thing as——"

"My son," said the hereditary monarch coolly, "you made a confession to me this morning that only leaves me one course. The honour of The Macnamaras is at stake, and as the representative of the family it's my duty to preserve it untarnished. When a son of mine confesses his affection for a lady, the only course he can pursue towards her is to marry her, let her even be a Gerald."

"I won't go on such a fool's errand," cried the young man. "She—her grandfather—they would laugh at such a proposal."

"The Desmond laughed, and what came of it, my boy?" said the Macnamara sternly.

"I will not go on any farther," cried Standish, unawed by the reference to the consequences of the inopportune hilarity of The Desmond. "How could you think that I would have the presumption to fancy for the least moment that—that—she—that is—that they would listen to—to anything I might say? Oh, the idea is absurd!"

"My boy, I am the head of the line of The Munster Macnamaras, and the head always decides in delicate matters like this. I'll not have the feeling's of the lady trifled with even by a son of my own. Didn't you confess all to me?"

"I will not go on," the young man cried again. "She—that is—they will think that we mean an affront—and it is a gross insult to her—to them— to even fancy that—oh, if we were anything but what we are there would be some hope—some chance; if I had only been allowed my own way I might have won her in time—long years perhaps, but still some time. But now— — "

"Recreant son of a noble house, have you no more spirit than a Saxon?" said the father, trying to assume a dignified position, an attempt that the jerking of the imperfect spring of the vehicle frustrated. "Mightn't the noblest family in Europe think it an honour to be allied with The Munster Macnamaras, penniless though we are?"

"Don't go to-day, father," said Standish, almost piteously; "no, not to-day. It is too sudden—my mind is not made up."

"But mine is, my boy. Haven't I prepared everything so that there can be no mistake?"—here he pressed his tall hat more firmly upon his forehead, and glanced towards Eugene's boots that projected a considerable way beyond the line of the car. "My boy," he continued, "The Macnamaras descend to ally themselves with any other family only for the sake of keeping up the race. It's their solemn duty.'

"I'll not go on any farther on such an errand—I will not be such a fool," said Standish, making a movement on his side of the car.

"My boy," said The Macnamara unconcernedly, "my boy, you can get off at any moment; your presence will make no difference in the matter. The matrimonial alliances of The Macnamaras are family matters, not individual. The head of the race only is accountable to posterity for the consequences of the acts of them under him. I'm the head of the race." He removed his hat and looked upward, somewhat jerkily, but still impressively.

Standish Macnamara's eyes flashed and his hands clenched themselves over the rail of the car, but he did not make any attempt to carry out his threat of getting off. He did not utter another word. How could he? It was torture to him to hear his father discuss beneath the ear of the boy Eugene such a question as his confession of love for a certain lady. It was terrible for him to observe the expression of interest which was apparent upon the ingenuous face of Eugene, and to see his nods of approval at the words of The Macnamara. What could poor Standish do beyond closing his teeth very tightly and clenching his hands madly as the car jerked its way along the coast of Lough Suangorm, in view of a portion of the loveliest scenery in the world?

CHAPTER III

How weary, stale, flat and unprofitable
Seem to me all the uses of this world.

Gather by him, as he is behaved,
If't be the affliction of his love or no
That thus he suffers for.

Break my heart, for I must hold my tongue.
Hamlet.

THE road upon which the car was driving was made round an elevated part of the coast of the lough. It curved away from where the castle of The Macnamaras was situated on one side of the water, to the termination of the lough. It did not slope downwards in the least at any part, but swept on to the opposite lofty shore, five hundred feet above the great rollers from the Atlantic that spent themselves amongst the half-hidden rocks.

The car jerked on in silence after The Macnamara had spoken his impressive sentence. Standish's hands soon relaxed their passionate hold upon the rail of the car, and, in spite of his consciousness of being twenty-three years of age, he found it almost impossible to restrain his tears of mortification from bursting their bonds. He knew how pure—how fervent—how exhaustless was the love that filled all his heart. He had been loving, not without hope, but without utterance, for years, and now all the fruit of his patience—of his years of speechlessness—would be blighted by the ridiculous action of his father. What would now be left for him in the world? he asked himself, and the despairing tears of his heart gave him his only answer.

He was on the seaward side of the car, which was now passing out of the green shade of the boughs that for three miles overhung the road. Then as the curve of the termination of the lough was approached, the full panorama of sea and coast leapt into view, with all the magical glamour those wizards Motion and Height can enweave round a scene. Far beneath, the narrow band of blue water lost itself amongst the steep cliffs. The double coasts of the lough that were joined at the point of vision, broadened out in undulating heights towards the mighty headlands of the entrance, that lifted up their hoary brows as the lion-waves of the Atlantic leapt between them and crouched in unwieldy bulk at their bases. Far away stretched that ocean, its horizon lost in mist; and above the line of rugged coast-cliff arose mountains—mighty masses tumbled together in black confusion, like Titanic gladiators locked in the close throes of the wrestle.

Never before had the familiar scene so taken Standish in its arms, so to speak, as it did now. He felt it. He looked down at the screen islands of the lough encircled with the floss of the moving waters; he looked along the slopes of the coasts with the ruins of ancient days on their summits, then his eyes went out to where the sun dipped towards the Atlantic, and he felt no more that passion of mortification which his reflections had aroused. Quickly as it had sprung into view the scene dissolved, as the car entered a glen, dim in the shadow of a great hill whose slope, swathed in purple heather to its highest peak, made a twilight at noon-day to all beneath. In the distance of the winding road beyond the dark edge of the mountain were seen the gray ridges of another range running far inland. With the twilight shadow of the glen, the shadow seemed to come again over the mind of Standish. He gave himself up to his own sad thoughts, and when, from a black tarn amongst the low pine-trees beneath the road, a tall heron rose and fled silently through the silent air to the foot of the slope, he regarded it ominously, as he would have done a raven.

There they sat speechless upon the car. The Macnamara, who was a short, middle-aged man with a rather highly-coloured face, and features that not even the most malignant could pronounce of a Roman or even of a Saxon type, was sitting in silent dignity of which he seemed by no means unconscious Standish, who was tall, slender almost to a point of lankness, and gray-eyed, was morosely speechless, his father felt. Nature had not given The Macnamara a son after his own heart. The young man's features, that had at one time showed great promise of developing into the pure Milesian, had not fulfilled the early hope they had raised in his father's bosom; they had within the past twelve years exhibited a downward tendency that was not in keeping with the traditions of The Macnamaras. If the direction of the caressing hand of Nature over the features of the family should be reversed, what would remain to distinguish The Macnamaras from their Saxon invaders? This was a question whose weight had for some time oppressed the representative of the race; and he could only quiet his apprehension by the assurance which forced itself upon his mind, that Nature would never persist in any course prejudicial to her own interests in the maintenance of an irreproachable type of manhood.

Then it was a great grief to the father to become aware of the fact that the speech of Standish was all unlike his own in accent; it was, indeed, terribly like the ordinary Saxon speech—at least it sounded so to The Macnamara, whose vowels were diphthongic to a marked degree. But of course the most distressing reflection of the head of the race had reference to the mental disqualifications of his son to sustain the position which he would some day have to occupy as The Macnamara; for Standish had of late shown a tendency to accept the position accorded to him by the enemies of his race, and to allow that there existed a certain unwritten statute of limitations in the maintenance of the divine right of monarchs. He actually seemed to be under the impression that because nine hundred years had elapsed since a Macnamara had been the acknowledged king of Munster, the claim to be regarded as a royal family should not be strongly urged. This was very terrible to The Macnamara. And now he reflected upon all these matters as he held in a fixed and fervent grasp the somewhat untrustworthy rail of the undoubtedly shaky vehicle.

Thus in silence the car was driven through the dim glen, until the slope on the seaward-side of the road dwindled away and once more the sea came in sight; and, with the first glimpse of the sea, the square tower of an old, though not an ancient, castle that stood half hidden by trees at the base of the purple mountain. In a few minutes the car pulled up at the entrance gate to a walled demesne.

"Will yer honours git off here?" asked Eugene, preparing to throw the reins down.

"Never!" cried The Macnamara emphatically. "Never will the head of the race descend to walk up to the door of a foreigner. Drive up to the very hall, Eugene, as the great Brian Macnamara would have done."

"An' it's hopin' I am that his car-sphrings wouldn't be mindid with hemp," remarked the boy, as he pulled the horse round and urged his mild career through the great pillars at the entrance.

Everything about this place gave signs of having been cared for. The avenue was long, but it could be traversed without any risk of the vehicle being lost in the landslip of a rut. The grass around the trees, though by no means trimmed at the edges, was still not dank with weeds, and the trees themselves, if old, had none of the gauntness apparent in all the timber about the castle of The Macnamara. As the car went along there was visible every now and again the flash of branching antlers among the green foliage, and more than once the stately head of a red deer appeared gazing at the visitors, motionless, as if the animal had been a painted statue.

The castle, opposite whose black oak door Eugene at last dropped his reins, was by no means an imposing building. It was large and square, and at one wing stood the square ivy-covered tower that was seen from the road.

Above it rose the great dark mountain ridge, and in front rolled the Atlantic, for the trees prevented the shoreway from being seen.

"Eugene, knock at the door of the Geralds," said The Macnamara from his seat on the car, with a dignity the emphasis of which would have been diminished had he dismounted.

Eugene—looked upward at this order, shook his head in wonderment, and then got down, but not with quite the same expedition as his boot, which could not sustain the severe test of being suspended for any time in the air. He had not fully secured it again on his bare foot before a laugh sounded from the balcony over the porch—a laugh that made Standish's face redder than any rose—that made Eugene glance up with a grin and touch his hat, even before a girl's voice was heard saying:

"Oh, Eugene, Eugene! What a clumsy fellow you are, to be sure."

"Ah, don't be a sayin' of that, Miss Daireen, ma'am," the boy replied, as he gave a final stamp to secure possession of the boot.

The Macnamara looked up and gravely removed his hat; but Standish having got down from the car turned his gaze seawards. Had he followed his father's example, he would have seen the laughing face and the graceful figure of a girl leaning over the balustrade of the porch surveying the group beneath her.

"And how do you do, Macnamara?" she said. "No, no, don't let Eugene knock; all the dogs are asleep except King Cormac, and I am too grateful to allow their rest to be broken. I'll go down and give you entrance."

She disappeared from the balcony, and in a few moments the hall door was softly sundered and the western sunlight fell about the form of the portress. The girl was tall and exquisitely moulded, from her little blue shoe to her rich brown hair, over which the sun made light and shade; her face was slightly flushed with her rapid descent and the quick kiss of the sunlight, and her eyes were of the most gracious gray that ever shone or laughed or wept. But her mouth—it was a visible song. It expressed all that song is capable of suggesting—passion of love or of anger, comfort of hope or of charity.

"Enter, O my king-," she said, giving The Macnamara her hand; then turning to Standish, "How do you do, Standish? Why do you not come in?"

But Standish uttered no word. He took her hand for a second and followed his father into the big square oaken hall. All were black oak, floor and wall and ceiling, only while the sunlight leapt through the open door was the sombre hue relieved by the flashing of the arms that lined the walls, and the glittering of the enormous elk-antlers that spread their branches over the lintels.

"And you drove all round the coast to see me, I hope," said the girl, as they stood together under the battle-axes of the brave days of old, when the qualifications for becoming a successful knight and a successful blacksmith were identical.

"We drove round to admire the beauty of the lovely Daireen," said The Macnamara, with a flourish of the hand that did him infinite credit.

"If that is all," laughed the girl, "your visit will not be a long one." She was standing listlessly caressing with her hand the coarse hide of King Corrnac, a gigantic Wolf-dog, and in that posture looked like a statue of the Genius of her country. The dog had been welcoming Standish a moment before, and the young man's hand still resting upon its head, felt the casual touch of the girl's fingers as she played with the animal's ears. Every touch sent a thrill of passionate delight through him.

"The beauty of the daughter of the Geralds is worth coming so far to see; and now that I look at her before me— —"

"Now you know that it is impossible to make out a single feature in this darkness," said Daireen. "So come along into the drawing-room."

"Go with the lovely Daireen, my boy," said The Macnamara, as the girl led the way across the hall. "For myself, I think I'll just turn in here." He opened a door at one side of the hall and exposed to view, within the room beyond, a piece of ancient furniture which was not yet too decrepit to sustain the burden of a row of square glass bottles and tumblers. But before he entered he whispered to Standish with an appropriate action, "Make it all right with her by the time come I back." And so he vanished.

"The Macnamara is right," said Daireen. "You must join him in taking a glass of wine after your long drive, Standish."

For the first time since he had spoken on the car Standish found his voice.

"I do not want to drink anything, Daireen," he said.

"Then we shall go round to the garden and try to find grandpapa, if you don't want to rest."

With her brown unbonneted hair tossing in its irregular strands about her neck, she went out by a door at the farther end of the square hall, and Standish followed her by a high-arched passage that seemed to lead right through the building. At the extremity was an iron gate which the girl unlocked, and they passed into a large garden somewhat wild in its growth, but with its few brilliant spots of colour well brought out by the general *feeling* of purple that forced itself upon every one beneath the shadow of the great mountain-peak. Very lovely did that world of heather seem now as the sun burned over against the slope, stirring up the wonderful secret hues of dark blue and crimson. The peak stood out in bold relief against the pale sky, and above its highest point an eagle sailed.

"I have such good news for you, Standish," said Miss Gerald. "You cannot guess what it is."

"I cannot guess what good news there could possibly be in store for me," he replied, with so much sadness in his voice that the girl gave a little start, and then the least possible smile, for she was well aware that the luxury of sadness was frequently indulged in by her companion.

"It is good news for you, for me, for all of us, for all the world, for— well, for everybody that I have not included. Don't laugh at me, please, for my news is that papa is coming home at last. Now, isn't that good news?"

"I am very glad to hear it," said Standish. "I am very glad because I know it will make you happy."

"How nicely said; and I know you feel it, my dear Standish. Ah, poor papa! he has had a hard time of it, battling with the terrible Indian climate and with those annoying people."

"It is a life worth living," cried Standish. "After you are dead the world feels that you have lived in it. The world is the better for your life."

"You are right," said Daireen. "Papa leaves India crowned with honours, as the newspapers say. The Queen has made him a C.B., you know. But—only think how provoking it is—he has been ordered by the surgeon of his regiment to return by long-sea, instead of overland, for the sake of his health; so that though I got his letter from Madras yesterday to tell me that he was at the point of starting, it will be another month before I can see him."

"But then he will no doubt have completely recovered," said Standish.

"That is my only consolation. Yes; he will be himself again—himself as I saw him five years ago in our bungalow—how well I remember it and its single plantain-tree in the garden where the officers used to hunt me for kisses."

Standish frowned. It was, to him, a hideous recollection for the girl to have. He would cheerfully have undertaken the strangulation of each of those sportive officers. "I should have learned a great deal during these five years that have passed since I was sent to England to school, but I'm afraid I didn't. Never mind, papa won't cross-examine me to see if his money has been wasted. But why do you look so sad, Standish? You do look sad, you know."

"I feel it too," he cried. "I feel more wretched than I can tell you. I'm sick of everything here—no, not here, you know, but at home. There I am in that cursed jail, shut out from the world, a beggar without the liberty to beg."

"Oh, Standish!"

"But it is the truth, Daireen. I might as well be dead as living as I am. Yes, better—I wish to God I was dead, for then there might be at least some chance of making a beginning in a new sort of life under different conditions."

"Isn't it wicked to talk that way, Standish?"

"I don't know," he replied doggedly. "Wickedness and goodness have ceased to be anything more to me than vague conditions of life in a world I have nothing to say to. I cannot be either good or bad here."

Daireen looked very solemn at this confession of impotence.

"You told me you meant to speak to The Mac-namara about going away or doing something," she said.

"And I did speak to him, but it came to the one end: it was a disgrace for the son of the——— bah, you know how he talks. Every person of any position laughs at him; only those worse than himself think that he is wronged. But I'll do something, if it should only be to enlist as a common soldier."

"Standish, do not talk that way, like a good boy," she said, laying her hand upon his arm. "I have a bright thought for the first time: wait just for another month until papa is here, and he will, you may be sure, tell you what is exactly right to do. Oh, there is grandpapa, with his gun as usual, coming from the hill."

They saw at a little distance the figure of a tall old man carrying a gun, and followed by a couple of sporting dogs.

"Daireen," said Standish, stopping suddenly as if a thought had just struck him. "Daireen, promise me that you will not let anything my father may say here to-day make you think badly of me."

"Good gracious! why should I ever do that? What is he going to say that is so dreadful?"

"I cannot tell you, Daireen; but you will promise me;" he had seized her by the hand and was looking with earnest entreaty into her eyes. "Daireen," he continued, "you will give me your word. You have been such a friend to me always—such a good angel to me."

"And we shall always be friends, Standish. I promise you this. Now let go my hand, like a good boy."

He obeyed her, and in a few minutes they had met Daireen's grandfather, Mr. Gerald, who had been coming towards them.

"What, The Macnamara here? then I must hasten to him," said the old gentleman, handing his gun to Standish.

No one knew better than Mr. Gerald the necessity that existed for hastening to The Macnamara, in case of his waiting for a length of time in that room the sideboard of which was laden with bottles.

CHAPTER IV

And now, Laertes, what's the news with you?
You told us of some suit: what is't, Laertes?

He hath, my lord, wrung from me my slow' leave
By laboursome petition; and at last,
Upon his will I sealed my hard consent.

Horatio. There's no offence, my lord.
Hamlet. Yes, by Saint Patrick, but there is, Horatio,
And much offence too.
— Hamlet.

THE Macnamara had been led away from his companionship in that old oak room by the time his son and Miss Gerald returned from the garden, and the consciousness of his own dignity seemed to have increased considerably since they had left him. This emotion was a variable possession with him: any one acquainted with his habits could without difficulty, from knowing the degree of dignity he manifested at any moment, calculate minutely the space of time, he must of necessity have spent in a room furnished similarly to that he had just now left.

He was talking pretty loudly in the room to which he had been led by Mr. Gerald when Daireen and Standish entered; and beside him was a whitehaired old lady whom Standish greeted as Mrs. Gerald and the girl called grandmamma—an old lady with very white hair but with large dark eyes whose lustre remained yet undimmed.

"Standish will reveal the mystery," said this old lady, as the young man shook hands with her. "Your father has been speaking in proverbs, Standish, and we want your assistance to read them."

"He is my son," said The Macnamara, waving his hand proudly and lifting up his head. "He will hear his father speak on his behalf. Head of the Geralds, Gerald-na-Tor, chief of the hills, the last of The Macnamaras, king's of Munster, Innishdermot, and all islands, comes to you."

"And I am honoured by his visit, and glad to find him looking so well." said Mr. Gerald. "I am only sorry you can't make it suit you to come oftener, Macnamara."

"It's that boy Eugene that's at fault," said The Macnamara, dropping so suddenly into a colloquial speech from his eloquent Ossianic strain that one might have been led to believe his opening words were somewhat forced. "Yes, my lad," he continued, addressing Mr. Gerald; "that Eugene is either breaking the springs or the straps or his own bones." Here he recollected that his mission was not one to be expressed in this ordinary vein. He straightened himself in an instant, and as he went on asserted even more dignity than before. "Gerald, you know my position, don't you? and you know your 'own; but you can't say, can you, that The Macnamara ever held himself aloof from your table by any show of pride? I mixed with you as if we were equals."

Again he waved his hand patronisingly, but no one showed the least sign of laughter. Standish was in front of one of the windows leaning his head upon his hand as he looked out to the misty ocean. "Yes, I've treated you at all times as if you had been born of the land, though this ground we tread on this moment was torn from the grasp of The Macnamaras by fraud."

"True, true—six hundred years ago," remarked Mr. Gerald. He had been so frequently reminded of this fact during his acquaintance with The Macnamara, he could afford to make the concession he now did.

"But I've not let that rankle in my heart," continued The Macnamara; "I've descended to break bread with you and to drink—drink water with you—ay, at times. You know my son too, and you know that if he's not the same as his father to the backbone, it's not his father that's to blame for it. It was the last wish of his poor mother—rest her soul!—that he should be schooled outside our country, and you know that I carried out her will, though it cost me dear. He's been back these four years, as you know—what's he looking out at at the window?—but it's only three since he found out the pearl of the Lough Suangorm—the diamond of Slieve Docas—the beautiful daughter of the Geralds. Ay, he confessed to me this morning where his soft heart had turned, poor boy. Don't be blushing, Standish; the blood of the Macnamaras shouldn't betray itself in their cheeks."

Standish had started away from the window before his father had ended; his hands were clenched, and his cheeks were burning with shame. He could not fail to see the frown that was settling down upon the face of Mr. Gerald. But he dared not even glance towards Daireen.

"My dear Macnamara, we needn't talk on this subject any farther just now," said the girl's grandfather, as the orator paused for an instant.

But The Macnamara only gave his hand another wave before he proceeded. "I have promised my boy to make him happy," he said, "and you know what the word of a Macnamara is worth even to his son; so, though I confess I was taken aback at first, yet I at last consented to throw over my natural family pride and to let my boy have his way. An alliance between the Macnamaras and the Geralds is not what would have been thought about a few years ago, but The Macnamaras have always been condescending."

"Yes, yes, you condescend to a jest now and again with us, but really this is a sort of mystery I have no clue to," said Mr. Gerald.

"Mystery? Ay, it will astonish the world to know that The Macnamara has given his consent to such an alliance; it must be kept secret for a while for fear of its effects upon the foreign States that have their eyes upon all our steps. I wouldn't like this made a State affair at all."

"My dear Macnamara, you are usually very lucid," said Mr. Gerald, "but to-day I somehow cannot arrive at your meaning."

"What, sir?" cried The Macnamara, giving his head an angry twitch. "What, sir, do you mean to tell me that you don't understand that I have given my consent to my son taking as his wife the daughter of the Geralds?—see how the lovely Daireen blushes like a rose."

Daireen was certainly blushing, as she left her seat and went over to the farthest end of the room. But Standish was deadly pale, his lips tightly closed.

"Macnamara, this is absurd—quite absurd!" said Mr. Gerald, hastily rising. "Pray let us talk no more in such a strain."

Then The Macnamara's consciousness of his own dignity asserted itself. He drew himself up and threw back his head. "Sir, do you mean to put an affront upon the one who has left his proper station to raise your family to his own level?"

"Don't let us quarrel, Macnamara; you know how highly I esteem you personally, and you know that I have ever looked upon the family of the Macnamaras as the noblest in the land."

"And it is the noblest in the land. There's not a drop of blood in our veins that hasn't sprung from the heart of a king," cried The Macnamara.

"Yes, yes, I know it; but—well, we will not talk any further to-day. Daireen, you needn't go away."

"Heavens! do you mean to say that I haven't spoken plainly enough, that——"

"Now, Macnamara, I must really interrupt you——"

"Must you?" cried the representative of the ancient line, his face developing all the secret resources of redness it possessed. "Must you interrupt the hereditary monarch of the country where you're but an immigrant when he descends to equalise himself with you? This is the reward of condescension! Enough, sir, you have affronted the family that were living in castles when your forefathers were like beasts in caves. The offer of an alliance ought to have come from you, not from me; but never again will it be said that The Macnamara forgot what was due to him and his family. No, by the powers, Gerald, you'll never have the chance again. I scorn you; I reject your alliance. The Macnamara seats himself once more upon his ancient throne, and he tramples upon you all. Come, my son, look at him that has insulted your family—look at him for the last time and lift up your head."

The grandeur with which The Macnamara uttered this speech was overpowering. He had at its conclusion turned towards poor Standish, and waved his hand in the direction of Mr. Gerald. Then Standish seemed to have recovered himself.

"No, father, it is you who have insulted this family by talking as you have done," he cried passionately.

"Boy!" shouted The Macnamara. "Recreant son of a noble race, don't demean yourself with such language!"

"It is you who have demeaned our family," cried the son still more energetically. "You have sunk us even lower than we were before." Then he turned imploringly towards Mr. Gerald. "You know—you know that I am only to be pitied, not blamed, for my father's words," he said quietly, and then went to the door.

"My dear boy," said the old lady, hastening towards him.

"Madam!" cried The Macnamara, raising his arm majestically to stay her.

She stopped in the centre of the room. Daireen had also risen, her pure eyes full of tears as she grasped her grandfather's hand while he laid his other upon her head.

From the door Standish looked with passionate gratitude back to the girl, then rushed out.

But The Macnamara stood for some moments with his head elevated, the better to express the scorn that was in his heart. No one made a motion, and then he stalked after his son.

CHAPTER V

What advancement may I hope from thee
That no revenue hast...
To feed and clothe thee?

Guildenstern. The King, sir, —
Hamlet. Ay, sir, what of him?
Guild. Is in his retirement marvellous distempered.
Hamlet. With drink, sir?
Guild. No, my lord, rather with choler.
Hamlet. The King doth wake to-night and takes his
rouse.
Keeps wassail, and the swaggering up-spring reels.

Horatio. Is it a custom?
Hamlet. Ay, marry is't:
But to my mind, though I am native here,
And to the manner born, it is a custom
More honour'd in the breach than the observance.
This heavy-headed revel...
Makes us traduced and taxed. — Hamlet.

TO do The Macnamara justice, while he was driving homeward upon that very shaky car round the lovely coast, he was somewhat disturbed in mind as he reflected upon the possible consequences of his quarrel with old Mr. Gerald. He was dimly conscious of the truth of the worldly and undeniably selfish maxim referring to the awkwardness of a quarrel with a neighbour. And if there is any truth in it as a general maxim, its value is certainly intensified when the neighbour in question has been the lender of sundry sums of money. A neighbour under these conditions should not be quarrelled with, he knew.

The Macnamara had borrowed from Mr. Gerald, at various times, certain moneys which had amounted in the aggregate to a considerable sum; for though Daireen's grandfather was not possessed of a very large income from the land that had been granted to his ancestors some few hundred years before, he had still enough to enable him from time to time to oblige

The Macnamara with a loan. And this reflection caused The Macnamara about as much mental uneasiness as the irregular motion of the vehicle did physical discomfort. By the time, however, that the great hill, whose heather slope was now wrapped in the purple shade of twilight, its highest peak alone being bathed in the red glory of the sunset, was passed, his mind was almost at ease; for he recalled the fact that his misunderstandings with Mr. Gerald were exactly equal in number to his visits; he never passed an hour at Suanmara without what would at any rate have been a quarrel but for Mr. Gerald's good nature, which refused to be ruffled. And as no reference had ever upon these occasions been made to his borrowings, The Macnamara felt that he had no reason to conclude that his present quarrel would become embarrassing through any action of Mr. Gerald's. So he tried to feel the luxury of the scorn that he had so powerfully expressed in the room at Suanmara.

"Mushrooms of a night's growth!" he muttered. "I trampled them beneath my feet. They may go down on their knees before me now, I'll have nothing to say to them." Then as the car passed out of the glen and he saw before him the long shadows of the hills lying amongst the crimson and yellow flames that swept from the sunset out on the Atlantic, and streamed between the headlands at the entrance to the lough, he became more fixed in his resolution. "The son of The Macnamara will never wed with the daughter of a man that is paid by the oppressors of the country, no, never!"

This was an allusion to the fact of Daireen's father being a colonel in the British army, on service in India. Then exactly between the headlands the sun went down in a gorgeous mist that was permeated with the glow of the orb it enveloped. The waters shook and trembled in the light, but the many islands of the lough remained dark and silent in the midst of the glow. The Macnamara became more resolute still. He had almost forgotten that he had ever borrowed a penny from Mr. Gerald. He turned to where Standish sat silent and almost grim.

"And you, boy," said the father—"you, that threw your insults in my face—you, that's a disgrace to the family—I've made up my mind what I'll do with you; I'll—yes, by the powers, I'll disinherit you."

But not a word did Standish utter in reply to this threat, the force of which, coupled with an expressive motion of the speaker, jeopardised the imperfect spring, and wrung from Eugene a sudden exclamation.

"Holy mother o' Saint Malachi, kape the sthring from breakin' yit awhile!" he cried devoutly.

And it seemed that the driver's devotion was efficacious, for, without any accident, the car reached the entrance to Innishdermot, as the residence of the ancient monarchs had been called since the days when the waters of Lough Suangorm had flowed all about the castle slope, for even the lough had become reduced in strength.

The twilight, rich and blue, was now swathing the mountains and overshadowing the distant cliffs, though the waters at their base were steel gray and full of light that seemed to shine upwards through their depth. Desolate, truly, the ruins loomed through the dimness. Only a single feeble light glimmered from one of the panes, and even this seemed agonising to the owls, for they moaned wildly and continuously from the round tower. There was, indeed, scarcely an aspect of welcome in anything that surrounded this home which one family had occupied for seven hundred years.

As the car stopped at the door, however, there came a voice from an unseen figure, saying, in even a more pronounced accent than The Macnamara himself gloried in, "Wilcome, ye noble sonns of noble soyers! Wilcome back to the anshent home of the gloryous race that'll stand whoile there's a sod of the land to bear it."

"It's The Randal himself," said The Macnamara, looking in the direction from which the sound came. "And where is it that you are, Randal? Oh, I see your pipe shining like a star out of the ivy."

From the forest of ivy that clung about the porch of the castle the figure of a small man emerged. One of his hands was in his pocket, the other removed a short black pipe, the length of whose stem in comparison to the breadth of its bowl was as the proportion of Falstaff's bread to his sack.

"Wilcome back, Macnamara," said this gentleman, who was indeed The Randal, hereditary chief of Suangorm. "An' Standish too, how are ye, my boy?" Standish shook hands with the speaker, but did not utter a word. "An' where is it ye're afther dhrivin' from?" continued The Randal.

"It's a long drive and a long story," said The Macnamara.

"Thin for hivin's sake don't begin it till we've put boy the dinner. I'm goin' to take share with ye this day, and I'm afther waitin' an hour and more."

"It's welcome The Randal is every day in the week," said The Macnamara, leading the way into the great dilapidated hall, where in the ancient days fifty men-at-arms had been wont to feast royally. Now it was black in night.

In the room where the dinner was laid there were but two candles, and their feeble glimmer availed no more than to make the blotches on the cloth more apparent: the maps of the British Isles done in mustard and gravy were numerous. At each end a huge black bottle stood like a sentry at the border of a snowfield.

By far the greater portion of the light was supplied by the blazing log in the fireplace. It lay not in any grate but upon the bare hearth, and crackled and roared up the chimney like a demon prostrate in torture. The Randal and his host stood before the blaze, while Standish seated himself in another part of the room. The ruddy flicker of the wood fire shone upon the faces of the two men, and the yellow glimmer of the candle upon the face of Standish. Here and there a polish upon the surface of the black oak panelling gleamed, but all the rest of the high room was dim.

Salmon from the lough, venison from the forest, wild birds from the moor made up the dinner. All were served on silver dishes strangely worked, and plates of the same metal were laid before the diners, while horns mounted on massive stands were the drinking vessels. From these dishes The Macnamaras of the past had eaten, and from these horns they had drunken, and though the present head of the family could have gained many years' income had he given the metal to be melted, he had never for an instant thought of taking such a step. He would have starved with that plate empty in front of him sooner than have sold it to buy bread.

Standish spoke no word during the entire meal, and the guest saw that something had gone wrong; so with his native tact he chatted away, asking questions, but waiting for no answer.

When the table was cleared and the old serving-woman had brought in a broken black kettle of boiling water, and had laid in the centre of the table an immense silver bowl for the brewing of the punch, The Randal drew up the remnant of his collar and said: "Now for the sthory of the droive, Macnamara; I'm riddy whin ye fill the bowl."

Standish rose from the table and walked away to a seat at the furthest end of the great room, where he sat hidden in the gloom of the corner. The Randal did not think it inconsistent with his chieftainship to wink at his host.

"Randal," said The Macnamara, "I've made up my mind. I'll disinherit that boy, I will."

"No," cried The Randal eagerly. "Don't spake so loud, man; if this should git wind through the counthry who knows what might happen? Disinhirit the boy; ye don't mane it, Macnamara," he continued in an excited but awe-stricken whisper.

"But by the powers, I do mean it," cried The Macnamara, who had been testing the potent elements of the punch.

"Disinherit me, will you, father?" came the sudden voice of Standish echoing strangely down the dark room. Then he rose and stood facing both men at the table, the red glare of the log mixing with the sickly candlelight upon his face and quivering hands. "Disinherit me?" he said again, bitterly. "You cannot do that. I wish you could. My inheritance, what is it? Degradation of family, proud beggary, a life to be wasted outside the world of life and work, and a death rejoiced over by those wretches who have lent you money. Disinherit me from all this, if you can."

"Holy Saint Malachi, hare the sonn of The Macnamaras talkin' loike a choild!" cried The Randal.

"I don't care who hears me," said Standish. "I'm sick of hearing about my forefathers; no one cares about them nowadays. I wanted years ago to go out into the world and work."

"Work—a Macnamara work!" cried The Randal horror-stricken.

"I told you so," said The Macnamara, in the tone of one who finds sudden confirmation to the improbable story of some enormity.

"I wanted to work as a man should to redeem the shame which our life as it is at present brings upon our family," said the young man earnestly— almost passionately; "but I was not allowed to do anything that I wanted. I was kept here in this jail wasting my best years; but to-day has brought everything to an end. You say you will disinherit me, father, but I have from this day disinherited myself—I have cast off my old existence. I begin life from to-day."

Then he turned away and went out of the room, leaving his father and his guest in dumb amazement before their punch. It was some minutes before either could speak. At last The Randal took adraught of the hot spirit, and shook his head thoughtfully.

"Poor boy! poor boy! he needs to be looked after till he gets over this turn," he said.

"It's all that girl—that Daireen of the Geralds," said The Macnamara. "I found a paper with poetry on it for her this morning, and when I forced him he confessed that he was in love with her."

"D'ye tell me that? And what more did ye do, Mac?"

"I'll tell you," said the hereditary prince, leaning over the table.

And he gave his guest all the details of the visit to the Geralds at length.

But poor Standish had rushed up the crumbling staircase and was lying on his bed with his face in his hands. It was only now he seemed to feel all the shame that had caused his face to be red and pale by turns in the drawing-room at Suanmara. He lay there in a passion of tears, while the great owls kept moaning and hooting in the tower just outside his window, making sympathetic melody to his ears.

At last he arose and went over to the window and stood gazing out through the break in the ivy armour of the wall. He gazed over the tops of the trees growing in a straggling way down the slope to the water's edge. He could see far away the ocean, whose voice he now and again heard as the wind bore it around the tower. Thousands of stars glittered above the water and trembled upon its moving surface. He felt strong now. He felt that he might never weep again in the world as he had just wept. Then he turned to another window and sent his eyes out to where that great peak of Slieve Docas stood out dark and terrible among the stars. He could not see the house at the base of the hill, but he clenched his hands as he looked out, saying "Hope."

It was late before he got into his bed, and it was still later when he awoke and heard, mingling with the cries of the night-birds, the sound of hoarse singing that floated upward from the room where he had left his father and The Randal. The prince and the chief were joining their voices in a native melody, Standish knew; and he was well aware that he would not be disturbed by the ascent of either during the night. The dormitory arrangements of the prince and the chief when they had dined in company were of the simplest nature.

Standish went to sleep again, and the ancient rafters, that had heard the tones of many generations of Macnamaras' voices, trembled for some hours with the echoes from the room below, while outside the ancient owls hooted and the ancient sea murmured in its sleep.

CHAPTER VI

What imports this song?
The wind sits in the shoulder of your sail
And you are stay'd for. There; my blessing with thee.

Hamlet. I do not set my life at a pin's fee...
It waves me forth again: I'll follow it.

Horatio. What if it tempt you toward the flood?...
Look whether he has not changed his colour.
—Hamlet.

THE sounds of wild harp-music were ascending at even from the depths of Glenmara. The sun had sunk, and the hues that had been woven round the west were wasting themselves away on the horizon. The faint shell-pink had drifted and dwindled far from the place of sunset. The woods of the slopes looked very dark now that the red glances from the west were withdrawn from their glossy foliage; but the heather-swathed mountains, towering through the soft blue air to the dark blue sky, were richly purple, as though the sunset hues had become entangled amongst the heather, and had forgotten to fly back to the west that had cast them forth.

The little tarn at the foot of the lowest crags was black and still, waiting for the first star-glimpse, and from its marge came the wild notes of a harp fitfully swelling and waning; and then arose the still wilder and more melancholy tones of a man's voice chanting what seemed like a weird dirge to the fading twilight, and the language was the Irish Celtic—that language every song of which sounds like a dirge sung over its own death:—

Why art thou gone from us, White Dove of the Irish woods?
Why art thou gone who made all the leaves tremulous with the low voice of love?
Love that tarried yet afar, though the fleet swallow had come back to us—
Love that stayed in the far lands though the primrose had cast its gold by the streams—

Love that heard not the voice sent forth from every new-
budded briar—
This love came only when thou earnest, and rapture thrilled
the heart of the green land.
Why art thou gone from us, White Dove of the Irish
woods?

This is a translation of the wild lament that arose in the twilight air and
stirred up the echoes of the rocks. Then the fitful melody of the harp made
an interlude:—

Why art thou gone from us, sweet Linnet of the Irish
woods?
Why art thou gone from us whose song brought the Spring
to our land?
Yea, flowers to thy singing arose from the earth in bountiful
bloom,
And scents of the violet, scents of the hawthorn—all scents
of the spring
Were wafted about us when thy voice was heard albeit in
autumn.
All thoughts of the spring—all its hopes woke and breathed
through our hearts,
Till our souls thrilled with passionate song and the perfume
of spring which is love.
Why art thou gone from us, sweet Linnet of the Irish
woods?

Again the chaunter paused and again his harp prolonged the wailing
melody. Then passing into a more sadly soft strain, he continued his song:—

Why art thou gone from us, Soul of all beauty and joy?
Now thou art gone the berry drops from the arbutus,
The wind comes in from the ocean with wail and the
autumn is sad,
The yellow leaves perish, whirled wild whither no one can
know.
As the crisp leaves are crushed in the woods, so our hearts
are crushed at thy parting;
As the woods moan for the summer departed, so we mourn
that we see thee no more.
Why art thou gone from us, Soul of all beauty and joy?

Into the twilight the last notes died away, and a lonely heron standing among the rushes at the edge of the tarn moved his head critically to one side as if waiting for another song with which to sympathise. But he was not the only listener. Far up among the purple crags Standish Macnamara was lying looking out to the sunset when he heard the sound of the chant in the glen beneath him. He lay silent while the dirge floated up the mountain-side and died away among the heather of the peak. But when the silence of the twilight came once more upon the glen, Standish arose and made his way downwards to where an old man with one of the small ancient Irish harps, was seated on a stone, his head bent across the strings upon which his fingers still rested. Standish knew him to be one Murrough O'Brian, a descendant of the bards of the country, and an old retainer of the Gerald family. A man learned in Irish, but not speaking an intelligible sentence in English.

"Why do you sing the Dirge of Tuathal on this evening, Murrough?" he asked in his native tongue, as he came beside the old man.

"What else is there left for me to sing at this time, Standish O'Dermot Macnamara, son of the Prince of Islands and all Munster?" said the bard. "There is nothing of joy left us now. We cannot sing except in sorrow. Does not the land seem to have sympathy with such songs, prolonging their sound by its own voice from every glen and mountain-face?"

"It is true," said Standish. "As I sat up among the cliffs of heather it seemed to me that the melody was made by the spirits of the glen bewailing in the twilight the departure of the glory of our land."

"See how desolate is all around us here," said the bard. "Glenmara is lonely now, where it was wont to be gay with song and laughter; when the nobles thronged the valley with hawk and hound, the voice of the bugle and the melody of a hundred harps were heard stirring up the echoes in delight."

"But now all are gone; they can only be recalled in vain dreams," said the second in this duet of Celtic mourners—the younger Marius among the ruins.

"The sons of Erin have left her in her loneliness while the world is stirred with their brave actions," continued the ancient bard.

"True," cried Standish; "outside is the world that needs Irish hands and hearts to make it better worth living in." The young man was so enthusiastic in the utterance of his part in the dialogue as to cause the bard to look suddenly up.

"Yes, the hands and the hearts of the Irish have done much," he said. "Let the men go out into the world for a while, but let our daughters be spared to us."

Standish gave a little start and looked inquiringly into the face of the bard.

"What do you mean, Murrough?" he asked slowly.

The bard leant forward as if straining to catch some distant sound.

"Listen to it, listen to it," he said. There was a pause, and through the silence the moan of the far-off ocean was borne along the dim glen.

"It is the sound of the Atlantic," said Standish. "The breeze from the west carries it to us up from the lough."

"Listen to it and think that she is out on that far ocean," said the old man. "Listen to it, and think that Daireen, daughter of the Geralds, has left her Irish home and is now tossing upon that ocean; gone is she, the bright bird of the South—gone from those her smile lightened!"

Standish neither started nor uttered a word when the old man had spoken; but he felt his feet give way under him. He sat down upon a crag and laid his head upon his hand staring into the black tarn. He could not comprehend at first the force of the words "She is gone." He had thought of his own departure, but the possibility of Daireen's had not occurred to him. The meaning of the bard's lament was now apparent to him, and even now the melody seemed to be given back by the rocks that had heard it:

Why art thou gone from us, Soul of all beauty and joy?

The words moaned through the dim air with the sound of the distant waters for accompaniment.

"Gone—gone—Daireen," he whispered. "And you only tell me of it now," he added almost fiercely to the old man, for he reflected upon the time he had wasted in that duet of lamentation over the ruins of his country. What a wretchedly trivial thing he felt was the condition of the country compared with such an event as the departure of Daireen Gerald.

"It is only since morning that she is gone," said the bard. "It was only in the morning that the letter arrived to tell her that her father was lying in a fever at some place where the vessel called on the way home. And now she is gone from us, perhaps for ever."

"Murrough," said the young man, laying his hand upon the other's arm, and speaking in a hoarse whisper. "Tell me all about her. Why did they allow her to go? Where is she gone? Not out to where her father was landed?"

"Why not there?" cried the old man, raising his head proudly. "Did a Gerald ever shrink from duty when the hour came? Brave girl she is, worthy to be a Gerald!"

"Tell me all—all."

"What more is there to tell than what is bound up in those three words 'She is gone'?" said the man. "The letter came to her grandfather and she saw him read it—I was in the hall—she saw his hand tremble. She stood up there beside him and asked him what was in the letter; he looked into her face and put the letter in her hand. I saw her face grow pale as she read it. Then she sat down for a minute, but no word or cry came from her until she looked up to the old man's face; then she clasped her hands and said only, 'I will go to him.' The old people talked to her of the distance, of the danger; they told her how she would be alone for days and nights among strangers; but she only repeated, 'I will go to him.' And now she is gone—gone alone over those waters."

"Alone!" Standish repeated. "Gone away alone, no friend near her, none to utter a word of comfort in her ears!" He buried his face in his hands as he pictured the girl whom he had loved silently, but with all his soul, since she had come to her home in Ireland from India where she had lived with her father since the death of his wife ten years ago. He pictured her sitting in her loneliness aboard the ship that was bearing her away to, perhaps, the land of her father's grave, and he felt that now at last all the bitterness that could be crowded upon his life had fallen on him. He gazed into the black tarn, and saw within its depths a star glittering as it glittered in the sky above, but it did not relieve his thoughts with any touch of its gold.

He rose after a while and gave his hand to Murrough.

"Thank you," he said. "You have told me all better than any one else could have done. But did she not speak of me, Murrough—only once perhaps? Did she not send me one little word of farewell?"

"She gave me this for you," said the old bard, producing a letter which Standish clutched almost wildly.

"Thank God, thank God!" he cried, hurrying away without another word. But after him swept the sound of the bard's lament which he commenced anew, with that query:

Why art thou gone from us, Soul of all beauty and joy?

It was not yet too dark outside the glen for Standish to read the letter which he had just received; and so soon as he found himself in sight of the sea he tore open the cover and read the few lines Daireen Gerald had written, with a tremulous hand, to say farewell to him.

"My father has been left ill with fever at the Cape, and I know that he will recover only if I go to him. I am going away to-day, for the steamer will leave Southampton in four days, and I cannot be there in time unless I start at once. I thought you would not like me to go without saying good-bye, and God bless you, dear Standish."

"You will say good-bye to The Macnamara for me. I thought poor papa would be here to give you the advice you want. Pray to God that I may be in time to see him."

He read the lines by the gray light reflected from the sea—he read them until his eyes were dim.

"Brave, glorious girl!" he cried. "But to think of her—alone—alone out there, while I—— oh, what a poor weak fool I am! Here am I—here, looking out to the sea she is gone to battle with! Oh, God! oh, God! I must do something for her—I must—but what—what?"

He cast himself down upon the heather that crawled from the slopes even to the road, and there he lay with his head buried in agony at the thought of his own impotence; while through the dark glen floated the wild, weird strain of the lament:

"Why art thou gone from us, Soul of all beauty and joy?"

CHAPTER VII

Hamlet. How chances it they travel? their residence,
both in reputation and profit, was better both ways.
Rosencrantz. I think their inhibition comes by the means
of the late innovation.

Many, wearing rapiers, are afraid of goose-quills.
What imports the nomination of this gentleman?
Hamlet.

AWAY from the glens and the heather-clad mountains, from the blue loughs and their islands of arbutus, from the harp-music, and from the ocean-music which makes those who hear it ripe for revolt; away from the land whose life is the memory of ancient deeds of nobleness; away from the land that has given birth to more heroes than any nation in the world, the land whose inhabitants live in thousands in squalor and look out from mud windows upon the most glorious scenery in the world; away from all these one must now be borne.

Upon the evening of the fourth day after the chanting of that lament by the bard O'Brian from the depths of Glenmara, the good steamship *Cardwell Castle* was making its way down Channel with a full cargo and heavy mails for Madeira, St. Helena, and the Cape. It had left its port but a few hours and already the coast had become dim with distance. The red shoreway of the south-west was now so far away that the level rays of sunlight which swept across the water were not seen to shine upon the faces of the rocks, or to show where the green fields joined the brown moorland; the windmills crowning every height were not seen to be in motion.

The passengers were for the most part very cheerful, as passengers generally are during the first couple of hours of a voyage, when only the gentle ripples of the Channel lap the sides of the vessel. The old voyagers, who had thought it prudent to dine off a piece of sea-biscuit and a glass of brandy and water, while they watched with grim smiles the novices trifling with roast pork and apricot-dumplings, were now sitting in seats they had arranged for themselves in such places as they knew would be well to leeward for the greater part of the voyage, and here they smoked their cigars and read their newspapers just as they would be doing every day for three weeks. To them the phenomenon of the lessening land was not particularly interesting. The novices were endeavouring to look as if they had been used to knock about the sea all their lives; they carried their telescopes under their arms quite jauntily, and gave critical glances aloft every now and again, consulting their pocket compasses gravely at regular intervals to convince themselves that they were not being trifled with in the navigation of the vessel.

Then there were, of course, those who had come aboard with the determination of learning in three weeks as much seamanship as should enable them to accept any post of marine responsibility that they might be called upon to fill in after life. They handled the loose tackle with a view of determining its exact utility, and endeavoured to trace stray lines to their source. They placed the captain entirely at his ease with them by asking him a number of questions regarding the dangers of boiler-bursting, and the perils of storms; they begged that he would let them know if there was any truth in the report which had reached them to the effect that the Atlantic was a very stormy place; and they left him with the entreaty that in case of any danger arising suddenly he would at once communicate with them; they then went down to put a few casual questions to the quartermaster who was at the wheel, and doubtless felt that they were making most of the people about them cheerful with their converse.

Then there were the young ladies who had just completed their education in England and were now on their way to join their relations abroad. Having read in the course of their studies of English literature the poems of the late Samuel Rogers, they were much amazed to find that the mariners were not leaning over the ship's bulwarks sighing to behold the sinking of their native land, and that not an individual had climbed the mast to partake of the ocular banquet with indulging in which the poet has accredited the sailor. Towards this section the glances of several male eyes were turned, for most of the young men had roved sufficiently far to become aware of the fact that the relief of the monotony of a lengthened voyage is principally dependent on—well, on the relieving capacities of the young ladies, lately sundered from school and just commencing their education in the world.

But far away from the groups that hung about the stern stood a girl looking over the side of the ship towards the west—towards the sun that was almost touching the horizon. She heard the laughter of the groups of girls and the silly questions of the uninformed, but all sounded to her like the strange voices of a dream; for as she gazed towards the west she seemed to see a fair landscape of purple slopes and green woods; the dash of the ripples against the ship's side came to her as the rustle of the breaking ripples amongst the shells of a blue lough upon whose surface a number of green islets raised their heads. She saw them all—every islet, with its moveless I shadow beneath it, and the light touching the edges of the leaves with red. Daireen Gerald it was who stood there looking out to the sunset, but seeing in the golden lands of the west the Irish land she knew so well.

She remained motionless, with her eyes far away and her heart still farther, until the red sun had disappeared, and the delicate twilight change was slipping over the bright gray water. With every change she seemed to see the shifting of the hues over the heather of Slieve Docas and the pulsating of the tremulous red light through the foliage of the deer ground. It was only now that the tears forced themselves into her eyes, for she had not wept at parting from her grandfather, who had gone with her from Ireland and had left her aboard the steamer a few hours before; and while her tears made everything misty to her, the light laughter of the groups scattered about the quarter-deck sounded in her ears. It did not come harshly to her, for it seemed to come from a world in which she had no part. The things about her were as the things of a dream. The reality in which she was living was that which she saw out in the west.

"Come, my dear," said a voice behind her—"Come and walk with me on the deck. I fancied I had lost you, and you may guess what a state I was in, after all the promises I made to Mr. Gerald."

"I was just looking out there, and wondering what they were all doing at home—at the foot of the dear old mountain," said Daireen, allowing herself to be led away.

"That is what most people would call moping, dear," said the lady who had come up. She was a middle-aged lady with a pleasant face, though her figure was hardly what a scrupulous painter would choose as a model for a Nausicaa.

"Perhaps I was moping, Mrs. Crawford," Daireen replied; "but I feel the better for it now."

"My dear, I don't disapprove of moping now and again, though as a habit it should not be encouraged. I was down in my cabin, and when I came on deck I couldn't understand where you had disappeared to. I asked the major, but of course, you know, he was quite oblivious to everything but the mutiny at Cawnpore, through being beside Doctor Campion."

"But you have found me, you see, Mrs. Crawford."

"Yes, thanks to Mr. Glaston; he knew where you had gone; he had been watching you." Daireen felt her face turning red as she thought of this Mr.

Glaston, whoever he was, with his eyes fixed upon her movements. "You don't know Mr. Glaston, Daireen?—I shall call you 'Daireen' of course, though we have only known each other a couple of hours," continued the lady. "No, of course you don't. Never mind, I'll show him to you." For the promise of this treat Daireen did not express her gratitude. She had come to think the most unfavourable things regarding this Mr. Glaston. Mrs. Crawford, however, did not seem to expect an acknowledgment. Her chat ran on as briskly as ever. "I shall point him out to you, but on no account look near him for some time—young men are so conceited, you know."

Daireen had heard this peculiarity ascribed to the race before, and so when her guide, as they walked towards the stern of the vessel, indicated to her that a young man sitting in a deck-chair smoking a cigar was Mr. Glaston, she certainly did not do anything that might possibly increase in Mr. Glaston this dangerous tendency which Mrs. Crawford had assigned to young men generally.

"What do you think of him, my dear?" asked Mrs. Crawford, when they had strolled up the deck once more.

"Of whom?" inquired Daireen.

"Good gracious," cried the lady, "are your thoughts still straying? Why, I mean Mr. Glaston, to be sure. What do you think of him?"

"I didn't look at him," the girl answered.

Mrs. Crawford searched the fair face beside her to find out if its expression agreed with her words, and the scrutiny being satisfactory she gave a little laugh. "How do you ever mean to know what he is like if you don't look at him?" she asked.

Daireen did not stop to explain how she thought it possible that contentment might exist aboard the steamer even though she remained in ignorance for ever of Mr. Glaston's qualities; but presently she glanced along the deck, and saw sitting at graceful ease upon the chair Mrs. Crawford had indicated, a tall man of apparently a year or two under thirty. He had black hair which he had allowed to grow long behind, and a black moustache which gave every indication of having been subjected to the most careful youthful training. His face would not have been thought expressive but for his eyes, and the expression that these organs gave out could hardly be called anything except a neutral one: they indicated nothing except that nothing was meant to be indicated by them. No suggestion of passion, feeling, or even thoughtfulness, did they give; and in fact the only possible result of looking at this face which some people called expressive, was a feeling that the man himself was calmly conscious of the fact that some people were in the habit of calling his face expressive.

"And what *do* you think of him now, my dear?" asked Mrs. Crawford, after Daireen had gratified her by taking that look.

"I really don't think that I think anything," she answered with a little laugh.

"That is the beauty of his face," cried Mrs. Crawford. "It sets one thinking."

"But that is not what I said, Mrs. Crawford."

"You said you did not think you were thinking anything, Daireen; and that meant, I know, that there was more in his face than you could read at a first glance. Never mind; every one is set thinking when one sees Mr. Glaston."

Daireen had almost become interested in this Mr. Glaston, even though she could not forget that he had watched her when she did not want to be watched. She gave another glance towards him, but with no more profitable conclusion than her previous look had attained.

"I will tell you all about him, my child," said Mrs. Crawford confidentially; "but first let us make ourselves comfortable. Dear old England, there is the last of it for us for some time. Adieu, adieu, dear old country!" There was not much sentimentality in the stout little lady's tone, as she looked towards the faint line of mist far astern that marked the English coast. She sat down with Daireen to the leeward of the deck-house where she had laid her rugs, and until the tea-bell rang Daireen had certainly no opportunity for moping.

Mrs. Crawford told her that this Mr. Glaston was a young man of such immense capacities that nothing lay outside his grasp either in art or science. He had not thought it necessary to devote his attention to any subject in particular; but that, Mrs. Crawford thought, was rather because there existed no single subject that he considered worthy of an expenditure of all his energies. As things unfortunately existed, there was nothing left for him but to get rid of the unbounded resources of his mind by applying them to a variety of subjects. He had, in fact, written poetry—never an entire volume of course, but exceedingly clever pieces that had been published in his college magazine. He was capable of painting a great picture if he chose, though he had contented himself with giving ideas to other men who had worked them out through the medium of pictures. He was one of the most accomplished of musicians; and if he had not yet produced an opera or composed even a song, instances were on record of his having performed impromptus that would undoubtedly have made the fame of a professor. He was the son of a Colonial Bishop, Mrs. Crawford told Daireen, and though he lived in England he was still dutiful enough to go out to pay a month's visit to his father every year.

"But we must not make him conceited, Daireen," said Mrs. Crawford, ending her discourse; "we must not, dear; and if he should look over and see us together this way, he would conclude that we were talking of him."

Daireen rose with her instructive companion with an uneasy sense of feeling that all they could by their combined efforts contribute to the conceit of a young man who would, upon grounds so slight, come to such a conclusion as Mrs. Crawford feared he might, would be but trifling.

Then the tea-bell rang, and all the novices who had enjoyed the roast pork and dumplings at dinner, descended to make a hearty meal of buttered toast and banana jelly. The sea air had given them an appetite, they declared with much merriment. The chief steward, however, being an experienced man, and knowing that in a few hours the Bay of Biscay would be entered, did not, from observing the hearty manner in which the novices were eating, feel uneasy on the matter of the endurance of the ship's stores. He knew it would be their last meal for some days at least, and he smiled grimly as he laid down another plate of buttered toast, and hastened off to send up some more brandy and biscuits to Major Crawford and Doctor Campion, whose hoarse chuckles called forth by pleasing reminiscences of Cawnpore were dimly heard from the deck through the cabin skylight.

CHAPTER VIII

An hour of quiet shortly shall we see;
Till then in patience our proceeding be.

We'll put on those shall praise your excellence
And set a double varnish on the fame
The Frenchman gave you, bring you in fine together.
... I know love is begun by time.

I know him well: he is the brooch indeed
And gem of all the nation.

He made confession of you,
And gave you such a masterly report
For art...'twould be a sight indeed
If one could match you.
　　　　　—Hamlet.

MRS. Crawford absolutely clung to Daireen all this evening. When the whist parties were formed in the cabin she brought the girl on deck and instructed her in some of the matters worth knowing aboard a passenger ship.

"On no account bind yourself to any whist set before you look about you: nothing could be more dangerous," she said confidentially. "Just think how terrible it would be if you were to join a set now, and afterwards to find out that it was not the best set. You would simply be ruined. Besides that, it is better to stay on deck as much as possible during the first day or two at sea. Now let us go over to the major and Campion."

So Daireen found herself borne onward with Mrs. Crawford's arm in her own to where Major Crawford and Doctor Campion were sitting on their battered deck-chairs lighting fresh cheroots from the ashes of the expiring ends.

"Don't tread on the tumblers, my dear," said the major as his wife advanced. "And how is Miss Gerald now that we have got under weigh? You didn't take any of that liquid they insult the Chinese Empire by calling tea, aboard ship, I hope?"

"Just a single cup, and very weak," said Mrs. Crawford apologetically.

"My dear, I thought you were wiser."

"You will take this chair, Mrs. Crawford?" said Doctor Campion, without making the least pretence of moving, however.

"Don't think of such a thing," cried the lady's husband; and to do Doctor Campion justice, he did not think of such a thing. "Why, you don't fancy these are our Junkapore days, do you, when Kate came out to our bungalow, and the boys called her the Sylph? It's a fact, Miss Gerald; my wife, as your father will tell you, was as slim as a lily. Ah, dear, dear! Time, they say, takes a lot away from us, but by Jingo, he's liberal enough in some ways. By Jingo, yes," and the gallant old man kept shaking his head and chuckling towards his comrade, whose features could be seen puckered into a grin though he uttered no sound.

"And stranger still, Miss Gerald," said the lady, "the major was once looked upon as a polite man, and politer to his wife than to anybody else. Go and fetch some chairs here, Campion, like a good fellow," she added to the doctor, who rose slowly and obeyed.

"That's how my wife takes command of the entire battalion, Miss Gerald," remarked the major. "Oh, your father will tell you all about her."

The constant reference to her father by one who was an old friend, came with a cheering influence to the girl. A terrible question as to what might be the result of her arrival at the Cape had suggested itself to her more than once since she had left Ireland; but now the major did not seem to fancy that there could be any question in the matter.

When the chairs were brought, and enveloped in karosses, as the old campaigners called the furs, there arose a chatter of bungalows, and punkahs, and puggarees, and calapashes, and curries, that was quite delightful to the girl's ears, especially as from time to time her father's name would be mentioned in connection with some elephant-trapping expedition, or, perhaps, a mess joke.

When at last Daireen found herself alone in the cabin which her grandfather had managed to secure for her, she did not feel that loneliness which she thought she should have felt aboard this ship full of strangers without sympathy for her.

She stood for a short time in the darkness, looking out of her cabin port over the long waters, and listening to the sound of the waves hurrying away from the ship and flapping against its sides, and once more she thought of the purple mountain and the green Irish Lough. Then as she moved away from the port her thoughts stretched in another direction—southward. Her heart was full of hope as she turned in to her bunk and went quietly asleep just as the first waves of the Bay of Biscay were making the good steamer a little uneasy, and bringing about a bitter remorse to those who had made merry over the dumplings and buttered toast.

Major Crawford was an officer who had served for a good many years in India, and had there become acquainted with Daireen's father and mother. When Mr. Gerald was holding his grandchild in his arms aboard the steamer saying good-bye, he was surprised by a strange lady coming up to him and begging to be informed if it was possible that Daireen was the daughter of Colonel Gerald. In another instant Mr. Gerald was overjoyed to know that Daireen would be during the entire voyage in the company of an officer and his wife who were old friends of her father, and had recognised her from her likeness to her mother, whom they had also known when she was little older than Daireen. Mr. Gerald left the vessel with a mind at rest; and that his belief that the girl would be looked after was well-founded is already known. Daireen was, indeed, in the hands of a lady who was noted in many parts of the world for her capacities for taking charge of young ladies. When she was in India her position at the station was very similiar to that of immigration-agent-general. Fond matrons in England, who had brought their daughters year after year to Homburg, Kissingen, and Nice, in the "open" season, and had yet brought them back in safety — matrons who had even sunk to the low level of hydropathic hunting-grounds without success, were accustomed to write pathetic letters to Junkapore and Arradambad conveying to Mrs. Crawford intelligence of the strange fancy that some of the dear girls had conceived to visit those parts of the Indian Empire, and begging Mrs. Crawford to give her valuable advice with regard to the carrying out of such remarkable freaks. Never in any of these cases had the major's wife failed. These forlorn hopes took passage to India and found in her a real friend, with tact, perseverance, and experience. The subalterns of the station were never allowed to mope in a wretched, companionless condition; and thus Mrs. Crawford had achieved for herself a certain fame, which it was her study to maintain. Having herself had men-children only, she had no personal interests to look after. Her boys had been swaddled in puggarees, spoon-fed with curry, and nurtured upon chutney, and had so developed into full-grown Indians ready for the choicest appointments, and they had succeeded very well indeed. Her husband had now received a command from the War Office to proceed to the Cape for the purpose of obtaining evidence on the subject of the regulation boots to be supplied to troops on active foreign service; a commission upon this most important subject having been ordered by a Parliamentary vote. Other officers of experience had been sent to various of the colonies, and much was expected to result from the prosecution of their inquiries, the opponents of the Government being confident that gussets would eventually be allowed to non-commissioned officers, and back straps to privates.

Of course Major Crawford could not set out on a mission so important without the companionship of his wife. Though just at the instant of Daireen's turning in, the major fancied he might have managed to get along pretty well even if his partner had been left behind him in England. He was inclined to snarl in his cabin at nights when his wife unfolded her plans to him and kept him awake to give his opinion as to the possibility of the tastes of various young persons becoming assimilated. To-night the major expressed his indifference as to whether every single man in the ship's company got married to every single woman before the end of the voyage, or whether they all went to perdition singly. He concluded by wishing fervently that they would disappear, married and single, by a supernatural agency.

"But think, how gratified poor Gerald would be if the dear girl could think as I do on this subject," said Mrs. Crawford persistently, alluding to the matter of certain amalgamation of tastes. At this point, however, the major expressed himself in words still more vigorous than he had brought to his aid before, and his wife thought it prudent to get into her bunk without pursuing any further the question of the possible gratification of Colonel Gerald at the unanimity of thought existing between his daughter and Mrs. Crawford.

CHAPTER IX

How dangerous is it that this man goes loose...
He's loved of the distracted multitude,
Who like not in their judgment but their eyes:
And where 'tis so the offender's scourge is weigh'd,
But never the offence.

Look here upon this picture, and on this.

Thus has he—and many more of the same breed that I know
the drossy age dotes on—only got the tune of the time... a
kind of yesty collection which carries them through and
through the most fond and winnowed opinions; and do but
blow them to their trial, the bubbles are out.—*Hamlet.*

THE uneasy bosom of the Bay of Biscay was throbbing with its
customary emotion beneath the good vessel, when Daireen awoke the next
morning to the sound of creaking timbers and rioting glasses. Above her
on the deck the tramp of a healthy passenger, who wore a pedometer and
walked three miles every morning before breakfast, was heard, now dilating
and now decreasing, as he passed over the cabins. He had almost completed
his second mile, and was putting on a spurt in order to keep himself up to
time; his spurt at the end of the first mile had effectually awakened all the
passengers beneath, who had yet remained undisturbed through the earlier
part of his tramp.

Mrs. Crawford, looking bright and fresh and good-natured, entered
Daireen's cabin before the girl was ready to leave it. She certainly seemed
determined that the confidence Mr. Gerald had reposed in her with regard
to the care of his granddaughter should not prove to have been misplaced.

"I am not going in, my dear," she said as she entered the cabin. "I
only stepped round to see that you were all right this morning. I knew
you would be so, though Robinson the steward tells me that even the little
sea there is on in the bay has been quite sufficient to make about a dozen
vacancies at the breakfast-table. People are such fools when they come
aboard a ship—eating boiled paste and all sorts of things, and so the sea is
grossly misrepresented. Did that dreadfully healthy Mr. Thompson awake

you with his tramping on deck? Of course he did; he's a dreadful man. If he goes on like this we'll have to petition the captain to lay down bark on the deck. Now I'll leave you. Come aloft when you are ready; and, by the way, you must take care what dress you put on—very great care."

"Why, I thought that aboard ship one might wear anything," said the girl.

"Never was there a greater mistake, my child. People say the same about going to the seaside: anything will do; but you know how one requires to be doubly particular there; and it's just the same in our little world aboard ship."

"You quite frighten me, Mrs. Crawford," said Daireen. "What advice can you give me on the subject?"

Mrs. Crawford was thoughtful. "If you had only had time to prepare for the voyage, and I had been beside you, everything might have been different. You must not wear anything pronounced—any distinct colour: you must find out something undecided—you understand?"

Daireen looked puzzled. "I'm sorry to say I don't."

"Oh, you have surely something of pale sage—no, that is a bad tone for the first days aboard—too like the complexions of most of the passengers—but, chocolate-gray? ah, that should do: have you anything in that to do for a morning dress?"

Daireen was so extremely fortunate as to be possessed of a garment of the required tone, and her kind friend left her arraying herself in its folds.

On going aloft Daireen found the deck occupied by a select few of the passengers. The healthy gentleman was just increasing his pace for the final hundred yards of his morning's walk, and Doctor Campion had got very near the end of his second cheroot, while he sat talking to a fair-haired and bronze-visaged man with clear gray eyes that had such a way of looking at things as caused people to fancy he was making a mental calculation of the cubic measure of everything; and it was probably the recollection of their peculiarity that made people fancy, when these eyes looked into a human face, that the mind of the man was going through a similar calculation with reference to the human object: one could not avoid feeling that he had a number of formulas for calculating the intellectual value of people, and that when he looked at a person he was thinking which formula should be employed for arriving at a conclusion regarding that person's mental capacity.

Mrs. Crawford was chatting with the doctor and his companion, but on Daireen's appearing, she went over to her.

"Perfect, my child," she said in a whisper—"the tone of the dress, I mean; it will work wonders."

While Daireen was reflecting upon the possibility of a suspension of the laws of nature being the result of the appearance of the chocolate-toned dress, she was led towards the doctor, who immediately went through a fiction of rising from his seat as she approached; and one would really have fancied that he intended getting upon his feet, and was only restrained at the last moment by a remonstrance of the girl's. Daireen acknowledged his courtesy, though it was only imaginary, and she was conscious that his companion had really risen.

"You haven't made the acquaintance of Miss Gerald, Mr. Harwood?" said Mrs. Crawford.

"I have not had the honour," said the man.

"Let me present you, Daireen. Mr. Harwood—Miss Gerald. Now take great care what you say to this gentleman, Daireen; he is a dangerous man— the most dangerous that any one could meet. He is a detective, dear, and the worst of all—a literary detective; the 'special' of the *Domnant Trumpeter*."

Daireen had looked into the man's face while she was being presented to him, and she knew it was the face of a man who had seen the people of more than one nation.

"This is not your first voyage, Miss Gerald, or you would not be on deck so early?" he said.

"It certainly is not," she replied. "I was born in India, so that my first voyage was to England; then I have crossed the Irish Channel frequently, going to school and returning for the holidays; and I have also had some long voyages on Lough Suangorm," she added with a little smile, for she did not think that her companion would be likely to have heard of the existence of the Irish fjord.

"Suangorm? then you have had some of the most picturesque voyages one can make in the course of a day in this world," he said. "Lough Suangorm is the most wonderful fjord in the world, let me tell you."

"Then you know it," she cried with a good deal of surprise. "You must know the dear old lough or you would not talk so." She did not seem to think that his assertion should imply that he had seen a good many other fjords also.

"I think I may say I know it. Yes, from those fine headlands that the Atlantic beats against, to where the purple slope of that great hill meets the little road."

"You know the hill—old Slieve Docas? How strange! I live just at the foot."

"I have a sketch of a mansion, taken just there," he said, laughing. "It is of a dark brown exterior."

"Exactly."

"It looks towards the sea."

"It does indeed."

"It is exceedingly picturesque."

"Picturesque?"

"Well, yes; the house I allude to is very much so. If I recollect aright, the one window of the wall was not glazed, and the smoke certainly found its way out through a hole in the roof."

"Oh, that is too bad," said Daireen. "I had no idea that the peculiarities of my country people would be known so far away. Please don't say anything about that sketch to the passengers aboard."

"I shall never be tempted to allude, even by the 'pronouncing of some doubtful phrase,' to the—the—peculiarities of your country people, Miss Gerald," he answered. "It is a lovely country, and contains the most hospitable people in the world; but their talent does not develop itself architecturally. Ah! there is the second bell. I hope you have an appetite."

"Have you been guarded enough in your conversation, Daireen?" said Mrs. Crawford, coming up with the doctor, whose rising at the summons of the breakfast-bell was by no means a fiction.

"The secrets of the Home Rule Confederation are safe in the keeping of Miss Gerald," said Mr. Harwood, with a smile which any one could see was simply the result of his satisfaction at having produced a well-turned sentence.

The breakfast-table was very thinly attended, more so even than Robinson the steward had anticipated when on the previous evening he had laid down that second plate of buttered toast before the novices.

Of the young ladies only three appeared at the table, and their complexions were of the softest amber shade that was ever worked in satin in the upholstery of mock-mediæval furniture. Major Crawford had just come out of the steward's pantry, and he greeted Daireen with all courtesy, as indeed he did the other young ladies at the table, for the major was gallant and gay aboard ship.

After every one had been seated for about ten minutes, the curtain that screened off one of the cabin entrances from the saloon was moved aside, and the figure of the young man to whom Mrs. Crawford had alluded as Mr. Glaston appeared. He came slowly forward, nodding to the captain and saying good-morning to Mrs. Crawford, while he elevated his eyebrows in recognition of Mr. Harwood, taking his seat at the table.

"You can't have an appetite coming directly out of your bunk," said the doctor.

"Indeed?" said Mr. Glaston, without the least expression.

"Quite impossible," said the doctor. "You should have been up an hour ago at least. Here is Mr. Thompson, who has walked more than three miles in the open air."

"Ah," said the other, never moving his eyes to see the modest smile that spread itself over the features of the exemplary Mr. Thompson. "Ah, I heard some one who seemed to be going in for that irrepressible thousand miles in a thousand hours. Yes, bring me a pear and a grape." The last sentence he addressed to the waiter, who, having been drilled by the steward on the subject of Mr. Glaston's tastes, did not show any astonishment at being asked for fruit instead of fish, but hastened off to procure the grape and the pear.

While Mr. Glaston was waiting he glanced across the table, and gave a visible start as his eyes rested upon one of the young ladies—a pleasant-looking girl wearing a pink dress and having a blue ribbon in her hair. Mr. Glaston gave a little shudder, and then turned away.

"That face—ah, where have I beheld it?" muttered Mr. Harwood to the doctor.

"Dam puppy!" said the doctor.

Then the plate and fruit were laid before Mr. Glaston, who said quickly, "Take them away." The bewildered waiter looked towards his chief and obeyed, so that Mr. Glaston remained with an empty plate. Robinson became uneasy.

"Can I get you anything, sir?—we have three peaches aboard and a pine-apple," he murmured.

"Can't touch anything now, Robinson," Mr. Glaston answered.

"The doctor is right," said Mrs. Crawford. "You have no appetite, Mr. Glaston."

"No," he replied; "not *now*," and he gave the least glance towards the girl in pink, who began to feel that all her school dreams of going forth into the world of men to conquer and overcome were being realised beyond her wildest anticipations.

Then there was a pause at the table, which the good major broke by suddenly inquiring something of the captain. Mr. Glaston, however, sat silent, and somewhat sad apparently, until the breakfast was over.

Daireen went into her cabin for a book, and remained arranging some volumes on the little shelf for a few minutes. Mr. Glaston was on deck when she ascended, and he was engaged in a very serious conversation with Mrs. Crawford.

"Something must be done. Surely she has a guardian aboard who is not so utterly lost to everything of truth and right as to allow that to go on unchecked."

These words Daireen could make out as she passed the young man and the major's wife, and the girl began to fear that something terrible was about to happen. But Mr. Harwood, who was standing above the major's chair, hastened forward as she appeared.

"Why, Major Crawford has been telling me that your father is Colonel Gerald," he said. "Mrs. Crawford never mentioned that fact, thinking that I should be able to guess it for myself."

"Did you know papa?" Daireen asked.

"I met him several times when I was out about the Baroda affair," said the "special."

"And as you are his daughter, I suppose it will interest you to know that he has been selected as the first governor of the Castaways."

Daireen looked puzzled. "The Castaways?" she said.

"Yes, Miss Gerald; the lovely Castaway Islands which, you know, have just been annexed by England. Colonel Gerald has been chosen by the Colonial Secretary as the first governor."

"But I heard nothing of this," said Daireen, a little astonished to receive such information in the Bay of Biscay.

"How could you hear anything of it? No one outside the Cabinet has the least idea of it."

"And you— —" said the girl doubtfully.

"Ah, my dear Miss Gerald, the resources of information possessed by the *Dominant Trumpeter* are as unlimited as they are trustworthy. You may depend upon what I tell you. It is not generally known that I am now bound for the Castaway group, to make the British public aware of the extent of the treasure they have acquired in these sunny isles. But I understood that Colonel Gerald was on his way from Madras?"

Daireen explained how her father came to be at the Cape, and Mr. Harwood gave her a few cheering words regarding his sickness. She was greatly disappointed when their conversation was interrupted by Mrs. Crawford.

"The poor fellow!" she said — "Mr. Glaston, I mean. I have induced him to go down and eat some grapes and a pear."

"Why couldn't he take them at breakfast and not betray his idiocy?" said Mr. Harwood.

"Mr. Harwood, you have no sympathy for sufferers from sensitiveness," replied the lady. "Poor Mr. Glaston! he had an excellent appetite, but he found it impossible to touch anything the instant he saw that fearful pink dress with the blue ribbon hanging over it."

"Poor fellow!" said Mr. Harwood.

"Dam puppy!" said the doctor.

"Campion!" cried Mrs. Crawford severely.

"A thousand pardons! my dear Miss Gerald," said the transgressor. "But what can a man say when he hears of such puppyism? This is my third voyage with that young man, and he has been developing into the full-grown puppy with the greatest rapidity."

"You have no fine feeling, Campion," said Mrs. Crawford. "You have got no sympathy for those who are artistically sensitive. But hush! here is the offending person herself, and with such a hat! Now admit that to look at her sends a cold shudder through you."

"I think her a devilish pretty little thing, by gad," said the doctor.

The young lady with the pink dress and the blue ribbon appeared, wearing the additional horror of a hat lined with yellow and encircled with mighty flowers.

"Something must be done to suppress her," said Mrs. Crawford decisively. "Surely such people must have a better side to their natures that one may appeal to."

"I doubt it, Mrs. Crawford," said Mr. Harwood, with only the least tinge of sarcasm in his voice. "I admit that one might not have been in utter despair though the dress was rather aggressive, but I cannot see anything but depravity in that hat with those floral splendours."

"But what is to be done?" said the lady. "Mr. Glaston would, no doubt, advocate making a Jonah of that young person for the sake of saving the rest of the ship's company. But, however just that might be, I do not suppose it would be considered strictly legal."

"Many acts of justice are done that are not legal," replied Harwood gravely. "From a legal standpoint, Cain was no murderer—his accuser being witness and also judge. He would leave the court without a stain on his character nowadays. Meantime, major, suppose we have a smoke on the bridge."

"He fancies he has said something clever," remarked Mrs. Crawford when he had walked away; and it must be confessed that Mr. Harwood had a suspicion to that effect.

CHAPTER X

His will is not his own;
For he himself is subject to his birth:
He may not, as unvalued persons do,
Carve for himself; for on his choice depends
The safety and the health of this whole state,
And therefore must his choice be circumscribed
Unto the voice and yielding of that body,
Whereof he is the head.

Osric.... Believe me, an absolute gentleman, full of most excellent differences, of very soft society and great showing; indeed, to speak feelingly of him, he is the card... of gentry.

Hamlet.... His definement suffers no perdition in you... But, in the verity of extolment I take him to be a soul of great article.—*Hamlet.*

THE information which Daireen had received on the unimpeachable authority of the special correspondent of the *Dominant Trumpeter* was somewhat puzzling to her at first; but as she reflected upon the fact hat the position of governor of the newly-acquired Castaway group must be one of importance, she could not help feeling some happiness; only in the midmost heart of her joy her recollection clasped a single grief—-a doubt about her father was still clinging to her heart. The letter her grandfather had received which caused her to make up her mind to set out for the Cape, merely stated that Colonel Gerald had been found too weak to continue the homeward voyage in the vessel that had brought him from India. He had a bad attack of fever, and was not allowed to be moved from where he lay at the Cape. The girl thought over all of this as she reflected upon what Mr. Harwood had told her, and looking over the long restless waters of the Bay of Biscay from her seat far astern, her eyes became very misty; the unhappy author represented by the yellow-covered book which she had been reading lay neglected upon her knee. But soon her brave, hopeful heart took courage, and she began to paint in her imagination the fairest pictures of the future—a future beneath the rich blue sky that was alleged by the Ministers who had brought about the annexation, evermore to overshadow the Castaway group—a future beneath the purple shadow of the giant Slieve Docas when her father would have discharged his duties at the Castaways.

She could not even pretend to herself to be reading the book she had brought up, so that Mrs. Crawford could not have been accused of an interruption when she drew her chair alongside the girl's, saying:

"We must have a little chat together, now that there is a chance for it. It is really terrible how much time one can fritter away aboard ship. I have known people take long voyages for the sake of study, and yet never open a single book but a novel. By the way, what is this the major has been telling me Harwood says about your father?"

Daireen repeated all that Harwood had said regarding the new island colony, and begged Mrs. Crawford to give an opinion as to the trustworthiness of the information.

"My dear child," said Mrs. Crawford, "you may depend upon its truth if Harwood told it to you. The *Dominant Trumpeter* sends out as many arms as an octopus, for news, and, like the octopus too, it has the instinct of only making use of what is worth anything. The Government have been very good to George—I mean Colonel Gerald—he was always 'George' with us when he was lieutenant. The Castaway governorship is one of the nice things they sometimes have to dispose of to the deserving. It was thought, you know, that George would sell out and get his brevet long ago, but what he often said to us after your poor mother died convinced me that he would not accept a quiet life. And so it was Mr. Harwood that gave you this welcome news," she continued, adding in a thoughtful tone, "By the way, what do you think of Mr. Harwood?"

"I really have not thought anything about him," Daireen replied, wondering if it was indeed a necessity of life aboard ship to be able at a moment's notice to give a summary of her opinion as to the nature of every person she might chance to meet.

"He is a very nice man," said Mrs. Crawford; "only just inclined to be conceited, don't you think? This is our third voyage with him, so that we know something of him. One knows more of a person at the end of a week at sea than after a month ashore. What can be keeping Mr. Glaston over his pears, I wonder? I meant to have presented him to you before. Ah, here he comes out of the companion. I asked him to return to me."

But again Mrs. Crawford's expectations were dashed to the ground. Mr. Glaston certainly did appear on deck, and showed some sign in a languid way of walking over to where Mrs. Crawford was sitting, but unfortunately before he had taken half a dozen steps he caught sight of that terrible pink dress and the hat with the jaundiced interior. He stopped short, and a look of martyrdom passed over his face as he turned and made his way to the bridge in the opposite direction to where that horror of pronounced tones sat quite unconscious of the agony her appearance was creating in the aesthetic soul of the young man.

Daireen having glanced up and seen the look of dismay upon his face, and the flight of Mr. Glaston, could not avoid laughing outright so soon as he had disappeared. But Mrs. Crawford did not laugh. On the contrary she looked very grave.

"This is terrible—terrible, Daireen," she said. "That vile hat has driven him away. I knew it must."

"Matters are getting serious indeed," said the girl, with only the least touch of mockery in her voice. "If he is not allowed to eat anything at breakfast in sight of the dress, and he is driven up to the bridge by a glimpse of the hat, I am afraid that his life will not be quite happy here."

"Happy! my dear, you cannot conceive the agonies he endures through his sensitiveness. I must make the acquaintance of that young person and try to bring her to see the error of her ways. Oh, how fortunate you had this chocolate-gray!"

"I must have thought of it in a moment of inspiration," said Daireen.

"Come, you really mustn't laugh," said the elder lady reprovingly. "It was a happy thought, at any rate, and I only hope that you will be able to sustain its effect by something good at dinner. I must look over your trunks and tell you what tone is most artistic."

Daireen began to feel rebellious.

"My dear Mrs. Crawford, it is very kind of you to offer to take so much trouble; but, you see, I do not feel it to be a necessity to choose the shade of my dress solely to please the taste of a gentleman who may not be absolutely perfect in his ideas."

Mrs. Crawford laughed. "Do not get angry, my dear," she said. "I admire your spirit, and I will not attempt to control your own good taste; you will never, I am sure, sink to such a depth of depravity as is manifested by that hat."

"Well, I think you may depend on me so far," said Daireen.

Shortly afterwards Mrs. Crawford descended to arrange some matters in her cabin, and Daireen had consequently an opportunity of returning to her neglected author.

But before she had made much progress in her study she was again interrupted, and this time by Doctor Campion, who had been smoking with Mr. Harwood on the ship's bridge. Doctor Campion was a small man, with a reddish face upon which a perpetual frown was resting. He had a jerky way of turning his head as if it was set upon a ratchet wheel only capable of shifting a tooth at a time. He had been in the army for a good many years, and had only accepted the post aboard the *Cardwell Castle* for the sake of his health.

"Young cub!" he muttered, as he came up to Daireen. "Infernal young cub!—I beg your pardon, Miss Gerald, but I really must say it. That fellow Glaston is getting out of all bounds. Ah, it's his father's fault—his father's fault. Keeps him dawdling about England without any employment. Why, it would have been better for him to have taken to the Church, as they call it, at once, idle though the business is."

"Surely you have not been wearing an inartistic tie, Doctor Campion?"

"Inartistic indeed! The puppy has got so much cant on his finger-ends that weak-minded people think him a genius. Don't you believe it, my dear; he's a dam puppy—excuse me, but there's really no drawing it mild here."

Daireen was amused at the doctor's vehemence, however shocked she may have been at his manner of getting rid of it.

"What on earth has happened with Mr. Glaston now?" she asked. "It is impossible that there could be another obnoxious dress aboard."

"He hasn't given himself any airs in that direction since," said the doctor. "But he came up to the bridge where we were smoking, and after he had talked for a minute with Harwood, he started when he saw a boy who had been sent up to clean out one of the hencoops—asked if we didn't think his head marvellously like Carlyle's—was amazed at our want of judgment—went up to the boy and cross-questioned him—found out that his father sells vegetables to the Victoria Docks—asked if it had ever been remarked before that his head was like Carlyle's—boy says quickly that if the man he means is the tailor in Wapping, anybody that says his head is like that man's is a liar, and then boy goes quietly down. 'Wonderful!' says our genius, as he comes over to us; 'wonderful head—exactly the same as Carlyle's, and language marvellously similar—brief—earnest—emphatic—full of powah!' Then he goes on to say he'll take notes of the boy's peculiarities and send them to a magazine. I couldn't stand any more of that sort of thing, so I left him with Harwood. Harwood can sift him."

Daireen laughed at this new story of the young man whose movements seemed to be regarded as of so much importance by every one aboard the steamer. She began really to feel interested in this Mr. Glaston; and she thought that perhaps she might as well be particular about the tone of the dress she would select for appearing in before the judicial eyes of this Mr. Glaston. She relinquished the design she had formed in her mind while Mrs. Crawford was urging on her the necessity for discrimination in this respect: she had resolved to show a recklessness in her choice of a dress, but now she felt that she had better take Mrs. Crawford's advice, and give some care to the artistic combinations of her toilette.

The result of her decision was that she appeared in such studious carelessness of attire that Mr. Glaston, sitting opposite to her, was enabled to eat a hearty dinner utterly regardless of the aggressive splendour of the imperial blue dress worn by the other young lady, with a pink ribbon flowing over it from her hair. This young lady's imagination was unequal to suggesting a more diversified arrangement than she had already shown. She thought it gave evidence of considerable strategical resources to wear that pink ribbon over the blue dress: it was very nearly as effective as the blue ribbon over the pink, of the morning. The appreciation of contrast as an important element of effect in art was very strongly developed in this young lady.

Mrs. Crawford did not conceal the satisfaction she felt observing the appetite of Mr. Glaston; and after dinner she took his arm as he went towards the bridge.

"I am so glad you were not offended with that dreadful young person's hideous colours," she said, as they strolled along.

"I could hardly have believed it possible that such wickedness could survive nowadays," he replied. "But I was, after the first few minutes, quite unconscious of its enormity. My dear Mrs. Crawford, your young protégée appeared as a spirit of light to charm away that fiend of evil. She sat before me—a poem of tones—a delicate symphony of Schumann's played at twilight on the brink of a mere of long reeds and water-flags, with a single star shining through the well-defined twigs of a solitary alder. That was her idea, don't you think?"

"I have no doubt of it," the lady replied after a little pause. "But if you allow me to present you to her you will have an opportunity of finding out. Now do let me."

"Not this evening, Mrs. Crawford; I do not feel equal to it," he answered. "She has given me too much to think about—too many ideas to work out. That was the most thoughtful and pure-souled toilette I ever recollect; but there are a few points about it I do not fully grasp, though I have an instinct of their meaning. No, I want a quiet hour alone. But you will do me the favour to thank the child for me."

"I wish you would come and do it yourself," said the lady. "But I suppose there is no use attempting to force you. If you change your mind, remember that we shall be here."

She left the young man preparing a cigarette, and joined Daireen and the major, who were sitting far astern: the girl with that fiction of a fiction still in her hand; her companion with a cheroot that was anything but insubstantial in his fingers.

"My dear child," whispered Mrs. Crawford, "I am so glad you took your own way and would not allow me to choose your dress for you. I could never have dreamt of anything so perfect and— —yes, it is far beyond what I could have composed."

Mrs. Crawford thought it better on the whole not to transfer to Daireen the expression of gratitude Mr. Glaston had begged to be conveyed to her. She had an uneasy consciousness that such a message coming to one who was as yet unacquainted with Mr. Glaston might give her the impression that he was inclined to have some of that unhappy conceit, with the possession of which Mrs. Crawford herself had accredited the race generally.

"Miss Gerald is an angel in whatever dress she may wear," said the major gallantly. "What is dress, after all?" he asked. "By gad, my dear, the finest women I ever recollect seeing were in Burmah, and all the dress they wore was the merest— —"

"Major, you forget yourself," cried his wife severely.

The major pulled vigorously at the end of his moustache, grinning and bobbing his head towards the doctor.

"By gad, my dear, the recollection of those beauties would make any fellow forget not only himself but his own wife, even if she was as fine a woman as yourself."

The doctor's face relapsed into its accustomed frown after he had given a responsive grin and a baritone chuckle to the delicate pleasantry of his old comrade.

CHAPTER XI

Look, with what courteous action
It waves you to a more removed ground:
But do not go with it.

The very place puts toys of desperation,
Without more motive, into every brain.

Horatio. What are they that would speak with me?

Servant. Sea-faring men, sir.—*Hamlet.*

WHO does not know the delightful monotony of a voyage southward, broken only at the intervals of anchoring beneath the brilliant green slopes of Madeira or under the grim shadow of the cliffs of St. Helena?

The first week of the voyage for those who are not sensitive of the uneasy motion of the ship through the waves of the Bay of Biscay is perhaps the most delightful, for then every one is courteous with every one else. The passengers have not become friendly enough to be able to quarrel satisfactorily. The young ladies have got a great deal of white about them, and they have not begun to show that jealousy of each other which the next fortnight so powerfully develops. The men, too, are prodigal in their distribution of cigars; and one feels in one's own heart nothing but the most generous emotions, as one sits filling a meerschaum with Latakia in the delicate twilight of time and of thought that succeeds the curried lobster and pilau chickens as prepared in the galley of such ships as the *Cardwell Castle*. Certainly for a week of Sabbaths a September voyage to Madeira must be looked to.

Things had begun to arrange themselves aboard the *Cardwell Castle*. The whist sets and the deck sets had been formed. The far-stretching arm of society had at least one finger in the construction of the laws of life in this Atlantic ship-town.

The young woman with the pronounced tastes in colour and the large resources of imagination in the arrangement of blue and pink had become less aggressive, as she was compelled to fall back upon the minor glories of her trunk, so that there was no likelihood of Mr. Glaston's perishing of starvation. Though very fond of taking-up young ladies, Mrs. Crawford had no great struggle with her propensity so far as this young lady was concerned. But as Mr. Glaston had towards the evening of the third day of the voyage found himself in a fit state of mind to be presented to Miss Gerald, Mrs. Crawford had nothing to complain of. She knew that the young man was invariably fascinating to all of her sex, and she could see no reason why Miss Gerald should not have at least the monotony of the voyage relieved for her through the improving nature of his conversation. To be sure, Mr. Harwood also possessed in his conversation many elements of improvement, but then they were of a more commonplace type in Mrs. Crawford's eyes, and she thought it as well, now and again when he was sitting beside Daireen, to make a third to their party and assist in the solution of any question they might be discussing. She rather wished that it had not been in Mr. Harwood's power to give Daireen that information about her father's appointment; it was a sort of link of friendship between him and the girl; but Mrs. Crawford recollected her own responsibility with regard to Daireen too well to allow such a frail link to become a bond to bind with any degree of force.

She was just making a mental resolution to this effect upon the day preceding their expected arrival at Madeira, when Mr. Harwood, who had before tiffin been showing the girl how to adjust a binocular glass, strolled up to where the major's wife sat resolving many things, reflecting upon her victories in quarter-deck campaigns of the past and laying out her tactics for the future.

"This is our third voyage together, is it not, Mrs. Crawford?" he asked.

"Let me see," said the lady. "Yes, it is our third. Dear, dear, how time runs past us!"

"I wish it did run past us; unfortunately it seems to remain to work some of its vengeance upon each of us. But do you think we ever had a more charming voyage so far as this has run, Mrs. Crawford?"

The lady became thoughtful. "That was a very nice trip in the P. & O.'s *Turcoman*, when Mr. Carpingham of the Gunners proposed to Clara Walton before he landed at Aden," she said. "Curiously enough, I was thinking about that very voyage just before you came up now. General Walton had placed Clara in my care, and it was I who presented her to young Carpingham." There was a slight tone of triumph in her voice as she recalled this victory of the past.

"I remember well," said Mr. Harwood. "How pleased every one was, and also how—well, the weather was extremely warm in the Red Sea just before he proposed. But I certainly think that this voyage is likely to be quite as pleasant. By the way, what a charming protégée you have got this time, Mrs. Crawford."

"She is a dear girl indeed, and I hope that she may find her father all right at the Cape. Think of what she must suffer."

Mr. Harwood glanced round and saw that Mr. Glaston had strolled up to Daireen's chair. "Yes, I have no doubt that she suffers," he said. "But she is so gentle, so natural in her thoughts and in her manner, I should indeed be sorry that any trouble would come to her." He was himself speaking gently now—so gently, in fact, that Mrs. Crawford drew her lips together with a slight pressure. "Perhaps it is because I am so much older than she that she talks to me naturally as she would to her father. I am old enough to be her father, I suppose," he added almost mournfully. But this only made the lady's lips become more compressed. She had heard men talk before now of being old enough to be young ladies' fathers, and she could also recollect instances of men who were actually old enough to be young ladies' grandfathers marrying those very young ladies.

"Yes," said Mrs. Crawford, "Daireen is a dear natural little thing." Into the paternal potentialities of Mr. Harwood's position towards this dear natural little thing Mrs. Crawford did not think it judicious to go just then.

"She is a dear child," he repeated. "By the way, we shall be at Funchal at noon to-morrow, and we do not leave until the evening. You will land, I suppose?"

"I don't think I shall, I know every spot so well, and those bullock sleighs are so tiresome. I am not so young as I was when I first made their acquaintance."

"Oh, really, if that is your only plea, my dear Mrs. Crawford, we may count on your being in our party."

"Our party!" said the lady.

"I should not say that until I get your consent," said Harwood quickly. "Miss Gerald has never been at the island, you see, and she is girlishly eager to go ashore. Miss Butler and her mother are also landing"—these were other passengers—"and in a weak moment I volunteered my services as guide. Don't you think you can trust me so far as to agree to be one of us?"

"Of course I can," she said. "If Daireen wishes to go ashore you may depend upon my keeping her company. But you will have to provide a sleigh for myself."

"You may depend upon the sleigh, Mrs. Crawford; and many thanks for your trusting to my guidance. Though I sleigh you yet you will trust me."

"Mr. Harwood, that is dreadful. I am afraid that Mrs. Butler will need one of them also."

"The entire sleigh service shall be impressed if necessary," said the "special," as he walked away.

Mrs. Crawford felt that she had not done anything rash. Daireen would, no doubt, be delighted with the day among the lovely heights of Madeira, and if by some little thoughtfulness it would be possible to hit upon a plan that should give over the guidance of some of the walking members of the party to Mr. Glaston, surely the matter was worth pursuing.

Mr. Glaston was just at this instant looking into, Daireen's face as he talked to her. He invariably kept his eyes fixed upon the faces of the young women to whom he was fond of talking. It did not argue any earnestness on his part, Mrs. Crawford knew. He seemed now, however, to be a little in earnest in what he was saying. But then Mrs. Crawford reflected that the subjects upon which his discourse was most impassioned were mostly those that other people would call trivial, such as the effect produced upon the mind of man by seeing a grape-green ribbon lying upon a pale amber cushion. "Every colour has got its soul," she once heard him say; "and though any one can appreciate its meaning and the work it has to perform in the world, the subtle thoughts breathed by the tones are too delicate to be understood except by a few. Colour is language of the subtlest nature, and one can praise God through that medium just as one can blaspheme through it." He had said this very earnestly at one time, she recollected, and as she now saw Daireen laugh she thought it was not impossible that it might be at some phrase of the same nature, the meaning of which her uncultured ear did not at once catch, that Daireen had laughed. Daireen, at any rate, did laugh in spite of his earnestness of visage.

In a few moments Mr. Glaston came over to Mrs. Crawford, and now his face wore an expression of sadness rather than of any other emotion.

"My dear Mrs. Crawford, you surely cannot intend to give your consent to that child's going ashore tomorrow. She tells me that that newspaper fellow has drawn her into a promise to land with a party—actually a party— and go round the place like a Cook's excursion."

"Oh, I hope we shall not be like that, Mr. Glaston," said Mrs. Crawford.

"But you have not given your consent?"

"If Daireen would enjoy it I do not see how I could avoid. Mr. Harwood was talking to me just now. He seems to think she will enjoy herself, as she has never seen the island before. Will you not be one of our party?"

"Oh, Mrs. Crawford, if you have got the least regard for me, do not say that word party; it means everything that is popular; it suggests unutterable horrors to me. No subsequent pleasure could balance the agony I should endure going ashore. Will you not try and induce that child to give up the idea? Tell her what dreadful taste it would be to join a party—that it would most certainly destroy her perceptions of beauty for months to come."

"I am very sorry I promised Mr. Harwood," said the lady; "if going ashore would do all of this it would certainly be better for Daireen to remain aboard. But they will be taking in coals here," she added, as the sudden thought struck her.

"She can shut herself in her cabin and neither see nor hear anything offensive. Who but a newspaper man would think of suggesting to cultured people the possibility of enjoyment in a party?"

But the newspaper man had strolled up to the place beside Daireen, which the aesthetic man had vacated. He knew something of the art of strategical defence, this newspaper man, and he was well aware that as he had got the promise of the major's wife, all the arguments that might be advanced by any one else would not cause him to be defrauded of the happiness of being by this girl's side in one of the loveliest spots of the world.

"I will find out what Daireen thinks," said Mrs. Crawford, in reply to Mr. Glaston; and just then she turned and saw the newspaper man beside the girl.

"Never mind him," said Mr. Glaston; "tell the poor child that it is impossible for her to go."

"I really cannot break my promise," replied the lady. "We must be resigned, it will only be for a few hours."

"This is the saddest thing I ever knew," said Mr. Glaston. "She will lose all the ideas she was getting—all through being of a party. Good heavens, a party!"

Mrs. Crawford could see that Mr. Glaston was annoyed at the presence of Harwood by the side of the girl, and she smiled, for she was too old a tactician not to be well aware of the value of a skeleton enemy.

"How kind of you to say you would not mind my going ashore," said Daireen, walking up to her. "We shall enjoy ourselves I am sure, and Mr.

Harwood knows every spot to take us to. I was afraid that Mr. Glaston might be talking to you as he was to me."

"Yes, he spoke to me, but of course, my dear, if you think you would like to go ashore I shall not say anything but that I will be happy to take care of you."

"You are all that is good," said Mr. Harwood. This was very pretty, the lady thought—very pretty indeed; but at the same time she was making up her mind that if the gentleman before her had conceived it probable that he should be left to exhibit any of the wonders of the island scenery to the girl, separate from the companionship of the girl's temporary guardian, he would certainly find out that he had reckoned without due regard to other contingencies.

Sadness was the only expression visible upon the face of Mr. Glaston for the remainder of this day; but upon the following morning this aspect had changed to one of contempt as he heard nearly all the cabin's company talking with expectancy of the joys of a few hours ashore. It was a great disappointment to him to observe the brightening of the face of Daireen Gerald, as Mr. Harwood came to tell her that the land was in sight.

Daireen's face, however, did brighten. She went up to the ship's bridge, and Mr. Harwood, laying one hand upon her shoulder, pointed out with the other where upon the horizon lay a long, low, gray cloud. Mrs. Crawford observing his action, and being well aware that the girl's range of vision was not increased in the smallest degree by the touch of his fingers upon her shoulder, made a resolution that she herself would be the first to show Daireen the earliest view of St. Helena when they should be approaching that island.

But there lay that group of cloud, and onward the good steamer sped. In the course of an hour the formless mass had assumed a well-defined outline against the soft blue sky. Then a lovely white bird came about the ship from the distance like a spirit from those Fortunate Islands. In a short time a gleam of sunshine was seen reflected from the flat surface of a cliff, and then the dark chasms upon the face of each of the island-rocks of the Dezertas could be seen. But when these were passed the long island of Madeira appeared gray and massive, and with a white cloud clinging about its highest ridges. Onward still, and the thin white thread of foam encircling the rocks was perceived. Then the outline of the cliffs stood defined against the fainter background of the island; but still all was gray and colourless.

Not for long, however, for the sunlight smote the clouds and broke their gray masses, and then fell around the ridges, showing the green heights of vines and slopes of sugar-canes. But it was not until the roll of the waves against the cliff-faces was heard that the cloud-veil was lifted and all the glad green beauty of the slope flashed up to the blue sky, and thrilled all those who stood on the deck of the vessel.

Along this lovely coast the vessel moved through the sparkling green ripples. Not the faintest white fleck of cloud was now in the sky, and the sunlight falling downwards upon the island, brought out every brown rock of the coast in bold relief against the brilliant green of the slope. So close to the shore the vessel passed, the nearer cliffs appeared to glide away as the land in their shade was disclosed, and this effect of soft motion was entrancing to all who experienced it. Then the low headland with the island-rock crowned with a small pillared building was reached and passed, and the lovely bay of Funchal came in view.

Daireen, who had lived among the sombre magnificence of the Irish scenery, felt this soft dazzling green as something marvellously strange and unexpected. Had not Mr. Glaston descended to his cabin at the earliest expression of delight that was forced from the lips of some young lady on the deck, he, would have been still more disappointed with Daireen, for her face was shining with happiness. But Mr. Harwood found more pleasure in watching her face than he did in gazing at the long crescent slope of the bay, and at the white houses that peeped from amongst the vines, or at the high convent of the hill. He did not speak a word to the girl, but only watched her as she drank in everything of beauty that passed before her.

Then the Loo rock at the farther point of the bay was neared, and as the engine slowed, the head of the steamer was brought round towards the white town of Funchal, spread all about the beach where the huge rollers were breaking. The tinkle of the engine-room telegraph brought a wonderful silence over everything as the propeller ceased. The voice of the captain giving orders about the lead line was heard distinctly, and the passengers felt inclined to speak in whispers. Suddenly with a harsh roar the great chain cable rushes out and the anchor drops into the water.

"This is the first stage of our voyage," said Mr. Harwood. "Now, while I select a boat, will you kindly get ready for landing? Oh, Mrs. Crawford, you will be with us at once, I suppose?"

"Without the loss of a moment," said the lady, going down to the cabins with Daireen.

The various island authorities pushed off from the shore in their boats, sitting under canvas awnings and looking unpleasantly like banditti. Doctor Campion answered their kind inquiries regarding the health of the passengers, for nothing could exceed the attentive courtesy shown by the government in this respect.

Then a young Scotchman, who had resolved to emulate Mr. Harwood's example in taking a party ashore, began making a bargain by signs with one of the boatmen, while his friends stood around. The major and the doctor having plotted together to go up to pay a visit to an hotel, pushed off in a government boat without acquainting any one with their movements. But long before the Scotchman had succeeded in reducing the prohibitory sum named by the man with whom he was treating for the transit of the party ashore, Mr. Harwood had a boat waiting at the rail for his friends, and Mrs. Butler and her daughter were in act to descend, chatting with the "special" who was to be their guide. Another party had already left for the shore, the young lady who had worn the blue and pink appearing in a bonnet surrounded with resplendent flowers and beads. But before the smiles of Mrs. Butler and Harwood had passed away, Mrs. Crawford and Daireen had come on deck again, the former with many apologies for her delay.

Mr. Harwood ran down the sloping rail to assist the ladies into the boat that rose and fell with every throb of the waves against the ship's side. Mrs. Crawford followed him and was safely stowed in a place in the stern. Then came Mrs. Butler and her daughter, and while Mr. Harwood was handing them off the last step Daireen began to descend. But she had not got farther down than to where a young sailor was kneeling to shift the line of one of the fruit boats, when she stopped suddenly with a great start that almost forced a cry from her.

"For God's sake go on—give no sign if you don't wish to make me wretched," said the sailor in a whisper.

"Come, Miss Gerald, we are waiting," cried Harwood up the long rail.

Daireen remained irresolute for a moment, then walked slowly down, and allowed herself to be handed into the boat.

"Surely you are not timid, Miss Gerald," said Harwood as the boat pushed off.

"Timid?" said Daireen mechanically.

"Yes, your hand was really trembling as I helped you down."

"No, no, I am not—not timid, only—I fear I shall not be very good company to-day; I feel——" she looked back to the steamer and did not finish her sentence.

Mr. Harwood glanced at her for a moment, thinking if it really could be possible that she was regretting the absence of Mr. Glaston. Mrs. Crawford also looked at her and came to the conclusion that, at the last moment, the girl was recalling the aesthetic instructions of the young man who was doubtless sitting lonely in his cabin while she was bent on enjoying herself with a "party."

But Daireen was only thinking how it was she had refrained from crying out when she saw the face of that sailor on the rail, and when she heard his voice; and it must be confessed that it was rather singular, taking into account the fact that she had recognised in the features and voice of that sailor the features and voice of Standish Macnamara.

CHAPTER XII

Your visitation shall receive such thanks
As fits... remembrance.

... Thus do we of wisdom and of reach,
With windlasses and with assays of bias,
By indirections find directions out.

More matter with less art. —*Hamlet.*

THE thin white silk thread of a moon was hanging in the blue twilight over the darkened western slope of the island, and almost within the horns of its crescent a planet was burning without the least tremulous motion. The lights of the town were glimmering over the waters, and the strange, wildly musical cries of the bullock-drivers were borne faintly out to the steamer, mingling with the sound of the bell of St. Mary's on the Mount.

The vessel had just begun to move away from its anchorage, and Daireen Gerald was standing on the deck far astern leaning over the bulwarks looking back upon the island slope whose bright green had changed to twilight purple. Not of the enjoyment of the day she had spent up among the vines was the girl thinking; her memory fled back to the past days spent beneath the shadow of a slope that was always purple, with a robe of heather clinging to it from base to summit.

"I hope you don't regret having taken my advice about going on shore, Miss Gerald," said Mr. Harwood, who had come beside her.

"Oh, no," she said; "it was all so lovely—so unlike what I ever saw or imagined."

"It has always seemed lovely to me," he said, "but to-day it was very lovely. I had got some pleasant recollections of the island before, but now the memories I shall retain will be the happiest of my life."

"Was to-day really so much pleasanter?" asked the girl quickly. "Then I am indeed fortunate in my first visit. But you were not at any part of the island that you had not seen before," she added, after a moment's pause.

"No," he said quietly. "But I saw all to-day under a new aspect."

"You had not visited it in September? Ah, I recollect now having heard that this was the best month for Madeira. You see I am fortunate."

"Yes, you are—fortunate," he said slowly. "You are fortunate; you are a child; I am—a man."

Daireen was quite puzzled by his tone; it was one of sadness, and she knew that he was not accustomed to be sad. He had not been so at any time through the day when they were up among the vineyards looking down upon the tiny ships in the harbour beneath them, or wandering through the gardens surrounding the villa at which they had lunched after being presented by their guide—no, he had certainly not displayed any sign of sadness then. But here he was now beside her watching the lights of the shore twinkling into dimness, and speaking in this way that puzzled her.

"I don't know why, if you say you will have only pleasant recollections of to-day, you should speak in a tone like that," she said.

"No, no, you would not understand it," he replied. If she had kept silence after he had spoken his previous sentence, he would have been tempted to say to her what he had on his heart, but her question made him hold back his words, for it proved to him what he told her—she would not understand him.

It is probable, however, that Mrs. Crawford, who by the merest accident, of course, chanced to come from the cabin at this moment, would have understood even the most enigmatical utterance that might pass from his lips on the subject of his future memories of the day they had spent on the island; she felt quite equal to the solution of any question of psychological analysis that might arise. But she contented herself now by calling Daireen's attention to the flashing of the phosphorescent water at the base of the cliffs round which the vessel was moving, and the observance of this phenomenon drew the girl's thoughts away from the possibility of discovering the meaning of the man's words. The major and his old comrade Doctor Campion then came near and expressed the greatest anxiety to learn how their friends had passed the day. Both major and doctor were in the happiest of moods. They had visited the hotel they agreed in stating, and no one on the deck undertook to prove anything to the contrary—no one, in fact, seemed to doubt in the least the truth of what they said.

In a short time Mrs. Crawford and Daireen were left alone; not for long, however, for Mr. Glaston strolled languidly up.

"I cannot say I hope you enjoyed yourself," he said. "I know very well you did not. I hope you could not."

Daireen laughed. "Your hopes are misplaced, I fear, Mr. Glaston," she answered. "We had a very happy day—had we not, Mrs. Crawford?"

"I am afraid we had, dear."

"Why, Mr. Harwood said distinctly to me just now," continued Daireen, "that it was the pleasantest day he had ever passed upon the island."

"Ah, he said so? well, you see, he is a newspaper man, and they all look at things from a popular standpoint; whatever is popular is right, is their motto; while ours is, whatever is popular is wrong."

He felt himself speaking as the representative of a class, no doubt, when he made use of the plural.

"Yes; Mr. Harwood seemed even more pleased than we were," continued the girl. "He told me that the recollection of our exploration to-day would be the—the—yes, the happiest of his life. He did indeed," she added almost triumphantly.

"Did he?" said Mr. Glaston slowly.

"My dear child," cried Mrs. Crawford, quickly interposing, "he has got that way of talking. He has, no doubt, said those very words to every person he took ashore on his previous visits. He has, I know, said them every evening for a fortnight in the Mediterranean."

"Then you don't think he means anything beyond a stupid compliment to us? What a wretched thing it is to be a girl, after all. Never mind, I enjoyed myself beyond any doubt."

"It is impossible—quite impossible, child," said the young man. "Enjoyment with a refined organisation such as yours can never be anything that is not reflective—it is something that cannot be shared with a number of persons. It is quite impossible that you could have any feeling in common with such a mind as this Mr. Harwood's or with the other people who went ashore. I heard nothing but expressions of enjoyment, and I felt really sad to think that there was not a refined soul among them all. They enjoyed themselves, therefore you did not."

"I think I can understand you," said Mrs. Crawford at once, for she feared that Daireen might attempt to question the point he insisted on. Of course when the superior intellect of Mr. Glaston demonstrated that they could not have enjoyed themselves, it was evident that it was their own sensations which were deceiving them. Mrs. Crawford trusted to the decision of the young man's intellect more implicitly than she did her own senses: just as Christopher Sly, old Sly's son of Burton Heath, came to believe the practical jesters.

"Should you enjoy the society and scenery of a desert island better than an inhabited one?" asked the girl, somewhat rebellious at the concessions of Mrs. Crawford.

"Undoubtedly, if everything was in good taste," he answered quietly.

"That is, if everything was in accordance with your own taste," came the voice of Mr. Harwood, who, unseen, had rejoined the party.

Mr. Glaston made no reply. He had previously become aware of the unsatisfactory results of making any answers to such men as wrote for newspapers. As he had always considered such men outside the world of art in which he lived and to the inhabitants of which he addressed himself, it was hardly to be expected that he would put himself on a level of argument with them. In fact, Mr. Glaston rarely consented to hold an argument with any one. If people maintained opinions different from his own, it was so much the worse for those people—that was all he felt. It was to a certain circle of young women in good society that he preferred addressing himself, for he knew that to each individual in that circle he appeared as the prophet and high priest of art. His tone-poems in the college magazine, his impromptus—musical *aquarellen* he called them—performed in secret and out of hearing of any earthly audience, his colour-harmonies, his statuesque idealisms—all these were his priestly ministrations; while the interpretation, not of his own works—this he never attempted—but of the works of three poets belonging to what he called his school, of one painter, and of one musical composer, was his prophetical service.

It was obviously impossible that such a man could put himself on that mental level which would be implied by his action should he consent to make any answer to a person like Mr. Harwood. But apart from these general grounds, Mr. Glaston had got concrete reasons for declining to discuss any subject with this newspaper man. He knew that it was Mr. Harwood who had called the tone-poems of the college magazine alliterative conundrums for young ladies; that it was Mr. Harwood who had termed one of the colour-harmonies a study in virulent jaundice; that it was Mr. Harwood who had, after smiling on being told of the *aquarellen* impromptus, expressed a desire to hear one of these compositions—all this Mr. Glaston knew well, and so when Mr. Harwood made that remark about taste Mr. Glaston did not reply.

Daireen, however, did not feel the silence oppressive. She kept her eyes fixed upon that thin thread of moon that was now almost touching the dark ridge of the island.

Harwood looked at her for a few moments, and then he too leaned over the side of the ship and gazed at that lovely moon and its burning star.

"How curious," he said gently—"how very curious, is it not, that the sight of that hill and that moon should bring back to me memories of Lough Suangorm and Slieve Docas?"

The girl gave a start. "You are thinking of them too? I am so glad. It makes me so happy to know that I am not the only one here who knows all about Suangorm." Suddenly another thought seemed to come to her. She turned her eyes away from the island and glanced down the deck anxiously.

"No," said Mr. Harwood very gently indeed; "you are not alone in your memories of the loveliest spot of the world."

Mrs. Crawford thought it well to interpose. "My dear Daireen, you must be careful not to take a chill now after all the unusual exercise you have had during the day. Don't you think you had better go below?"

"Yes, I had much better," said the girl quickly and in a startled tone; and she had actually gone to the door of the companion before she recollected that she had not said good-night either to Glaston or Harwood. She turned back and redeemed her negligence, and then went down with her good guardian.

"Poor child," thought Mr. Glaston, "she fears that I am hurt by her disregard of my advice about going ashore with those people. Poor child! perhaps I was hard upon her!"

"Poor little thing," thought Mr. Harwood. "She begins to understand."

"It would never do to let that sort or thing go on," thought Mrs. Crawford, as she saw that Daireen got a cup of tea before retiring. Mrs. Crawford fully appreciated Mr. Harwood's cleverness in reading the girl's thought and so quickly adapting his speech to the requirements of the moment; but she felt her own superiority of cleverness.

Each of the three was a careful and experienced observer, but there are certain conditional influences to be taken into account in arriving at a correct conclusion as to the motives of speech or action of every human subject under observation; and the reason that these careful analysts of motives were so utterly astray in tracing to its source the remissness of Miss Gerald, was probably because none of the three was aware of the existence of an important factor necessary for the solution of the interesting problem they had worked out so airily; this factor being the sudden appearance of Standish Macnamara beside the girl in the morning, and her consequent reflections upon the circumstance in the evening.

But as she sat alone in her cabin, seeing through the port the effect of the silver moonlight upon the ridge of the hill behind which the moon itself had now sunk, she was wondering, as she had often wondered during the day, if indeed it was Standish whom she had seen and whose voice she had heard. All had been so sudden—so impossible, she thought, that the sight of him and the hearing of his voice seemed to her but as the memories of a dream of her home.

But now that she was alone and capable of reflecting upon the matter, she felt that she had not been deceived. By some means the young man to whom she had written her last letter in Ireland was aboard the steamer. It was very wonderful to the girl to reflect upon this; but then she thought if he was aboard, why should she not be able to find him and ask him all about himself?

CHAPTER XIII

Providence
Should have kept short, restrained, and out of haunt
This mad young man...
His very madness, like some ore
Among a mineral of metals base,
Shows itself pure.

Pity me not, but lend thy serious hearing
To what I shall unfold.

It is common for the younger sort
To lack discretion.

Queen.... Whereon do you look?

Hamlet. On him, on him! look you, how pale he glares.
... It is not madness
That I have uttered: bring me to the test.—*Hamlet*

THE question which suggested itself to Daireen as to the possibility of seeing Standish aboard the steamer, was not the only one that occupied her thoughts. How had he come aboard, and why had he come aboard, were further questions whose solution puzzled her. She recollected how he had told her on that last day she had seen him, while they walked in the garden after leaving The Macnamara in that side room with the excellent specimen of ancient furniture ranged with glass vessels, that he was heartily tired of living among the ruins of the castle, and that he had made up his mind to go out into the world of work. She had then begged of him to take no action of so much importance until her father should have returned to give him the advice he needed; and in that brief postscript which she had added to the farewell letter given into the care of the bard O'Brian, she had expressed her regret that this counsel of hers had been rendered impracticable. Was it possible, however, that Standish placed so much confidence in the likelihood of valuable advice being given to him by her father that he had resolved to go out to the Cape and speak with him on the subject face to face, she thought; but it struck her that there would be something like an inconsistency in the young man's travelling six thousand miles to take an opinion as to the propriety of his leaving his home.

What was she to do? She felt that she must see Standish and have from his own lips an explanation of how he had come aboard the ship; but in that, sentence he had spoken to her he had entreated of her to keep silence, so that she dared not seek for him under the guidance of Mrs. Crawford or any of her friends aboard the vessel. It would be necessary for her to find him alone, and she knew that this would be a difficult thing to do, situated as she was. But let the worst come, she reflected that it could only result in the true position of Standish being-known. This was really all that the girl believed could possibly be the result if a secret interview between herself and a sailor aboard the steamer should be discovered; and, thinking of the worst consequences so lightly, made her all the more anxious to hasten on such an interview if she could contrive it.

She seated herself upon her little sofa and tried to think by what means she could meet with Standish, and yet fulfil his entreaty for secrecy. Her imagination, so far as inventing plans was concerned, did not seem to be inexhaustible. After half an hour's pondering over the matter, no more subtle device was suggested to her than going on deck and walking alone towards the fore-part of the ship between the deck-house and the bulwarks, where it might possibly chance that Standish would be found. This was her plan, and she did not presume to think to herself that its intricacy was the chief element of its possible success. Had she been aware of the fact that Standish was at that instant standing in the shadow of that deck-house looking anxiously astern in the hope of catching a glimpse of her—had she known that since the steamer had left the English port he had every evening stood with the same object in the same place, she would have been more hopeful of her simple plan succeeding.

At any rate she stole out of her cabin and went up the companion and out upon the deck, with all the caution that a novice in the art of dissembling could bring to her aid.

The night was full of softness—softness of gray reflected light from the waters that were rippling along before the vessel—softness of air that seemed saturated with the balm of odorous trees growing upon the slopes of those Fortunate Islands. The deck was deserted by passengers; only Major Crawford, the doctor, and the special correspondent were sitting in a group in their cane chairs, smoking their cheroots and discussing some action of a certain colonel that had not yet been fully explained, though it had taken place fifteen years previously. The group could not see her, she knew; but even if they had espied her and demanded an explanation, she felt that she had progressed sufficiently far in the crooked ways of deception to be able to lull their suspicions by her answers. She could tell them that she had a headache, or put them off with some equally artful excuse.

She walked gently along until she was at the rear of the deck-house where the stock of the mainmast was standing with all its gear. She looked down the dark tunnel passage between the side of the house and the bulwarks, but she felt her courage fail her: she dared do all that might become a woman, but the gloom of that covered place, and the consciousness that beyond it lay the mysterious fore-cabin space, caused her to pause. What was she to do?

Suddenly there came the sound of a low voice at her ear.

"Daireen, Daireen, why did you come here?" She started and looked around trembling, for it was the voice of Standish, though she could not see the form of the speaker. It was some moments before she found that he was under the broad rail leading to the ship's bridge.

"Then it is you, Standish, indeed?" she said. "How on earth did you come aboard?—Why have you come?—Are you really a sailor?—Where is your father?—Does he know?—Why don't you shake hands with me, Standish?"

These few questions she put to him in a breath, looking between the steps of the rail.

"Daireen, hush, for Heaven's sake!" he said anxiously. "You don't know what you are doing in coming to speak with me here—I am only a sailor, and if you were seen near me it would be terrible. Do go back to your cabin and leave me to my wretchedness."

"I shall not go back," she said resolutely. "I am your friend, Standish, and why should I not speak to you for an hour if I wish? You are not the quartermaster at the wheel. What a start you gave me this morning! Why did you not tell me you were coming in this steamer?"

"I did not leave Suangorm until the next morning after I heard you had gone," he answered in a whisper. "I should have died—I should indeed, Daireen, if I had remained at home while you were gone away without any one to take care of you."

"Oh, Standish, Standish, what will your father say?—What will he think?"

"I don't care," said Standish. "I told him on that day when we returned from Suanmara that I would go away. I was a fool that I did not make up my mind long ago. It was, indeed, only when you left that I carried out my resolution. I learned what ship you were going in; I had as much money as brought me to England—I had heard of people working their passage abroad; so I found out the captain of the steamer, and telling him all about myself that I could—not of course breathing your name, Daireen—I begged him to allow me to work my way as a sailor, and he agreed to give me the passage. He wanted me to become a waiter in the cabin, but I couldn't do that; I didn't mind facing all the hardships that might come, so long as I was near you—and—able to get your father's advice. Now do go back, Daireen."

"No one will see us," said the girl, after a pause, in which she reflected on the story he had told her. "But all is so strange, Standish," she continued—"all is so unlike anything I ever imagined possible. Oh, Standish, it is too dreadful to think of your being a sailor—just a sailor—aboard the ship."

"There's nothing so very bad in it," he replied. "I can work, thank God; and I mean to work. The thought of being near you—that is, near the time when I can get the advice I want from your father—makes all my labour seem light."

"But if I ask the captain, he will, I am sure, let you become a passenger," said the girl suddenly. "Do let me ask him, Standish. It is so—so hard for you to have to work as a sailor."

"It is no harder than I expected it would be," he said; "I am not afraid to work hard: and I feel that I am doing something—I feel it. I should be more wretched in the cabin. Now do not think of speaking to me for the rest of the voyage, Daireen; only, do not forget that you have a friend aboard the ship—a friend who will be willing to die for you."

His voice was very tremulous, and she could see his tearful eyes glistening in the gray light as he put out one of his hands to her. She put her own hand into it and felt his strong earnest grasp as he whispered, "God bless you, Daireen! God bless you!"

"Make it six bells, quartermaster," came the voice of the officer on watch from the bridge. In fear and trembling Daireen waited until the man came aft and gave the six strokes upon the ship's bell that hung quite near where she was standing—Standish thinking it prudent to remain close in the shade of the rail. The quartermaster saw her, but did not, of course, conceive it to be within the range of his duties to give any thought to the circumstance of a passenger being on deck at that hour. When the girl turned round after the bell had been struck, she found that Standish had disappeared. All she could do was to hasten back to her cabin with as much caution as it was possible for her to preserve, for she could still hear the hoarse tones of the major's voice coming from the centre of the group far astern, who were regaled with a very pointed chronicle of a certain station in the empire of Hindustan.

Daireen reached her cabin and sat once more upon her sofa, breathing a sigh of relief, for she had never in her life had such a call upon her courage as this to which she had just responded.

Her face was flushed and hot, and her hands were trembling, so she threw open the pane of the cabin port-hole and let the soft breeze enter. It moved about her hair as she stood there, and she seemed to feel the fingers of a dear friend caressing her forehead. Then she sat down once more and thought over all that had happened since the morning when she had gone on deck to see that gray cloud-land brighten into the lovely green slope of Madeira.

She thought of all that Standish had told her about himself, and she felt her heart overflowing, as were her eyes, with sympathy for him who had cast aside his old life and was endeavouring to enter upon the new.

As she sat there in her dreaming mood all the days of the past came back to her, with a clearness she had never before known. All the pleasant hours returned to her with even a more intense happiness than she had felt at first. For out of the distance of these Fortunate Islands the ghosts of the blessed departed hours came and moved before her, looking into her face with their own sweet pale faces; thus she passed from a waking dream into a dream of sleep as she lay upon her sofa, and the ghost shapes continued to float before her. The fatigue of the day, the darkness of the cabin, and the monotonous washing of the ripples against the side of the ship, had brought on her sleep before she had got into her berth.

With a sudden start she awoke and sprang to her feet in instantaneous consciousness, for the monotony of the washing waves was broken by a sound that was strange and startling to her ears—the sound of something hard tapping at irregular intervals upon the side of the ship just at her ear.

She ran over to the cabin port and looked out fearfully—looked out and gave a cry of terror, for beneath her—out from those gray waters there glanced up to her in speechless agony the white face of a man; she saw it but for a moment, then it seemed to be swept away from her and swallowed up in the darkness of the deep waters.

CHAPTER XIV

... Rashly,
And praised be rashness for it....
Up from my cabin,
My sea-gown scarf'd about me, in the dark
Groped I to find out them... making so bold,
My fears forgetting manners.

Give me leave: here lies the water; good: here stands the
man; good.
Let us know
Our indiscretion sometimes serves us well
... and that should learn us
There's a divinity that shapes our ends
Rough-hew them how we will. — *Hamlet.*

ASINGLE cry of terror was all that Daireen uttered as she fell back upon her berth. An instant more and she was standing with white lips, and hands that were untrembling as the rigid hand of a dead person. She knew what was to be done as plainly as if she saw everything in a picture. She rushed into the saloon and mounted the companion to the deck. There sat the little group astern just as she had seen them an hour before, only that the doctor had fallen asleep under the influence of one of the less pointed of the major's stories.

"God bless my soul!" cried the major, as the girl clutched the back of his chair.

"Good heavens, Miss Gerald, what is the matter?" said Harwood, leaping to his feet.

She pointed to the white wake of the ship.

"There—there," she whispered—"a man—drowning—clinging to something—a wreck—I saw him!"

"Dear me! dear me!" said the major, in a tone of relief, and with a breath of a smile.

But the special correspondent had looked into the girl's face. It was his business to understand the difference between dreaming and waking. He was by the side of the officer on watch in a moment. A few words were enough to startle the officer into acquiescence with the demands of the "special." The unwonted sound of the engine-room telegraph was heard, its tinkle shaking the slumbers of the chief engineer as effectively as if it had been the thunder of an alarum peal.

The stopping of the engine, the blowing off of the steam, and the arrival of the captain upon the deck, were simultaneous occurrences. The officer's reply to his chief as he hurried aft did not seem to be very satisfactory, judging from the manner in which it was received.

But Harwood had left the officer to explain the stoppage of the vessel, and was now kneeling by the side of the chair, back upon which lay the unconscious form of Daireen, while the doctor was forcing some brandy—all that remained in the major's tumbler—between her lips, and a young sailor—the one who had been at the rail in the morning—chafed her pallid hand. The major was scanning the expanse of water by aid of his pilot glass, and the quartermaster who had been steering went to the line of the patent log to haul it in—his first duty at any time on the stopping of the vessel, to prevent the line—the strain being taken off it—fouling with the propeller.

When the steamer is under weigh it is the work of two sailors to take in the eighty fathoms of log-line, otherwise, however, the line is of course quite slack; it was thus rather inexplicable to the quartermaster to find much more resistance to his first haul than if the vessel were going full speed ahead.

"The darned thing's fouled already," he murmured for his own satisfaction. He could not take in a fathom, so great was the resistance.

"Hang it all, major," said the captain, "isn't this too bad? Bringing the ship to like this, and—ah, here they come! All the ship's company will be aft in a minute."

"Rum, my boy, very rum," muttered the sympathetic major.

"What's the matter, captain?" said one voice.

"Is there any danger?" asked a tremulous second.

"If it's a collision or a leak, don't keep it from us, sir," came a stern contralto. For in various stages of toilet incompleteness the passengers were crowding out of the cabin.

But before the "unhappy master" could utter a word of reply, the sailor had touched his cap and reported to the third mate:

"Log-line fouled on wreck, sir."

"By gad!" shouted the major, who was twisting the log-line about, and peering into the water. "By gad, the girl was right! The line has fouled on some wreck, and there is a body made fast to it."

The captain gave just a single glance in the direction indicated. .

"Stand by gig davits and lower away," he shouted to the watch, who had of course come aft.

The men ran to where the boat was hanging, and loosened the lines.

"Oh, Heaven preserve us! they are taking to the boats!" cried a female passenger.

"Don't be a fool, my good woman," said Mrs. Crawford tartly. The major's wife had come on deck in a most marvellous costume, and she was already holding a sal-volatile bottle to Daireen's nose, having made a number of inquiries of Mr. Harwood and the doctor.

All the other passengers had crowded to the ship's side, and were watching the men in the boat cutting at something which had been reached at the end of the log-line. They could see the broken stump of a mast and the cross-trees, but nothing further.

"They have got it into the boat," said the major, giving the result of his observation through the binocular.

"For Heaven's sake, ladies, go below!" cried the captain. But no one moved.

"If you don't want to see the ghastly corpse of a drowned man gnawed by fishes for weeks maybe, you had better go down, ladies," said the chief officer. Still no one stirred.

The major, who was an observer of nature, smiled and winked sagaciously at the exasperated captain before he said:

"Why should the ladies go down at all? it's a pleasant night, and begad, sir, a group of nightcaps like this isn't to be got together more than once in a lifetime." Before the gallant officer had finished his sentence the deck was cleared of women; but, of course, the luxury of seeing a dead body lifted from the boat being too great to be missed, the starboard cabin ports had many faces opposite them.

The doctor left Daireen to the care of Mrs. Crawford, saying that she would recover consciousness in a few minutes, and he hastened with a kaross to the top of the boiler, where he had shouted to the men in the boat to carry the body.

The companion-rail having been lowered, it was an easy matter for the four men to take the body on deck and to lay it upon the tiger-skin before the doctor, who rubbed his hands—an expression which the seamen interpreted as meaning satisfaction.

"Gently, my men, raise his head—so—throw the light on his face. By George, he doesn't seem to have suffered from the oysters; there's hope for him yet."

And the compassionate surgeon began cutting the clothing from the limbs of the body.

"No, don't take the pieces away," he said to one of the men; "let them remain here Now dry his arms carefully, and we'll try and get some air into his lungs, if they're not already past work."

But before the doctor had commenced his operations the ship's gig had been hauled up once more to the davits, and the steamer was going ahead at slow speed.

"Keep her at slow until the dawn," said the captain to the officer on watch. "And let there be a good lookout; there may be others floating upon the wreck. Call me if the doctor brings the body to life."

The captain did not think it necessary to view the body that had been snatched from the deep. The captain was a compassionate man and full of tender feeling; he was exceedingly glad that he had had it in his power to pick up that body, even with the small probability there was of being able to restore life to its frozen blood; but he would have been much more grateful to Providence had it been so willed that it should have been picked up without the necessity of stopping the engines of the steamer for nearly a quarter of an hour. It was explained to him that Miss Gerald had been the first to see the face of the man upon the wreck, but he could scarcely understand how it was possible for her to have seen it from her cabin. He was also puzzled to know how it was that the log-line had not been carried away so soon as it was entangled in such a large mass of wreck when the steamer was going at full speed. He, however, thought it as well to resume his broken slumbers without waiting to solve either of these puzzling questions.

But the chief officer who was now on watch, when the deck was once more deserted—Daireen having been taken down to her cabin—made the attempt to account for both of these occurrences. He found that the girl's cabin was not far astern of the companion-rail that had been lowered during the day, and he saw that, in the confusion of weighing anchor in the dimness, a large block with its gear which was used in the hauling of the vegetable baskets aboard, had been allowed to hang down the side of the ship between the steps of the rail; and upon the hook of the block, almost touching the water, he found some broken cordage. He knew then that the hook had caught fast in the cordage of the wreck as the steamer went past, and the wreck had swung round until it was just opposite the girl's cabin, when the cordage had given way; not, however, until some of the motion of the ship had been communicated to the wreck so that there was no abrupt strain put on the log-line when it had become entangled. It was all plain to the chief officer, as no doubt it would have been to the captain had he waited to search out the matter.

So soon as the body had been brought aboard the ship all the interest of the passengers seemed to subside, and the doctor was allowed to pursue his experiments of resuscitation without inquiry. The chief officer being engaged at his own business of working out the question of the endurance of the log-line, and keeping a careful lookout for any other portions of wreck, had almost forgotten that the doctor and two of the sailors were applying a series of restoratives to the body of the man who had been detached from the wreck. It was nearly two hours after he had come on watch that one of the sailors—the one who had been kneeling by the side of Daireen—came up to the chief officer presenting Doctor Campion's compliments, with the information that the man was breathing.

In accordance with the captain's instructions, the chief officer knocked at the cabin door and repeated the message.

"Breathing is he?" said the captain rather sleepily. "Very good, Mr. Holden; I'm glad to hear it. Just call me again in case he should relapse."

The captain had hitherto, in alluding to the man, made use of the neuter pronoun, but now that breath was restored he acknowledged his right to a gender.

"Very good, sir," replied the officer, closing the door.

CHAPTER XV

Be thou a spirit of health, or goblin damn'd,
Bring with thee airs from heaven or blasts from hell,
Be thy intents wicked or charitable,
Thou com'st in such a questionable shape.

What may this mean
That thou, dead corse, again...
Revisit'st thus...?

I hope your virtues
Will bring him to his wonted way again.—*Hamlet.*

IT was the general opinion in the cabin that Miss Gerald—the young lady who was in such an exclusive set—had shown very doubtful taste in being the first to discover the man upon the wreck. Every one had, of course, heard the particulars of the matter from the steward's assistants, who had in turn been in communication with the watch on deck. At any rate, it was felt by the ladies that it showed exceedingly bad taste in Miss Gerald to take such steps as eventually led to the ladies appearing on deck in incomplete toilettes. There was, indeed, a very pronounced feeling against Miss Gerald; several representatives of the other sections of the cabin society declaring that they could not conscientiously admit Miss Gerald into their intimacy. That dreadful designing old woman, the major's wife, might do as she pleased, they declared, and so might Mrs. Butler and her daughter, who were only the near relatives of some Colonial Governor, but such precedents should be by no means followed, the ladies of this section announced to each other. But as Daireen had never hitherto found it necessary to fall back upon any of the passengers outside her own set, the resolution of the others, even if it had come to her ears, would not have caused her any great despondency.

The captain made some inquiries of the doctor in the morning, and learned that the rescued man was breathing, though still unconscious. Mr. Harwood showed even a greater anxiety to hear from Mrs. Crawford about Daireen, after the terrible night she had gone through, and he felt no doubt proportionately happy when he was told that she was now sleeping, having passed some hours in feverish excitement. Daireen had described to Mrs. Crawford how she had seen the face looking up to her from the water, and Mr. Harwood, hearing this, and making a careful examination of the outside of the ship in the neighbourhood of Daireen's cabin, came to the same conclusion as that at which the chief officer had arrived.

Mrs. Crawford tried to make Mr. Glaston equally interested in her protégée, but she was scarcely successful.

"How brave it was in the dear child, was it not, Mr. Glaston?" she asked. "Just imagine her glancing casually out of the port—thinking, it maybe, of her father, who is perhaps dying at the Cape"—the good lady felt that this bit of poetical pathos might work wonders with Mr. Glaston—"and then," she continued, "fancy her seeing that terrible, ghastly thing in the water beneath her! What must her feelings have been as she rushed on deck and gave the alarm that caused that poor wretch to be saved! Wonderful, is it not?"

But Mr. Glaston's face was quite devoid of expression on hearing this powerful narrative. The introduction of the pathos even did not make him wince; and there was a considerable pause before he said the few words that he did.

"Poor child," he murmured. "Poor child. It was very melodramatic—terribly melodramatic; but she is still young, her taste is—ah—plastic. At least I hope so."

Mrs. Crawford began to feel that, after all, it was something to have gained this expression of hope from Mr. Glaston, though her warmth of feeling did undoubtedly receive a chill from his manner. She did not reflect that there is a certain etiquette to be observed in the saving of the bodies as well as the souls of people, and that the aesthetic element, in the opinion of some people, should enter largely into every scheme of salvation, corporeal as well as spiritual.

The doctor was sitting with Major Crawford when the lady joined them a few minutes after her conversation with Mr. Glaston, and never had Mrs. Crawford fancied that her husband's old friend could talk in such an affectionate way as he now did about the rescued man. She could almost bring herself to believe that she saw the tears of emotion in his eyes as he detailed the circumstances of the man's resuscitation. The doctor felt personally obliged to him for his handsome behaviour in bearing such testimony to the skill of his resuscitator.

When the lady spoke of the possibilities of a relapse, the doctor's eyes glistened at first, but under the influence of maturer thought, he sighed and shook his head. No, he knew that there are limits to the generosity of even a half-strangled man—a relapse was too much to hope for; but the doctor felt at that instant that if this "case" should see its way to a relapse, and subsequently to submit to be restored, it would place itself under a lasting obligation to its physician.

Surely, thought Mrs. Crawford, when the doctor talks of the stranger with such enthusiasm he will go into raptures about Daireen; so she quietly alluded to the girl's achievement. But the doctor could see no reason for becoming ecstatic about Miss Gerald. Five minutes with the smelling-bottle had restored her to consciousness.

"Quite a trifle—overstrung nerves, you know," he said, as he lit another cheroot.

"But think of her bravery in keeping strong until she had told you all that she had seen!" said the lady. "I never heard of anything so brave! Just fancy her looking out of the port—thinking of her father perhaps"—the lady went on to the end of that pathetic sentence of hers, but it had no effect upon the doctor.

"True, very true!" he muttered, looking at his watch.

But the major was secretly convulsed for some moments after his wife had spoken her choice piece of pathos, and though he did not betray himself, she knew well all that was in his mind, and so turned away without a further word. So soon as she was out of hearing, the major exchanged confidential chuckles with his old comrade.

"He is not what you'd call a handsome man as he lies at present, Campion," remarked Mr. Harwood, strolling up later in the day. "But you did well not to send him to the forecastle, I think; he has not been a sailor."

"I know it, my boy," said the doctor. "He is not a handsome man, you say, and I agree with you that he is not seen to advantage just now; but I made up my mind an hour after I saw him that he was not for the forecastle, or even the forecabin."

"I dare say you are right," said Harwood. "Yes; there is a something in his look that half drowning could not kill. That was the sort of thing you felt, eh?"

"Nothing like it," said the mild physician. "It was this," he took out of his pocket an envelope, from which he extracted a document that he handed to Harwood.

It was an order for four hundred pounds, payable by a certain bank in England, and granted by the Sydney branch of the Australasian Banking Company to one Mr. Oswin Markham.

"Ah, I see; he is a gentleman," said Harwood, returning the order. It had evidently suffered a sea-change, but it had been carefully dried by the doctor.

"Yes, he is a gentleman," said the doctor. "That is what I remarked when I found this in a flask in one of his pockets. Sharp thing to do, to keep a paper free from damp and yet to have it in a buoyant case. Devilish sharp thing!"

"And the man's name is this—Oswin Markham?" said the major.

"No doubt about it," said the doctor.

"None whatever; unless he stole the order from the rightful owner, and meant to get it cashed at his leisure," remarked Harwood.

"Then he must have stolen the shirt, the collar, and the socks of Oswin Markham," snarled the doctor. "All these things of his are marked as plain as red silk can do it."

"Any man who would steal an order for four hundred pounds would not hesitate about a few toilet necessaries."

"Maybe you'll suggest to the skipper the need to put him in irons as soon as he is sufficiently recovered to be conscious of an insult," cried the doctor in an acrid way that received a sympathetic chuckle from the major. "Young man, you've got your brain too full of fancies—a devilish deal, sir; they do well enough retailed for the readers of the *Dominant Trumpeter*, but sensible people don't want to hear them."

"Then I won't force them upon you and Crawford, my dear Campion," said Harwood, walking away, for he knew that upon some occasions the doctor should be conciliated, and in the matter of a patient every allowance should be made for his warmth of feeling. So long as one of his "cases" paid his skill the compliment of surviving any danger, he spoke well of the patient; but when one behaved so unhandsomely as to die, it was with the doctor *De mortuis nil nisi malum*. Harwood knew this, and so he walked away.

And now that he found himself—or rather made himself—alone, he thought over all the events of the previous eventful day; but somehow there did not seem to be any event worth remembering that was not associated with Daireen Gerald. He recollected how he had watched her when they had been together among the lovely gardens of the island slope. As she turned her eyes seaward with an earnest, sad, *questioning* gaze, he felt that he had never seen a picture so full of beauty.

The words he had spoken to her, telling her that the day he had spent on the island was the happiest of his life, were true indeed; he had never felt so happy; and now as he reflected upon his after-words his conscience smote him for having pretended to her that he was thinking of the place where he knew her thoughts had carried her: he had seen from her face that she was dreaming about her Irish home, and he had made her feel that the recollection of the lough and the mountains was upon his mind also. He felt now how coarse had been his deception.

He then recalled the final scene of the night, when, as he was trying to pursue his own course of thought, and at the same time pretend to be listening to the major's thrice-told tale of a certain colonel's conduct at the Arradambad station, the girl had appeared before them like a vision. Yes, it was altogether a remarkable day even for a special correspondent. The reflection upon its events made him very thoughtful during the entire of this afternoon. Nor was he at all disturbed by the information Doctor Campion brought vo him just when he was going for his usual smoke upon the bridge, while the shore of Palma was yet in view not far astern.

"Good fellow he is," murmured the doctor. "Capital fellow! opened his eyes just now when I was in his cabin—recovered consciousness in a moment."

"Ah, in a moment?" said Harwood dubiously. "I thought it always needed the existence of some link of consciousness between the past and the present to bring about a restoration like this—some familiar sight—some well-known sound."

"And, by George, you are right, my boy, this time, though you are a 'special,'" said the doctor, grinning. "Yes, I was standing by the fellow's bunk when I heard Crawford call for another bottle of soda. Robinson got it for him, and bang went the cork, of course; a faint smile stole over the haggard features, my boy, the glassy eyes opened full of intelligence and with a mine of pleasant recollections. That familiar sound of the popping of the cork acted as the link you talk of. He saw all in a moment, and tried to put out his hand to me. 'My boy,' I said, 'you've behaved most handsomely, and I'll get you a glass of brandy out of another bottle, but don't you try to speak for another day.' And I got him a glass from Crawford, though, by George, sir, Crawford grudged it; he didn't see the sentiment of the thing, sir, and when I tried to explain it, he said I was welcome to the cork."

"Capital tale for an advertisement of the brandy," said Harwood.

Then the doctor with many smiles hastened to spread abroad the story of the considerate behaviour of his patient, and Harwood was left to continue his twilight meditations alone once more. He was sitting in his deck-chair on the ship's bridge, and he could but dimly hear the laughter and the chat of the passengers far astern. He did not remain for long in this dreamy mood of his, for Mrs. Crawford and Daireen Gerald were seen coming up the rail, and he hastened to meet them. The girl was very pale but smiling, and in the soft twilight she seemed very lovely.

"I am so glad to see you," he said, as he settled a chair for her. "I feared a great many things when you did not appear to-day."

"We must not talk too much," said Mrs. Crawford, who had not expected to find Mr. Harwood alone in this place. "I brought Miss Gerard up here in order that she might not be subjected to the gaze of those colonists on the deck; a little quiet is what she needs to restore her completely from her shock."

"It was very foolish, I am afraid you think—very foolish of me to behave as I did," said Daireen, with a faint little smile. "But I had been asleep in my cabin, and I—I was not so strong as I should have been. The next time I hope I shall not be so very stupid."

"My dear Miss Gerald," said Harwood, "you behaved as a heroine. There is no woman aboard the ship—Mrs. Crawford of course excepted—who would have had courage to do what you did."

"And he," said the girl somewhat eagerly—"he—is he really safe?—has he recovered? Tell me all, Mr. Harwood."

"No, no!" cried Mrs. Crawford, interposing. "You must not speak a word about him. Do you want to be thrown into a fresh state of excitement, my dear, now that you are getting on so nicely?"

"But I am more excited remaining as I am in doubt about that poor man. Was he a sailor, Mr. Harwood?"

"It appears-not," said Harwood. "The doctor, however, is returning; he will tell all that is safe to be told."

"I really must protest," said Mrs. Crawford. "Well, I will be a good girl and not ask for any information whatever," said Daireen.

But she was not destined to remain in complete ignorance on the subject which might reasonably be expected to interest her, for the doctor on seeing her hastened up, and, of course, Mrs. Crawford's protest was weak against his judgment.

"My dear young lady," he cried, shaking Daireen warmly by the hand. "You are anxious to know the sequel of the romance of last night, I am sure?"

"No, no, Doctor Campion," said Daireen almost mischievously; "Mrs. Crawford says I must hear nothing, and think about nothing, all this evening. Did you not say so, Mrs. Crawford?"

"My dear child, Doctor Campion is supposed to know much better than myself how you should be treated in your present nervous condition. If he chooses to talk to you for an hour or two hours about drowning wretches, he may do so on his own responsibility."

"Drowning wretches!" said the doctor. "My dear madam, you have not been told all, or you would not talk in this way. He is no drowning wretch, but a gentleman; look at this—ah, I forgot it's not light enough for you to see the document, but Harwood there will tell you all that it contains."

"And what does that wonderful document contain, Mr. Harwood?" asked Mrs. Crawford. "Tell us, please, and we shall drop the subject."

"That document," said Harwood, with affected solemnity; "it is a guarantee of the respectability of the possessor; it is a bank order for four hundred pounds, payable to one Oswin Markham, and it was, I understand, found upon the person of the man who has just been resuscitated through the skill of our good friend Doctor Campion."

"Now you will not call him a poor wretch, I am sure," said the doctor. "He has now fully recovered consciousness, and, you see, he is a gentleman."

"You see that, no doubt, Mrs. Crawford," said Harwood, in a tone that made the good physician long to have him for a few weeks on the sick list— the way the doctor had of paying off old scores.

"Don't be sarcastic, Mr. Harwood," said Daireen. Then she added, "What did you say the name was?—Oswin Markham? I like it—I like it very much."

"Hush," said Mrs. Crawford. "Here is Mr. Glaston." And it was indeed Mr. Glaston who ascended the rail with a languor of motion in keeping with the hour of twilight. With a few muttered words the doctor walked away.

"I hear," said Mr. Glaston, after he had shaken hands with Daireen—"I hear that there was some wreck or other picked up last night with a man clinging to it—a dreadfully vulgar fellow he must be to carry about with him a lot of money—a man with a name like what one would find attached to the hero of an East End melodrama."

There was a rather lengthened silence in that little group before Harwood spoke.

"Yes," he said; "it struck me that it showed very questionable taste in the man to go about flaunting his money in the face of every one he met. As for his name—well, perhaps we had better not say anything about his name. You recollect what Tennyson makes Sir Tristram say to his Isolt—I don't mean you, Glaston, I know you only read the pre-Raphaelites—

"Let be thy Mark, seeing he is not thine."

But no one seemed to remember the quotation, or, at any rate, to see the happiness of its present application.

CHAPTER XVI

It beckons you to go away with it,
As if it some impartment did desire
To you alone.

... Weigh what loss
If with too credent ear you list his songs
Or lose your heart...
Fear it, Ophelia, fear it. —*Hamlet.*

IT could hardly be expected that there should be in the mind of Daireen Gerald a total absence of interest in the man who by her aid had been rescued from the deep. To be sure, her friend Mrs. Crawford had given her to understand that people of taste might pronounce the episode melodramatic, and as this word sounded very terrible to Daireen, as, indeed, it did to Mrs. Crawford herself, whose apprehension of its meaning was about as vague as the girl's, she never betrayed the anxiety she felt for the recovery of this man, who was, she thought, equally accountable for the dubious taste displayed in the circumstances of his rescue. She began to feel, as Mr. Glaston in his delicacy carefully refrained from alluding to this night of terror, and as Mrs. Crawford assumed a solemn expression of countenance upon the least reference to the girl's participation in the recovery of the man with the melodramatic name, that there was a certain bond of sympathy between herself and this Oswin Markham; and now and again when she found the doctor alone, she ventured to make some inquiries regarding him. In the course of a few days she learned a good deal.

"He is behaving handsomely—most handsomely, my dear," said the doctor, one afternoon about a week after the occurrence. "He eats everything that is given to him and drinks in a like proportion."

The girl felt that this was truly noble on the part of the man, but it was scarcely the exact type of information she would have liked.

"And he—is he able to speak yet?" she asked.

"Speak? yes, to be sure. He asked me how he came to be picked up, and I told him," continued the doctor, with a smile of gallantry of which Daireen did not believe him capable, "that he was seen by the most charming young lady in the world,—yes, yes, I told him that, though I ran a chance of retarding his recovery by doing so." This was, of course, quite delightful to hear, but Daireen wanted to know even more about the stranger than the doctor's speech had conveyed to her.

"The poor fellow was a long time in the water, I suppose?" she said artfully, trying to find out all that the doctor had learned.

"He was four days upon that piece of wreck," said the doctor.

The girl gave a start that seemed very like a shudder, as she repeated the words, "Four days."

"Yes; he was on his way home from Australia, where he had been living for some years, and the vessel he was in was commanded by some incompetent and drunken idiot who allowed it to be struck by a tornado of no extraordinary violence, and to founder in mid-ocean. As our friend was a passenger, he says, the crew did not think it necessary to invite him to have a seat in one of the boats, a fact that accounts for his being alive to-day, for both boats were swamped and every soul sent to the bottom in his view. He tells me he managed to lash a broken topmast to the stump of the mainmast that had gone by the board, and to cut the rigging so that he was left drifting when the hull went down. That's all the story, my dear, only we know what a hard time of it he must have had during the four days."

"A hard time—a hard time," Daireen repeated musingly, and without a further word she turned away.

Mr. Glaston, who had been pleased to take a merciful view of her recent action of so pronounced a type, found that his gracious attempts to reform her plastic taste did not, during this evening, meet with that appreciation of which they were undoubtedly deserving. Had he been aware that all the time his eloquent speech was flowing on the subject of the consciousness of hues—a theme attractive on account of its delicacy—the girl had before her eyes only a vision of heavy blue skies overhanging dark green seas terrible in loneliness—the monotony of endless waves broken only by the appearance in the centre of the waste of a broken mast and a ghastly face and clinging lean hands upon it, he would probably have withdrawn the concession he had made to Mrs. Crawford regarding the taste of her protégée.

And indeed, Daireen was not during any of these days thinking about much besides this Oswin Markham, though she never mentioned his name even to the doctor. At nights when she would look out over the flashing phosphorescent waters, she would evermore seem to see that white face looking up at her; but now she neither started nor shuddered as she was used to do for a few nights after she had seen the real face there. It seemed to her now as a face that she knew—the face of a friend looking into her face from the dim uncertain surface of the sea of a dream.

One morning a few days after her most interesting chat with Doctor Campion, she got up even earlier than usual—before, in fact, the healthy pedestrian gentleman had completed his first mile, and went on deck. She had, however, just stepped out of the companion when she heard voices and a laugh or two coming from the stern. She glanced in the direction of the sounds and remained motionless at the cabin door. A group consisting of the major, the doctor, and the captain of the steamer were standing in the neighbourhood of the wheel; but upon a deck-chair, amongst a heap of cushions, a stranger was lying back—a man with a thin brown face and large, somewhat sunken eyes, and a short brown beard and moustache; he was holding a cigar in the fingers of his left hand that drooped over the arm of the chair—a long, white hand—and he was looking up to the face of the major, who was telling one of his usual stories with his accustomed power. None of the other passengers were on deck, with the exception of the pedestrian, who came into view every few minutes as he reached the after part of the ship.

She stood there at the door of the companion without any motion, looking at that haggard face of the stranger. She saw a faint smile light up his deep eyes and pass over his features as the major brought out the full piquancy of his little anecdote, which was certainly not *virginibus puerisque*. Then she turned and went down again to her cabin without seeing how a young sailor was standing gazing at her from the passage of the ship's bridge. She sat down in her cabin and waited until the ringing of the second bell for breakfast.

"You are getting dreadfully lazy, my dear," said Mrs. Crawford, as she took her seat by the girl's side. "Why were you not up as usual to get an appetite for breakfast?" Then without waiting for an answer, she whispered, "Do you see the stranger at the other side of the table? That is our friend Mr. Oswin Markham; his name does not sound so queer when you come to know him. The doctor was right, Daireen: he is a gentleman."

"Then you have——"

"Yes, I have made his acquaintance this morning already. I hope Mr. Glaston may not think that it was my fault."

"Mr. Glaston?" said Daireen. .

"Yes; you know he is so sensitive in matters like this; he might fancy that it would be better to leave this stranger by himself; but considering that he will be parting from the ship in a week, I don't think I was wrong to let my husband present me. At any rate he is a gentleman—that is one satisfaction."

Daireen felt that there was every reason to be glad that she was not placed in the unhappy position of having taken steps for the rescue of a person not accustomed to mix in good society. But she did not even once glance down towards the man whose standing had been by a competent judge pronounced satisfactory. She herself talked so little, however, that she could hear him speak in answer to the questions some good-natured people at the bottom of the table put to him, regarding the name of his ship and the circumstances of the catastrophe that had come upon it. She also heard the young lady who had the peculiar fancy for blue and pink beg of him to do her the favour of writing his name in her birthday book.

During the hours that elapsed before tiffin Daireen sat with a novel in her hand, and she knew that the stranger was on the ship's bridge with Major Crawford. The major found his company exceedingly agreeable, for the old officer had unfortunately been prodigal of his stories through the first week of the voyage, and lately he had been reminded that he was repeating himself when he had begun a really choice anecdote. This Mr. Markham, however, had never been in India, so that the major found in him an appreciative audience, and for the satisfactory narration of a chronicle of Hindustan an appreciative audience is an important consideration. The major, however, appeared alone at tiffin, for Mr. Markham, he said, preferred lying in the sun on the bridge to eating salad in the cabin. The young lady with the birthday book seemed a little disappointed, for she had just taken the bold step of adding to her personal decorations a large artificial moss-rose with glass beads sewed all about it in marvellous similitude to early dew, and it would not bear being trifled with in the matter of detaching from her dress.

Whether or not Mrs. Crawford had conferred with Mr. Glaston on the subject of the isolation of Mr. Markham, Daireen, on coming to sit down to the dinner-table, found Mrs. Crawford and Mr. Markham standing in the saloon just at the entrance to her cabin. She could feel herself flushing as she looked up to the man's haggard face while Mrs. Crawford pronounced their names, and she knew that the hand she put in his thin fingers was trembling. Neither spoke a single word: they only looked at each other. Then the doctor came forward with some remark that Daireen did not seem to hear, and soon the table was surrounded with the passengers.

"He says he feels nearly as strong as he ever did," whispered Mrs. Crawford to the girl as they sat down together. "He will be able to leave us at St. Helena next week without doubt."

On the same evening Daireen was sitting in her usual place far astern. The sun had set some time, and the latitude being only a few degrees south of the equator, the darkness had already almost come down upon the waters. It was dimmer than twilight, but not the solid darkness of a tropical night. The groups of passengers had all dispersed or gone forward, and the only sounds were the whisperings of the water in the wake of the steamer, and the splashing of the flying fish.

Suddenly from the cabin there came the music of the piano, and a low voice singing to its accompaniment—so faint it came that Daireen knew no one on deck except herself could hear the voice, for she was sitting just beside the open fanlight of the saloon; but she heard every word that was sung:

I.

When the vesper gold has waned:
When the passion-hues of eve
Breathe themselves away and leave
Blue the heaven their crimson stained,
But one hour the world doth grieve,
For the shadowy skies receive
Stars so gracious-sweet that they
Make night more beloved than day.

II

From my life the light has waned:
Every golden gleam that shone
Through the dimness now las gone.
Of all joys has one remained?
Stays one gladness I have known?
Day is past; I stand, alone,
Here beneath these darkened skies,
Asking—"Doth a star arise?"

IT ended so faintly that Daireen Gerald could not tell when the last note had come. She felt that she was in a dream and the sounds she had heard were but a part of her dream—sounds? were these sounds, or merely the effect of breathing the lovely shadowy light that swathed the waters? The sounds seemed to her the twilight expressed in music.

Then in the silence she heard a voice speaking her name. She turned and saw Oswin Markham standing beside her.

"Miss Gerald," he said, "I owe my life to you. I thank you for it."

He could hardly have expressed himself more simply if he had been thanking her for passing him a fig at dinner, and yet his words thrilled her.

"No, no; do not say that," she said, in a startled voice. "I did nothing—nothing that any one else might not have done. Oh, do not talk of it, please."

"I will not," he said slowly, after a pause. "I will never talk of it again. I was a fool to speak of it to you. I know now that you understand—that there is no need for me to open my lips to you."

"I do indeed," she said, turning her eyes upon his face. "I do understand." She put out her hand, and he took it in his own—not fervently, not with the least expression of emotion, his fingers closed over it. A long time passed before she saw his face in front of her own, and felt his eyes looking into her eyes as his words came in a whisper, "Child—child, there is a bond between us—a bond whose token is silence."

She kept her eyes fixed upon his as he spoke, and long after his words had come. She knew he had spoken the truth: there was a bond between them. She understood it.

She saw the gaunt face with its large eyes close to her own; her own eyes filled with tears, and then came the first token of their bond—silence. She felt his grasp unloosed, she heard him moving away, and she knew that she was alone in the silence.

CHAPTER XVII

Give him heedful note;
For I mine eyes will rivet to his face,
And after we will both our judgments join.

Thou wouldst not think how ill all's here about my heart:
but it is no matter.

You must needs have heard, how I am punish'd
With sore distraction. What I have done
I here proclaim was madness.—*Hamlet.*

IT was very generally thought that it was a fortunate circumstance for Mr. Oswin Markham that there chanced to be in the fore-cabin of the steamer an enterprising American speculator who was taking out some hundred dozens of ready-made garments for disposal to the diamond miners—and an equal quantity of less durable clothing, in which he had been induced to invest some money with a view to the ultimate adoption of clothing by the Kafir nation. He explained how he had secured the services of a hard-working missionary whom he had sent as agent in advance to endeavour to convince the natives that if they ever wished to gain a footing among great nations, the auxiliary of clothing towards the effecting of their object was worth taking into consideration. When the market for these garments would thus be created, the speculator hoped to arrive on the scene and make a tolerable sum of money. In rear of his missionary, he had scoured most of the islands of the Pacific with very satisfactory results; and he said he felt that, if he could but prevail upon his missionary in advance to keep steady, a large work of evangelisation could be done in South Africa.

By the aid of this enterprising person, Mr. Markham was able to clothe himself without borrowing from any of the passengers. But about the payment for his purchases there seemed likely to be some difficulty. The bank order for four hundred pounds was once again in the possession of Mr. Markham, but it was payable in England, and how then could he effect the transfer of the few pounds he owed the American speculator, when he was to leave the vessel at St. Helena? There was no agency of the bank at this island, though there was one at the Cape, and thus the question of payment became somewhat difficult to solve.

"Do you want to leave the craft at St. Helena, mister?" asked the American, stroking his chin thoughtfully.

"I do," said Mr. Markham. "I must leave at the island and take the first ship to England."

"It's the awkwardest place on God's footstool, this St. Helena, isn't it?" said the American.

"I don't see that it is; why do you say so?"

"Only that I don't see why you want so partickler to land thar, mister. Maybe you'll change yer mind, eh?"

"I have said that I must part from this ship there," exclaimed Mr. Markham almost impatiently. "I must get this order reduced to money somehow."

"Wal, I reckon that's about the point, mister." said the speculator. "But you see if you want to fly it as you say, you'll not breeze about that it's needful for you to cut the craft before you come to the Cape. I'd half a mind to try and trade with you for that bit of paper ten minutes ago, but I reckon that's not what's the matter with me now. No, *sir*; if you want to get rid of that paper without much trouble, just you give out that you don't care if you do go on to the Cape; maybe a nibble will come from that."

"I don't know what you mean, my good fellow," said Markham; "but I can only repeat that I will not go on to the Cape. I shall get the money somehow and pay you before I leave, for surely the order is as good as money to any one living in the midst of civilisation. I don't suppose a savage would understand it, but I can't see what objection any one in business could make to receiving it at its full value."

The American screwed up his mouth in a peculiar fashion, and smiled in a still more peculiar fashion. He rather fancied he had a small piece of tobacco in his waistcoat pocket, nor did the result of a search show that he was mistaken; he extracted the succulent morsel and put it into his mouth. Then he winked at Mr. Markham, put his hands in his pockets, and walked slowly away without a word.

Markham looked after him with a puzzled expression. He did not know what the man meant to convey by his nods and his becks and his wreathed smiles. But just at this moment Mr. Harwood came up; he had of course previously made the acquaintance of Markham.

"I suppose we shall soon be losing you?" said Harwood, offering him a cigar. "You said, I think, that you would be leaving us at St. Helena?"

"Yes, I leave at St. Helena, and we shall be there in a few days. You see, I am now nearly as strong as ever, thanks to Campion, and it is important for me to get to England at once."

"No doubt," said Harwood; "your relatives will be very anxious if they hear of the loss of the vessel you were in."

Markham gave a little laugh, as he said, "I have no relatives; and as for friends—well, I suppose I shall have a number now."

"Now?"

"Yes; the fact is I was on my way home from Australia to take up a certain property which my father left to me in England. He died six months ago, and the solicitors for the estate sent me out a considerable sum of money in case I should need it in Australia—this order for four hundred pounds is what remains of it."

"I can now easily understand your desire to be at home and settled down," said Harwood.

"I don't mean to settle down," replied Markham. "There are a good many places to be seen in the world, small as it is."

"A man who has knocked about in the Colonies is generally glad to settle down at home," remarked Harwood.

"No doubt that is the rule, but I fear I am all awry so far as rules are concerned. I haven't allowed my life to be subject to many rules, hitherto. Would to God I had! It is not a pleasant recollection for a son to go through life with, Harwood, that his father has died without becoming reconciled to him—especially when he knows that his father has died leaving him a couple of thousands a year."

"And you——"

"I am such a son," said Markham, turning round suddenly. "I did all that I could to make my father's life miserable till—a climax came, and I found myself in Australia three years ago with an allowance sufficient to keep me from ever being in want. But I forget, I'm not a modern Ancient Mariner, wandering about boring people with my sad story."

"No," said Harwood, "you are not, I should hope. Nor am I so pressed for time just now as the wedding guest. You did not go in for a sheep-run in Australia?"

"Nothing of the sort," laughed the other. "The only thing I went in for was getting through my allowance, until that letter came that sobered me— that letter telling me that my father was dead, and that every penny he had possessed was mine. Harwood, you have heard of people's hair turning white in a few hours, but you have not often heard of natures changing from black to white in a short space; believe me it was so with me. The idea that theologians used to have long ago about souls passing from earth to heaven in a moment might well be believed by me, knowing as I do how my soul was transformed by that letter. I cast my old life behind me, though I did not tell any one about me what had happened. I left my companions and said to them that I was going up country. I did go up country, but I returned in a few days and got aboard the first ship that was sailing for England, and—here I am."

"And you mean to renew your life of wandering when you reach England?" said Harwood, after a pause.

"It is all that there is left for me," said the man bitterly, though a change in his tone would have made his words seem very pitiful. "I am not such a fool as to fancy that a man can sow tares and reap wheat. The spring of my life is over, and also the summer, the seed-time and the ripening; shall the harvest be delayed then? No, I am not such a fool."

"I cannot see that you might not rest at home," said Harwood. "Surely you have some associations in England."

"Not one that is not wretched."

"But a man of good family with some money is always certain to make new associations for himself, no matter what his life has been. Marriage, for instance; it is, I think, an exceedingly sure way of squaring a fellow up in life."

"A very sure way indeed," laughed Markham. "Never mind; in another week I shall be away from this society which has already become so pleasant to me. Perhaps I shall knock up against you in some of the strange places of the earth, Harwood."

"I heartily hope so," said the other. "But I still cannot see why you should not come on with us to the Cape. The voyage will completely restore you, you can get your money changed there, and a steamer of this company's will take you away two days after you land."

"I cannot remain aboard this steamer," said Markham quickly. "I must leave at St. Helena." Then he walked away with that shortness of ceremony which steamer voyagers get into a habit of showing to each other without giving offence.

"Poor beggar!" muttered Harwood. "Wrecked in sight of the haven—a pleasant haven—yes, if he is not an uncommonly good actor." He turned round from where he was leaning over the ship's side smoking, and saw the man with whom he had been talking seated in his chair by the side of Daireen Gerald. He watched them for some time—for a long time—until his cigar was smoked to the very end. He looked over the side thoughtfully as he dropped the remnant and heard its little hiss in the water; then he repeated his words, "a wreck." Once more he glanced astern, and then he added thoughtfully, "Yes, he is right; he had much better part at St. Helena—very much better."

Mr. Markham seemed quite naturally to have found his place in Mrs. Crawford's set, exclusive though it was; for somehow aboard ship a man amalgamates only with that society for which he is suited; a man is seldom to be found out of place on account of certain considerations such as one meets on shore. Not even Mr. Glaston could raise any protest against Mr. Markham's right to take a place in the midst of the elect of the cabin. But the young lady in whose birthday book Mr. Markham had inscribed his name upon the first day of his appearance at the table, thought it very unkind of him to join the band who had failed to appreciate her toilet splendours.

During the day on which he gave Harwood his brief autobiographical outline, Mr. Oswin Markham was frequently by the side of Miss Gerald and Mrs. Crawford. But towards night the major felt that it would be unjust to allow him to be defrauded of the due amount of narratory entertainment so necessary for his comfort; and with these excellent intentions drew him away from the others of the set, and, sitting on the secluded bridge, brought forth from the abundant resources of his memory a few well-defined anecdotes of that lively Arradambad station. But all the while the major was narrating the stories he could see that Markham's soul was otherwhere, and he began to be disappointed in Mr. Markham.

"I mustn't bore you, Markham, my boy," he said as he rose, after having whiled away about two hours of the night in this agreeable occupation. "No, I mustn't bore you, and you look, upon my soul, as if you had been suffering."

"No, no, I assure you, I never enjoyed anything more than that story of—of—the Surgeon-General and the wife of—of—the Commissary."

"The Adjutant-General, you mean," interrupted the major.

"Of course, yes, the Adjutant; a deucedly good story!"

"Ah, not bad, is it? But there goes six bells; I must think about turning in. Come and join me in a glass of brandy-and-water."

"No, no; not to-night—not to-night. The fact is I feel—I feel queer."

"You're not quite set on your feet yet, my boy," said the major critically. "Take care of yourself." And he walked away, wondering if it was possible that he had been deceived in his estimate of the nature of Mr. Markham.

But Mr. Markham continued sitting alone in the silence of the deserted deck. His thoughts were truly otherwhere. He lay back upon his seat and kept his eyes fixed upon the sky—the sky of stars towards which he had looked in agony for those four nights when nothing ever broke in upon the dread loneliness of the barren sea but those starlights. The terrible recollection of every moment he had passed returned to him.

Then he thought how he had heard of men becoming, through sufferings such as his, oblivious of everything of their past life—men who were thus enabled to begin life anew without being racked by any dread memories, the agony that they had endured being acknowledged by Heaven as expiation of their past deeds. That was justice, he felt, and if this justice had been done to these men, why had it been withheld from him?

"Could God Himself have added to what I endured?" he said, in passionate bitterness. "God! did I not suffer until my agony had overshot its mark by destroying in me the power of feeling agony—my agony consumed itself; I was dead—dead; and yet I am denied the power of beginning my new life under the conditions which are my due. What more can God want of man than his life? have I not paid that debt daily for four days?" He rose from his chair and stood upright upon the deck with clenched hands and lips. "It is past," he said, after a long pause. "From this hour I throw the past beneath my feet. It is my right to forget all, and—I have forgotten all—all."

Mr. Harwood had truly reason to feel surprised when, on the following day, Oswin Markham came up to him, and said quietly:

"I believe you are right, Harwood: after all, it would be foolish for me to part from the ship at St. Helena. I have decided to take your advice and run on to the Cape."

Harwood looked at him for a few moments before he answered slowly:

"Ah, you have decided."

"Yes; you see I am amenable to reason: I acknowledge the wisdom of my counsellors." But Harwood made no answer, only continued with his eyes fixed upon his face. "Hang it all," exclaimed Markham, "can't you congratulate me upon my return to the side of reason? Can't you acknowledge that you have been mistaken in me—that you find I am not so pig-headed as you supposed?"

"Yes," said Harwood; "you are not pig-headed." And, taking all things into consideration, it can hardly be denied that Mr. Oswin Markham's claim to be exempted from the class of persons called pig-headed was well founded.

CHAPTER XVIII

'Tis told me he hath very oft of late
Given private time to you: and you yourself
Have of your audience been most free and bounteous.

Do you believe his tenders, as you call them? —*Hamlet.*

MRS. Crawford felt that she was being unkindly dealt with by Fate in many matters. She had formed certain plans on coming aboard the steamer and on taking in at a glance the position of every one about her—it was her habit to do so on the occasion of her arrival at any new station in the Indian Empire—and hitherto she had generally had the satisfaction of witnessing the success of her plans; but now she began to fear that if things continued to diverge so widely from the paths which it was natural to expect them to have kept, her skilful devices would be completely overthrown.

Mrs. Crawford had within the first few hours of the voyage communicated to her husband her intention of surprising Colonel Gerald on the arrival of his daughter at the Cape; for he could scarcely fail to be surprised and, of course, gratified, if he were made aware of the fact that his daughter had conceived an attachment for a young man so distinguished in many ways as the son of the Bishop of the Calapash Islands and Metropolitan of the Salamander Archipelago—the style and titles of the father of Mr. Glaston.

But Daireen, instead of showing herself a docile subject and ready to act according to the least suggestion of one who was so much wiser and more experienced than herself, had begun to think and to act most waywardly. Though she had gone ashore at Madeira contrary to Mr. Glaston's advice, and had even ventured to assert, in the face of Mr. Glaston's demonstration to the contrary, that she had spent a pleasant day, yet Mrs. Crawford saw that it would be quite possible, by care and thoughtfulness in the future, to overcome all the unhappy influences her childishness would have upon the mind of Mr. Glaston.

Being well aware of this, she had for some days great hope of her protégée; but then Daireen had apparently cast to the winds all her sense of duty to those who were qualified to instruct her, for she had not only disagreed from Mr. Glaston upon a theory he had expressed regarding the symbolism of a certain design having for its chief elements sections of pomegranates and conventionalised daisies—Innocence allured by Ungovernable Passion was the parable preached through the union of some tones of sage green and saffron, Mr. Glaston assured the circle whom he had favoured with his views on this subject—but she had also laughed when Mr. Harwood made some whispered remark about the distressing diffusion of jaundice through the floral creation.

This was very sad to Mrs. Crawford. She was nearly angry with Daireen, and if she could have afforded it, she would have been angry with Mr. Harwood; she was, however, mindful of the influence of the letters she hoped the special correspondent of the *Dominant Trumpeter* would be writing regarding the general satisfaction that was felt throughout the colonies of South Africa that the Home Government had selected so efficient and trustworthy an officer to discharge the duties in connection with the Army Boot Commission, so she could not be anything but most friendly towards Mr. Harwood.

Then it was a great grief to Mrs. Crawford to see the man who, though undoubtedly well educated and even cultured, was still a sort of adventurer, seating himself more than once by the side of Daireen on the deck, and to notice that the girl talked with him even when Mr. Glaston was near—Mr. Glaston, who had referred to his sudden arrival aboard the ship as being melodramatic. But on the day preceding the expected arrival of the steamer at St. Helena, the well-meaning lady began to feel almost happy once more, for she recollected how fixed had been Mr. Markham's determination to leave the steamer at the island. Being almost happy, she thought she might go so far as to express to the man the grief which reflecting upon his departure excited.

"We shall miss you from our little circle, I can assure you, Mr. Markham," she said. "Your coming was so—so"—she thought of a substitute for melodramatic—"so unexpected, and so—well, almost romantic, that indeed it has left an impression upon all of us. Try and get into a room in the hotel at James Town that the white ants haven't devoured; I really envy you the delicious water-cress you will have every day."

"You will be spared the chance of committing that sin, Mrs. Crawford, though I fear the penance which will be imposed upon you for having even imagined it will be unjustly great. The fact is, I have been so weak as to allow myself to be persuaded by Doctor Campion and Harwood to go on to the Cape."

"To go on to the Cape!" exclaimed the lady.

"To go on to the Cape, Mrs. Crawford; so you see you will be bored with me for another week."

Mrs. Crawford looked utterly bewildered, as, indeed, she was. Her smile was very faint as she said:

"Ah, how nice; you have been persuaded. Ah, very pleasant it will be; but how one may be deceived in judging of another's character! I really formed the impression that you were firmness itself, Mr. Markham!"

"So I am, Mrs. Crawford, except when my inclination tends in the opposite direction to my resolution; then, I assure you, I can be led with a strand of floss."

This was, of course, very pleasant chat, and with the clink of compliment about it, but it was anything but satisfactory to the lady to whom it was addressed. She by no means felt in the mood for listening to mere colloquialisms, even though they might be of the most brilliant nature, which Mr. Markham's certainly were not.

"Yes, I fancied that you were firmness itself," she repeated. "But you allowed your mind to be changed by—by the doctor and Mr. Harwood."

"Well, not wholly, to say the truth, Mrs. Crawford," he interposed. "It is pitiful to have to confess that I am capable of being influenced by a monetary matter; but so it is: the fact is, if I were to land now at St. Helena, I should be not only penniless myself, but I should be obliged also to run in debt for these garments that my friend Phineas F. Fulton of Denver City supplied me with, not to speak of what I feel I owe to the steamer itself; so I think it is better for me to get my paper money turned into cash at the Cape, and then hurry homewards."

"No doubt you understand your own business," said the lady, smiling faintly as she walked away.

Mr. Oswin Markham watched her for some moments in a thoughtful way. He had known for a considerable time that the major's wife understood her business, at any rate, and that she was also quite capable of comprehending—nay, of directing as well—the business of every member of her social circle. But how was it possible, he asked himself, that she should have come to look upon his remaining for another week aboard the steamer as a matter of concern? He was a close enough observer to be able to see from her manner that she did so; but he could not understand how she should regard him as of any importance in the arrangement of her plans for the next week, whatever they might be.

But Mrs. Crawford, so soon as she found herself by the side of Daireen in the evening, resolved to satisfy herself upon the subject of the influences which had been brought to bear upon Mr. Oswin Markham, causing his character for determination to be lost for ever.

Daireen was sitting alone far astern, and had just finished directing some envelopes for letters to be sent home the next day from St. Helena.

"What a capital habit to get into of writing on that little case on your knee!" said Mrs. Crawford. "You have been on deck all day, you see, while the other correspondents are shut down in the saloon. You have had a good deal to tell the old people at that wonderful Irish lake of yours since you wrote at Madeira."

Daireen thought of all she had written regarding Standish, to prevent his father becoming uneasy about him.

"Oh, yes, I have had a good deal of news that will interest them," she said. "I have told them that the Atlantic is not such a terrible place after all. Why, we have not had even a breeze yet."

"No, *we* have not, but you should not forget, Daireen, the tornado that at least one ship perished in." She looked gravely at the girl, though she felt very pleased indeed to know that her protégée had not remembered this particular storm. "You have mentioned in your letters, I hope, how Mr. Markham was saved?"

"I believe I devoted an entire page to Mr. Markham," Daireen replied with a smile.

"That is right, my dear. You have also said, I am sure, how we all hope he is—a—a gentleman."

"*Hope?*" said Daireen quickly. Then she added after a pause, "No, Mrs. Crawford, I don't think I said that. I only said that he would be leaving us to-morrow."

Mrs. Crawford's nicely sensitive ear detected, she fancied, a tinge of regret in the girl's last tone.

"Ah, he told you that he had made up his mind to leave the ship at St. Helena, did he not?" she asked.

"Of course he is to leave us there, Mrs. Crawford. Did you not understand so?"

"I did indeed; but I am disappointed in Mr. Markham. I thought that he was everything that is firm. Yes, I am disappointed in him."

"How?" said Daireen, with a little flush and an anxious movement of her eyes. "How do you mean he has disappointed you?"

"He is not going to leave us at St. Helena, Daireen; he is coming on with us to the Cape."

With sorrow and dismay Mrs. Crawford noticed Daireen's face undergo a change from anxiety to pleasure; nor did she allow the little flush that came to the girl's forehead to escape her observation. These changes of countenance were almost terrifying to the lady. "It is the first time I have had my confidence in him shaken," she added. "In spite of what Mr. Harwood said of him I had not the least suspicion of this Mr. Markham, but now — —"

"What did! Mr. Harwood say of him?" asked Daireen, with a touch of scorn in her voice.

"You need not get angry, Daireen, my child," replied Mrs. Crawford.

"Angry, Mrs. Crawford? How could you fancy I was angry? Only what right had this Mr. Harwood to say anything about Mr. Markham? Perhaps Mr. Glaston was saying something too. I thought that as Mr. Markham was a stranger every one here would treat him with consideration, and yet, you see — —"

"Good gracious, Daireen, what can you possibly mean?" cried Mrs. Crawford. "Not a soul has ever treated Mr. Markham except in good taste from the day he came aboard this vessel. Of course young men will talk, especially young newspaper men, and more especially young *Dominant. Trumpeter* men. For myself, you saw how readily I admitted Mr. Markham into our set, though you will allow that, all things considered, I need not have done so at all."

"He was a stranger," said Daireen.

"But he is not therefore an angel unawares, my dear," said Mrs. Crawford, smiling as she patted the girl's hand in token of amity. "So long as he meant, to be a stranger of course we were justified in making him as pleasant as possible; but now, you see, he is not going to be a stranger. But why should we talk upon so unprofitable a subject? Tell me all the rest that you have been writing about."

Daireen made an attempt to recollect what were the topics of her letters, but she was not very successful in recalling them.

"I told them about the—the albatross, how it has followed us so faithfully," she said; "and how the Cape pigeons came to us yesterday."

"Ah, indeed. Very nice it will be for the dear old people at home. Ah, Daireen, how happy you are to have some place you can look back upon and think of as your home. Here am I in my old age still a vagabond upon the face of the earth. I have no home, dear." The lady felt that this piece of pathos should touch the girl deeply.

"No, no, don't say that, my dear Mrs. Crawford," Daireen said gently. "Say that your dear kind goodnature makes you feel at home in every part of the world."

This was very nice Mrs. Crawford felt, as she kissed the face beside her, but she did not therefore come to the conclusion that it would be well to forget that little expression of pleasure which had flashed over this same face a few minutes before.

At this very hour upon the evening following the anchors were being weighed, and the good steamer was already backing slowly out from the place it had occupied in the midst of the little fleet of whale-ships and East Indiamen beneath the grim shadow of that black ocean rock, St. Helena. The church spire of James Town was just coming into view as the motion of the ship disclosed a larger space of the gorge where the little town is built. The flag was being hauled down from the spar at the top of Ladder Hill, and the man was standing by the sunset gun aboard H.M.S. *Cobra*. The last of the shore-boats was cast off from the rail, and then, the anchor being reported in sight, the steamer put on full speed ahead, the helm was made hard-a-starboard, and the vessel swept round out of the harbour.

Mr. Harwood and Major Crawford were in anxious conversation with an engineer officer who had been summoned to the Cape to assist in a certain council which was to be held regarding the attitude of a Kafir chief who was inclined to be defiant of the lawful possessors of the country. But Daireen was standing at the ship's side looking at that wonderful line of mountain-wall connecting the batteries round the island. Her thoughts were not, however, wholly of the days when there was a reason why this little island should be the most strongly fortified in the ocean. As the steamer moved gently round the dark cliffs she was not reflecting upon what must have been the feelings of the great emperor-general who had been accustomed to stand upon these cliffs and to look seaward. Her thoughts were indeed undefined in their course, and she knew this when she heard the voice of Oswin Markham beside her.

"Can you fancy what would be my thoughts at this time if I had kept to my resolution—and if I were now up there among those big rocks?" he asked.

She shook her head, but did not utter a word in answer.

"I wonder what would yours have been now if I had kept to my resolution," he then said.

"I cannot tell you, indeed," she answered. "I cannot fancy what I should be thinking."

"Nor can I tell you what my thought would be," he said after a pause. He was leaning with one arm upon the moulding of the bulwarks, and she had her eyes still fixed upon the ridges of the island. He touched her and pointed out over the water. The sun like a shield of sparkling gold had already buried half its disc beneath the horizon. They watched the remainder become gradually less and less until only a thread of gold was on the water; in another instant this had dwindled away. "I know now how I should have felt," he said, with his eyes fixed upon the blank horizon.

The girl looked out to that blank horizon also.

Then from each fort on the cliffs there leaped a little flash of light, and the roar of the sunset guns made thunder all along the hollow shore; before the echoes had given back the sound, faint bugle-calls were borne out to the ocean as fort answered fort all along that line of mountain-wall. The girl listened until the faintest farthest thin sound dwindled away just as the last touch of sunlight had waned into blankness upon the horizon.

CHAPTER XIX

Polonius. What treasure had he, my lord?
Hamlet. Why,
"One fair daughter and no more,
The which he loved passing well."
O my old friend, thy face is valanced since I saw thee last.... What, my young lady and mistress! By'r lady, your ladyship is nearer to heaven than when I saw you last.... You are all welcome.—*Hamlet.*

HOWEVER varying, indefinite, and objectless the thoughts of Daireen Gerald may have been—and they certainly were—during the earlier days of the voyage, they were undoubtedly fixed and steadfast during the last week. She knew that she could not hear anything of her father until she would arrive at the Cape, and so she had allowed herself to be buoyed up by the hopeful conversation of the major and Mrs. Crawford, who seemed to think of her meeting with her father as a matter of certainty, and by the various little excitements of every day. But now when she knew that upon what the next few days would bring forth all the happiness of her future life depended, what thought—what prayer but one, could she have?

She was certainly not good company during these final days. Mr. Harwood never got a word from her. Mr. Glaston did not make the attempt, though he attributed her silence to remorse at having neglected his artistic instructions. Major Crawford's gallantries received no smiling recognition from her; and Mrs. Crawford's most motherly pieces of pathos went by unheeded so far as Daireen was concerned.

What on earth was the matter, Mrs. Crawford thought; could it be possible that her worst fears were realised? she asked herself; and she made a vow that even if Mr. Harwood had spoken a single word on the subject of affection to Daireen, he should forfeit her own friendship for ever.

"My dear Daireen," she said, two days after leaving St. Helena, "you know I love you as a daughter, and I have come to feel for you as a mother might. I know something is the matter—what is it? you may confide in me; indeed you may."

"How good you are!" said the child of this adoption; "how very good! You know all that is the matter, though you have in your kindness prevented me from feeling it hitherto."

"Good gracious, Daireen, you frighten me! No one can have been speaking to you surely, while I am your guardian——"

"You know what a wretched doubt there is in my mind now that I know a few days will tell me all that can be told—you know the terrible question that comes to me every day—every hour—shall I see him?—shall he be—alive?"

Even the young men, with no touches of motherly pathos about them, had appreciated the girl's feelings in those days more readily than Mrs. Crawford.

"My poor dear little thing," she now said, fondling her in a way whose soothing effect the combined efforts of all the young men could never have approached. "Don't let the doubt enter your mind for an instant—it positively must not. Your father is as well as I am to-day, I can assure you. Can you disbelieve me? I know him a great deal better than you do; and I know the Cape climate better than you do. Nonsense, my dear, no one ever dies at the Cape—at least not when they go there to recover. Now make your mind easy for the next three days."

But for just this interval poor Daireen's mind was in a state of anything but repose.

During the last night the steamer would be on the voyage she found it utterly impossible to go to sleep. She heard all of the bells struck from watch to watch. Her cabin became stifling to her though a cool breeze was passing through the opened port. She rose, dressed herself, and went on deck though it was about two o'clock in the morning. It was a terrible thing for a girl to do, but nothing could have prevented Daireen's taking that step. She stood just outside the door of the companion, and in the moonlight and soft air of the sea more ease of mind came to her than she had yet felt on this voyage.

While she stood there in the moonlight listening to the even whisperings of the water as it parted away before the ship, and to the fitful flights of the winged fish, she seemed to hear some order as she thought, given from the forward part of the vessel. In another minute the officer on watch hastened past her. She heard him knock at the captain's cabin which was just aft of the deck-house, and make the report.

"Fixed light right ahead, sir."

She knew then that the first glimpse of the land which they were approaching had been obtained, and her anxiety gave place to peace. That message of the light seemed to be ominous of good to her. She returned to her cabin, and found it cool and tranquil, so that she fell asleep at once; and when she next opened her eyes she saw a tall man standing with folded arms beside her, gazing at her. She gave but one little cry, and then that long drooping moustache of his was down upon her face and her bare arms were about his neck.

"Thank you, thank you, Dolly; that is a sufficiently close escape from strangulation to make me respect your powers," said the man; and at the sound of his voice Daireen turned her face to her pillow, while the man shook out with spasmodic fingers his handkerchief from its folds and endeavoured to repair the injury done to his moustache by the girl's embrace.

"Now, now, my Dolly," he said, after some convulsive mutterings which Daireen could, of course, not hear; "now, now, don't you think it might be as well to think of making some apology for your laziness instead of trying to go asleep again?"

Then she looked up with wondering eyes.

"I don't understand anything at all," she cried. "How could I go asleep when we were within four hours of the Cape? How could any one be so cruel as to let me sleep so dreadfully? It was wicked of me: it was quite wicked."

"There's not the least question about the enormity of the crime, I'm afraid," he answered; "only I think that Mrs. Crawford may be responsible for a good deal of it, if her confession to me is to be depended upon. She told me how you were—but never mind, I am the ill-treated one in the matter, and I forgive you all."

"And we have actually been brought into the dock?"

"For the past half-hour, my love; and I have been waiting for much longer. I got the telegram you sent to me, by the last mail from Madeira, so that I have been on the lookout for the *Cardwell Castle* for a week. Now don't be too hard on an old boy, Dolly, with all of those questions I see on your lips. Here, I'll take them in the lump, and think over them as I get through a glass of brandy-and-water with Jack Crawford and the Sylph— by George, to think of your meeting with the poor old hearty Sylph—ah, I forgot you never heard that we used to call Mrs. Crawford the Sylph at our station before you were born. There, now I have got all your questions, my darling—my own darling little Dolly."

She only gave him a little hug this time, and he hastened up to the deck, where Mrs. Crawford and her husband were waiting for him.

"Now, did I say anything more of her than was the truth, George?" cried Mrs. Crawford, so soon as Colonel Gerald got on deck.

But Colonel Gerald smiled at her abstractedly and pulled fiercely at the ends of his moustache. Then seeing Mr. Harwood at the other side of the skylight, he ran and shook hands with him warmly; and Harwood, who fancied he understood something of the theory of the expression of emotion in mankind, refrained from hinting to the colonel that they had already had a chat together since the steamer had come into dock.

Mrs. Crawford, however, was not particularly well pleased to find that her old friend George Gerald had only answered her with that vague smile, which implied nothing; she knew that he had been speaking for half an hour before with Harwood, from whom he had heard the first intelligence of his appointment to the Castaway group. When Colonel Gerald, however, went the length of rushing up to Doctor Campion and violently shaking hands with him also, though they had been in conversation together before, the lady began to fear that the attack of fever from which it was reported Daireen's father had been suffering had left its traces upon him still.

"Rather rum, by gad," said the major, when his attention was called to his old comrade's behaviour. "Just like the way a boy would behave visiting his grandmother, isn't it? Looks as if he were working off his feelings, doesn't it? By gad, he's going back to Harwood!"

"I thought he would," said Mrs. Crawford. "Harwood can tell him all about his appointment. That's what George, like all the rest of them nowadays, is anxious about. He forgets his child—he has no interest in her, I see."

"That's devilish bad, Kate, devilish bad! by Jingo! But upon my soul, I was under the impression that his wildness just now was the effect of having been below with the kid."

"If he had the least concern about her, would he not come to me, when he knows very well that I could tell him all about the voyage? But no, he prefers to remain by the side of the special correspondent."

"No, he doesn't; here he comes, and hang me if he isn't going to shake hands with both of us!" cried the major, as Colonel Gerald, recognising him, apparently for the first time, left Harwood's side and hastened across the deck with extended hand.

"George, dear old George," said Mrs. Crawford, reflecting upon the advantages usually attributed to the conciliatory method of treatment. "Isn't it like the old time come back again? Here we stand together—Jack, Campion, yourself and myself, just as we used to be in—ah, it cannot have been '58!—yes, it was, good gracious, '58! It seems like a dream."

"Exactly like a dream, by Jingo, my dear," said the major pensively, for he was thinking what an auxiliary to the realistic effect of the scene a glass of brandy-and-water, or some other Indian cooling drink, would be. "Just like a vision, you know, George, isn't it? So if you'll come to the smoking-room, we'll have that light breakfast we were talking about."

"He won't go, major," said the lady severely.

"He wishes to have a talk with me about the dear child. Don't you, George?"

"And about your dear self, Kate," replied Colonel Gerald, in the Irish way that brought back to the lady still more vividly all the old memories of the happy station on the Himalayas.

"Ah, how like George that, isn't it?" she whispered to her husband.

"My dear girl, don't be a tool," was the parting request of the major as he strolled off to where the doctor was, he knew, waiting for some sign that the brandy and water were amalgamating.

"I'm glad that we are alone, George," said Mrs. Crawford, taking Colonel Gerald's arm. "We can talk together freely about the child—about Daireen."

"And what have we to say about her, Kate? Can you give me any hints about her temper, eh? How she needs to be managed, and that sort of thing? You used to be capital at that long ago."

"And I flatter myself that I can still tell all about a girl after a single glance; but, my dear George, I never indeed knew what a truly perfect nature was until I came to understand Daireen. She is an angel, George."

"No," said the colonel gently; "not Daireen—she is not the angel; but her face, when I saw it just now upon its pillow, sent back all my soul in thought of one—one who is—who always was an angel—my good angel."

"That was my first thought too," said Mrs. Crawford. "And her nature is the same. Only poor Daireen errs on the side of good nature. She is a child in her simplicity of thought about every one she meets. She wants some one near her who will be able to guide her tastes in—in—well, in different matters. By the way, you remember Austin Glaston, who was chaplain for a while on the *Telemachus*, and who got made Bishop of the Salamanders; well, that is his son, that tall handsome youngman—I must present you. He is one of the most distinguished men I ever met."

"Ah, indeed? Does he write for a newspaper?"

"Oh, George, I am ashamed of you. No, Mr. Glaston is a—a—an artist and a poet, and—well, he does nearly everything much better than any one else, and if you take my advice you will give him an invitation to dinner, and then you will find out all."

Before Colonel Gerald could utter a word he was brought face to face with Mr. Glaston, and felt his grasp responded to by a gentle pressure.

"I'm very glad to meet you, Mr. Glaston; your father and I were old friends. If you are staying at Cape Town, I hope you will not neglect to call upon my daughter and myself," said the colonel.

"You are extremely kind," returned the young man: "I shall be delighted."

Thus Daireen on coming on deck found her father in conversation with Mr. Glaston, and already acquainted with every member of Mrs. Crawford's circle.

"Mr. Glaston has just promised to pay you a visit on shore, my dear," said the major's wife, as she came up.

"How very kind," said Daireen. "But can he tell me where I live ashore, for no one has thought fit to let me know anything about myself. I will never forgive you, Mrs. Crawford, for ordering that I was not to be awakened this morning. It was too cruel."

"Only to be kind, dear; I knew what a state of nervousness you were in."

"And now of course," continued the girl, "when I come on deck all the news will have been told—even that secret about the Castaway Islands."

"Heavens':" said the colonel, "what about the Castaway Islands? Have they been submerged, or have they thrown off the British yoke already?"

"I see you know all," she said mournfully, "and I had treasured up all that Mr. Harwood said no one in the world but himself knew, to be the first to tell you. And now, too, you know every one aboard except—ah, I have my secret to tell at last. There he stands, and even you don't remember him, papa. Come here, Standish, and let me present you. This, papa, is Standish Macnamara, and he is coming out with us now to wherever we are to live."

"Good gracious, Daireen!" cried Mrs. Crawford.

"What, Standish, Prince of Innishdermot!" said the colonel. "My dear boy, I am delighted to welcome you to this strange place. I remember you when your curls were a good deal longer, my boy."

Poor Standish, who was no longer in his sailor's jacket, but in the best attire his Dublin tailor could provide, blushed most painfully as every one gazed at him—every one with the exception of Daireen, who was gazing anxiously around the deck as though she expected to see some one still.

"This is certainly a secret," murmured Mrs. Crawford.

"Now, Daireen, to the shore," said Colonel Gerald. "You need not say good-bye to any one here. Mrs. Crawford will be out to dine with us to-morrow. She will bring the major and Doctor Campion, and Mr. Harwood says he will ride one of my horses till he gets his own. So there need be no tears. My man will look after the luggage while I drive you out."

"I must get my bag from my cabin," Daireen said, going slowly towards the companion. In a few moments she reappeared with her dressing-bag, and gave another searching glance around the deck.

"Now," she said, "I am ready."

CHAPTER XX

(Note: The following four chapters were taken from a print copy of a different edition as these chapters were missing from the 1889 print edition from which the rest of the Project Gutenberg edition was taken. In the inserted four chapters it will be noted that the normal double quotation marks were printed as single quote marks.)

> Something have you heard
> Of Hamlet's transformation; so call it—
> ... What it should be...
> I cannot dream or
>
> ... gather
> So much as from occasion you may glean
> Whether aught to us unknown afflicts him.
>
> At night we'll feast together:
> Most welcome home!
> Most fair return of greetings.*Hamlet.*

WHAT an extraordinary affair!' said Mrs. Crawford, turning from where she had been watching the departure of the colonel and his daughter and that tall handsome young friend of theirs whom they had called Standish MacDermot.

'I would not have believed it of Daireen. Standish MacDermot—what a dreadful Irish name! But where can he have been aboard the ship? He cannot have been one of those terrible fore-cabin passengers. Ah, I would not have believed her capable of such disingenuousness. Who is this young man, Jack?'

'My dear girl, never mind the young man or the young woman just now. We must look after the traps and get them through the Custom-house.' replied the major.

'Mr. Harwood, who is this young man with the terrible Irish name?' she asked in desperation of the special correspondent. She felt indeed in an extremity when she sought Harwood for an ally.

'I never was so much astonished in all my life,' he whispered in answer. 'I never heard of him. She never breathed a word about him to me.'

Mrs. Crawford did not think this at all improbable, seeing that Daireen had never breathed a word about him to herself.

'My dear Mr. Harwood, these Irish are too romantic for us. It is impossible for us ever to understand them.' And she hastened away to look after her luggage. It was not until she was quite alone that she raised her hands, exclaiming devoutly, 'Thank goodness Mr. Glaston had gone before this second piece of romance was disclosed! What on earth would he have thought!'

The reflection made the lady shudder. Mr. Glaston's thoughts, if he had been present while Daireen was bringing forward this child of mystery, Standish MacDermot, would, she knew, have been too terrible to be contemplated.

As for Mr. Harwood, though he professed to be affected by nothing that occurred about him, still he felt himself uncomfortably surprised by the sudden appearance of the young Irishman with whom Miss Gerald and her father appeared to be on such familiar terms; and as he stood looking up to that marvellous hill in whose shadow Cape Town lies, he came to the conclusion that it would be as well for him to find out all that could be known about this Standish MacDermot. He had promised Daireen's father to make use of one of his horses so long as he would remain at the Cape, and it appeared from all he could gather that the affairs in the colony were becoming sufficiently complicated to compel his remaining here instead of hastening out to make his report of the Castaway group. The British nation were of course burning to hear all that could be told about the new island colony, but Mr. Harwood knew very well that the heading which would be given in the columns of the '*Dominant Trumpeter*' to any information regarding the attitude of the defiant Kafir chief would be in very much larger type than that of the most flowery paragraph descriptive of the charms of the Castaway group; and so he had almost made up his mind that it would be to the advantage of the newspaper that he should stay at the Cape. Of course he felt that he had at heart no further interests, and so long as it was not conflicting with those interests he would ride Colonel Gerald's horse, and, perhaps, walk with Colonel Gerald's daughter.

But all the time that he was reflecting in this consistent manner the colonel and his daughter and Standish were driving along the base of Table Mountain, while on the other side the blue waters of the lovely bay were sparkling between the low shores of pure white sand, and far away the dim mountain ridges were seen.

'Shall I ever come to know that mountain and all about it as well as I know our own dear Slieve Docas?' cried the girl, looking around her. 'Will you, do you think, Standish?'

'Nothing here can compare with our Irish land,' cried Standish.

'You are right my boy,' said Daireen's father. 'I have knocked about a good deal, and I have seen a good many places, and, after all, I have come to the conclusion that our own Suangorm is worth all that I have seen for beauty.'

'We can all sympathise with each other here,' said the girl laughing. 'We will join hands and say that there is no place in the world like our Ireland, and then, maybe, the strangers here will believe us.'

'Yes,' said her father, 'we will think of ourselves in the midst of a strange country as three representatives of the greatest nation in, the world. Eh, Standish, that would please your father.'

But Standish could not make any answer to this allusion to his father. He was in fact just now wondering what Colonel Gerald would say when he would hear that Standish had travelled six thousand miles for the sake of obtaining his advice as to the prudence of entertaining the thought of leaving home. Standish was beginning to fear that there was a flaw somewhere in the consistency of the step he had taken, complimentary though it undoubtedly was to the judgment of Colonel Gerald. He could hardly define the inconsistency of which he was conscious, but as the phaeton drove rapidly along the red road beside the high peak of the mountain he became more deeply impressed with the fact that it existed somewhere.

Passing along great hedges of cactus and prickly-pear, and by the side of some well-wooded grounds with acres of trim green vineyards, the phaeton proceeded for a few miles. The scene was strange to Daireen and Standish; only for the consciousness of that towering peak they were grateful. Even though its slope was not swathed in heather, it still resembled in its outline the great Slieve Docas, and this was enough to make them feel while passing beneath it that it was a landmark breathing of other days. Half way up the ascent they could see in a ravine a large grove of the silver-leaf fir, and the sun-glints among the exquisite white foliage were very lovely. Further down the mighty aloes threw forth their thick green branches in graceful divergence, and then along the road were numerous bullock waggons with Malay drivers—eighteen or twenty animals running in a team. Nothing could have added to the strangeness of the scene to the girl and her companion, and yet the shadow of that great hill made the land seem no longer weary.

At last, just at the foot of the hill, Colonel Gerald turned his horses to where there was a broad rough avenue made through a grove of pines, and after following its curves for some distance, a broad cleared space was reached, beyond which stood a number of magnificent Australian oaks and fruit trees surrounding a long low Dutch-built house with an overhanging roof and the usual stoëp—the raised stone border—in front.

'This is our house, my darling,' said the girl's father as he pulled up at the door. 'I had only a week to get it in order for you, but I hope you will like it.'

'Like it?' she cried; 'it is lovelier than any we had in India, and then the hill—the hill—oh, papa, this is home indeed.'

'And for me, my own little Dolly, don't you think it is home too?' he said when he had his arms about her in the hall. 'With this face in my hands at last I feel all the joy of home that has been denied to me for years. How often have I seen your face, Dolly, as I sat with my coffee in the evening in my lonely bungalow under the palms? The sight of it used to cheer me night after night, darling,' but now that I have it here—here——'

'Keep it there,' she cried. 'Oh, papa, papa, why should we be miserable apart ever again? I will stay with you now wherever you go for ever.'

Colonel Gerald looked at her for a minute, he kissed her once again upon the face, and then burst into a laugh.

'And this is the only result of a voyage made under the protection of Mrs. Crawford!' he said. 'My dear, you must have used some charm to have resisted her power; or has she lost her ancient cunning? Why, after a voyage with Mrs. Crawford I have seen the most devoted daughters desert their parents. When I heard that you were coming out with her I feared you would allow yourself to be schooled by her into a sense of your duty, but it seems you have been stubborn.'

'She was everything that is kind to me, and I don't know what I should have done without her,' said the girl. 'Only, I'll never forgive her for not having awakened me to meet you this morning. But last night I suppose she thought I was too nervous. I was afraid, you know, lest—lest—but never mind, here we are together at home—for there is the hill—yes, at home.'

But when Daireen found herself in the room to which she had been shown by the neat little handmaiden provided by Colonel Gerald, and had seated herself in sight of a bright green cactus that occupied the centre of the garden outside, she had much to think about. She just at this moment realised that all her pleasant life aboard the steamer was at an end. More than a touch of sadness was in her reflection, for she had come to think of the good steamer as something more than a mere machine; it had been a home to her for twenty-five days, and it had contained her happiness and sorrow during that time as a home would have done. Then how could she have parted from it an hour before with so little concern? she asked herself. How could she have left it without shaking hands with—with all those who had been by her side for many days on the good old ship? Some she had said goodbye to, others she would see again on the following day, but still there were some whom she had left the ship without seeing—some who had been associated with her happiness during part of the voyage, at any rate, and she might never see them again. The reflection made her very sad, nor did the feeling pass off during the rest of the day spent by her father's side.

The day was very warm, and, as Daireens father was still weak, he did not stray away from the house beyond the avenue of shady oaks leading down to a little stream that moved sluggishly on its way a couple of hundred yards from the garden. They had, of course, plenty to talk about; for Colonel Gerald was somewhat anxious to hear how his friend Standish had come out. He had expressed the happiness he felt on meeting with the young man as soon as his daughter had said that he would go out to wherever they were to live, but he thought it would increase his satisfaction if his daughter would tell him how it came to pass that this young man was unacquainted with any of the passengers.

Daireen now gave him the entire history of Standish's quarrel with his father, and declared that it was solely to obtain the advice of Colonel Gerald he had made the voyage from Ireland.

The girl's father laughed when he heard of this characteristic action on the part of the young man; but he declared that it proved he meant to work for himself in the world, and not be content to live upon the traditions of The Mac-Dermots; and then he promised the girl that something should be done for the son of the hereditary prince.

CHAPTER XXI

The nights are wholesome;
No fairy takes, nor witch hath power to charm,
So hallowed and so gracious is the time.

What, has this thing appeared again to-night?—Hamlet.

WHEN evening came Daireen and her father sat out upon their chairs on the stoëp in front of the house. The sun had for long been hidden by the great peak, though to the rest of the world not under its shadow he had only just sunk. The twilight was very different from the last she had seen on land, when the mighty Slieve Docas had appeared in his purple robe. Here the twilight was brief and darkly blue as it overhung the arched aloes and those large palm plants whose broad leaves waved not in the least breeze. Far in the mellow distance a large star was glittering, and the only sound in the air was the shrill whistle of one of the Cape field crickets.

Then began the struggle between moonlight and darkness. The leaves of the boughs that were clasped above the little river began to be softly silvered as the influence of the rising light made itself apparent, and then the highest ridges of the hill gave back a flash as the beams shot through the air.

These changes were felt by the girl sitting silently beside her father—the changes of the twilight and of the moonlight, before the full round shield of the orb appeared above the trees, and the white beams fell around the broad floating leaves beneath her feet.

'Are you tired, Dolly?' asked her father.

'Not in the least, papa; it seems months since I was at sea.'

'Then you will ride with me for my usual hour? I find it suits me better to take an hour's exercise in the cool of the evening.'

'Nothing could be lovelier on such an evening,' she cried. 'It will complete our day's happiness.'

She hastened to put on her habit while her father went round to the stables to give directions to the groom regarding the saddling of a certain little Arab which had been bought within the week. In a short time Standish was left to gaze in admiration at the fine seat of the old officer in his saddle, and in rapture at the delicately shaped figure of the girl, as they trotted down the avenue between those strange trees.

They disappeared among the great leaves; and when the sound of their horses' hoofs had died away, Standish, sitting there upon the raised ground in front of the house, had his own hour of thought. He felt that he had hitherto not accomplished much in his career of labour. He had had an idea that there were a good many of the elements of heroism in joining as he did the vessel in which the girl was going abroad. Visions of wrecks, of fires, of fallings overboard, nay of pirates even, had floated before his mind, with himself as the only one near to save the girl from each threatening calamity. He had heard of such things taking place daily, and he was prepared to risk himself for her sake, and to account himself happy if the chance of protecting her should occur.

But so soon as he had been a few days at sea, and had found that such a thing as danger was not even hinted at any more than it would be in a drawing-room on shore—when in fact he saw how like a drawing-room on shore was the quarter-deck of the steamer, he began to be disappointed. Daireen was surrounded by friends who would, if there might chance to be the least appearance of danger, resent his undertaking to save the girl whom he loved with every thought of his soul. He would not, in fact, be permitted to play the part of the hero that his imagination had marked out for himself.

Yes, he felt that the heroic elements in his position aboard the steamer had somehow dwindled down to a minimum; and now here he had been so weak as to allow himself to be induced to come out to live, even though only for a short time, at this house. He felt that his acceptance of the sisterly friendship of the girl was making it daily more impossible for him to kneel at her feet, as he meant one day to do, and beg of her to accept of some heroic work done on her behalf.

'She is worthy of all that a man could do with all his soul,' Standish cried as he stood there in the moonlight. But what can I do for her? What can I do for her? Oh, I am the most miserable wretch in the whole world!'

This was not a very satisfactory conclusion for him to come to; but on the whole it did not cause him much despondency. In his Irish nature there were almost unlimited resources of hope, and it would have required a large number of reverses of fortune to cast him down utterly.

While he was trying in vain to make himself feel as miserable as he knew his situation demanded him to be, Daireen and her father were riding along the road that leads from Cape Town to the districts of Wynberg and Constantia. They went along through the moonlight beneath the splendid avenue of Australian oaks at the old Dutch district of Bondebosch, and then they turned aside into a narrow lane of cactus and prickly pear which brought them to that great sandy plain densely overgrown with blossoming heath and gorse called The Mats, along which they galloped for some miles. Turning their horses into the road once more, they then walked them back towards their house at Mowbray.

Daireen felt that she had never before so enjoyed a ride. All was so strange. That hill whose peak was once again towering above them; that long dark avenue with the myriads of fire-flies sparkling amongst the branches; the moonlight that was flooding the world outside; and then her companion, her father, whose face she had been dreaming over daily and nightly. She had never before so enjoyed a ride.

They had gone some distance through the oak avenue when they turned their horses aside at the entrance to one of the large vineyards that are planted in such neat lines up the sloping ground.

'Well, Dolly, are you satisfied at last?' said Colonel Gerald, looking into the girl's face that the moonlight was glorifying, though here and there the shadow of a leaf fell upon her.

'Satisfied! Oh, it is all like a dream,' she said. 'A strange dream of a strange place. When I think that a month ago I was so different, I feel inclined to—to—ask you to kiss me again, to make sure I am not dreaming.'

'If you are under the impression that you are a sleeping beauty, dear, and that you can only be roused by that means, I have no objection.'

'Now I am sure it is all reality,' she said with a little laugh. 'Oh, papa, I am so happy. Could anything disturb our happiness?'

Suddenly upon the dark avenue behind them there came the faint sound of a horses hoof, and then of a song sung carelessly through the darkness— one she had heard before.

The singer was evidently approaching on horseback, for the last notes were uttered just opposite where the girl and her father were standing their horses behind the trees at the entrance to the vineyard. The singer too seemed to have reined in at this point, though of course he could not see either of the others, the branches were so close. Daireen was mute while that air was being sung, and in another instant she became aware of a horse being pushed between the trees a few yards from her. There was only a small space to pass, so she and her father backed their horses round and the motion made the stranger start, for he had not perceived them before.

'I beg you will not move on my account. I did not know there was anyone here, or I should not have— —'

The light fell upon the girl's face, and her father saw the stranger give another little start.

'You need not make an apology to us, Mr. Markham,' said Daireen. 'We had hidden ourselves, I know. Papa, this is Mr. Oswin Markham. How odd it is that we should meet here upon the first evening of landing! The Cape is a good deal larger than the quarterdeck of the "Cardwell Castle."'

'You were a passenger, no doubt, aboard the steamer my daughter came out in, Mr. Markham?' said Colonel Gerald.

Mr. Markham laughed.

'Upon my word I hardly know that I am entitled to call myself a passenger,' he said. 'Can you define my position, Miss Gerald? it was something very uncertain. I am a castaway—a waif that was picked up in a half-drowned condition from a broken mast in the Atlantic, and sheltered aboard the hospitable vessel.'

'It is very rarely that a steamer is so fortunate as to save a life in that way,' said Colonel Gerald. 'Sailing vessels have a much better chance.'

'To me it seems almost a miracle—a long chain of coincidences was necessary for my rescue, and yet every link was perfect to the end.'

'It is upon threads our lives are constantly hanging,' said the colonel, backing his horse upon the avenue. 'Do you remain long in the colony, Mr. Markham?' he asked when they were standing in a group at a place where the moonlight broke through the branches.

'I think I shall have to remain for some weeks,' he answered. 'Campion tells me I must not think of going to England until the violence of the winter there is past.'

'Then we shall doubtless have the pleasure of meeting you frequently. We have a cottage at Mowbray, where we would be delighted to see you. By the way, Mrs. Crawford and a few of my other old friends are coming out to dine with us to-morrow, my daughter and myself would be greatly pleased if you could join us.'

'You are exceedingly kind,' said Mr. Markham. 'I need scarcely say how happy I will be.'

'Our little circle on board the good old ship is not yet to be dispersed, you see, Mr. Markham,' said Daireen with a laugh. 'For once again, at any rate, we will be all together.'

'For once again,' he repeated as he raised his hat, the girl's horse and her father's having turned. 'For once again, till when goodbye, Miss Gerald.'

'Goodbye, Mr. Markham,' said the colonel. 'By the way, we dine early I should have told you—half past six.'

Markham watched them ride along the avenue and reappear in the moonlight space beyond. Then he dropped the bridle on his horse's neck and listlessly let the animal nibble at the leaves on the side of the road for a long time. At last he seemed to start into consciousness of everything. He gathered up the bridle and brought the horse back to the avenue.

'It is Fate or Providence or God this time,' he muttered as if for his own satisfaction. 'I have had no part in the matter; I have not so much as raised my hand for this, and yet it has come.'

He walked his horse back to Cape Town in the moonlight.

'I don't think you mentioned this Mr. Markham's name to me, Dolly,' said Colonel Gerald as they returned to Mowbray.

'I don't think I did, papa; but you see he had gone ashore when I came on deck to you this morning, and I did not suppose we should ever meet again.'

'I hope you do not object to my asking him to dinner, dear?'

'I object, papa? Oh, no, no; I never felt so glad at anything. He does not talk affectedly like Mr. Glaston, nor cleverly like Mr. Harwood, so I prefer him to either of them. And then, think of his being for a week tossing about the Atlantic upon that wreck.'

'All very good reasons for asking him to dine to-morrow,' said her father. 'Now suppose we try a trot.'

'I would rather walk if it is the same to you, papa,' she said. 'I don't feel equal to another trot now.'

'Why, surely, you have not allowed yourself to become tired, Daireen? Yes, my dear, you look it. I should have remembered that you are just off the sea. We will go gently home, and you will get a good sleep.'

They did go very gently, and silently too, and in a short time Daireen was lying on her bed, thinking not of the strange moonlight wonders of her ride, but of that five minutes spent upon the avenue of Australian oaks down which had echoed that song.

It seemed that poor Mrs. Crawford was destined to have enigmas of the most various sorts thrust upon her for her solution; at any rate she regarded the presence of Mr. Oswin Markham at Colonel Crawford's little dinner the next, evening as a question as puzzling as the mysterious appearance of the young man called Standish MacDermot. She, however, chatted with Mr. Markham as usual, and learned that he also was going to a certain garden party which was to be held at Government House in a few days.

'And you will come too, Daireen?' she said. 'You must come, for Mr. Glaston has been so good as to promise to exhibit in one of the rooms a few of his pictures he spoke to us about. How kind of him, isn't it, to try and educate the taste of the colony?' The bishop has not yet arrived at the Cape, but Mr. Glaston says he will wait for him for a fortnight.'

'For a fortnight? Such filial devotion will no doubt bring its own reward,' said Mr. Harwood.

CHAPTER XXII

Being remiss,
Most generous and free from all contriving.
A heart unfortified,
An understanding simple and unschooled.

A violet in the youth of primy nature.

O'tis most sweet
When in one line two crafts directly meet.

Soft,—let me see:—
We'll make a solemn wager on your cunnings.—*Hamlet.*

THE band of the gallant Bayonetteers was making the calm air of Government House gardens melodious with the strains of an entrancing German valse not more than a year old, which had convulsed society at Cape Town when introduced a few weeks previously; for society at Cape Town, like society everywhere else, professes to understand everything artistic, even to the delicacies of German dance music. The evening was soft and sunny, while the effect of a very warm day drawing near its close was to be seen everywhere around. The broad leaves of the feathery plants were hanging dry and languid across the walks, and the grass was becoming tawny as that on the Lion's Head—that strangely curved hill beside Table Mountain. The giant aloes and plantains were, however, defiant of the heat and spread their leaves out mightily as ever.

The gardens are always charming in the southern spring, but never so charming as when their avenues are crowded with coolly dressed girls of moderate degrees of prettiness whose voices are dancing to the melody of a German valse not more than a year old. How charming it is to discuss all the absorbing colonial questions—such as how the beautiful Van der Veldt is looking this evening; and if Miss Van Schmidt, whose papa belongs to the Legislative Council and is consequently a voice in the British Empire, has really carried out his threat of writing home to the War Office to demand the dismissal of that young Mr. Westbury from the corps of Royal Engineers on account of his conduct towards Miss Van Schmidt; or perhaps a question of art, such as how the general's daughters contrive to have Paris bonnets several days previous to the arrival of the mail with the patterns; or a question of diplomacy, such as whether His Excellency's private secretary will see his way to making that proposal to the second eldest daughter of one of the Supreme Court judges. There is no colony in the world so devoted to discussions of this nature as the Cape, and in no part of the colony may a discussion be carried out with more spirit than in the gardens around Government House.

But upon the afternoon of this garden party there was an unusual display of colonial beauty and colonial young men—the two are never found in conjunction—and English delicacy and Dutch *gaucherie*, for the spring had been unusually damp, and this was the first garden party day that was declared perfect. There were, of course, numbers of officers, the military with their wives—such as had wives, and the naval with other people's wives, each branch of the service grumbling at the other's luck in this respect. And then there were sundry civil servants of exalted rank—commissioners of newly founded districts, their wives and daughters, and a brace of good colonial bishops also, with their partners in their mission labours, none of whom objected to Waldteufel or Gung'l.

On the large lawn in front of the balcony at the Residence there was a good deal of tennis being played, and upon the tables laid out on the balcony there were a good many transactions in the way of brandy and soda carried on by special commissioners and field officers, whose prerogative it was to discuss the attitude of the belligerent Kafir chief who, it was supposed, intended to give as much trouble as he could without inconvenience to himself. And then from shady places all around the avenues came the sounds of girlish laughter and the glimmer of muslin. Behind this scene the great flat-faced, flat-roofed mountain stood dark and bold, and through it all the band of the Bayonetteers brayed out that inspiriting valse.

Major Crawford was, in consequence of the importance of his mission to the colony, pointed out to the semi-Dutch legislators, each of whom had much to tell him on the burning boot question; and Mr. Harwood was naturally enough, regarded with interest, for the sounds of the 'Dominant Trumpeter' go forth into all the ends of the earth. Mr. Glaston, too, as son of the Metropolitan of the Salamander Archipelago, was entitled to every token of respectful admiration, even if he had not in the fulness of his heart allowed a few of his pictures to be hung in one of the reception rooms. But perhaps Daireen Gerald had more eyes fixed upon her than anyone in the gardens.

Everyone knew that she was the daughter of Colonel Gerald who had just been gazetted Governor-General of the new colony of the Castaway

Islands, but why she had come out to the Cape no one seemed to know exactly. Many romances were related to account for her appearance, the Cape Town people possessing almost unlimited resources in the way of romance making; but as no pains were taken to bring about a coincidence of stories, it was impossible to say who was in the right.

She was dressed so perfectly according to Mr. Glaston's theories of harmony that he could not refrain from congratulating her—or rather commending her—upon her good taste, though it struck Daireen that there was not much good taste in his commendation. He remained by her side for some time lamenting the degradation of the colony in being shut out from Art—the only world worth living in, as he said; then Daireen found herself with some other people to whom she had been presented, and who were anxious to present her to some relations.

The girl's dress was looked at by most of the colonial young ladies, and her figure was gazed at by all of the men, until it was generally understood that to have made the acquaintance of Miss Gerald was a happiness gained.

'My dear George,' said Mrs. Crawford to Colonel Gerald when she had contrived to draw him to her side at a secluded part of the gardens,—'My dear George, she is far more of a success than even I myself anticipated. Why, the darling child is the centre of all attraction.'

'Poor little Dolly! that is not a very dizzy point to reach at the Cape, is it, Kate?'

'Now don't be provoking, George. We all know well enough, of course, that it is here the same as at any place else: the latest arrival has the charm of novelty. But it is not so in Daireen's case. I can see at once—and I am sure you will give me credit for some power of perception in these things— that she has created a genuine impression. George, you may depend on her receiving particular attention on all sides.' The lady's voice lowered confidentially until her last sentence had in it something of the tone of a revelation.

'That will make the time pass in a rather lively way for Dolly,' said George, pulling his long iron-grey moustache as he smiled thoughtfully, looking into Mrs. Crawford's face.

'Now, George, you must fully recognise the great responsibility resting with you—I certainly feel how much devolves upon myself, being as I am, her father's oldest friend in the colony, and having had the dear child in my care during the voyage.'

'Nothing could be stronger than your claims.'

'Then is it not natural that I should feel anxious about her, George? This is not India, you must remember.'

'No, no,' said the colonel thoughtfully; 'it's not India.' He was trying to grasp the exact thread of reasoning his old friend was using in her argument. He could not at once see why the fact of Cape Town not being situated in the Empire of Hindustan should cause one's responsible duties to increase in severity.

'You know what I mean, George. In India marriage is marriage, and a certain good, no matter who is concerned in it. It is one's duty there to get a girl married, and there is no blame to be attached to one if everything doesn't turn out exactly as one could have wished.'

'Ah, yes, exactly,' said the colonel, beginning to comprehend. 'But I think you have not much to reproach yourself with, Kate; almost every mail brought you out an instalment of the youth and beauty of home, and I don't think that one ever missed fire—failed to go off, you know.'

'Well, yes, I may say I was fortunate, George,' she replied, with a smile of reflective satisfaction. 'But this is not India, George; we must be very careful. I observed Daireen carefully on the voyage, and I can safely say that the dear child has yet formed no attachment.'

'Formed an attachment? You mean—oh Kate, the idea is too absurd,' said Colonel Gerald. 'Why, she is a child—a baby.'

'Of course all fathers think such things about their girls,' said the lady with a pitying smile. 'They understand their boys well enough, and take good care to make them begin to work not a day too late, but their girls are all babies. Why, George, Daireen must be nearly twenty.'

Colonel Gerald was thoughtful for some moments. 'So she is,' he said; 'but she is still quite a baby.'

'Even so,' said the lady, 'a baby's tastes should be turned in the right direction. By the way, I have been asked frequently who is this young Mr. MacDermot who came out to you in such a peculiar fashion. People are beginning to talk curiously about him.'

'As people at the Cape do about everyone,' said the colonel. 'Poor Standish might at least have escaped criticism.'

'I scarcely think so, George, considering how he came out.'

'Well, it was rather what people who do not understand us call an Irish idea. Poor boy!'

'Who is he, George?' 'The son of one of our oldest friends. The friendship has existed between his family and mine for some hundreds of years.'

'Why did he come out to the Cape in that way?'

'My dear Kate, how can I tell you everything?' said the puzzled colonel. 'You would not understand if I were to try and explain to you how this Standish MacDermot's father is a genuine king, whose civil list unfortunately does not provide for the travelling expenses of the members of his family, so that the young man thought it well to set out as he did.' 'I hope you are not imposing on me, George. Well, I must be satisfied, I suppose. By the way, you have not yet been to the room where Mr. Glaston's pictures are hung; we must not neglect to see them. Mr. Glaston told me just now he thought Daireen's taste perfect.'

'That was very kind of Mr. Glaston.'

'If you knew him as I do, George—in fact as he is known in the most exclusive drawing-rooms in London—you would understand how much his commendation is worth,' said Mrs. Crawford.

'I have no doubt of it. He must come out to us some evening to dinner. For his father's sake I owe him some attention, if not for his remark to you just now.'

'I hope you may not forget to ask him,' said Mrs. Crawford. 'He is a most remarkable young man. Of course he is envied by the less accomplished, and you may hear contradictory reports about him. But, believe me, he is looked upon in London as the leader of the most fashionable—that is—the most—not most learned—no, the most artistic set in town. Very exclusive they are, but they have done ever so much good—designing dados, you know, and writing up the new pomegranate cottage wall-paper.'

'I am afraid that Mr. Glaston will find my Hutch cottage deficient in these elements of decoration,' remarked the colonel.

'I wanted to talk to you about him for a long time,' said Mrs. Crawford. 'Not knowing how you might regard the subject, I did not think it well to give him too much encouragement on the voyage, George, so that perhaps he may have thought me inclined to repel him, Daireen being in my care; but I am sure that all may yet be well. Hush! who is it that is laughing so loud? they are coming this way. Ah, Mr. Markham and that little Lottie Vincent. Good gracious, how long that girl is in the field, and how well she wears her age! Doesn't she look quite juvenile?'

Colonel Gerald could not venture an answer before the young lady, who was the eldest daughter of the deputy surgeon-general, tripped up to Mrs. Crawford, and cried, clasping her four-button strawberry-ice-coloured gloves over the elder lady's plump arm, 'Dear good Mrs. Crawford, I have come to you in despair to beg your assistance. Promise me that you will do all you can to help me.' 'If your case is so bad, Lottie, I suppose I must. But what am I to do?'

'You are to make Mr. Markham promise that he will take part in our theatricals next month. He can act—I know he can act like Irving or Salvini or Terry or Mr. Bancroft or some of the others, and yet he will not promise to take any part. Could anything be more cruel?'

'Nothing, unless I were to take some part,' said Mr. Markham, laughing.

'Hush, sir,' cried the young lady, stamping her Pinet shoe upon the ground, and taking care in the action to show what a remarkably well-formed foot she possessed.

'It is cruel of you to refuse a request so offered, Mr. Markham,' said Mrs. Crawford. 'Pray allow yourself to be made amenable to reason, and make Miss Vincent happy for one evening.'

'Since you put it as a matter of reason, Mrs. Crawford, there is, I fear, no escape for me,' said Mr. Markham.

'Didn't I talk to you about reason, sir?' cried the young lady in very pretty mock anger.

'You talked *about* it,' said Markham, 'just as we walked about that centre bed of cactus, we didn't once touch upon it, you know. You talk very well about a subject, Miss Vincent.'

'Was there ever such impertinence? Mrs. Crawford, isn't it dreadful? But we have secured him for our cast, and that is enough. You will take a dozen tickets of course, Colonel Gerald?'

'I can confidently say the object is most worthy,' said Markham.

'And he doesn't know what it is yet,' said Lottie.

'That's why I can confidently recommend it.'

'Now do give me five minutes with Colonel Gerald, like a good dear,' cried the young lady to Mrs. Crawford! 'I must persuade him.'

'We are going to see Mr. Glaston's pictures,' replied Mrs. Crawford.

'How delightful! That is what I have been so anxious to do all the afternoon: one feels so delightfully artistic, you know, talking about pictures; and people think one knows all about them. Do let us go with you, Mrs. Crawford. I can talk to Colonel Gerald while you go on with Mr. Markham.'

'You are a sad little puss,' said Mrs. Crawford, shaking her finger at the artless and ingenuous maiden; and as she walked on with Mr. Markham she could not help remembering how this little puss had caused herself to be pretty hardly spoken about some ten years before at the Arradambad station in the Himalayahs.

How well she was wearing her age to be sure, Mrs. Crawford thought. It is not many young ladies who, after ten years' campaigning, can be called sad little pusses; but Miss Vincent still looked quite juvenile—in fact, *plus Arabe qu'en Arabie*—more juvenile than a juvenile. Everyone knew her and talked of her in various degrees of familiarity; it was generally understood that an acquaintanceship of twenty-four hours' duration was sufficient to entitle any field officer to call her by the abbreviated form of her first name, while a week was the space allowed to subalterns.

CHAPTER XXIII

I have heard of your paintings too.

Hamlet. His form and cause conjoined, preaching to stones,
Would make them capable. Do not look upon me,
Lest... what I have to do
Will want true colour....
Do you see nothing there?

Queen. No, nothing but ourselves.

Hamlet. Why, look you there...
Look, where he goes, even now, out at the portal.
Hamlet.

IAM so glad to be beside some one who can tell me all I want to know' said Lottie, looking up to Colonel Gerald's bronzed face when Mrs. Crawford and Markham had walked on.

'My dear Lottie, you know very well that you know as much as I do,' he answered, smiling down at her.

'Oh, Colonel Gerald, how can you say such a thing?' she cried innocently. 'You know I am always getting into scrapes through my simplicity.'

'You have managed to get out of a good many in your time, my dear. Is it by the same means you got out of them, Lottie-your simplicity?'

'Oh, you are as amusing as ever,' laughed the young thing. 'But you must not be hard upon poor little me, now that I want to ask you so much. Will you tell me, like a dear good colonel—I know you can if you choose—what is the mystery about this Mr. Markham?'

'Mystery? I don't hear of any mystery about him.'

'Why, all your friends came out in the some steamer as he did. They must have told you. Everybody here is talking about him. That's why I want him for our theatricals: everyone will come to see him.'

'Well, if the mystery, whatever it may be, remains unrevealed up to the night of the performance, you will have a house all the more crowded.'

'But I want to know all about it for myself. Is it really true that he had fallen overboard from another ship, and was picked up after being several weeks at sea?'

'You would be justified in calling that a mystery, at any rate,' said Colonel Gerald.

'That is what some people here are saying, I can assure you,' she cried quickly. 'Others say that he was merely taken aboard the steamer at St. Helena, after having been wrecked; but that is far too unromantic.'

'Oh, yes, far too unromantic.'

'Then you do know the truth? Oh, please tell it to me. I have always said I was sure it was true that a girl on the steamer saw him floating on the horizon with an unusually powerful pilot-glass.'

'Rather mysterious for a fellow to be floating about on the horizon with a pilot-glass, Lottie.'

'What a shame to make fun of me, especially as our performance is in the cause of charity, and I want Mr. Markham's name to be the particular attraction! Do tell me if he was picked up at sea.'

'I believe he was.'

'How really lovely! Floating about on a wreck and only restored after great difficulty! Our room should be filled to the doors. But what I can't understand, Colonel Gerald, is where he gets the money he lives on here. He could not have had much with him when he was picked up. But people say he is very rich.'

'Then no doubt people have been well informed, my dear. But all I know is that this Mr. Markham was on his way from New Zealand, or perhaps Australia, and his vessel having foundered, he was picked up by the "Cardwell Castle" and brought to the Cape. He had a note for a few hundred pounds in his pocket which he told me he got cashed here without any difficulty, and he is going to England in a short time. Here we are at the room where these pictures are said to be hanging. Be sure you keep up the mystery, Lottie.'

'Ah, you have had your little chat, I hope,' said Mrs. Crawford, waiting at the door of Government House until Colonel Gerald and Lottie had come up.

'A delightful little chat, as all mine with Colonel Gerald are,' said Lottie, passing over to Mr. Markham. 'Are you going inside to see the pictures, Mrs. Crawford?'

'Not just yet, my dear; we must find Miss Gerald,' said Mrs. Crawford, who had no particular wish to remain in close attachment to Miss Vincent for the rest of the evening.

'Mr. Markham and I are going in,' said Lottie. 'I do so dote upon pictures, and Mr. Markham can explain them I know; so *au revoir*.'

She kissed the dainty tips of her gloves and passed up to the small piazza at the House, near where Major Crawford and some of the old Indians were sitting drinking their brandy and soda and revolving many memories.

'Let us not go in for a while, Mr. Markham,' she said. 'Let us stay here and watch them all. Isn't it delightfully cool here? How tell me all that that dreadful old Mrs. Crawford was saying to you about me.'

'Upon my word,' said Markham smiling, 'it *is* delightfully cool up here.'

'I know she said ever so much; she does so about everyone who has at any time run against her and her designs. She's always designing.'

'And you ran against her, you think?'

'Of course I did,' cried Lottie, turning round and giving an almost indignant look at the man beside her. 'And she has been saying nasty things about me ever since; only of course they have never injured me, as people get to understand her in a very short time. But what did she say just now?'

'Nothing, I can assure you, that was not very much in favour of the theatrical idea I have just promised to work out with you, Miss Vincent: she told me you were a—a capital actress.'

'She said that, did she? Spiteful old creature! Just see how she is all smiles and friendliness to Mr. Harwood because she thinks he will say something about her husband's appointment and the satisfaction it is giving in the colony in his next letter to the "Trumpeter." That is Colonel Gerald's daughter with them now, is it not?'

'Yes, that is Miss Gerald,' answered Markham, looking across the lawn to where Daireen was standing with Mr. Harwood and some of the tennis-players as Mrs. Crawford and her companion came up with Mr. Glaston, whom they had discovered and of whom the lady had taken possession. The girl was standing beneath the broad leaf of a plantain with the red sunlight falling behind her and lighting up the deep ravine of the mountain beyond. Oswin thought he had never before seen her look so girlishly lovely.

'How people here do run after every novelty!' remarked Miss Vincent, who was certainly aware that she herself was by no means a novelty. 'Just because they never happen to have seen that girl before, they mob her to death. Isn't it too bad? What extremes they go to in their delight at having found something new! I actually heard a gentleman say to-day that he thought Miss Geralds face perfect. Could anything be more absurd, when one has only to see her complexion to know that it is extremely defective, while her nose is—are you going in to the pictures so soon?'

'Well, I think so,' said Markham. 'If we don't see them now it will be too dark presently.'

'Why, I had no idea you were such a devotee of Art,' she cried. 'Just let me speak to papa for a moment and I will submit myself to your guidance.' And she tripped away to where the surgeon-general was smoking among the old Indians.

Oswin Markham waited at the side of the balcony, and then Mrs. Crawford with her entire party came up, Mr. Glaston following with Daireen, who said, just as she was beside Mr. Markham, 'We are all going to view the pictures, Mr. Markham; won't you join us?'

'I am only waiting for Miss Vincent,' he answered. Then Daireen and her companion passed into the room containing the four works meant to be illustrative of that perfect conception of a subject, and of the only true method of its treatment, which were the characteristics assigned to themselves by a certain section of painters with whom Mr. Glaston enjoyed communion.

The pictures had, by Mr. Glaston's direction, been hung in what would strike an uncultured mind as being an eccentric fashion. But, of course, there was a method in it. Each painting was placed obliquely at a window; the natural view which was to be obtained at a glance outside being supposed to have a powerful influence upon the mind of a spectator in preparing him to receive the delicate symbolism of each work.

'One of our theories is, that a painting is not merely an imitation of a part of nature, but that it becomes, if perfectly worked out in its symbolism, a pure creation of Nature herself,' said Mr. Glaston airily, as he condescended to explain his method of arrangement to his immediate circle. There were only a few people in the room when Mrs. Crawford's party entered. Mr. Glaston knew, of course, that Harwood was there, but he felt that he could, with these pictures about him, defy all the criticism of the opposing school.

'It is a beautiful idea,' said Mrs. Crawford; 'is it not, Colonel Gerald?'

'Capital idea,' said the colonel.

'Rubbish!' whispered Harwood to Markham, who entered at this moment with Lottie Vincent.

'The absurdity—the wickedness—of hanging pictures in the popular fashion is apparent to every thoughtful mind,' said the prophet of Art.

'Putting pictures of different subjects in a row and asking the public to admire them is something too terrible to think about. It is the act of a nation of barbarians. To hold a concert and perform at the same instant selections from Verdi, Wagner, Liszt, and the Oxford music-hall would be as consistent with the principles of Art as these Gallery exhibitions of pictures.'

'How delightful!' cried Lottie, lifting up her four-buttoned gloves in true enthusiasm. 'I have often thought exactly what he says, only I have never had courage to express myself.'

'It needs a good deal of courage,' remarked Harwood.

'What a pity it is that people will continue to be stupid!' said Mrs. Crawford. 'For my own part, I will never enter an Academy exhibition again. I am ashamed to confess that I have never missed a season when I had the chance, but now I see the folly of it all. What a lovely scene that is in the small black frame! Is it not, Daireen?'

'Ah, you perceive the Idea?' said Mr. Glaston as the girl and Mrs. Crawford stood before a small picture of a man and a woman in a pomegranate grove in a grey light, the man being in the act of plucking the fruit. 'You understand, of course, the symbolism of the pomegranate and the early dawn-light among the boughs?'

'It is a darling picture,' said Lottie effusively.

'I never saw such carelessness in drawing before,' said Harwood so soon as Mr. Glaston and his friends had passed on to another work.

'The colour is pretty fair, but the drawing is ruffianly.'

'Ah, you terrible critic!' cried Lottie.

'You spoil one's enjoyment of the pictures. But I quite agree with you; they are fearful daubs,' she added in a whisper. 'Let us stay here and listen to the gushing of that absurd old woman; we need not be in the back row in looking at that wonderful work they are crowding about.'

'I am not particularly anxious to stand either in the front or the second row,' said Harwood. 'The pavement in the picture is simply an atrocity. I saw the thing before.'

So Harwood, Lottie, and Markham stood together at one of the open windows, through which were borne the brazen strains of the distant band, and the faint sounds of the laughter of the lawn-tennis players, and the growls of the old Indians on the balcony. Daireen and the rest of the party had gone to the furthest window from which at an oblique angle one of the pictures was placed. Miss Vincent and Harwood soon found themselves chatting briskly; but Markham stood leaning against the wall behind them, with his eyes fixed upon Daireen, who was looking in a puzzled way at the picture. Markham wondered what was the element that called for this puzzled—almost troubled expression upon her face, but he could not see anything of the work.

'How very fine, is it not, George?' said Mrs. Crawford to Colonel Gerald as they stood back to gaze upon the painting.

'I think I'll go out and have a smoke,' replied the colonel smiling.

Mrs. Crawford cast a reproachful glance towards him as he turned away, but Mr. Glaston seemed oblivious to every remark.

'Is it not wonderful, Daireen?' whispered Mrs. Crawford to the girl.

'Yes,' said Daireen, 'I think it is—wonderful,' and the expression upon her face became more troubled still.

The picture was composed of a single figure—a half-naked, dark-skinned female with large limbs and wild black hair. She was standing in a high-roofed oriental kiosk upon a faintly coloured pavement, gazing with fierce eyes upon a decoration of the wall, representing a battle in which elephants and dromedaries were taking part. Through one of the arched windows of the building a purple hill with a touch of sunset crimson upon its ridge was seen, while the Evening Star blazed through the dark blue of the higher heaven.

Daireen looked into the picture, and when she saw the wild face of the woman she gave a shudder, though she scarcely knew why.

'All but the face,' she said. 'It is too terrible—there is nothing of a woman about it.'

'My dear child, that is the chief wonder of the picture,' said Mr. Glaston. 'You recognise the subject, of course?'

'It might be Cleopatra,' said Daireen dubiously.

'Oh, hush, hush! never think of such a thing again,' said Mr. Glaston with an expression that would have meant horror if it had not been tempered with pity. 'Cleopatra is vulgar—vulgar—popular. That is Aholibah.'

'You remember, of course, my dear,' said Mrs. Crawford; 'she is a young woman in the Bible—one of the old parts—Daniel or Job or Hezekiah, you know. She was a Jewess or an Egyptian or something of that sort, like Judith, the young person who drove a nail into somebody's brain—they were always doing disagreeable things in those days. I can't recollect exactly what this dreadful creature did, but I think it was somehow connected with the head of John the Baptist.'

'Oh, no, no,' said Daireen, still keeping her eyes fixed upon the face of the figure as though it had fascinated her.

'Aholibah the painter has called it,' said

Mr. Glaston. 'But it is the symbolism of the picture that is most valuable. Wonderful thought that is of the star—Astarte, you know —shedding the light by which the woman views the picture of one of her lovers.'

'Oh!' exclaimed Mrs. Crawford in a shocked way, forgetting for the moment that they were talking on Art. Then she recollected herself and added apologetically, 'They were dreadful young women, you know, dear.'

'Marvellous passion there is in that face,' continued the young man. 'It contains a lifetime of thought—of suffering. It is a poem—it is a precious composition of intricate harmonies.'

'Intricate! I should think it is,' said Harwood to Lottie, in the distant window.

'Hush!' cried the girl, 'the high-priest is beginning to speak.'

'The picture is perhaps the only one in existence that may be said to be the direct result of the three arts as they are termed, though we prefer to think that there is not the least distinction between the methods of painting, poetry, and music,' said Mr. Glaston. 'I chanced to drop in to the studio of my friend who painted this, and I found him in a sad state of despondency. He had nearly all of the details of the picture filled in; the figure was as perfect as it is at present—all except the expression of the face. "I have been thinking about it for days," said the poor fellow, and I could see that his face was haggard with suffering; "but only now and again has the expression I want passed across my mind, and I have been unable to catch it." I looked at the unfinished picture,' continued Mr. Glaston, 'and I saw what he wanted. I stood before the picture in silence for some time, and then I composed and repeated a sonnet which I fancied contained the missing expression of passion. He sprang up and seized my hand, and his face brightened with happiness: I had given him the absent idea, and I left him painting enthusiastically. A few days after, however, I got a line from him entreating me to come to him. I was by his side in an hour, and I found him in his former state of despondency. "It has passed away again," he said, "and I want you to repeat your sonnet." Unfortunately I had forgotten every line of the sonnet, and when I told him so he was in agony. But I begged of him not to despair. I brought the picture and placed it before me on a piano. I looked at it and composed an impromptu that I thought suggested the exact passion he wanted for the face. The painter stood listening with his head bowed down to his hands. When I ended he caught up the picture. "I see it all clearly," he cried; "you have saved me—you have saved the picture." Two days afterwards he sent it to me finished as it is now.'

'Wonderful! is it not, Daireen?' said Mrs. Crawford, as the girl turned away after a little pause.

'The face,' said Daireen gently; 'I don't want ever to see it again. Let us look at something else.'

They turned away to the next picture; but Markham, who had been observing the girl's face, and had noticed that little shudder come over her, felt strangely interested in the painting, whatever it might be, that had produced such an impression upon her. He determined to go unobserved over to the window where the work was hanging so soon as everyone would have left it.

'It requires real cleverness to compose such a story as that of Mr. Glaston's,' said Lottie Vincent to Mr. Harwood.

'It sounded to me all along like a clever bit of satire, and I daresay it was told to him as such,' said Harwood. 'It only needed him to complete the nonsense by introducing another of the fine arts in the working out of that wonderfully volatile expression.'

'Which is that?' said Lottie; 'do tell me, like a good fellow,' and she laid the persuasive finger of a four-buttoned glove upon his arm.

'Certainly. I will finish the story for you,' said Harwood, giving the least little imitation of the lordly manner of Mr. Glaston. 'Yes, my friend the painter sent a telegram to me a few years after I had performed that impromptu, and I was by his side in an hour. I found him at least twenty years older in appearance, and he was searching with a lighted candle in every corner of the studio for that expression of passion which had once more disappeared.

What could I do? I had exhausted the auxiliaries of poetry and music, but fortunately another art remained to me; you have heard of the poetry of motion? In an instant I had mounted the table and had gone through a breakdown of the most æsthetic design, when I saw his face lighten—his grey hairs turned once more to black—long artistic oily black. "I have found it," he cried, seizing the hearthbrush and dipping it into the paint just as I completed the final attitude: it was found—but—what is the matter, Miss Vincent?'

'Look!' she whispered. 'Look at Mr. Markham.'

'Good heavens!' cried Harwood, starting up, 'is he going to fall? No, he has steadied himself by the window. I thought he was beside us.'

'He went over to the picture a second ago, and I saw that pallor come over him,' said Lottie.

Harwood hastened to where Oswin Markham was standing, his white face turned away from the picture, and his hand clutching the rail of a curtain.

'What is the matter, Markham?' said Harwood quietly. 'Are you faint?'

Markham turned his eyes upon him with a startled expression, and a smile that was not a smile came upon his face.

'Faint? yes,' he said. 'This room after the air. I'll be all right. Don't make a scene, for God's sake.'

'There is no need,' said Harwood. 'Sit down here, and I'll get you a glass of brandy.'

'Not here,' said Markham, giving the least little side glance towards the picture. 'Not here, but at the open window.'

Harwood helped him over to the open window, and he fell into a seat beside it and gazed out at the lawn-tennis players, quite regardless of Lottie Vincent standing beside him and enquiring how he felt.

In a few minutes Harwood returned with some brandy in a glass.

'Thanks, my dear fellow,' said the other, drinking it off eagerly. 'I feel better now—all right, in fact.'

'This, of course, you perceive,' came the voice of Mr. Glaston from the group who were engrossed over the wonders of the final picture,—'This is an exquisite example of a powerful mind endeavouring to subdue the agony of memory. Observe the symbolism of the grapes and vine leaves.'

In the warm sunset light outside the band played on, and Miss Vincent flitted from group to group with the news that this Mr. Markham had added to the romance which was already associated with his name, by fainting in the room with the pictures. She was considerably surprised and mortified to see him walking with Miss Gerald to the colonel's carriage in half an hour afterwards.

'I assure you,' she said to some one who was laughing at her,—'I assure you I saw him fall against the window at the side of one of the pictures. If he was not in earnest, he will make our theatricals a great success, for he must be a splendid actor.'

CHAPTER XXIV

Rightly to be great
Is not to stir without great argument.

So much was our love
We would not understand what was most fit.

She is so conjunctive to my life and soul
That, as the star moves not but in his sphere,
I could not but by her.

How should I your true love know
From another one? — *Hamlet.*

ALL was not well with Mr. Standish MacDermot in these days. He was still a guest at that pleasant little Dutch cottage of Colonel Gerald's at Mowbray, and he received invitations daily to wherever Daireen and her father were going. This was certainly all that he could have expected to make him feel at ease in the strange land; but somehow he did not feel at ease. He made himself extremely pleasant everywhere he went, and he was soon a general favourite, though perhaps the few words Mrs. Crawford now and again let fall on the subject of his parentage had as large an influence as his own natural charm of manner in making the young Irishman popular. Ireland was a curious place most of the people at the Cape thought. They had heard of its rebellions and of its secret societies, and they had thus formed an idea that the island was something like a British colony of which the aborigines had hardly been subdued. The impression that Standish was the son of one of the kings of the land, who, like the Indian maharajahs, they believed, were allowed a certain revenue and had their titles acknowledged by the British Government, was very general; and Standish had certainly nothing to complain of as to his treatment. But still all was not well with Standish.

He had received a letter from his father a week after his arrival imploring him to return to the land of his sires, for The MacDermot had learned from the ancient bard O'Brian, in whom the young man had confided, that Standish's destination was the Cape, and so he had been able to write to some address. The MacDermot promised to extend his forgiveness to his son, and to withdraw his threat of disinheritance, if he would return; and he concluded his letter by drawing a picture of the desolation of the neighbourhood owing to the English projectors of a railway and a tourists' hotel having sent a number of surveyors to the very woods of Innishdermot to measure and plan and form all sorts of evil intentions about the region. Under these trying circumstances, The Mac-Dermot implored his son to grant him the consolation of his society once more. What was still more surprising to Standish was the enclosure in the letter of an order for a considerable sum of money, for he fancied that his father had previously exhausted every available system of leverage for the raising of money.

But though it was very sad for Standish to hear of the old man sitting desolate beside the lonely hearth of Innishdermot castle, he made up his mind not to return to his home. He had set out to work in the world, and he would work, he said. He would break loose from this pleasant life he was at present leading, and he would work. Every night he made this resolution, though as yet the concrete form of the thought as to what sort of work he meant to set about had not suggested itself. He would work nobly and manfully for her, he swore, and he would never tell her of his love until he could lay his work at her feet and tell her that it had been done all for her. Meantime he had gone to that garden party at Government House and to several other entertainments, while nearly every day he had been riding by the side of Daireen over The Flats or along the beautiful road to Wynberg.

And all the time that Standish was resolving not to open his lips in an endeavour to express to Daireen all that was in his heart, another man was beginning to feel that it would be necessary to take some step to reveal himself to the girl. Arthur Harwood had been analyzing his own heart every day since he had gazed out to the far still ocean from the mountain above Funchal with Daireen beside him, and now he fancied he knew every thought that was in his heart.

He knew that he had been obliged to deny himself in his youth the luxury of love. He had been working himself up to his present position by his own industry and the use of the brains that he felt must be his capital in life, and he knew he dared not even think of falling in love. But, when he had passed the age of thirty and had made a name and a place for himself in the world, he was aware that he might let his affections go fetterless; but, alas, it seemed that they had been for too long in slavery: they refused to taste the sweets of freedom, and it appeared that his nature had become hard and unsympathetic. But it was neither, he knew in his own soul, only he had been standing out of the world of softness and of sympathy, and had built up for himself unconsciously an ideal whose elements were various and indefinable, his imagination only making it a necessity that not one of these elements of his ideal should be possible to be found in the nature of any of the women with whom he was acquainted and whom he had studied.

When he had come to know Daireen Gerald—and he fancied he had come to know her—he felt that he was no longer shut out from the world of love with his cold ideal. He had thought of her day by day aboard the steamer as he had thought of no girl hitherto in his life, and he had waited for her to think of him and to become conscious that he loved her. Considering that one of the most important elements of his vague ideal was a complete and absolute unconsciousness of any passion, it was scarcely consistent for him now to expect that Daireen should ever perceive the feeling of his secret heart.

He had, however, made up his mind to remain at the Cape instead of going on to the Castaway Islands; and he had written long and interesting letters to the newspaper which he represented, on the subject of the attitude of the Kafir chief who, he heard, had been taking an attitude. Then he had had several opportunities of riding the horse that Colonel Gerald had placed at his disposal; but though he had walked and conversed frequently with the daughter of Colonel Gerald, he felt that it would be necessary for him to speak more directly what he at least fancied was in his heart; so that while poor Standish was swearing every night to keep his secret, Mr. Harwood was thinking by what means he could contrive to reveal himself and find out what were the girl's feelings with regard to himself.

In the firmness of his resolution Standish was one afternoon, a few days after the garden party, by the side of Daireen on the furthest extremity of The Flats, where there was a small wood of pines growing in a sandy soil of a glittering whiteness. They pulled up their horses here amongst the trees, and Daireen looked out at the white plain beyond; but poor Standish could only gaze upon her wistful face.

'I like it,' she said musingly. 'I like that snow. Don't you think it is snow, Standish?'

'It is exactly the same,' he answered. 'I can feel a chill pass over me as I look upon it. I hate it.'

'Oh!' cried the girl, 'don't say that when I have said I like it.'

'Why should that matter?' he said sternly, for he was feeling his resolution very strong within him.

She laughed. 'Why, indeed? Well, hate it as much as you wish, Standish, it won't interfere with my loving it, and thinking of how I used to enjoy the white winters at home. Then, you know, I used to be thinking of places like this—places with plants like those aloes that the sun is glittering over.'

'And why I hate it,' said Standish, 'is because it puts me in mind of the many wretched winters I spent in the miserable idleness of my home. While others were allowed some chance of making their way in the world—making names for themselves—there was I shut up in that gaol. I have lost every chance I might have had—everyone is before me in the race.'

'In what race, Standish? In the race for fame?'

'Yes, for fame,' cried Standish; 'not that I value fame for its own sake,' he added. 'No, I don't covet it, except that—Daireen, I think there is nothing left for me in the world—I am shut out from every chance of reaching anything. I was wretched at home, but I feel even more wretched here.'

'Why should you do that, Standish?' she asked, turning her eyes upon him. 'I am sure everyone here is very kind.'

'I don't want their kindness, Daireen; it is their kindness that makes me feel an impostor. What right have I to receive their kindness? Yes, I had better take my father's advice and return by next mail. I am useless in the world—it doesn't want me.'

'Don't talk so stupidly—so wickedly,' said the girl gravely. 'You are not a coward to set out in the world and turn back discouraged even before you have got anything to discourage you.'

'I am no coward,' he said; 'but everything has been too hard for me. I am a fool—a wretched fool to have set my heart—my soul, upon an object I can never reach.'

'What do you mean, Standish? You haven't set your heart upon anything that you may not gain in time. You will, I know, if you have courage, gain a good and noble name for yourself.'

'Of what use would it be to me, Daireen? It would only be a mockery to me—a bitter mockery unless—Oh, Daireen, it must come, you have forced it from me—I will tell you and then leave you for ever—Daireen, I don't care for anything in the world but to have you love me—a little, Daireen. What would a great name be to me unless——'

'Hush, Standish,' said the girl with her face flushed and almost angry. 'Do not ever speak to me like this again. Why should all our good friendship come to an end?' She had softened towards the close of her sentence, and she was now looking at him in tenderness.

'You have forced me to speak,' he said. 'God knows how I have struggled to hold my secret deep down in my heart—how I have sworn to hold it, but it forced itself out—we are not masters of ourselves, Daireen. Now tell me to leave you—I am prepared for it, for my dream, I knew, was bound to vanish at a touch.'

'Considering that I am four miles from home and in a wood, I cannot tell you to do that,' she said with a laugh, for all her anger had been driven away. 'Besides that, I like you far too well to turn you away; but, Standish, you must never talk so to me again. Now, let us return.'

'I know I must not, because I am a beggar,' he said almost madly. 'You will love some one who has had a chance of making a name for himself in the world. I have had no chance.'

'Standish, I am waiting for you to return.'

'Yes, I have seen them sitting beside you aboard the steamer,' continued Standish bitterly, 'and I knew well how it would be.' He looked at her almost fiercely. 'Yes, I knew it—you have loved one of them.'

Daireen's face flushed fearfully and then became deathly pale as she looked at him. She did not utter a word, but looked into his face steadily with an expression he had never before seen upon hers. He became frightened.

'Daireen—dearest Daireen, forgive me,' he cried. I am a fool—no, worse—I don't know what I say. Daireen, pity me and forgive me. Don't look at me that way, for God's sake. Speak to me.'

'Come away,' she said gently. 'Come away, Standish.'

'But tell me you forgive me, Daireen,' he pleaded.

'Come away,' she said.

She turned her horse's head towards the track which was made through that fine white sand and went on from amongst the pines. He followed her with a troubled mind, and they rode side by side over the long flats of heath until they had almost reached the lane of cactus leading to Mowbray. In a few minutes they would be at the Dutch cottage, and yet they had not interchanged a word. Standish could not endure the silence any longer. He pulled up his horse suddenly.

'Daireen,' he said. 'I have been a fool—a wicked fool, to talk to you as I did. I cannot go on until you say you forgive me.'

Then she turned round and smiled on him, holding out her hand.

'We are very foolish, Standish,' she said. 'We are both very foolish. Why should I think anything of what you said? We are still good friends, Standish.'

'God bless you!' he cried, seizing her hand fervently. 'I will not make myself a fool again.' 'And I,' said the girl, 'I will not be a fool again.'

So they rode back together. But though Standish had received forgiveness he was by no means satisfied with the girl's manner. There was an expression that he could not easily read in that smile she had given him. He had meant to be very bitter towards her, but had not expected her to place him in a position requiring forgiveness. She had forgiven him, it was true, but then that smile of hers—what was that sad wistful expression upon her face? He could not tell, but he felt that on the whole he had not gained much by the resolutions he had made night after night. He was inclined to be dissatisfied with the result of his morning's ride, nor was this feeling perceptibly decreased by seeing beneath one of the broad-leaved trees that surrounded the cottage the figure of Mr. Arthur Harwood by the side of Colonel Gerald.

Harwood came forward as Daireen reined up on the avenue.

'I have come to say good-bye to you,' he said, looking up to her face.

'Good-bye?' she answered. 'Why, you haven't said good-morning yet.'

Mr. Harwood was a clever man and he knew it; but his faculty for reading what was passing in another person's mind did not bring him happiness always. He had made use of what he meant to be a test sentence to Daireen, and the result of his observation of its effect was not wholly pleasant to him. He had hoped for a little flush—a little trembling of the hand, but neither had come; a smile was on her face, and the pulses of the hand she held out to him were unruffled. He knew then that the time had not yet come for him to reveal himself.

But why should you say good-bye?' she asked after she had greeted him.

'Well, perhaps I should only say *au revoir*, though, upon my word, the state of the colony is becoming so critical that one going up country should always say good-bye. Yes, my duties call me to leave all this pleasant society, Miss Gerald. I am going among the Zulus for a while.'

'I have every confidence in you, Mr. Harwood,' she said. 'You will return in safety. We will miss you greatly, but I know how much the people at home will be benefited by hearing the result of your visit; so we resign ourselves to your absence. But indeed we shall miss you.'

'And if a treacherous assegai should transfix me, I trust my fate will draw a single tear,' he said.

There was a laugh as Daireen rode round to dismount and Harwood went in to lunch. It was very pleasant chat he felt, but he was as much dissatisfied with her laugh as Standish had been with her smile.

CHAPTER XXV

Sure, He that made us with such large discourse,
Looking before and after, gave us not
That capability and godlike reason
To fust in us unused.

Yet do I believe
The origin and commencement of his grief
Sprung from neglected love.

... he repulsed—a short tale to make—
Fell into a sadness, then into a fast,
Thence to a watch, thence into a weakness,
Thence to a lightness; and by this declension
Into the madness.—*Hamlet.*

THE very pleasantness of the lunch Harwood had at the Dutch cottage
made his visit seem more unsatisfactory to him. He had come up to the girl
with that sentence which should surely have sounded pathetic even though
spoken with indifference. He was beside her to say good-bye. He had given
her to understand that he was going amongst the dangers of a disturbed
part of the country, but the name of the barbarous nation had not made her
cheek pale. It was well enough for himself to make light of his adventurous
undertaking, but he did not think that her smiles in telling him that she
would miss him were altogether becoming.

Yes, as he rode towards Cape Town he felt that the time had not yet
come for him to reveal himself to Daireen Gerald. He would have to be
patient, as he had been for years.

Thus far he had found out negatively how Daireen felt towards himself:
she liked him, he knew, but only as most women liked him, because he could
tell them in an agreeable way things that they wanted to know—because
he had travelled everywhere and had become distinguished. He was not
a conceited man, but he knew exactly how he stood in the estimation of
people, and it was bitter for him to reflect that he did not stand differently
with regard to Miss Gerald. But he had not attempted to discover what were

Daireen's feelings respecting any one else. He was well aware that Mrs. Crawford was anxious to throw Mr. Glaston in the way of the girl as much as possible; but he felt that it would take a long time for Mr. Glaston to make up his mind to sacrifice himself at Daireen's feet, and Daireen was far too sensible to be imposed upon by his artistic flourishes. As for this young Mr. Standish Macnamara, Harwood saw at once that Daireen regarded him with a friendliness that precluded the possibility of love, so he did not fear the occupation of the girl's heart by Standish. But when Harwood began to think of Oswin Markham—he heard the sound of a horse's hoofs behind him, and Oswin Markham himself trotted up, looking dusty and fatigued.

"I thought I should know your animal," said Markham, "and I made an effort to overtake you, though I meant to go easily into the town."

Harwood looked at him and then at his horse.

"You seem as if you owed yourself a little ease," he said. "You must have done a good deal in the way of riding, judging from your appearance."

"A great deal too much," replied Markham. "I have been on the saddle since breakfast."

"You have been out every morning for the past three days before I have left my room. I was quite surprised when I heard it, after the evidence you gave at the garden party of your weakness."

"Of my weakness, yes," said Markham, with a little laugh. "It was wretchedly weak to allow myself to be affected by the change from the open air to that room, but it felt stifling to me."

"I didn't feel the difference to be anything considerable," said Harwood; "so the fact of your being overcome by it proves that you are not in a fit state to be playing with your constitution. Where did you ride to-day?"

"Where? Upon my word I have not the remotest idea," said Markham. "I took the road out to Simon's Bay, but I pulled up at a beach on the nearer side of it, and remained there for a good while."

"Nothing could be worse than riding about in this aimless sort of way. Here you are completely knocked up now, as you have been for the past three evenings. Upon my word, you seem indifferent as to whether or not you ever leave the colony alive. You are simply trifling with yourself."

"You are right, I suppose," said Markham wearily. "But what is a fellow to do in Cape Town? One can't remain inactive beyond a certain time."

"It is only within the past three days you have taken up this roving notion," said Harwood. "It is in fact only since that Government House affair." Markham turned and looked at him eagerly for a moment. "Yes, since your weakness became apparent to yourself, you have seemed bound to prove your strength to the furthest. But you are pushing it too far, my boy. You'll find out your mistake."

"Perhaps so," laughed the other. "Perhaps so. By the way, is it true that you are going up country, Harwood?"

"Quite true. The fact is that affairs are becoming critical with regard to our relations with the Zulus, and unless I am greatly mistaken, this colony will be the centre of interest before many months have passed."

"There is nothing I should like better than to go up with you, Harwood."

Harwood shook his head. "You are not strong enough, my boy," he said.

There was a pause before Markham said slowly:

"No, I am not strong enough."

Then they rode into Cape Town together, and dismounted at their hotel; and, certainly, as he walked up the stairs to his room, Oswin Markham looked anything but strong enough to undertake a journey into the Veldt. Doctor Campion would probably have spoken unkindly to him had he seen him now, haggard and weary, with his day spent on an exposed road beneath a hot sun.

"He is anything but strong enough," said Harwood to himself as he watched the other man; and then he recollected the tone in which Markham had repeated those words, "I am not strong enough." Was it possible, he asked himself, that Markham meant that his strength of purpose was not sufficiently great? He thought over this question for some time, and the result of his reflection was to make him wish that he had not thought the conduct of that defiant chief of such importance as demanded the personal observation of the representative of the *Dominant Trumpeter*. He felt that he would like to search out the origin of the weakness of Mr. Oswin Markham.

But all the time these people were thinking their thoughts and making their resolutions upon various subjects, Mr. Algernon Glaston was remaining in the settled calm of artistic rectitude. He was awaiting with patience the arrival of his father from the Salamander Archipelago, though he had given the prelate of that interesting group to understand that circumstances would render it impossible for his son to remain longer than a certain period at the Cape, so that if he desired the communion of his society it would be necessary to allow the mission work among the Salamanders to take care of itself. For Mr. Glaston was by no means unaware of the sacrifice he was in the habit of making annually for the sake of passing a few weeks with his father in a country far removed from all artistic centres. The Bishop of the Calapash Islands and Metropolitan of the Salamander Archipelago had it several times urged upon him that his son was a marvel of filial duty for undertaking this annual journey, so that he, no doubt, felt convinced of the fact; and though this visit added materially to the expenses of his son's mode of life, which, of course, were defrayed by the bishop, yet the bishop felt that this addition was, after all, trifling compared with the value of the sentiment of filial affection embodied in the annual visit to the Cape.

Mr. Glaston had allowed his father a margin of three weeks for any impediments that might arise to prevent his leaving the Salamanders, but a longer space he could not, he assured his father, remain awaiting his arrival from the sunny islands of his see. Meantime he was dining out night after night with his friends at the Cape, and taking daily drives and horse-exercise for the benefit of his health. Upon the evening when Harwood and Markham entered the hotel together, Mr. Glaston was just departing to join a dinner-party which was to assemble at the house of a certain judge, and as Harwood was also to be a guest, he was compelled to dress hastily.

Oswin Markham was not, however, aware of the existence of the hospitable judge, so he remained in the hotel. He was tired almost to a point of prostration after his long aimless ride, but a bath and a dinner revived him, and after drinking his coffee he threw himself upon a sofa and slept for some hours. When he awoke it was dark, and then lighting a cigar he went out to the balcony that ran along the upper windows, and seated himself in the cool air that came landwards from the sea.

He watched the soldiers in white uniform crossing the square; he saw the Malay population who had been making a holiday, returning to their quarter of the town, the men with their broad conical straw hats, the women with marvellously coloured shawls; he saw the coolies carrying their burdens, and the Hottentots and the Kafirs and all the races blended in the motley population of Cape Town. He glanced listlessly at all, thinking his own thoughts undisturbed by any incongruity of tongues or of races beneath him, and he was only awakened from the reverie into which he had fallen by the opening of one of the windows near him and the appearance on the balcony of Algernon Glaston in his dinner dress and smoking a choice cigar.

The generous wine of the generous judge had made Mr. Glaston particularly courteous, for he drew his chair almost by the side of Markham's and inquired after his health.

"Harwood was at that place to-night," he said, "and he mentioned that you were killing yourself. Just like these newspaper fellows to exaggerate fearfully for the sake of making a sensation. You are all right now, I think."

"Quite right," said Markham. "I don't feel exactly like an elephant for vigour, but you know what it is to feel strong without having any particular strength. I am that way."

"Dreadfully brutal people I met to-night," continued Mr. Glaston reflectively. "Sort of people Harwood could get on with. Talking actually about some wretched savage—some Zulu chief or other from whom they expect great things; as if the action of a ruffianly barbarian could affect any one. It was quite disgusting talk. I certainly would have come away at once only I was lucky enough to get by the side of a girl who seems to know something of Art—a Miss Vincent—she is quite fresh and enthusiastic on the subject—quite a child indeed."

Markham thought it prudent to light a fresh cigar from the end of the one he had smoked, at the interval left by Mr. Glaston for his comment, so that a vague "indeed" was all that came through his closed lips.

"Yes, she seems rather a tractable sort of little thing. By the way, she mentioned something about your having become faint at Government House the other day, before you had seen all my pictures."

"Ah, yes," said Markham. "The change from the open air to that room."

"Ah, of course. Miss Vincent seems to understand something of the meaning of the pictures. She was particularly interested in one of them, which, curiously enough, is the most wonderful of the collection. Did you study them all?"

"No, not all; the fact was, that unfortunate weakness of mine interfered with my scrutiny," said Markham. "But the single glance I had at one of the pictures convinced me that it was a most unusual work. I felt greatly interested in it."

"That was the Aholibah, no doubt."

"Yes, I heard your description of how if came to be painted."

"Ah, but that referred only to the marvellous expression of the face—so saturate—so devoured—with passion. You saw how Miss Gerald turned away from it with a shudder?"

"Why did she do that?" said Markham.

"Heaven knows," said Glaston, with a little sneer.

"Heaven knows," said Markham, after a pause and without any sneer.

"She could not understand it," continued Glaston. "All that that face means cannot be apprehended in a glance. It has a significance of its own—it is a symbol of a passion that withers like a fire—a passion that can destroy utterly all the beauty of a life that might have been intense with beauty. You are not going away, are you?"

Markham had risen from his seat and turned away his head, grasping the rail of the balcony. It was some moments before he started and looked round at the other man. "I beg your pardon," he said; "I'm not going away, I am greatly interested. Yes, I caught a glimpse of the expression of the face."

"It is a miracle of power," continued Glaston. "Miss Gerald felt, but she could not understand why she should feel, its power."

There was a long pause, during which Markham stared blankly across the square, and the other leant back in his chair and watched the curling of his cigar clouds through the still air. From the garrison at the castle there came to them the sound of a bugle-call.

"I am greatly interested in that picture," said Markham at length. "I should like to know all the details of its working out."

"The expression of the face——"

"Ah, I know all of that. I mean the scene—that hill seen through the arch—the pavement of the oriental apartment—the—the figure—how did the painter bring them together?"

"That is of little consequence in the study of the elements of the symbolism," said Mr. Glaston.

"Yes, of course it is; but still I should like to know."

"I really never thought of putting any question to the painter about these matters," replied Glaston. "He had travelled in the East, and the kiosk was amongst his sketches; as for the model of the figure, if I do not mistake, I saw the study for the face in an old portfolio of his he brought from Sicily."

"Ah, indeed."

"But these are mere accidents in the production of the picture. The symbolism is the picture."

Again there was a pause, and the chatter of a couple of Malays in the street became louder, and then fainter, as the speakers drew near and passed away.

"Glaston," said Markham at length, "did you remove the pictures from Government House?"

"They are in one of my rooms," said Glaston. "Would you think it a piece of idle curiosity if I were to step upstairs and take a look at that particular work?"

"You could not see it by lamplight. You can study them all in the morning."

"But I feel in the mood just now, and you know how much depends upon the mood."

"My room is open," said Glaston. "But the idea that has possessed you is absurd."

"I dare say, I dare say, but I have become interested in all that you have told me; I must try and—and understand the symbolism."

He left the balcony before Mr. Glaston had made up his mind as to whether there was a touch of sarcasm in his voice uttering the final sentence.

"Not worse than the rest of the uneducated world," murmured the Art prophet condescendingly.

But in Mr. Glaston's private room upstairs Oswin Markham was standing holding a lighted lamp up to that interesting picture and before that wonderful symbolic expression upon the face of the figure; the rest of the room was in darkness. He looked up to the face that the lamplight gloated over. The remainder of the picture was full of reflections of the light.

"A power that can destroy utterly all the beauty of a life," he said, repeating the analysis of Mr. Glaston. He continued looking at it before he repeated another of that gentleman's sentences—"She felt, but could not understand, its power." He laid the lamp on the table and walked over to the darkened window and gazed out. But once more he returned to the picture. "A passion that can destroy utterly all the beauty of life," he said again. "Utterly! that is a lie!" He remained with his eyes upon the picture for some moments, then he lifted the lamp and went to the door. At the door he stopped, glanced at the picture and laughed.

In the Volsunga Saga there is an account of how a jealous woman listens outside the chamber where a man whom she once loved is being murdered in his wife's arms; hearing the cry of the wife in the chamber the woman at the door laughs. A man beside her says, "Thou dost not laugh because thy heart is made glad, or why moves that pallor upon thy face?"

Oswin Markham left the room and thanked Mr. Glaston for having gratified his whim.

CHAPTER XXVI

... What he spake, though it lacked form a little,
Was not like madness. There's something in his soul
O'er which his melancholy sits on brood.

Purpose is but the slave to memory.
Most necessary 'tis that we forget.—*Hamlet.*

THE long level rays of the sun that was setting in crimson splendour were touching the bright leaves of the silver-fir grove on one side of the ravine traversing the slope of the great peaked hill which makes the highest point of Table Mountain, but the other side was shadowy. The flat face of the precipice beneath the long ridge of the mountain was full of fantastic gleams of red in its many crevices, and far away a thin waterfall seemed a shimmering band of satin floating downwards through a dark bed of rocks. Table Bay was lying silent and with hardly' a sparkle upon its ripples from where the outline of Robbin Island was seen at one arm of its crescent to the white sand of the opposite shore. The vineyards of the lower slope, beneath which the red road crawled, were dim and colourless, for the sunset bands had passed away from them and flared only upon the higher slopes.

Upon the summit of the ridge of the silver-fir ravine Daireen Gerald sat looking out to where the sun was losing itself among the ridges of the distant kloof, and at her feet was Oswin Markham. Behind them rose the rocks of the Peak with their dark green herbage. Beneath them the soft rustle of a songless bird was heard through the foliage.

But it remains to be told how those two persons came to be watching together the phenomenon of sunset from the slope.

It was Mrs. Crawford who had upon the very day after the departure of Arthur Harwood organised one of those little luncheon parties which are so easily organised and give promise of pleasures so abundant. She had expressed to Mr. Harwood the grief she felt at his being compelled by duty to depart from the midst of their circle, just as she had said to Mr. Markham how bowed down she had been at the reflection of his leaving the steamer at St. Helena; and Harwood had thanked her for her kind expressions, and made a mental resolve that he would say something sarcastic regarding the Army Boot Commission in his next communication to the *Dominant Trumpeter*. But the hearing of the gun of the mail steamer that was to convey the special correspondent to Natal was the pleasantest sensation Mrs. Crawford had experienced for long. She had been very anxious on Harwood's account for some time. She did not by any means think highly of the arrangement which had been made by Colonel Gerald to secure for one of his horses an amount of exercise by allowing Mr. Harwood to ride it; for she was well aware that Mr. Harwood would think it quite within the line of his duty to exercise the animal at times when Miss Gerald would be riding out. She knew that most girls liked Mr. Harwood, and whatever might be Mr. Harwood's feelings towards the race that so complimented him, she could not doubt that he admired to a perilous point the daughter of Colonel Gerald. If, then, the girl would return his feeling, what would become of Mrs. Crawford's hopes for Mr. Glaston?

It was the constant reflection upon this question that caused the sound of the mail gun to fall gratefully upon the ears of the major's wife. Harwood was to be away for more than a month at any rate, and in a month much might be accomplished, not merely by a special correspondent, but by a lady with a resolute mind and a strategical training. So she had set her mind to work, and without delay had organised what gave promise of being a delightful little lunch, issuing half a dozen invitations only three days in advance.

Mr. Algernon Glaston had, after some persuasion, promised to join the party. Colonel Gerald and his daughter expressed the happiness they would have at being present, and Mr. Standish Macnamara felt certain that nothing could interfere with his delight. Then there were the two daughters of a member of the Legislative Council who were reported to look with fond eyes upon the son of one of the justices of the Supreme Court, a young gentleman who was also invited. Lastly, by what Mrs. Crawford considered a stroke of real constructive ability, Mr. Oswin Markham and Miss Lottie Vincent were also begged to allow themselves to be added to the number of the party. Mrs. Crawford disliked Lottie, but that was no reason why Lottie should not exercise the tactics Mrs. Crawford knew she possessed, to take care of Mr. Oswin Markham for the day.

They would have much to talk about regarding the projected dramatic entertainment of the young lady, so that Mr. Glaston should be left solitary in that delightful listless after-space of lunch, unless indeed—and the contingency was, it must be confessed, suggested to the lady—Miss Gerald might chance to remain behind the rest of the party; in that case it would not seem beyond the bounds of possibility that the weight of Mr. Glaston's loneliness would be endurable.

Everything had been carried out with that perfect skill which can be gained only by experience. The party had driven from Mowbray for a considerable way up the hill. The hampers had been unpacked and the lunch partaken of in a shady nook which was supposed to be free from the venomous reptiles that make picnics somewhat risky enjoyments in sunny lands; and then the young people had trooped away to gather Venus-hair ferns at the waterfall, or silver leaves from the grove, or bronze-green lizards, or some others of the offspring of nature which have come into existence solely to meet the requirements of collectors. Mr. Glaston and Daireen followed more leisurely, and Mrs. Crawford's heart was happy. The sun would be setting in an hour, she reflected, and she had great confidence in the effect of fine sunsets upon the hearts of lovers—. nay, upon the raw material that might after a time develop into the hearts of lovers. She was quite satisfied seeing the young people depart, for she was not aware how much more pleasant than Oswin Markham Lottie Vincent had found Mr. Glaston at that judge's dinner-party a few evenings previous, nor how much more plastic than Miss Gerald Mr. Glaston had found Lottie Vincent upon the same occasion.

Mrs. Crawford did not think it possible that Lottie could be so clever, even if she had had the inclination, as to effect the separation of the party as it had been arranged. But Lottie had by a little manouvre waited at the head of the ravine until Mr. Glaston and Daireen had come up, and then she had got into conversation with Mr. Glaston upon a subject that was a blank to the others, so that they had walked quietly on together until that pleasant space at the head of the ravine was reached. There Daireen had seated herself to watch the west become crimson with sunset, and at her feet Oswin had cast himself to watch her face.

Had Mrs. Crawford been aware of this, she would scarcely perhaps have been so pleasant to her friend Colonel Gerald, or to her husband far down on the slope.

It was very silent at the head of that ravine. The delicate splash of the water that trickled through the rocks far away was distinctly heard. The rosy bands that had been about the edges of the silver leaves had passed off. Daireen's face was at last left in shadow, and she turned to watch the rays move upwards, until soon only the dark Peak was enwound in the red light that made its forehead like the brows of an ancient Bacchanal encircled with a rose-wreath. Then quickly the red dwindled away, until only a single rose-leaf was upon the highest point; an instant more and it had passed, leaving the hill dark and grim in outline against the pale blue.

Then succeeded that time of silent conflict between light and darkness—a time of silence and of wonder.

Upon the slope of the Peak it was silent enough. The girl's eyes went out across the shadowy plain below to where the water was shining in its own gray light, but she uttered not a word. The man leant his head upon his hand as he looked up to her face.

"What is the 'Ave' you are breathing to the sunset, Miss Gerald?" he said at length, and she gave a little start and looked at him. "What is the vesper hymn your heart has been singing all this time?"

She laughed. "No hymn, no song."

"I saw it upon your face," he said. "I saw its melody in your eyes; and yet—yet I cannot understand it—I am too gross to be able to translate it. I suppose if a man had sensitive hearing the wind upon the blades of grass would make good music to him, but most people are dull to everything but the rolling of barrels and such-like music."

"I had not even a musical thought," said the girl. "I am afraid that if all I thought were translated into words, the result would be a jumble: you know what that means."

"Yes. Heaven is a jumble, isn't it? A bit of wonderful blue here, and a shapeless cloud there—a few faint breaths of music floating about a place of green, and an odour of a field of flowers. Yes, all dreams are jumbles."

"And I was dreaming?" she said. "Yes, I dare say my confusion of thought without a single idea may be called by courtesy a dream."

"And now have you awakened?"

"Dreams must break and dissolve some time, I suppose, Mr. Markham."

"They must, they must," he said. "I wonder when will my awaking come."

"Have you a dream?" she asked, with a laugh.

"I am living one," he answered.

"Living one?"

"Living one. My life has become a dream to me. How am I beside you? How is it possible that I could be beside you? Either of two things must be a dream—either my past life is a dream, or I am living one in this life."

"Is there so vast a difference between them?" she asked, looking at him. His eyes were turned away from her.

"Vast? Vast?" he repeated musingly. Then he rose to his feet and looked out oceanwards. "I don't know what is vast," he said. Then he looked down to her. "Miss Gerald, I don't believe that my recollection of my past is in the least correct. My memory is a falsehood utterly. For it is quite impossible that this body of mine—this soul of mine—could have passed through such a change as I must have passed through if my memory has got anything of truth in it. My God! my God! The recollections that come to me are, I know, impossible."

"I don't understand you, Mr. Markham," said Daireen.

Once more he threw himself on the short tawny herbage beside her.

"Have you not heard of men being dragged back when they have taken a step beyond the barrier that hangs between life and death—men who have had one foot within the territory of death?"

"I have heard of that."

"And you know it is not the same old life that a man leads when he is brought from that dominion of death. He begins life anew. He knows nothing of the past. He laughs at the faces that were once familiar to him; they mean nothing to him. His past is dead. Think of me, child. Day by day I suffered all the agonies of death and hell, and shall I not have granted to me that most righteous gift of God? Shall not my past be utterly blotted out? Yes, these vague memories that I have are the memories of a dream. God has not been so just to me as to others, for there are some realities of the past still with me I know, and thus I am at times led to think it might be possible that all my recollections are true—but no, it is impossible—utterly impossible." Again he leapt to his feet and clasped his hands over his head. "Child—child, if you knew all, you would pity me," he said, in a tone no louder than a whisper.

She had never heard anything so pitiful before. Seeing the agony of the man, and hearing him trying to convince himself of that at which his reason rebelled, was terribly pitiful to her. She never before that moment knew how she felt towards this man to whom she had given life.

"What can I say of comfort to you?" she said. "You have all the sympathy of my heart. Why will you not ask me to help you? What is my pity?"

He knelt beside her. "Be near me," he said. "Let me look at you now. Is there not a bond between us?—such a bond as binds man to his God? You gave me my life as a gift, and it will be a true life now. God had no pity for me, but you have more than given me your pity. The life you have given me is better than the life given me by God."

"Do not say that," she said. "Do not think that I have given you anything. It is your God who has changed you through those days of terrible suffering."

"Yes, the suffering is God's gift," he cried bitterly. "Torture of days and nights, and then not utter forgetfulness. After passing through the barrier of death, I am denied the blessings that should come with death."

"Why should you wish to forget anything of the past?" she asked. "Has everything been so very terrible to you?"

"Terrible?" he said, clasping his hands over one of his knees and gazing out to the conflict of purple and shell-pink in the west. "No, nothing was terrible. I am no Corsair with a hundred romantic crimes to give me so much remorseful agony as would enable me to act the part of Count Lara with consistency. I am no Lucifer encircled with a halo of splendid wickedness. It is only the change that has passed over me since I felt myself looking at you that gives me this agony of thought. Wasted time is my only sin—hours cast aside—years trampled upon. I lived for myself as I had a chance—as thousands of others do, and it did not seem to me anything terrible that I should make my father's days miserable to him. I did not feel myself to be the curse to him that I now know myself to have been. I was a curse to him. He had only myself in the world—no other son, and yet I could leave him to die alone—yes, and to die offering me his forgiveness—offering it when it was not in my power to refuse to accept it. This is the memory that God will not take away. Nay, I tell you it seems that instead of being blotted out by my days of suffering it is but intensified."

He had bowed down his face upon his hands as he sat there. Her eyes were full of tears of sympathy and compassion—she felt with him, and his sufferings were hers.

"I pity you—with all my soul I pity you," she said, laying her hand upon his shoulder.

He turned and took her hand, holding it not with a fervent grasp; but in his face that looked up to her tearful eyes there was a passion of love and adoration.

"As a man looks to his God I look to you," he said. "Be near me that the life you have given me may be good. Let me think of you, and the dead Past shall bury its dead."

What answer could she make to him? The tears continued to come to her eyes as she sat while he looked into her face.

"You know," she said—"you know I feel for you. You know that I understand you."

"Not all," he said slowly. "I am only beginning to understand myself; I have never done so in all my life hitherto."

Then they watched the delicate shadowy dimness—not gray, but full of the softest azure—begin to swathe the world beneath them. The waters of the bay were reflecting the darkening sky, and out over the ocean horizon a single star was beginning to breathe through the blue.

"Daireen," he said at length, "is the bond between us one of love?"

There was no passion in his voice, nor was his hand that held hers trembling as he spoke. She gave no start at his words, nor did she withdraw her hand. Through the silence the splash of the waterfall above them was heard clearly. She looked at him through the long pause.

"I do not know," she said. "I cannot answer you yet——No, not yet—not yet."

"I will not ask," he said quietly. "Not yet—not yet." And he dropped her hand.

Then he rose and looked out to that star, which was no longer smothered in the splendid blue of the heavens, but was glowing in passion until the waters beneath caught some of its rays.

There was a long pause before a voice sounded behind them on the slope—the musical voice of Miss Lottie Vincent.

"Did you ever see such a sentimental couple?" she cried, raising her hands with a very pretty expression of mock astonishment. "Watching the twilight as if you were sitting for your portraits, while here we have been searching for you over hill and dale. Have we not, Mr. Glaston?"

Mr. Glaston thought it unnecessary to corroborate a statement made with such evident ingenuousness.

"Well, your search met with its reward, I hope, Miss Vincent," said Oswin.

"What, in finding you?"

"I am not so vain as to fancy it possible that you should accept that as a reward, Miss Vincent," he replied.

The young lady gave him a glance that was meant to read his inmost soul. Then she laughed.

"We must really hasten back to good Mamma Crawford," she said, with a seriousness that seemed more frivolous than her frivolity. "Every one will be wondering where we have been."

"Lucky that you will be able to tell them," remarked Oswin.

"How?" she said quickly, almost apprehensively.

"Why, you know you can say 'Over hill, over dale,' and so satisfy even the most sceptical in a moment."

Miss Lottie made a little pause, then laughed again; she did not think it necessary to make any reply.

And so they all went down by the little track along the edge of the ravine, and the great Peak became darker above them as the twilight dwindled into evening.

CHAPTER XXVII

I have remembrances of yours—
... words of so sweet breath composed
As made the things more rich.

Hamlet.... You do remember all the circumstance?
Horatio. Remember it, my lord?
Hamlet. Sir, in my heart there was a kind of fighting
That would not let me sleep.

... poor Ophelia,
Divided from herself and her fair judgment.

Sleep rock thy brain,
And never come mischance.—*Hamlet.*

MRS. Crawford was not in the least apprehensive of the safety of the young people who had been placed under her care upon this day. She had been accustomed in the good old days at Arradambad, when the scorching inhabitants had lifted their eyes unto the hills, and had fled to their cooling slopes, to organise little open-air tiffins for the benefit of such young persons as had come out to visit the British Empire in the East under the guidance of the major's wife, and the result of her experience went to prove that it was quite unnecessary to be in the least degree nervous regarding the ultimate welfare of the young persons who were making collections of the various products of Nature. It was much better for the young persons to learn self-dependence, she thought, and though many of the maidens under her care had previously, through long seasons at Continental watering-places, become acquainted with a few of the general points to be observed in maintaining a course of self-dependence, yet the additional help that came to them from the hills was invaluable.

As Mrs. Crawford now gave a casual glance round the descending party, she felt that her skill as a tactician was not on the wane. They were walking together, and though Lottie was of course chatting away as flippantly as ever, yet both Markham and Mr. Glaston was very silent, she saw, and her conclusions were as rapid as those of an accustomed campaigner should be. Mr. Glaston had been talking to Daireen in the twilight, so that Lottie's floss-chat was a trouble to him; while Oswin Markham was wearied with having listened for nearly an hour to her inanities, and was seeking for the respite of silence.

"You naughty children, to stray away in that fashion!" she cried. "Do you fancy you had permission to lose yourselves like that?"

"Did we lose ourselves, Miss Vincent?" said Markham.

"We certainly did not," said Lottie, and then Mrs. Crawford's first suggestions were confirmed: Lottie and Markham spoke of themselves, while Daireen and Mr. Glaston were mute.

"It was very naughty of you," continued the matron. "Why, in India, if you once dared do such a thing— —"

"We should do it for ever," cried Lottie. "Now, you know, my dear good Mrs. Crawford, I have been in India, and I have had experience of your picnics when we were at the hills—oh, the most delightful little affairs— every one used to look forward to them."

Mrs. Crawford laughed gently as she patted Lottie on the cheek. "Ah, they were now and again successes, were they not? How I wish Daireen had been with us."

"Egad, she would not be with us now, my dear," said the major. "Eh, George, what do you say, my boy?"

"For shame, major," cried Mrs. Crawford, glancing towards Lottie.

"Eh, what?" said the bewildered Boot Commissioner, who meant to be very gallant indeed. It was some moments before he perceived how Miss Vincent could construe his words, and then he attempted an explanation, which made matters worse. "My dear, I assure you I never meant that your attractions were not—not—ah—most attractive, they were, I assure you— you were then most attractive."

"And so far from having waned," said Colonel Gerald, "it would seem that every year has but— —"

"Why, what on earth is the meaning of this raid of compliments on poor little me?" cried the young lady in the most artless manner, glancing from the major to the colonel with uplifted hands.

"Let us hasten to the carriages, and leave these old men to talk their nonsense to each other," said Mrs. Crawford, putting her arm about one of the daughters of the member of the Legislative Council—a young lady who had found the companionship of Standish Macnamara quite as pleasant as her sister had the guidance of the judge's son up the ravine—and so they descended to where the carriages were waiting to take them towards Cape Town. Daireen and her father were to walk to the Dutch cottage, which was but a short distance away, and with them, of course, Standish.

"Good-bye, my dear child," said Mrs. Crawford, embracing Daireen, while the others talked in a group. "You are looking pale, dear, but never mind; I will drive out and have a long chat with you in a couple of days," she whispered, in a way she meant to be particularly impressive.

Then the carriage went off, and Daireen put her hand through her father's arm, and walked silently in the silent evening to the house among the aloes and Australian oaks, through whose leaves the fireflies were flitting in myriads.

"She is a good woman," said Colonel Gerald. "An exceedingly good woman, only her long experience of the sort of girls who used to be sent out to her at India has made her rather misjudge the race, I think."

"She is so good," said Daireen. "Think of all the trouble she was at to-day for our sake."

"Yes, for our sake," laughed her father. "My dear Dolly, if you could only know the traditions our old station retains of Mrs. Crawford, you would think her doubly good. The trouble she has gone to for the sake of her friends—her importations by every mail—is simply astonishing. But what did you think of that charming Miss Van der Veldt you took such care of, Standish, my boy? Did you make much progress in Cape Dutch?"

But Standish could not answer in the same strain of pleasantry. He was thinking too earnestly upon the visions his fancy had been conjuring up during the entire evening—visions of Mr. Glaston sitting by the side of Daireen gazing out to that seductive, though by no means uncommon, phenomenon of sunset. He had often wished, when at the waterfall gathering Venus-hair for Miss Van der Veldt, that he could come into possession of the power of Joshua at the valley of Gibeon to arrest the descent of the orb. The possibly disastrous consequences to the planetary system seemed to him but trifling weighed against the advantages that would accrue from the fact of Mr. Glaston's being deprived of a source of conversation that was both fruitful and poetical. Standish knew well, without having read Wordsworth, that the twilight was sovereign of one peaceful hour; he had in his mind quite a store of unuttered poetical observations upon sunset, and he felt that Mr. Glaston might possibly be possessed of similar resources which he could draw upon when occasion demanded such a display. The thought of Mr. Glaston sitting at the feet of Daireen, and with her drinking in of the glory of the west, was agonising to Standish, and so he could not enter into Colonel Gerald's pleasantry regarding the attractive daughter of the member of the Legislative Council.

When Daireen had shut the door of her room that night and stood alone in the darkness, she found the relief that she had been seeking since she had come down from the slope of that great Peak—relief that could not be found even in the presence of her father, who had been everything to her a few days before. She found relief in being alone with her thoughts in the silence of the night. She drew aside the curtains of her window, and looked out up to that Peak which was towering amongst the brilliant stars. She could know exactly the spot upon the edge of the ravine where she had been sitting—where they had been sitting. What did it all mean? she asked herself. She could not at first recollect any of the words she had heard upon that slope, she could not even think what they should mean, but she had a childlike consciousness of happiness mixed with fear. What was the mystery that had been unfolded to her up there? What was the revelation that had been made to her? She could not tell. It seemed wonderful to her how she could so often have looked up to that hill without feeling anything of what she now felt gazing up to its slope.

It was all too wonderful for her to understand. She had a consciousness of nothing but that all was wonderful. She could not remember any of his words except those he had last uttered. The bond between them—was it of love? How could she tell? What did she know of love? She could not answer him when he had spoken to her, nor was she able even now, as she stood looking out to those brilliant stars that crowned the Peak and studded the dark edges of the slope which had been lately overspread with the poppy-petals of sunset. It was long before she went into her bed, but she had arrived at no conclusion to her thoughts—all that had happened seemed mysterious; and she knew not whether she felt happy beyond all the happiness she had ever known, or sad beyond the sadness of any hour of her life. Her sleep swallowed up all her perplexity.

But the instant she awoke in the bright morning she went softly over to the window and looked out from a corner of her blind to that slope and to the place where they had sat. No, it was not a dream. There shone the silver leaves and there sparkled the waterfall. It was the loveliest hill in the world, she felt—lovelier even than the purple heather-clad Slieve Docas. This was a terrible thought to suggest itself to her mind, she felt all the time she was dressing, but still it remained with her and refused to be shaken off.

CHAPTER XXVIII

Since my dear soul was mistress of her choice
... her election
Hath sealed thee for herself.

Adieu, adieu, adieu! Remember me.

Yea, from the table of my memory
I'll wipe away all trivial fond records...
That youth and observation copied there,
And thy commandment all alone shall live
Unmixed with baser matter; yes, by heaven!—*Hamlet.*

COLONEL Gerald was well aware of Mrs. Crawford's strategical skill, and he had watched its development and exercise during the afternoon of that pleasant little luncheon party on the hill. He remembered what she had said to him so gravely at the garden-party at Government House regarding the responsibility inseparable from the guardianship of Daireen at the Cape, and he knew that Mrs. Crawford had in her mind, when she organised the party to the hill, such precepts as she had previously enunciated. He had watched and admired her cleverness in arranging the collecting expeditions, and he felt that her detaining of Mr. Glaston as she had under some pretext until all the others but Daireen had gone up the ravine was a master stroke. But at this point Colonel Gerald's observation ended. His imagination had been much less vivid than either Mrs. Crawford's or Standish's. He did not attribute any subtle influence to the setting sun, nor did he conjure up any vision of Mr. Glaston sitting at the feet of Daireen and uttering words that the magic of the sunset glories alone could inspire.

The fact was that he knew much better than either Mrs. Crawford or Standish how his daughter felt towards Mr. Glaston, and he was not in the least concerned in the result of her observation of the glowing west by the side of the Art prophet. When Mrs. Crawford looked narrowly into the girl's face on her descent Colonel Gerald had only laughed; he did not feel any distressing weight of responsibility on the subject of the guardianship of his daughter, for he had not given a single thought to the accident of his daughter's straying up the ravine with Algernon Glaston, nor was he impressed by his daughter's behaviour on the day following. They had driven out together to pay some visits, and she had been even more affectionate to him than usual, and he justified Mrs. Crawford's accusation of his ignorance and the ignorance of men generally, by feeling, from this fact, more assured that Daireen had passed unscathed through the ordeal of sunset and the drawing on of twilight on the mount.

On the next day to that on which they had paid their visits, however, Daireen seemed somewhat abstracted in her manner, and when her father asked her if she would ride with him and Standish to The Flats she, for the first time, brought forward a plea—the plea of weariness—to be allowed to remain at home.

Her father looked at her, not narrowly nor with the least glance of suspicion, only tenderly, as he said:

"Certainly, stay at home if you wish, Dolly. You must not overtax yourself, or we shall have to get a nurse for you."

He sat by her side on the chair on the stoep of the Dutch cottage and put his arm about her. In an instant she had clasped him round the neck and had hidden her face upon his shoulder in something like hysterical passion. He laughed and patted her on the back in mock protest at her treatment. It was some time before she unwound her arms and he got upon his feet, declaring that he would not submit to such rough handling. But all the same he saw that her eyes were full of tears; and as he rode with Standish over the sandy plain made bright with heath, he thought more than once that there was something strange in her action and still stranger in her tears.

Standish, however, felt equal to explaining everything that seemed unaccountable. He felt there could be no doubt that Daireen was wearying of these rides with him: he was nothing more than a brother—a dull, wearisome, commonplace brother to her, while such fellows as Glaston, who had made fame for themselves, having been granted the opportunity denied to others, were naturally attractive to her. Feeling this, Standish once more resolved to enter upon that enterprise of work which he felt to be ennobling. He would no longer linger here in silken-folded idleness, he would work—work—work—steadfastly, nobly, to win her who was worth all the labour of a man's life. Yes, he would no longer remain inactive as he had been, he would—well, he lit another cigar and trotted up to the side of Colonel Gerald.

But Daireen, after the departure of her father and Standish, continued sitting upon the chair under the lovely creeping plants that twined themselves around the lattice of the projecting roof. It was very cool in the gracious shade while all the world outside was red with heat. The broad leaves of the plants in the garden were hanging languidly, and the great black bees plunged about the mighty roses that were bursting into bloom with the first breath of the southern summer. From the brink of the little river at the bottom of the avenue of Australian oaks the chatter of the Hottentot washerwomen came, and across the intervening space of short tawny grass a Malay fruitman passed, carrying his baskets slung on each end of a bamboo pole across his shoulders.

She looked out at the scene—so strange to her even after the weeks she had been at this place; all was strange to her—as the thoughts that were in her mind. It seemed to her that she had been but one day at this place, and yet since she had heard the voice of Oswin Markham how great a space had passed! All the days she had been here were swallowed up in the interval that had elapsed since she had seen this man—since she had seen him? Why, there he was before her very eyes, standing by the side of his horse with the bridle over his arm. There he was watching her while she had been thinking her thoughts.

She stood amongst the blossoms of the trellis, white and lovely as a lily in a land of red sun. He felt her beauty to be unutterably gracious to look upon. He threw his bridle over a branch and walked up to her.

"I have come to say good-bye," he said as he took her hand.

These were the same words that she had heard from Harwood a few days before and that had caused her to smile. But now the hand Markham was not holding was pressed against her heart. Now she knew all. There was no mystery between them. She knew why her heart became still after beating tumultuously for a few seconds; and he, though he had not designed the words with the same object that Harwood had, and though he spoke them without the same careful observance of their effect, in another instant had seen what was in the girl's heart.

"To say good-bye?" she repeated mechanically.

"For a time, yes; for a long time it will seem to me—for a month."

He saw the faint smile that came to her face, and how her lips parted as a little sigh of relief passed through them.

"For a month?" she said, and now she was speaking in her own voice, and sitting down. "A month is not a long time to say good-bye for, Mr. Markham. But I am so sorry that papa is gone out for his ride on The Flats."

"I am fortunate in finding even you here, then," he said.

"Fortunate! Yes," she said. "But where do you mean to spend this month?" she continued, feeling that he was now nothing more than a visitor.

"It is very ridiculous—very foolish," he replied. "I promised, you know, to act in some entertainment Miss Vincent has been getting up, and only yesterday her father received orders to proceed to Natal; but as all the fellows who had promised her to act are in the company of the Bayonetteers that has also been ordered off, no difference will be made in her arrangements, only that the performance will take place at Pietermaritzburg instead of at Cape Town. But she is so unreasonable as to refuse to release me from my promise, and I am bound to go with them."

"It is a compliment to value your services so highly, is it not?"

"I would be glad to sacrifice all the gratification I find from thinking so for the sake of being released. She is both absurd and unreasonable."

"So it would certainly strike any one hearing only of this," said Daireen. "But it will only be for a month, and you will see the place."

"I would rather remain seeing this place," he said. "Seeing that hill above us." She flushed as though he had told her in those words that he was aware of how often she had been looking up to that slope since they had been there together——

There was a long pause, through which the voices and laughter of the women at the river-bank were heard.

"Daireen," said the man, who stood up bareheaded before her. "Daireen, that hour we sat up there upon that slope has changed all my thoughts of life. I tell you the life which you restored to me a month ago I had ceased to regard as a gift. I had come to hope that it would end speedily. You cannot know how wretched I was."

"And now?" she said, looking up to him. "And now?"

"Now," he answered. "Now—what can I tell you? If I were to be cut off from life and happiness now, I should stand before God and say that I have had all the happiness that can be joined to one life on earth. I have had that one hour with you, and no God or man can take it from me: I have lived that hour, and none can make me unlive it. I told you I would say no word of love to you then, but I have come to say the word now. Child, I dared not love you as I was—I had no thought worthy to be devoted to loving you. God knows how I struggled with all my soul to keep myself from doing you the injustice of thinking of you; but that hour at your feet has given me something of your divine nature, and with that which I have caught from you, I can love you. Daireen, will you take the love I offer you? It it yours—all yours."

He was not speaking passionately, but when she looked up and saw his face haggard with earnestness she was almost frightened—she would have been frightened if she had not loved him as she now knew she did. "Speak," he said, "speak to me—one word."

"One word?" she repeated. "What one word can I say?"

"Tell me all that is in your heart, Daireen."

She looked up to him again. "All?" she said with a little smile. "All? No, I could never tell you all. You know a little of it. That is the bond between us."

He turned away and actually took a few steps from her. On his face was an expression that could not easily have been read. But in an instant he seemed to recover himself. He took her hand in his.

"My darling," he said, "the Past has buried its dead. I shall make myself worthy to think of you—I swear it to you. You shall have a true man to love." He was almost fierce in his earnestness, and her hand that he held was crushed for an instant. Then he looked into her face with tenderness. "How have you come to answer my love with yours?" he said almost wonderingly. "What was there in me to make you think of my existence for a single instant?"

She looked at him. "You were—*you*," she said, offering him the only explanation in her power. It had seemed to her easy enough to explain as she looked at him. Who else was worth loving with this love in all the world, she thought. He alone was worthy of all her heart.

"My darling, my darling," he said, "I am unworthy to have a single thought of you."

"You are indeed if you continue talking so," she said with a laugh, for she felt unutterably happy.

"Then I will not talk so. I will make myself worthy to think of you by— by—thinking of you. For a month, Daireen,—for a month we can only think of each other. It is better that I should not see you until the last tatter of my old self is shred away."

"It cannot be better that you should go away," she said. "Why should you go away just as we are so happy?"

"I must go, Daireen," he said. "I must go—and now. I would to God I could stay! but believe me, I cannot, darling; I feel that I must go."

"Because you made that stupid promise?" she said.

"That promise is nothing. What is such a promise to me now? If I had never made it I should still go."

He was looking down at her as he spoke. "Do not ask me to say anything more. There is nothing more to be said. Will you forget me in a month, do you think?"

Was it possible that there was a touch of anxiety in the tone of his question? she thought for an instant. Then she looked into his face and laughed.

"God bless you, Daireen!" he said tenderly, and there was sadness rather than passion in his voice.

"God keep you, Daireen! May nothing but happiness ever come to you!"

He held out his hand to her, and she laid her own trustfully in his.

"Do not say good-bye," she pleaded. "Think that it is only for a month — less than a month, it must be. You can surely be back in less than a month."

"I can," he replied; "I can, and I will be back within a month, and then — — God keep you, Daireen, for ever!"

He was holding her hand in his own with all gentleness. His face was bent down close to hers, but he did not kiss her face, only her hand. He crushed it to his lips, and then dropped it. She was blinded with her tears, so that she did not see him hasten away through the avenue of oaks. She did not even hear his horse's tread, nor could she know that he had not once turned round to give her a farewell look.

It was some minutes before she seemed to realise that she was alone. She sprang to her feet and stood looking out over those deathly silent broad leaves, and those immense aloes, that seemed to be the plants in a picture of a strange region. She heard the laughter of the Hottentot women at the river, and the unmusical shriek of a bird in the distance. She clasped her hands over her head, looking wistfully through the foliage of the oaks, but she did not utter a word. He was gone, she knew now, for she felt a loneliness that overwhelmed every other feeling. She seemed to be in the middle of a bare and joyless land. The splendid shrubs that branched before her eyes seemed dead, and the silence of the warm scented air was a terror to her.

He was gone, she knew, and there was nothing left for her but this loneliness. She went into her room in the cottage and seated herself upon her little sofa, hiding her face in her hands, and she felt it good to pray for him — for this man whom she had come to love, she knew not how. But she knew she loved him so that he was a part of her own life, and she felt that it would always be so. She could scarcely think what her life had been before she had seen him. How could she ever have fancied that she loved her father before this man had taught her what it was to love? Now she felt how dear beyond all thought her father was to her. It was not merely love for himself that she had learnt from Oswin Markham, it was the power of loving truly and perfectly that he had taught her.

Thus she dreamed until she heard the pleasant voice of her friend Mrs. Crawford in the hall. Then she rose and wondered if every one would not notice the change that had passed over her. Was it not written upon her face? Would not every touch of her hand—every word of her voice, betray it?

Then she lifted up her head and felt equal to facing even Mrs. Crawford, and to acknowledging all that she believed the acute observation of that lady would read from her face as plainly as from the page of a book.

But it seemed that Mrs. Crawford's eyes were heavy this afternoon, for though she looked into Daireen's face and kissed her cheek affectionately, she made no accusation.

"I am lucky in finding you all alone, my dear," she said. "It is so different ashore from aboard ship. I have not really had one good chat with you since we landed. George is always in the way, or the major, you know—ah, you think I should rather say the colonel and Jack, but indeed I think of your father only as Lieutenant George. And you enjoyed our little lunch on the hill, I hope? I thought you looked pale when you came down. Was it not a most charming sunset?"

"It was indeed," said Daireen, straining her eyes to catch a glimpse through the window of the slope where the red light had rested.

"I knew you would enjoy it, my dear. Mr. Glaston is such good company—ah, that is, of course, to a sympathetic mind. And I don't think I am going too far, Daireen, when I say that I am sure he was in company with a sympathetic mind the evening before last."

Mrs. Crawford was smiling as one smiles passing a graceful compliment.

"I think he was," said Daireen. "Miss Vincent and he always seemed pleased with each other's society."

"Miss Vincent?—Lottie Vincent?" cried the lady in a puzzled but apprehensive way. "What do you mean, Daireen? Lottie Vincent?"

"Why, you know Mr. Glaston and Miss Vincent went away from us, among the silver leaves, and only returned as we were coming down the hill."

Mrs. Crawford was speechless for some moments. Then she looked at the girl, saying, "We,—who were *we?*"

"Mr. Markham and myself," replied Daireen without faltering.

"Ah, indeed," said the other pleasantly. Then there was a pause before she added, "That ends my association with Lottie Vincent. The artful, designing little creature! Daireen, you have no idea what good nature it required on my part to take any notice of that girl, knowing so much as I do of her; and this is how she treats me! Never mind; I have done with her." Seeing the girl's puzzled glance, Mrs. Crawford began to recollect that it could not be expected that Daireen should understand the nature of Lottie's offence; so she added, "I mean, you know, dear, that that girl is full of spiteful, designing tricks upon every occasion. And yet she had the effrontery to come to me yesterday to beg of me to take charge of her while her father would be at Natal. But I was not quite so weak. Never mind; she leaves tomorrow, thank goodness, and that is the last I mean to see of her. But about Mr. Markham: I hope you do not think I had anything to say in the matter of letting you be with him, Daireen. I did not mean it, indeed."

"I am sure of it," said Daireen quietly—so quietly that Mrs. Crawford began to wonder could it be possible that the girl wished to show that she had been aware of the plans which had been designed on her behalf. Before she had made up her mind, however, the horses of Colonel Gerald and Standish were heard outside, and in a moment afterwards the colonel entered the room.

"Papa," said Daireen almost at once, "Mr. Markham rode out to see you this afternoon."

"Ah, indeed? I am sorry I missed him," he said quietly. But Mrs. Crawford stared at the girl, wondering what was coming.

"He came to say good-bye, papa."

Mrs. Crawford's heart began to beat again.

"What, is he returning to England?" asked the colonel.

"Oh, no; he is only about to follow Mr. Harwood's example and go up to Natal."

"Then he need not have said good-bye, anymore than Harwood," remarked the colonel; and his daughter felt it hard to restrain herself from throwing her arms about his neck.

"Ah," said Mrs. Crawford, "Miss Lottie has triumphed! This Mr. Markham will go up in the steamer with her, and will probably act with her in this theatrical nonsense she is always getting up."

"He is to act with her certainly," said Daireen. "Ah! Lottie has made a success at last," cried the elder lady. "Mr. Markham will suit her admirably. They will be engaged before they reach Algoa Bay."

"My dear Kate, why will you always jump at conclusions?" said the colonel. "Markham is a fellow of far too much sense to be in the least degree led by such a girl as Lottie."

Daireen had hold of her father's arm, and when he had spoken she turned round and kissed him. But it was not at all unusual for her to kiss him in this fashion on his return from a ride.

CHAPTER XXIX

Haply the seas and countries different
With variable objects shall expel
This something-settled matter in his heart,
Whereon his brain still beating puts him thus
From fashion of himself.—*Hamlet*

HE had got a good deal to think about, this Mr. Oswin Markham, as he stood on the bridge of the steamer that was taking him round the coast to Natal, and looked back at that mountain whose strange shape had never seemed stranger than it did from the distance of the Bay.

Table Mountain was of a blue dimness, and the white walls of the houses at its base were quite hidden; Robbin Island lighthouse had almost dwindled out of sight; and in the water, through the bright red gold shed from a mist in the west that the falling sun saturated with light, were seen the black heads of innumerable seals swimming out from the coastway of rocks. Yes, Mr. Oswin Markham had certainly a good deal to think about as he looked back to the flat-ridged mountain, and, mentally, upon all that had taken place since he had first seen its ridges a few weeks before.

He had thought it well to talk of love to that girl who had given him the gift of the life he was at present breathing—to talk to her of love and to ask her to love him. Well, he had succeeded; she had put her hand trustfully in his and had trusted him with all her heart, he knew; and yet the thought of it did not make him happy. His heart was not the heart of one who has triumphed. It was only full of pity for the girl who had listened to him and replied to him.

And for himself he felt what was more akin to shame than any other feeling—shame, that, knowing all he did of himself, he had still spoken those words to the girl to whom he owed the life that was now his.

"God! was it not forced upon me when I struggled against it with all my soul?" he said, in an endeavour to strangle his bitter feeling. "Did not I make up my mind to leave the ship when I saw what was coming upon me, and was I to be blamed if I could not do so? Did not I rush away from her without a word of farewell? Did not we meet by chance that night in the moonlight? Were those words that I spoke to her thought over? Were not they forced from me against my own will, and in spite of my resolution?" There could be no doubt that if any one acquainted with all the matters to which he referred had been ready to answer him, a satisfactory reply would have been received by him to each of his questions. But though, of course, he was aware of this, yet he seemed to find it necessary to alter the ground of the argument he was advancing for his own satisfaction. "I have a right to forget the wretched past," he said, standing upright and looking steadfastly across the glowing waters. "Have not I died for the past? Is not this life a new one? It is God's justice that I am carrying out by forgetting all. The past is past, and the future in all truth and devotion is hers."

There were, indeed, some moments of his life—and the present was one of them—when he felt satisfied in his conscience by assuring himself, as he did now, that as God had taken away all remembrance of the past from many men who had suffered the agonies of death, he was therefore entitled to let his past life and its recollections drift away on that broken mast from which he had been cut in the middle of the ocean; but the justice of the matter had not occurred to him when he got that bank order turned into money at the Cape, nor at the time when he had written to the agents of his father's property in England, informing them of his escape. He now stood up and spoke those words of his, and felt their force, until the sun, whose outline had all the afternoon been undefined in the mist, sank beneath the horizon, and the gorgeous colours drifted round from his sinking place and dwindled into the dark green of the waters. He watched the sunset, and though Lottie Vincent came to his side in her most playful mood, her fresh and artless young nature found no response to its impulses in him. She turned away chilled, but no more discouraged than a little child, who, desirous of being instructed on the secret of the creative art embodied in the transformation of a handkerchief into a rabbit, finds its mature friend reflecting upon a perplexing point in the theory of Unconscious Cerebration. Lottie knew that her friend Mr. Oswin Markham sometimes had to think about matters of such a nature as caused her little pleasantries to seem incongruous. She thought that now she had better turn to a certain Lieutenant Clifford, who, she knew, had no intricate mental problems to work out; and she did turn to him, with great advantage to herself, and, no doubt, to the officer as well. However forgetful Oswin Markham may have been of his past life, he could still recollect a few generalities that had struck him in former years regarding young persons of a nature similar to this pretty little Miss Vincent's. She had insisted on his fulfilling his promise to act with her, and he would fulfil it with a good grace; but at this point his contract terminated; he would not be tempted into making another promise to her which he might find much more embarrassing to carry out with consistency.

It had been a great grief to Lottie to be compelled, through the ridiculous treatment of her father by the authorities in ordering him to Natal, to transfer her dramatic entertainment from Cape Town to Pietermaritzburg. However, as she had sold a considerable number of tickets to her friends, she felt that "the most deserving charity," the augmentation of whose funds was the avowed object of the entertainment, would be benefited in no inconsiderable degree by the change of venue. If the people of Pietermaritzburg would steadfastly decline to supply her with so good an audience as the Cape Town people, there still would be a margin of profit, since her friends who had bought tickets on the understanding that the performance would take place where it was at first intended, did not receive their money back. How could they expect such a concession, Lottie asked, with innocent indignation; and begged to be informed if it was her fault that her father was ordered to Natal. Besides this one unanswerable query, she reminded those who ventured to make a timid suggestion regarding the returns, that it was in aid of a most deserving charity the tickets had been sold, so that it would be an act of injustice to give back a single shilling that had been paid for the tickets. Pursuing this very excellent system, Miss Lottie had to the credit of the coming performance a considerable sum which would provide against the contingencies of a lack of dramatic enthusiasm amongst the inhabitants of Pietermaritzburg.

It was at the garden-party at Government House that Markham had by accident mentioned to Lottie that he had frequently taken part in dramatic performances for such-like objects as Lottie's was designed to succour, and though he at first refused to be a member, of her company, yet at Mrs. Crawford's advocacy of the claims of the deserving object, he had agreed to place his services and experience at the disposal of the originator of the benevolent scheme.

At Cape Town he had not certainly thrown himself very heartily into the business of creating a part in the drama which had been selected. He was well aware that if a good performance of the nature designed by Lottie is successful, a bad performance is infinitely more so; and that any attempt on the side of an amateur to strike out a new character from an old part is looked upon with suspicion, and is generally attended with disaster; so he had not given himself any trouble in the matter.

"My dear Miss Vincent," he had said in reply to a pretty little remonstrance from the young lady, "the department of study requiring most attention in a dramatic entertainment of this sort is the financial. Sell all the tickets you can, and you will be a greater benefactress to the charity than if you acted like a Kemble."

Lottie had taken his advice; but still she made up her mind that Mr. Markham's name should be closely associated with the entertainment, and consequently, with her own name. Had she not been at pains to put into circulation certain stories of the romance surrounding him, and thus disposed of an unusual number of stalls? For even if one is not possessed of any dramatic inclinations, one is always ready to pay a price for looking at a man who has been saved from a shipwreck, or who has been the co-respondent in some notorious law case.

When the fellows of the Bayonetteers, who had been indulging in a number of surmises regarding Lottie's intentions with respect to Markham, heard that the young lady's father had been ordered to proceed to Natal without delay, the information seemed to give them a good deal of merriment. The man who offered four to one that Lottie should not be able to get any lady friend to take charge of her in Cape Town until her father's return, could get no one to accept his odds; but his proposal of three to one that she would get Markham to accompany her to Natal was eagerly taken up; so that there were several remarks made at the mess reflecting upon the acuteness of Mr. Markham's perception when it was learned that he was going with the young lady and her father.

"You see," remarked the man who had laid the odds, "I knew something of Lottie in India, and I knew what she was equal to."

"Lottie is a devilish smart child, by Jove," said one of the losers meditatively.

"Yes, she has probably cut her eye-teeth some years ago," hazarded another subaltern.

There was a considerable pause before a third of this full bench delivered final judgment as the result of the consideration of the case.

"Poor beggar!" he remarked; "poor beggar! he's a finished coon."

And that Mr. Oswin Markham was, indeed, a man whose career had been defined for him by another in the plainest possible manner, no member of the mess seemed to doubt.

During the first couple of days of the voyage round the coast, when Miss Lottie would go to the side of Mr. Markham for the purpose of consulting him on some important point of detail in the intended performance, the shrewd young fellows of the regiment of Bayonetteers pulled their phantom shreds of moustaches, and brought the muscles of their faces about the eyes into play to a remarkable extent, with a view of assuring one another of the possession of an unusual amount of sagacity by the company to which they belonged. But when, after the third day of rehearsals. Lottie's manner of gentle persuasiveness towards them altered to nasty bitter upbraidings of the young man who had committed the trifling error of overlooking an entire scene here and there in working out the character he was to bring before the audience, and to a most hurtful glance of scorn at the other aspirant who had marked off in the margin of his copy of the play all the dialogue he was to speak, but who, unfortunately, had picked up a second copy belonging to a young lady in which another part had been similarly marked, so that he had, naturally enough, perfected himself in the dialogue of the lady's rôle without knowing a letter of his own—when, for such trifling slips as these, Lottie was found to be so harsh, the deep young fellows made their facial muscles suggest a doubt as to whether it might not be possible that Markham was of a sterner and less malleable nature then they had at first believed him.

The fact was that since Lottie had met with Oswin Markham she had been in considerable perplexity of mind. She had found out that he was in by no means indigent circumstances; but even with her guileless, careless perceptions, she was not long in becoming aware that he was not likely to be moulded according to her desires; so, while still behaving in a fascinating manner towards him, she had had many agreeable half-hours with Mr. Glaston, who was infinitely more plastic, she could see; but so soon as the order had come for her father to go up to Natal she had returned in thought to Oswin Markham, and had smiled to see the grins upon the expressive faces of the officers of the Bayonetteers when she found herself by the side of Oswin Markham. She rather liked these grins, for she had an idea—in her own simple way, of course—that there is a general tendency on the part of young people to associate when their names have been previously associated. She knew that the fact of her having persuaded this Mr. Markham to accompany her to Natal would cause his name to be joined with hers pretty frequently, and in her innocence she had no objection to make to this.

As for Markham himself, he knew perfectly well what remarks people would make on the subject of his departure in the steamer with Lottie Vincent; he knew before he had been a day on the voyage that the Bayonetteers regarded him as somewhat deficient in firmness; but he felt that there was no occasion for him to be utterly broken down in spirit on account of this opinion being held by the Bayonetteers. He was not so blind but that he caught a glimpse now and again of a facial distortion on the part of a member of the company. He felt that it was probable these far-seeing fellows would be disappointed at the result of their surmises.

And indeed the fellows of the regiment were beginning, before the voyage was quite over, to feel that this Mr. Oswin Markham was not altogether of the yielding nature which they had ascribed to him on the grounds of his having promised Lottie Vincent to accompany her and her father to Natal at this time. About Lottie herself there was but one opinion expressed, and that was of such a character as any one disposed to ingratiate himself with the girl by means of flattery would hardly have hastened to communicate to her; for the poor little thing had been so much worried of late over the rehearsals which she was daily conducting aboard the steamer, that, failing to meet with any expression of sympathy from Oswin Markham, she had spoken very freely to some of the company in comment upon their dramatic capacity, and not even an amateur actor likes to receive unreserved comment of an unfavourable character upon his powers.

"She is a confounded little humbug," said one of the subalterns to Oswin in confidence on the last day of the voyage. "Hang me if I would have had anything to say to this deuced mummery if I had known what sort of a girl she was. By George, you should hear the stories Kirkham has on his fingers' ends about her in India."

Oswin laughed quietly. "It would be rash, if not cruel, to believe all the stories that are told about girls in India," he said. "As for Miss Vincent, I believe her to be a charming girl—as an actress."

"Yes," said the lieutenant, who had not left his grinder on English literature long enough to forget all that he had learned of the literature of the past century—"yes; she is an actress among girls, and a girl among actresses."

"Good," said Oswin; "very good. What is it that somebody or other remarked about Lord Chesterfield as a wit?"

"Never mind," said the other, ceasing the laugh he had commenced. "What I say about Lottie is true."

CHAPTER XXX

This world is not for aye, nor'tis not strange
That even our loves should with our fortunes change;
For'tis a question left us yet to prove,
Whether love lead fortune, or else fortune love.

Diseases desperate grown
By desperate appliance are relieved,
Or not at all.
... so you must take your husbands.

It is our trick. Nature her custom holds
Let shame say what it will: when these are gone
The woman will be out. —*Hamlet.*

OF course," said Lottie, as she stood by the side of Oswin Markham when the small steamer which had been specially engaged to take the field-officers of the Bayonetteers over the dreaded bar of Durban harbour was approaching the quay—"of course we shall all go together up to Pietermaritzburg. I have been there before, you know. We shall have a coach all to ourselves from Durban." She looked up to his face with only the least questioning expression upon her own. But Mr. Markham thought that he had made quite enough promises previously: it would be unwise to commit himself even in so small a detail as the manner of the journey from the port of Durban to the garrison town of Pietermaritzburg, which he knew was at a distance of upwards of fifty miles.

"I have not the least idea what I shall do when we land," he said. "It is probable that I shall remain at the port for some days. I may as well see all that there is on view in this part of the colony."

This was very distressing to the young lady.

"Do you mean to desert me?" she asked somewhat reproachfully.

"Desert you?" he said in a puzzled way. "Ah, those are the words in a scene in your part, are they not?"

Lottie became irritated almost beyond the endurance of a naturally patient soul.

"Do you mean to leave me to stand alone against all my difficulties, Mr. Markham?"

"I should be sorry to do that, Miss Vincent. If you have difficulties, tell me what they are; and if they are of such a nature that they can be curtailed by me, you may depend upon my exerting myself."

"You know very well what idiots these Bayonetteers are," cried Lottie.

"I know that most of them have promised to act in your theatricals," replied Markham quietly; and Lottie tried to read his soul in another of her glances to discover the exact shade of the meaning of his words, but she gave up the quest.

"Of course you can please yourself, Mr. Markham," she said, with a coldness that was meant to appal him.

"And I trust that I may never be led to do so at the expense of another," he remarked.

"Then you will come in our coach?" she cried, brightening up.

"Pray do not descend to particulars when we are talking in this vague way on broad matters of sentiment, Miss Vincent."

"But I must know what you intend to do at once."

"At once? I intend to go ashore, and try if it is possible to get a dinner worth eating. After that—well, this is Tuesday, and on Thursday week your entertainment will take place; before that day you say you want three rehearsals, then I will agree to be by your side at Pietermaritzburg on Saturday next."

This business-like arrangement was not what Lottie on leaving Cape Town had meant to be the result of the voyage to Natal. There was a slight pause before she asked:

"What do you mean by treating me in this way? I always thought you were my friend. What will papa say if you leave me to go up there alone?"

This was a very daring bit of dialogue on the part of Miss Lottie, but they were nearing the quay where she knew Oswin would be free; aboard the mail steamer of course he was—well, scarcely free. But Mr. Markham was one of those men who are least discomfited by a daring stroke. He looked steadfastly at the girl so soon as she uttered her words.

"The problem is too interesting to be allowed to pass, Miss Vincent," he said. "We shall do our best to have it answered. By Jove, doesn't that man on the quay look like Harwood? It is Harwood indeed, and I thought him among the Zulus."

The first man caught sight of on the quay was indeed the special correspondent of the *Dominant Trumpeter*. Lottie's manner changed instantly on seeing him, and she gave one of her girlish laughs on noticing the puzzled expression upon his face as he replied to her salutations while yet afar. She was very careful to keep by the side of Oswin until the steamer was at the quay; and when at last Harwood recognised the features of the two persons who had been saluting him, she saw him look with a little smile first to herself, then to Oswin, and she thought it prudent to give a small guilty glance downwards and to repeat her girlish laugh.

Oswin saw Harwood's glance and heard Lottie's laugh. He also heard the young lady making an explanation of certain matters, to which Harwood answered with a second little smile.

"Kind? Oh, exceedingly kind of him to come so long a distance for the sake of assisting you. Nothing could be kinder."

"I feel it to be so indeed," said Miss Vincent. "I feel that I can never repay Mr. Markham."

Again that smile came to Mr. Harwood as he said: "Do not take such a gloomy view of the matter, my dear Miss Vincent; perhaps on reflection some means may be suggested to you."

"What can you mean?" cried the puzzled little thing, tripping away.

"Well, Harwood, in spite of your advice to me, you see I am here not more than a week behind yourself."

"And you are looking better than I could have believed possible for any one in the condition you were in when I left," said Harwood. "Upon my word, I did not expect much from you as I watched you go up the stairs at the hotel after that wild ride of yours to and from no place in particular. But, of course, there are circumstances under which fellows look knocked up, and there are others that combine to make them seem quite the contrary; now it seems to me you are subject to the influence of the latter just at present." He glanced as if by accident over to where Lottie was making a pleasant little fuss about some articles of her luggage.

"You are right," said Markham—"quite right. I have reason to be particularly elated just now, having got free from that steamer and my fellow-passengers."

"Why, the fellows of the Bayonetteers struck me as being particularly good company," said Harwood.

"And so they were. Now I must look after this precious portmanteau of mine."

"And assist that helpless little creature to look after hers," muttered Harwood when the other had left him. "Poor little Lottie! is it possible that you have landed a prize at last? Well, no one will say that you don't deserve something for your years of angling."

Mr. Harwood felt very charitably inclined just at this instant, for his reflections on the behaviour of Markham during the last few days they had been at the same hotel at Cape Town had not by any means been quieted since they had parted. He was sorry to be compelled to leave Cape Town without making any discovery as to the mental condition of Markham. Now, however, he knew that Markham had been strong enough to come on to Natal, so that the searching out of the problem of his former weakness would be as uninteresting as it would be unprofitable. If there should chance to be any truth in that vague thought which had been suggested to him as to the possibility of Markham having become attached to Daireen Gerald, what did it matter now? Here was Markham, having overcome his weakness, whatever it may have been, by the side of Lottie Vincent; not indeed appearing to be in great anxiety regarding the welfare of the young lady's luggage which was being evil-treated, but still by her side, and this made any further thought on his behalf unnecessary.

Mr. Markham had given his portmanteau into the charge of one of the Natal Zulus, and then he turned to Harwood.

"You don't mind my asking you what you are doing at Durban instead of being at the other side of the Tugela?" he said.

"The Zulus of this province require to be treated of most carefully in the first instance, before the great question of Zulus in their own territory can be fully understood by the British public," replied the correspondent. "I am at present making the Zulu of Durban my special study. I suppose you will be off at once to Pietermaritzburg?"

"No," said Markham. "I intend remaining at Durban to study the—the Zulu characteristics for a few days."

"But Lottie—I beg your pardon—Miss Vincent is going on at once."

There was a little pause, during which Markham stared blankly at his friend.

"What on earth has that got to say to my remaining here?" he said.

Harwood looked at him and felt that Miss Lottie was right, even on purely artistic grounds, in choosing Oswin Markham as one of her actors.

"Nothing—nothing of course," he replied to Markham's question.

But Miss Lottie had heard more than a word of this conversation. She tripped up to Mr. Harwood.

"Why don't you make some inquiry about your old friends, you most ungrateful of men?" she cried. "Oh, I have such a lot to tell you. Dear old Mrs. Crawford was in great grief about your going away, you know—oh, such great grief that she was forced to give a picnic the second day after you left, for fear we should all have broken down utterly."

"That was very kind of Mrs. Crawford," said Harwood; "and it only remains for me to hope fervently that the required effect was produced."

"So far as I was concerned, it was," said Lottie. "But it would never do for me to speak for other people."

"Other people?"

"Yes, other people—the charming Miss Gerald, for instance; I cannot speak for her, but Mr. Markham certainly can, for he lay at her feet during the entire of the afternoon when every one else had wandered away up the ravine. Yes, Mr. Markham will tell you to a shade what her feelings were upon that occasion. Now, bye-bye. You will come to our little entertainment next week, will you not? And you will turn up on Saturday for rehearsal?" she added, smiling at Oswin, who was looking more stern than amused. "Don't forget—Saturday. You should be very grateful for my giving you liberty for so long."

Both men went ashore together without a word; nor did they fall at once into a fluent chat when they set out for the town, which was more than two miles distant; for Mr. Harwood was thinking out another of the problems which seemed to suggest themselves to him daily from the fact of his having an acute ear for discerning the shades of tone in which his friends uttered certain phrases. He was just now engaged linking fancy unto fancy, thinking if it was a little impulse of girlish jealousy, meant only to give a mosquito-sting to Oswin Markham, that had caused Miss Lottie Vincent to make that reference to Miss Gerald, or if it was a piece of real bitterness designed to wound deeply. It was an interesting problem, and Mr. Harwood worked at its solution very patiently, weighing all his recollections of past words and phrases that might tend to a satisfactory result.

But the greatest amount of satisfaction was not afforded to Mr. Harwood by the pursuit of the intricacies of the question he had set himself to work out, but by the reflection that at any rate Markham's being at Natal and not within easy riding distance of a picturesque Dutch cottage at Mowbray, was a certain good. What did it signify now if Markham had previously been too irresolute to tear himself away from the association of that cottage? Had he not afterwards proved himself sufficiently strong? And if this strength had come to him through any conversation he might have had with Miss Gerald on the hillside to which Lottie had alluded, or elsewhere, what business was it to anybody? Here was Markham—there was Durban, and this was satisfactory. Only—what did Lottie mean exactly by that little bit of spitefulness or bitterness?

CHAPTER XXXI

Polonius. The actors are come hither, my lord.

Hamlet. Buz, buz.

Polonius. Upon my honour.

Hamlet. Then came each actor on his ass.

Polonious. The best actors in the world, either for tragedy, comedy, history, pastoral-comical, historical-pastoral, scene individable or poem unlimited... these are the only men.

Being thus benetted round with villanies,—
Or I could make a prologue to my brains,
They had begun the play,—I sat me down.
... Wilt thou know
The effect...?—*Hamlet.*

UPON the evening of the Thursday week after the arrival of that steamer with two companies of the Bayonetteers at Durban, the town of Pietermaritzburg was convulsed with the prospect of the entertainment that was to take place in its midst, for Miss Lottie Vincent had not passed the preceding week in a condition of dramatic abstraction. She was by no means so wrapped up in the part she had undertaken to represent as to be unable to give the necessary attention to the securing of an audience.

It would seem to a casual *entrepreneur* visiting Pietermaritzburg that a large audience might be assured for an entertainment possessing even the minimum of attractiveness, for the town appears to be of an immense size—that is, for a South African town. The colonial Romulus and Remus have shown at all times very lordly notions on the subject of boundaries, and, being subject to none of those restrictions as to the cost of every square foot of territory which have such a cramping influence upon the founders of municipalities at home, they exercise their grand ideas in the most extensive way. The streets of an early colonial town are broad roads, and the spaces between the houses are so great as almost to justify the criticism of those narrow-minded visitors who call the town straggling. At one time Pietermaritzburg may have been straggling, but it certainly did not strike Oswin Markham as being so when he saw it now for the first time on his arrival. He felt that it had got less of a Dutch look about it than Cape Town, and though that towering and overshadowing impression which Table Mountain gives to Cape Town was absent, yet the circle of hills about Pietermaritzburg seemed to him—and his fancy was not particularly original—to give the town almost that nestling appearance which by tradition is the natural characteristic of an English village.

But if an *entrepreneur* should calculate the probable numerical value of an audience in Pietermaritzburg from a casual walk through the streets, he would find that his assumption had been founded upon an erroneous basis. The streets are long and in fact noble, but the inhabitants available for fulfilling the duties of an audience at a dramatic entertainment are out of all proportion few. Two difficulties are to be contended with in making up audiences in South Africa: the first is getting the people in, and the second is keeping people out. As a rule the races of different colour do not amalgamate with sufficient ease to allow of a mixed audience being pervaded with a common sympathy. A white man seated between a Hottentot and a Kafir will scarcely be brought to admit that he has had a pleasant evening, even though the performance on the stage is of a choice character. A single Zulu will make his presence easily perceptible in a room full of white people, even though he should remain silent and in a secluded corner; while a Hottentot, a Kafir, and a Zulu constitute a *bouquet d'Afrique*, the savour of which is apt to divert the attention of any one in their neighbourhood from the realistic effect of a garden scene upon the stage.

Miss Lottie, being well aware that the audience-forming material in the town was small in proportion to the extent of the streets, set herself with her usual animation about the task of disposing of the remaining tickets. She fancied that she understood something of the system to be pursued with success amongst the burghers. She felt it to be her duty to pay a round of visits to the houses where she had been intimate in the days of her previous residence at the garrison; and she contrived to impress upon her friends that the ties of old acquaintance should be consolidated by the purchase of a number of her tickets. She visited several families who, she knew, had been endeavouring for a long time to work themselves into the military section of the town's society, and after hinting to them that the officers of the Bayonetteers would remain in the lowest spirits until they had made the acquaintance of the individual members of each of those families, she invariably disposed of a ticket to the individual member whose friendship was so longed for at the garrison. As for the tradesmen of the town, she managed without any difficulty, or even without forgetting her own standing, to make them aware of the possible benefits that would accrue to the business of the town under the patronage of the officers of the Bayonetteers; and so, instead of having to beg of the tradesmen to support the deserving charity on account of which she was taking such a large amount of trouble, she found herself thanked for the permission she generously accorded to these worthy men to purchase places for the evening.

She certainly deserved well of the deserving charity, and the old field-officers, who rolled their eyes and pulled their moustaches, recollecting the former labours of Miss Lottie, had got as imperfect a knowledge of the proportions of her toil and reward as the less good-natured of their wives who alluded to the trouble she was taking as if it was not wholly disinterested. Lottie certainly took a vast amount of trouble, and if Oswin Markham only appeared at the beginning of each rehearsal and left at the conclusion, the success of the performance was not at all jeopardised by his action.

For the entire week preceding the evening of the performance little else was talked about in all sections of Maritzburgian society but the prospects of its success. The ladies in the garrison were beginning to be wearied of the topic of theatricals, and the colonel of the Bayonetteers was heard to declare that he would not submit any longer to have the regimental parades only half-officered day by day, and that the plea of dramatic study would be insufficient in future to excuse an absentee. But this vigorous action was probably accelerated by the report that reached him of a certain lieutenant, who had only four lines to speak in the play, having escaped duty for the entire week on the grounds of the necessity for dramatic study.

At last the final nail was put in the fastenings of the scenery on the stage, which a number of the Royal Engineers, under the guidance of two officers and a clerk of the works, had erected; the footlights were after considerable difficulty coaxed into flame. The officers of the garrison and their wives made an exceedingly good front row in the stalls, and a number of the sergeants and privates filled up the back seats, ready to applaud, without reference to their merits at the performance, their favourite officers when they should appear on the stage; the intervening seats were supposed to be booked by the general audience, and their punctuality of attendance proved that Lottie's labours had not been in vain.

Mr. Harwood having tired of Durban, had been some days in the town, and he walked from the hotel with Markham; for Mr. Markham, though the part he was to play was one of most importance in the drama, did not think it necessary to hang about the stage for the three hours preceding the lifting of the curtain, as most of the Bayonetteers who were to act believed to be prudent. Harwood took a seat in the second row of stalls, for he had promised Lottie and one of the other young ladies who was in the cast, to give each of them a candid opinion upon their representations. For his own part he would have preferred giving his opinion before seeing the representations, for he knew what a strain would be put upon his candour after they were over.

When the orchestra—which was a great feature of the performance—struck up an overture, the stage behind the curtain was crowded with figures in top-boots and with noble hats encircled with ostrich feathers—the element of brigandage entering largely into the construction of the drama of the evening. Each of the figures carried a small pamphlet which he studied every now and again, for in spite of the many missed parades, a good deal of uncertainty as to the text of their parts pervaded the minds of the histrionic Bayonetteers. Before the last notes of the overture had crashed, Lottie Vincent, radiant in pearl powder and pencilled eyebrows, wearing a plain muslin dress and white satin shoes, her fair hair with a lovely white rose shining amongst its folds, tripped out. Her character in the first act being that of a simple village maiden, she was dressed with becoming consistency, every detail down to those white satin shoes being, of course, in keeping with the ordinary attire of simple village maidens wherever civilisation has spread.

"For goodness' sake leave aside your books," she said to the young men as she came forward. "Do you mean to bring them out with you and read from them? Surely after ten rehearsals you might be perfect."

"Hang me, if I haven't a great mind not to appear at all in this rot," said one of the gentlemen in the top-boots to his companions. He had caught a glimpse of himself in a mirror a minute previously and he did not like the picture. "If it was not for the sake of the people who have come I'd cut the whole affair."

"She has done nothing but bully," remarked a second of these desperadoes in top-boots.

"All because that fellow Markham has shown himself to be no idiot," said a third.

"Count Rodolph loves her, but I'll spare him not: he dies to-night," remarked another, but he was only refreshing his memory on the dialogue he was to speak.

When the gentleman who was acting as prompter saw that the stage was cleared, he gave the signal for the orchestra to play the curtain up. At the correct moment, and with a perfection of stage management that would have been creditable to any dramatic establishment in the world, as one of the Natal newspapers a few days afterwards remarked with great justice, the curtain was raised, and an excellent village scene was disclosed to the enthusiastic audience. Two of the personages came on at once, and so soon as their identity was clearly established, the soldiers began to applaud, which was doubtless very gratifying to the two officers, from a regimental standpoint, though it somewhat interfered with the progress of the scene. The prompter, however, hastened to the aid of the young men who had lost themselves in that whirlwind of applause, and the dialogue began to run easily.

Lottie had made for herself a little loophole in the back drop-scene through which she observed the audience. She saw that the place was crowded to the doors—English-speaking and Dutch-speaking burghers were in the central seats; she smiled as she noticed the aspirants to garrison intimacies crowding up as close as possible to the officers' wives in the front row, and she wondered if it would be necessary to acknowledge any of them for longer than a week. Then she saw Harwood with the faintest smile imaginable upon his face, as the young men on the stage repeated the words of their parts without being guilty either of the smallest mistake or the least dramatic spirit; and this time she wondered if, when she would be going through her part and she would look towards Harwood, she should find the same sort of smile upon his face. She rather thought not. Then, as the time for her call approached, she hastened round to her entrance, waiting until the poor stuff the two young men were speaking came to an end; then, not a second past her time, she entered, demure and ingenuous as all village maidens in satin slippers must surely be.

She was not disappointed in her reception by the audience. The ladies in the front stalls who had spoken, it might be, unkindly of her in private, now showed their good nature in public, and the field officers forgot all the irregularities she had caused in the regiment and welcomed her heartily; while the tradesmen in the middle rows made their applause a matter of business. The village maiden with the satin shoes smiled in the timid, fluttered, dovelike way that is common amongst the class, and then went on with her dialogue. She felt altogether happy, for she knew that the young lady who was to appear in the second scene could not possibly meet with such an expression of good feeling as she had obtained from the audience.

And now the play might be said to have commenced in earnest. It was by no means a piece of French frivolity, this drama, but a genuine work of English art as it existed thirty years ago, and it was thus certain to commend itself to the Pietermaritzburghers who liked solidity even when it verged upon stolidity.

Throne or Spouse was the title of the play, and if its incidents were somewhat improbable and its details utterly impossible, it was not the less agreeable to the audience. The two young men who had appeared in top-boots on the village green had informed each other, the audience happily overhearing, that they had been out hunting with a certain Prince, and that they had got separated from their companions.

They embraced the moment as opportune for the discussion of a few court affairs, such as the illness ot the monarch, and the Prince's prospects of becoming his successor, and then they thought it would be as well to try and find their way back to the court; so off they went. Then Miss Vincent came on the village green and reminded herself that her name was Marie and that she was a simple village maiden; she also recalled the fact that she lived alone with her mother in Yonder Cottage. It seemed to give her considerable satisfaction to reflect that, though poor, she was, and she took it upon her to say that her mother was also, strictly virtuous, and she wished to state in the most emphatic terms that though she was wooed by a certain Count Rodolph, yet, as she did not love him, she would never be his. Lottie was indeed very emphatic at this part, and her audience applauded her determination as Marie. Curiously enough, she had no sooner expressed herself in this fashion than one of the Bayonetteers entered, and at the sight of him Lottie called out, "Ah, he is here! Count Rodolph!" This the audience felt was a piece of subtle constructive art on the part of the author. Then the new actor replied, "Yes, Count Rodolph is here, sweet Marie, where he would ever be, by the side of the fairest village maiden," etc.

The new actor was attired in one of the broad hats of the period—whatever it may have been—with a long ostrich feather. He had an immense black moustache, and his eyebrows were exceedingly heavy. He also wore top-boots, a long sword, and a black cloak, one fold of which he now and again threw over his left shoulder when it worked its way down his arm. It was not surprising that further on in the drama the Count was found to be a dissembler; his costume fostered any proclivities in this way that might otherwise have remained dormant.

The village maiden begged to know why the Count persecuted her with his attentions, and he replied that he did so on account of his love for her. She then assured him that she could never bring herself to look on him with favour; and this naturally drew from him the energetic declaration of his own passion for her. He concluded by asking her to be his: she cried with emphasis, "Never!" He repeated his application, and again she cried "Never!" and told him to begone. "You shall be mine," he cried, catching her by the arm. "Wretch, leave me," she said, in all her village-maiden dignity; he repeated his assertion, and clasped her round the waist with ardour.

Then she shrieked for help, and a few simple villagers rushed hurriedly on the stage, but the Count drew his sword and threatened with destruction any one who might advance. The simple villagers thought it prudent to retire. "Ha! now, proud Marie, you are in my power," said the Count. "Is there no one to save me?" shrieked Marie. "Yes, here is some one who will save you or perish in the attempt," came a voice from the wings, and with an agitation pervading the sympathetic orchestra, a respectable young man in a green hunting-suit with a horn by his side and a drawn sword in his hand, rushed on, and was received with an outburst of applause from the audience who, in Pietermaritzburg, as in every place else, are ever on the side of virtue. This new actor was Oswin Markham, and it seemed that Lottie's stories regarding the romance associated with his appearance were successful, for not only was there much applause, but a quiet hum of remark was heard amongst the front stalls, and it was some moments before the business of the stage could be proceeded with.

So soon as he was able to speak, the Count wished to know who was the intruder that dared to face one of the nobles of the land, and the intruder replied in general terms, dwelling particularly upon the fact that only those were noble who behaved nobly. He expressed an inclination to fight with the Count, but the latter declined to gratify him on account of the difference there was between their social standing, and he left the stage saying, "Farewell, proud beauty, we shall meet again." Then he turned to the stranger, and, laying his hand on his sword-hilt after he had thrown his cloak over his shoulder, he cried, "We too shall meet again."

The stranger then made some remarks to himself regarding the manner in which he was stirred by Marie's beauty. He asked her who she was, and she replied, truthfully enough, that she was a simple village maiden, and that she lived in Yonder Cottage. He then told her that he was a member of the Prince's retinue, and that he had lost his way at the hunt; and he begged the girl to conduct him to Yonder Cottage. The girl expressed her pleasure at being able to show him some little attention, but she remarked that the stranger would find Yonder Cottage very humble. She assured him, however, of the virtue of herself, and again went so far as to speak for her mother. The stranger then made a nice little speech about the constituents of true nobility, and went out with Marie as the curtain fell.

The next scene was laid in Yonder Cottage; the virtuous mother being discovered knitting, and whiling away the time by talking to herself of the days when she was nurse to the late Queen. Then Marie and the stranger entered, and there was a pleasant family party in Yonder Cottage. The stranger was evidently struck with Marie, and the scene ended by his swearing to make her his wife. The next act showed the stranger in his true character as the Prince; his royal father has heard of his attachment to Marie, and not being an enthusiast on the subject of simple village maidens becoming allied to the royal house, he threatens to cut off the entail of the kingdom—which it appeared he had power to do—if the Prince does not relinquish Marie, and he dies leaving a clause in his will to this effect.

The Prince rushes to Yonder Cottage—hears that Marie is carried off by the Count—rescues her—marries her—and then the virtuous mother confesses that the Prince is her own child, and Marie is the heiress to the throne. No one appeared to dispute the story—Marie is consequently Queen and her husband King, having through his proper treatment of the girl gained the kingdom; and the curtain falls on general happiness, Count Rodolph having committed suicide.

"Nothing could have been more successful," said Lottie, all tremulous with excitement, to Oswin, as they went off together amid a tumult of applause, which was very sweet to her ears.

"I think it went off very well indeed," said Oswin. "Your acting was perfection, Miss Vincent."

"Call me Marie," she said playfully. "But we must really go before the curtain; hear how they are applauding."

"I think we have had enough of it," said Oswin.

"Come along," she cried; "I dislike it above all things, but there is nothing for it."

The call for Lottie and Oswin was determined, so after the soldiers had called out their favourite officers, Oswin brought the girl forward, and the enthusiasm was very great. Lottie then went off, and for a few moments Markham remained alone upon the stage. He was most heartily applauded, and, after acknowledging the compliment, he was just stepping back, when from the centre of the seats a man's voice came, loud and clear:

"Bravo, old boy! you're a trump wherever you turn up."

There was a general moving of heads, and some laughter in the front rows.

But Oswin Markham looked from where he was standing on the stage down to the place whence that voice seemed to come. He neither laughed nor smiled, only stepped back behind the curtain.

The stage was now crowded with the actors and their friends; everybody was congratulating everybody else. Lottie was in the highest spirits.

"Could anything have been more successful?" she cried again to Oswin Markham. He looked at her without answering for some moments. "I don't know," he said at last. "Successful? perhaps so."

"What on earth do you mean?" she asked; "are you afraid of the Natal critics?"

"No, I can't say I am."

"Of what then?"

"There is a person at the door who wishes to speak to you, Mr. Markham," said one of the servants coming up to Oswin. "He says he doesn't carry cards, but you will see his name here," and he handed Oswin an envelope.

Oswin Markham read the name on the envelope and crushed it into his pocket, saying to the servant:

"Show the—gentleman up to the room where I dressed."

So Miss Lottie did not become aware of the origin of Mr. Markham's doubt as to the success of the great drama *Throne or Spouse*.

CHAPTER XXXII

Good my lord, what is your cause of distemper? You do
surely bar the door upon your own liberty if you deny your
griefs to your friend.

... tempt him with speed aboard;
Delay it not; I'll have him hence to-night.

Indeed this counsellor
Is now most still, most secret, and most grave,
Who was in life a foolish prating knave.

This sudden sending him away must seem
Deliberate.—*Hamlet.*

IN the room where he had assumed the dress of the part he had just
played, Oswin Markham was now standing idle, and without making any
attempt to remove the colour from his face or the streaks from his eyebrows.
He was still in the dress of the Prince when the door was opened and a man
entered the room eagerly.

"By Jingo! yes, I thought you'd see me," he cried before he had closed the
door. All the people outside—and there were a good many—who chanced
to hear the tone of the voice knew that the speaker was the man who had
shouted those friendly words when Oswin was leaving the stage. "Yes, old
fellow," he continued, slapping Markham on the back and grasping him by
the hand, "I thought I might venture to intrude upon you. Right glad I was
to see you, though, by heavens! I thought I should have shouted out when
I saw you—you, of all people, here. Tell us how it comes, Oswin. How the
deuce do you appear at this place? Why, what's the matter with you? Have
you talked so much in that tall way on the boards that you haven't a word
left to say here? You weren't used to be dumb in the good old days—-good
old nights, my boy."

"You won't give me a chance," said Oswin; and he did not even smile
in response to the other's laughter.

"There then, I've dried up," said the stranger. "But, by my soul, I tell
you I'm glad to see you. It seems to me, do you know, that I'm drunk now,

and that when I sleep off the fit you'll be gone. I've fancied queer things when I've been drunk, as you well know. But it's you yourself, isn't it?"

"One need have no doubt about your identity," said Oswin. "You talk in the same infernally muddled way that ever Harry Despard used to talk."

"That's like yourself, my boy," cried the man, with a loud laugh. "I'm beginning to feel that it's you indeed, though you are dressed up like a Prince—by heavens! you played the part well. I couldn't help shouting out what I did for a lark. I wondered what you'd think when you heard my voice. But how did you manage to turn up at Natal? tell me that. You left us to go up country, didn't you?"

"It's a long story," replied Oswin. "Very long, and I am bound to change this dress. I can't go about in this fashion for ever."

"No more you can," said the other. "And the sooner you get rid of those togs the better, for by God, it strikes me that they give you a wrong impression about yourself. You're not so hearty by a long way as you used to be. I'll tell you what I'll do; I'll go on to the hotel and wait there until you are in decent rig. I'll only be in this town until to-morrow evening, and we must have a night together."

For the first time since the man had entered the room Oswin brightened up.

"Only till to-morrow night, Hal?" he cried. "Then we must have a few jolly hours together before we part. I won't let you even go to the hotel now. Stay here while I change, like a decent fellow."

"Now that sounds like your old form, my boy; hang me if I don't stay with you. Is that a flask in the portmanteau? It is, by Jingo, and if it's not old Irish may I be—and cigars too. Yes, I will stay, old fellow, for auld langsyne. This is like auld langsyne, isn't it? Why, where are you off to?"

"I have to give a message to some one in another room," said Oswin, leaving the man alone. He was a tall man, apparently about the same age as Markham. So much of his face as remained unconcealed by a shaggy, tawny beard and whiskers was bronzed to a copper colour. His hair was short and tawny, and his mouth was very coarse. His dress was not shabby, but the largeness of the check on the pattern scarcely argued the possession of a subdued taste on the part of the wearer.

He had seated himself upon a table in the room though there were plenty of chairs, and when Oswin went out he filled the flask cup and emptied it with a single jerk of his head; then he snatched up the hat which had been worn by Oswin on the stage; he threw it into the air and caught it on one of his feet, then with a laugh he kicked it across the floor.

But Oswin had gone to the room where Captain Howard, who had acted as stage manager, was smoking after the labours of the evening. "Howard," Said Markham, "I must be excused from your supper to-night."

"Nonsense," said Howard. "It would be too ridiculous for us to have a supper if you who have done the most work to-night should be away. What's the matter? Have you a doctor's certificate?"

"The fact is a — a — sort of friend of mine — a man I knew pretty intimately some time ago, has turned up here most unexpectedly."

"Then bring your sort of friend with you."

"Quite impossible," said Markham quickly. "He is not the kind of man who would make the supper agreeable either to himself or to any one else. You will explain to the other fellows how I am compelled to be away."

"But you'll turn up some time in the course of the night, won't you?"

"I am afraid to say I shall. The fact is, my friend requires a good deal of attention to be given to him in the course of a friendly night. If I can manage to clear myself of him in decent time I'll be with you."

"You must manage it," said Howard as Oswin went back to the room, where he found his friend struggling to pull on the green doublet in which the Prince had appeared in the opening scene of the play.

"Hang me if I couldn't do the part like one o'clock," he cried; "the half of it is in the togs. You weren't loud enough, Oswin, when you came on; you wouldn't have brought down the gods even at Ballarat. This is how you should have done it: 'I'll save you or — —'"

"For Heaven's sake don't make a fool of yourself, Hal."

"I was only going to show you how it should be done to rouse the people; and as for making a fool of myself — —"

"You have done that so often you think it not worth the caution. Come now, stuff those things into the portmanteau, and I'll have on my mufti in five minutes."

"And then off to the hotel, and you bet your pile, as we used to say at Chokeneck Gulch, we'll have more than a pint bottle of Bass. By the way, how about your bronze; does the good old governor still stump up?"

"My allowance goes regularly to Australia," said Os win, with a stern look coming to his face.

"And where else should it go, my boy? By the way, that's a tidy female that showed what neat ankles she had as Marie. By my soul, I envied you squeezing her. 'What right has he to squeeze her?' I said to myself, and then I thought if— —"

"But you haven't told me how you came here," said Oswin, interrupting him.

"No more I did. It's easily told, my lad. It was getting too warm for me in Melbourne, and as I had still got some cash I thought I'd take a run to New York city—at least that's what I made up my mind to do when I awoke one fine morning in the cabin of the *Virginia* brig a couple of hundred miles from Cape Howe. I remembered going into a saloon one evening and finding a lot of men giving general shouts, but beyond that I had no idea of anything."

"That's your usual form," said Oswin. "So you are bound for New York?"

"Yes, the skipper of the *Virginia* had made Natal one of his ports, and there we put in yesterday, so I ran up to this town, under what you would call an inspiration, or I wouldn't be here now ready to slip the tinsel from as many bottles of genuine Moët as you choose to order. But you—what about yourself?"

"I am here, my Hal, to order as many bottles as you can slip the tinsel off," cried Oswin, his face flushed more deeply than when it had been rouged before the footlights.

"Spoken in your old form, by heavens!" cried the other, leaping from the table. "You always were a gentleman amongst us, and you never failed us in the matter of drink. Hang me if I don't let the *Virginia* brig—go—to—to New York without me; I'll stay here in company with my best friend."

"Come along," said Oswin, leaving the room. "Whether you go or stay we'll have a night of it at the hotel."

They passed out together and walked up to the hotel, hearing all the white population discussing the dramatic performance of the evening, for it had created a considerable stir in the town. There was no moon, but the stars were sparkling over the dark blue of the hills that almost encircle the town. Tall Zulus stood, as they usually do after dark, talking at the corners in their emphatic language, while here and there smaller white men speaking Cape Dutch passed through the streets smoking their native cigars.

"Just what you would find in Melbourne or in the direction of Geelong, isn't it, Oswin?" said the stranger, who had his arm inside Markham's.

"Yes, with a few modifications," said Oswin.

"Why, hang it all, man," cried the other. "You aren't getting sentimental, are you? A fellow would think from the way you've been talking in that low, hollow, parson's tone that you weren't glad I turned up. If you're not, just say so. You won't need to give Harry Despard a nod after you've given him a wink."

"What an infernal fool you do make of yourself," said Oswin. "You know that I'm glad to have you beside me again, old fellow,—yes, devilish glad. Confound it, man, do you fancy I've no feeling—no recollection? Haven't we stood by each other in the past, and won't we do it in the future?"

"We will, by heavens, my lad! and hang me if I don't smash anything that comes on the table tonight except the sparkling. And look here, the *Virginia* brig may slip her cable and be off to New York. I'll stand by you while you stay here, my boy. Yes, say no more, my mind is made up."

"Spoken like a man!" cried Oswin, with a sudden start. "Spoken like a man! and here we are at the hotel. We'll have one of our old suppers together, Hal——"

"Or perish in the attempt," shouted the other.

The stranger went upstairs, while Oswin remained below to talk to the landlord about some matters that occupied a little time.

Markham and Harwood had a sitting-room for their exclusive use in the hotel, but it was not into this room that Oswin brought his guest, it was into another apartment at a different quarter of the house. The stranger threw his hat into a corner and himself down upon a sofa with his legs upon a chair that he had tilted back.

"Now we'll have a general shout," he said. "Ask all the people in the house what they'll drink. If you acted the Prince on the stage to-night, I'll act the part here now. I've got the change of a hundred samples of the Sydney mint, and I want to ease myself of them. Yes, we'll have a general shout."

"A general shout in a Dutchman's house? My boy, this isn't a Ballarat saloon," said Oswin. "If we hinted such a thing we'd be turned into the street. Here is a bottle of the sparkling by way of opening the campaign."

"I'll open the champagne and you open the campaign, good! The sight of you, Oswin, old fellow—well, it makes me feel that life is a joke. Fill up your glass and we'll drink to the old times. And now tell me all about yourself. How did you light here, and what do you mean to do? Have you had another row in the old quarter?"

Oswin had drained his glass of champagne and had stretched himself upon the second sofa. His face seemed pale almost to ghastliness, as persons' faces do after the use of rouge. He gave a short laugh when the other had spoken.

"Wait till after supper," he cried. "I haven't a word to throw to a dog until after supper."

"Curse that Prince and his bluster on the stage; you're as hoarse as a rook now, Oswin," remarked the stranger.

In a brief space the curried crayfish and penguins' eggs, which form the opening dishes of a Cape supper, appeared; and though Oswin's friend seemed to have an excellent appetite, Markham himself scarcely ate anything. It did not, however, appear that the stranger's comfort was wholly dependent upon companionship. He ate and drank and talked loudly whether Oswin fasted or remained mute; but when the supper was removed and he lighted a cigar, he poured out half a bottle of champagne into a tumbler, and cried:

"Now, my gallant Prince, give us all your eventful history since you left Melbourne five months ago, saying you were going up country. Tell us how you came to this place, whatever its infernal Dutch name is."

And Oswin Markham, sitting at the table, told him.

But while this tète-à-tète supper was taking place at the hotel, the messroom of the Bayonetteers was alight, and the regimental cook had excelled himself in providing dishes that were wholly English, without the least colonial flavour, for the officers and their guests, among whom was Harwood.

Captain Howard's apology for Markham was not freely accepted, more especially as Markham did not put in an appearance during the entire of the supper. Harwood was greatly surprised at his absence, and the story of a friend having suddenly turned up he rejected as a thing devised as an excuse. He did not return to the hotel until late—more than an hour past midnight. He paused outside the hotel door for some moments, hearing the sound of loud laughter and a hoarse voice singing snatches of different songs.

"What is the noisy party upstairs?" he asked of the man who opened the door.

"That is Mr. Markham and his friend, sir. They have taken supper together," said the servant.

Harwood did not express the surprise he felt. He took his candle, and went to his own room, and, as he smoked a cigar before going to bed, he heard the intermittent sounds of the laughter and the singing.

"I shall have a talk with this old friend of Mr. Markham's in the morning," he said, after he had stated another of his problems to sleep over.

Markham and he had been accustomed to breakfast together in their sitting-room since they had come up from Durban; but when Harwood awoke the next morning, and came in to breakfast, he found only one cup upon the table.

"Why is there not a cup for Mr. Markham?" he asked of the servant.

"Mr. Markham, sir, left with his friend for Durban at four o'clock this morning," said the man.

"What, for Durban?"

"Yes, sir. Mr. Markham had ordered a Cape cart and team to be here at that time. I thought you might have awakened as they were leaving."

"No, I did not," said Mr. Harwood quietly; and the servant left the room.

Here was something additional for the special correspondent of the *Dominant Trumpeter* to ponder over and reduce to the terms of a problem. He reflected upon his early suspicions of Oswin Markham. Had he not even suggested that Markham's name was probably something very different from what he had called himself? Mr. Harwood knew well that men have a curious tendency to call themselves by the names of the persons to whom bank orders are made payable, and he believed that such a subtle sympathy might exist between the man who had been picked up at sea and the document that was found in his possession. Yes, Mr. Harwood felt that his instincts were not perhaps wholly in error regarding Mr. Oswin Markham, cleverly though he had acted the part of the Prince in that stirring drama on the previous evening.

On the afternoon of the following day, however, Oswin Markham entered the hotel at Pietermaritzburg and walked into the room where Harwood was working up a letter for his newspaper, descriptive of life among the Zulus.

"Good heavens!" cried the "special," starting up; "I did not expect you back so soon. Why, you could only have stayed a few hours at the port."

"It was enough for me," said Oswin, a smile lighting up his pale face; "quite enough for me. I only waited to see the vessel with my friend aboard safely over the bar. Then I returned."

"You went away from here in something of a hurry, did you not, Markham?"

Oswin laughed as he threw himself into a chair.

"Yes, something of a hurry. My friend is—let us say, eccentric. We left without going to bed the night before last. Never mind, Harwood, old fellow; he is gone, and here I am now, ready for anything you propose— an excursion across the Tugela or up to the Transvaal—anywhere— anywhere—I'm free now and myself again."

"Free?" said Harwood curiously. "What do you mean by free?"

Oswin looked at him mutely for a moment, then he laughed, saying:

"Free—yes, free from that wretched dramatic affair. Thank Heaven, it's off my mind!"

CHAPTER XXXIII

Horatio. My lord, the King your father.
Hamlet. The King—my father?
Horatio. Season your admiration for a while.

In what particular thought to work I know not;
But in the gross and scope of mine opinion
This bodes some strange eruption to our state.

Our last King,
Whose image even but now appear'd to us,
... by a sealed compact
Did forfeit... all those his lands
Which he stood seized of, to the conqueror.

Hamlet.

MY son," said The Macnamara, "you ought to be ashamed of your threatment of your father. The like of your threatment was never known in the family of the Macnamaras, or, for that matter, of the O'Dermots. A stain has been thrown upon the family that centuries can't wash out."

"It is no stain either upon myself or our family for me to have set out to do some work in the world," said Standish proudly, for he felt capable of maintaining the dignity of labour. "I told you that I would not pass my life in the idleness of Innishdermot. I— — — — —-"

"It's too much for me, Standish O'Dermot Macnamara—to hear you talk lightly of Innishdermot is too much for the blood of the representative of the ancient race. Don't, my boy, don't."

"I don't talk lightly of it; when you told me it was gone from us I felt it as deeply as any one could feel it."

"It's one more wrong added to the grievances of our thrampled counthry," cried the hereditary monarch of the islands with fervour. "And yet you have never sworn an oath to be revenged. You even tell me that you mean to be in the pay of the nation that has done your family this wrong— that has thrampled The Macnamara into the dust. This is the bitterest stroke of all."

"I have told you all," said Standish. "Colonel Gerald was kinder to me than words could express. He is going to England in two months, but only to remain a week, and then he will leave for the Castaway Islands. He has already written to have my appointment as private secretary confirmed, and I shall go at once to have everything ready for his arrival. It's not much I can do, God knows, but what I can do I will for him. I'll work my best."

"Oh, this is bitter—bitter—to hear a Macnamara talk of work; and just now, too, when the money has come to us."

"I don't want the money," said Standish indignantly.

"Ye're right, my son, so far. What signifies fifteen thousand pounds when the feelings of an ancient family are outraged?"

"But I can't understand how those men had power to take the land, if you did not wish to give it to them, for their railway and their hotel."

"It's more of the oppression, my son—more of the thrampling of our counthry into the dust. I rejected their offers with scorn at first; but I found out that they could get power from the oppressors of our counthry to buy every foot of the ground at the price put on it by a man they call an arbithrator—so between thraitors and arbithrators I knew I couldn't hold out. With tears in my eyes I signed the papers, and now all the land from the mouth of Suangorm to Innishdermot is in the hands of the English company—all but the castle—thank God they couldn't wrest that from me. If you'd only been by me, Standish, I would have held out against them all; but think of the desolate old man sitting amongst the ruins of his home and the tyrants with the gold—I could do nothing."

"And then you came out here. Well, father, I'm glad to see you, and Colonel Gerald will be so too, and—Daireen."

"Aye," said The Macnamara. "Daireen is here too. And have you been talking to the lovely daughter of the Geralds, my boy? Have you been confessing all you confessed to me, on that bright day at Innishdermot? Have you——"

"Look here, father," said Standish sternly; "you must never allude to anything that you forced me to say then. It was a dream of mine, and now it is past."

"You can hold your head higher than that now, my boy," said The Macnamara proudly. "You're not a beggar now, Standish; money's in the family."

"As if money could make any difference," said Standish.

"It makes all the difference in the world, my boy," said The Macnamara; but suddenly recollecting his principles, he added, "That is, to some people; but a Macnamara without a penny might aspire to the hand of the noblest in the land. Oh, here she comes—the bright snowdhrop of Glenmara—the arbutus-berry of Craig-Innish; and her father too—oh, why did he turn to the Saxons?"

The Macnamara, Prince of Innishdermot, Chief of the Islands and Lakes, and King of all Munster, was standing with his son in the coffee-room of the hotel, having just come ashore from the steamer that had brought him out to the Cape. The patriot had actually left his land for the first time in his life, and had proceeded to the colony in search of his son, and he found his son waiting for him at the dock gates.

That first letter which Standish received from his father had indeed been very piteous, and if the young man had not been so resolute in his determination to work, he would have returned to Innishdermot once more, to comfort his father in his trials. But the next mail brought a second communication from The Macnamara to say that he could endure no longer the desolation of the lonely hearth of his ancestral castle, but would set out in search of his lost offspring through all the secret places of the earth. Considering that he had posted this letter to the definite address of his offspring, the effect of the vagueness of his expressed resolution was somewhat lessened.

Standish received the letter with dismay, and Colonel Gerald himself felt a little uneasiness at the prospect of having The Macnamara quartered upon him for an uncertain period. He was well aware of the largeness of the ideas of The Macnamara on many matters, and in regard to the question of colonial hospitality he felt that the views of the hereditary prince would be liberal to an inconvenient degree. It was thus with something akin to consternation that he listened to the eloquent letter which Standish read with flushed face and trembling hands.

"We shall be very pleased to see The Macnamara here," said Colonel Gerald; and Daireen laughed, saying she could not believe that Standish's father would ever bring himself to depart from his kingdom. It was on the next day that Colonel Gerald had an interview of considerable duration with Standish on a matter of business, he said; and when it was over and the young man's qualifications had been judged of, Standish found himself in a position either to accept or decline the office of private secretary to the new governor of the lovely Castaway group. With tears he left the presence of the governor, and went to his room to weep the fulness from his mind and to make a number of firm resolutions as to his future of hard work; and that very evening Colonel Gerald had written to the Colonial Office nominating Standish to the appointment; so that the matter was considered settled, and Standish felt that he did not fear to face his father.

But when Standish had met The Macnamara on the arrival of the mail steamer a week after he had received that letter stating his intentions, the young man learned, what apparently could not be included in a letter without proving harassing to its eloquence, that the extensive lands along the coastway of the lough had been sold to an English company of speculators who had come to the conclusion that a railway made through the picturesque district would bring a fortune to every one who might be so fortunate as to have money invested in the undertaking. So a railway was to be made, and a gigantic hotel built to overlook the lough. The shooting and fishing rights—in fact every right and every foot of ground, had been sold for a large sum to the company by The Macnamara. And though Standish had at first felt the news as a great blow to him, he subsequently became reconciled to it, for his father's appearance at the Cape with several thousand pounds was infinitely more pleasing to him than if the representative of The Macnamaras had come in his former condition, which was simply one of borrowing powers.

"It's the snowdhrop of Glenmara," said The Macnamara, kissing the hand of Daireen as he met her at the door of the room. "And you, George, my boy," he continued, turning to her father; "I may shake hands with you as a friend, without the action being turned to mean that I forgive the threatment my counthry has received from the nation whose pay you are still in. Yes, only as a friend I shake hands with you, George."

"That is a sufficient ground for me, Macnamara," said the colonel. "We won't go into the other matters just now."

"I cannot believe that this is Cape Town," said Daireen. "Just think of our meeting here to-day. Oh, if we could only have a glimpse of the dear old Slieve Docas!"

"Why shouldn't you see it, white dove?" said The Macnamara in Irish to the girl, whose face brightened at the sound of the tongue that brought back so many pleasant recollections to her. "Why shouldn't you?" he continued, taking from one of the boxes of his luggage an immense bunch of purple heather in gorgeous bloom. "I gathered it for you from the slope of the mountain. It brings you the scent of the finest hill in the world."

The girl caught the magnificent bloom in both her hands and put her face down to it. As the first breath of the hill she loved came to her in this strange land they saw her face lighten. Then she turned away and buried her head in the scents of the hills—in the memories of the mountains and the lakes, while The Macnamara spoke on in the musical tongue that lived in her mind associated with all the things of the land she loved.

"And Innishdermot," said Colonel Gerald at length, "how is the seat of our kings?"

"Alas, my counthry! thrampled on—bethrayed—crushed to the ground!" said The Macnamara. "You won't believe it, George—no, you won't. They have spoiled me of all I possessed—they have driven me out of the counthry that my sires ruled when the oppressors were walking about in the skins of wild beasts. Yes, George, Innishdermot is taken from me and I've no place to shelter me."

Colonel Gerald began to look grave and to feel much graver even than he looked. The Macnamara shelterless was certainly a subject for serious consideration.

"Yes," said Standish, observing the expression on his face, "you would wonder how any company could find it profitable to pay fifteen thousand pounds for the piece of land. That is what the new railway people paid my father."

Once more the colonel's face brightened, but The Macnamara stood up proudly, saying:

"Pounds! What are pounds to the feelings of a true patriot? What can money do to heal the wrongs of a race?"

"Nothing," said the colonel; "nothing whatever. But we must hasten out to our cottage. I'll get a coolie to take your luggage to the railway station. We shall drive out. My dear Dolly, come down from yonder mountain height where you have gone on wings of heather. I'll take out the bouquet for you."

"No," said Daireen. "I'll not let any one carry it for me."

And they all went out of the hotel to the carriage.

The *maître d'hôtel*, who had been listening to the speech of The Macnamara in wonder, and had been finally mystified by the Celtic language, hastened to the visitors' book in which The Macnamara had written his name; but this last step certainly did not tend to make everything clear, for in the book was written:

"Macnamara, Prince of the Isles, Chief of Innish-dermot and the Lakes, and King of Munster."

"And with such a nose!" said the *maître d'hôtel*.

CHAPTER XXXIV

Tis sweet and commendable in your nature,
To give these... duties to your father.

In that and all things we show our duty.

King. What wouldst thou beg, Laertes?
What wouldst thou have?

Laertes. Your leave and favour to ret urn — *Hamlet*.

TO these four exiles from Erin sitting out on the stoep of the Dutch cottage after dinner very sweet it was to dream of fatherland. The soft light through which the broad-leaved, motionless plants glimmered was, of course, not to be compared with the long dwindling twilights that were wont to overhang the slopes of Lough Suangorm; and that mighty peak which towered above them, flanked by the long ridge of Table Mountain, was a poor thing in the eyes of those who had witnessed the glories of the heather-swathed Slieve Docas.

The cries ot the bullock wagoners, which were faintly heard from the road, did not interfere with the musings of any of the party, nor with the harangue of The Macnamara.

Very pleasant it was to hear The Macnamara talk about his homeless condition as attributable to the long course of oppression persisted in by the Saxon Monarchy — at least so Colonel Gerald thought, for in a distant colony a harangue on the subject of British tyranny in Ireland does not sound very vigorous, any more than does a burning revolutionary ode when read a century or so after the revolution has taken place.

But poor Standish, who had spent a good many years of his life breathing in of the atmosphere of harangue, began to feel impatient at his sire's eloquence. Standish knew very well that his father had made a hard bargain with the railway and hotel company that had bought the land; nay, he even went so far as to conjecture that the affectionate yearning which had caused The Macnamara to come out to the colony in search of his son might be more plainly defined as an impulse of prudence to escape from certain of his creditors before they could hear of his having received a large sum of money. Standish wondered how Colonel Gerald could listen to all that his father was saying when he could not help being conscious of the nonsense of it all, for the young man was not aware of the pleasant memories of his youth that were coming back to the colonel under the influence of The Macnamara's speech.

The next day, however, Standish had a conversation of considerable length with his father, and The Macnamara found that he had made rapid progress in his knowledge of the world since he had left his secluded home. In the face of his father he insisted on his father's promising to remove from the Dutch cottage at the end of a few days. The Macnamara's notions of hospitality were very large, and he could not see why Colonel Gerald should have the least feeling except of happiness in entertaining a shelterless monarch; but Standish was firm, and Colonel Gerald did not resist so stoutly as The Macnamara felt he should have done; so that at the end of the week Daireen and her father were left alone for the first time since they had come together at the Cape.

They found it very agreeable to be able to sit together and ride together and talk without reserve. Standish Macnamara was, beyond doubt, very good company, and his father was even more inclined to be sociable, but no one disputed the wisdom of the young man's conduct in curtailing his visit and his father's to the Dutch cottage. The Macnamara had his pockets filled with money, and as Standish knew that this was a strange experience for him, he resolved that the weight of responsibility which the preservation of so large a sum was bound to entail, should be reduced; so he took a cottage at Rondebosch for his father and himself, and even went the length of buying a horse. The lordliness of the ideas of the young man who had only had a few months' experience of the world greatly impressed his father, and he paid for everything without a murmur.

Standish had, at the intervals of his father's impassioned discourses, many a long and solitary ride and many a lengthened reverie amongst the pines that grow beside The Flats. The resolutions he made as to his life at the Castaway group were very numerous, and the visions that floated before his eyes were altogether very agreeable. He was beginning to feel that he had accomplished a good deal of that ennobling hard work in the world which he had resolved to set about fulfilling. His previous resolutions had not been made carelessly: he had grappled with adverse Fate, he felt, and was he not getting the better of this contrary power?

But not many days after the arrival of The Macnamara another personage of importance made his appearance in Cape Town. The Bishop of the Calapash Islands and Metropolitan of the Salamander Archipelago had at last found a vessel to convey him to where his dutiful son was waiting for him.

The prelate felt that he had every reason to congratulate himself upon the opportuneness of his arrival, for Mr. Glaston assured his father, after the exuberance of their meeting had passed away, that if the vessel had not appeared within the course of another week, he would have been compelled to defer the gratification of his filial desires for another year.

"A colony is endurable for a week," said Mr. Glaston; "it is wearisome at the end of a fortnight; but a month spent with colonists has got a demoralising effect that years perhaps may fail to obliterate."

The bishop felt that indeed he had every reason to be thankful that unfavourable winds had not prolonged the voyage of his vessel.

Mrs. Crawford was, naturally enough, one of the first persons at the Cape to visit the bishop, for she had known him years before—she had indeed known most Colonial celebrities in her time—and she took the opportunity to explain to him that Colonel Gerald had been counting the moments until the arrival of the vessel from the Salamanders, so great was his anxiety to meet with the Metropolitan of that interesting archipelago, with whom he had been acquainted a good many years before. This was very gratifying to the bishop, who liked to be remembered by his friends; he had an idea that even the bishop of a distant colony runs a chance of being forgotten in the world unless he has written an heretical book, so he was glad when, a few days after his arrival at Cape Town, he received a visit from Colonel Gerald and an invitation to dinner.

This was very pleasing to Mrs. Crawford, for, of course, Algernon Glaston was included in the invitation, and she contrived without any difficulty that he should be seated by the side of Miss Gerald. Her skill was amply rewarded, she felt, when she observed Mr. Glaston and Daireen engaged in what sounded like a discussion on the musical landscapes of Liszt; to be engaged—even on a discussion of so subtle a nature—was something, Mrs. Crawford thought.

In the course of this evening, she herself, while the bishop was smiling upon Daireen in a way that had gained the hearts, if not the souls, of the Salamanderians, got by the side of Mr. Glaston, intent upon following up the advantage the occasion offered.

"I am so glad that the bishop has taken a fancy to Daireen," she said. "Daireen is a dear good girl—is she not?"

Mr. Glaston raised his eyebrows and touched the extreme point of his moustache before he answered a question so pronounced. "Ah, she is—improving," he said slowly. "If she leaves this place at once she may improve still."

"She wants some one to be near her capable of moulding her tastes—don't you think?"

"She *needs* such a one. I should not like to say *wants*," remarked Mr. Glaston.

"I am sure Daireen would be very willing to learn, Mr. Glaston; she believes in you, I know," said Mrs. Crawford, who was proceeding on an assumption of the broad principles she had laid down to Daireen regarding the effect of flattery upon the race. But her words did not touch Mr. Glaston deeply: he was accustomed to be believed in by girls.

"She has taste—some taste," he replied, though the concession was not forced from him by Mrs. Crawford's revelation to him. "Yes; but of what value is taste unless it is educated upon the true principles of Art?"

"Ah, what indeed?"

"Miss Gerald's taste is as yet only approaching the right tracks of culture. One shudders, anticipating the effect another month of life in such a place as this may have upon her. For my own part, I do not suppose that I shall be myself again for at least a year after I return. I feel my taste utterly demoralised through the two months of my stay here; and I explained to my father that it will be necessary for him to resign his see if he wishes to have me near him at all. It is quite impossible for me to come out here again. The three months' absence from England that my visit entails is ruinous to me."

"I have always thought of your self-sacrifice as an example of true filial duty, Mr. Glaston. I know that Daireen thinks so as well."

But Mr. Glaston did not seem particularly anxious to talk of Daireen.

"Yes; my father must resign his see," he continued.

"The month I have just passed has left too terrible recollections behind it to allow of my running a chance of its being repeated. The only person I met in the colony who was not hopelessly astray was that Miss Vincent."

"Oh!" cried Mrs. Crawford, almost shocked. "Oh, Mr. Glaston! you surely do not mean that! Good gracious!—Lottie Vincent!"

"Miss Vincent was the only one who, I found, had any correct idea of Art; and yet, you see, how she turned out."

"Turned out? I should think so indeed. Lottie Vincent was always turning out since the first time I met her."

"Yes; the idea of her acting in company of such a man as this Markham—a man who had no hesitation in going to view a picture by candlelight—it is too distressing."

"My dear Mr. Glaston, I think they will get on very well together. You do not know Lottie Vincent as I know her. She has behaved with the most shocking ingratitude towards me. But we are parted now, and I shall take good care she does not impose upon me again."

"It scarcely matters how one's social life is conducted if one's artistic life is correct," said Mr. Glaston.

At this assertion, which she should have known to be one of the articles of Mr. Glaston's creed, Mrs. Crawford gave a little start. She thought it better, however, not to question its soundness. As a matter of fact, the bishop himself, if he had heard his son enunciate such a precept, would not have questioned its soundness; for Mr. Glaston spake as one having authority, and most people whose robustness was not altogether mental, believed his Gospel of Art.

"No doubt what you say is—ah—very true," said Mrs. Crawford. "But I do wish, Mr. Glaston, that you could find time to talk frequently to Daireen on these subjects. I should be so sorry if the dear child's ideas were allowed to run wild. Your influence might work wonders with her. There is no one here now who can interfere with you."

"Interfere with me, Mrs. Crawford?"

"I mean, you know, that Mr. Harwood, with his meretricious cleverness, might possibly—ah—well, you know how easily girls are led."

"If there would be a possibility of Miss Gerald's being influenced in a single point by such a man as that Mr. Harwood, I fear not much can be hoped for her," said Mr. Glaston.

"We should never be without hope," said Mrs. Crawford. "For my own part, I hope a great deal—a very great deal—from your influence over Daireen; and I am exceedingly happy that the bishop seems so pleased with her."

The good bishop was indeed distributing his benedictory smiles freely, and Daireen came in for a share of his favours. Her father wondered at the prodigality of the churchman's smiles; for as a chaplain he was not wont to be anything but grave. The colonel did not reflect that while smiling may be a grievous fault in a chaplain, it can never be anything but ornamental to a bishop.

A few days afterwards Mrs. Crawford called upon the bishop, and had an interesting conversation with him on the subject of his son's future—a question to which of late the bishop himself had given a good deal of thought; for in the course of his official investigations on the question of human existence he had been led to believe that the duration of life has at all times been uncertain; he had more than once communicated this fact to dusky congregations, and by reducing the application of the painful truth, he had come to feel that the life of even a throned bishop is not exempt from the fatalities of mankind.

As the bishop's son was accustomed to spend half of the revenues of his father's see, his father was beginning to have an anxiety about the future of the young man; for he did not think that his successor to the prelacy of the Calapash Islands would allow Mr. Glaston to draw, as usual, upon the income accruing to the office. The bishop was not so utterly unworldly in his notions but that he knew there exist other means of amassing wealth than by writing verses in a pamphlet-magazine, or even composing delicate impromptus in minor keys for one's own hearing, His son had not felt it necessary to occupy his mind with any profession, so that his future was somewhat difficult to foresee with any degree of clearness.

Mrs. Crawford, however, spoke many comforting words to the bishop regarding a provision for his son's future. Daireen Gerald, she assured him, besides being one of the most charming girls in the world, was the only child of her father, and her father's estates in the South of Ireland were extensive and profitable.

When Mrs. Crawford left him, the bishop felt glad that he had smiled so frequently upon Miss Gerald. He had heard that no kindly smile was bestowed in vain, but the truth of the sentiment had never before so forced itself upon his mind. He smiled again in recollection of his previous smiles. He felt that indeed Miss Gerald was a charming girl, and Mrs. Crawford was most certainly a wonderful woman; and it can scarcely be doubted that the result of the bishop's reflections proved the possession on his part of powerful mental resources, enabling him to arrive at subtle conclusions on questions of perplexity.

CHAPTER XXXV

Too much of water had'st thou, poor Ophelia.

How can that be unless she drowned herself?

If the man go to this water... it is, will he, nill he, he goes; mark you that.—*Hamlet*.

STANDISH Macnamara had ridden to the Dutch cottage, but he found it deserted. Colonel Gerald, one of the servants informed him, had early in the day driven to Simon's Town, and had taken Miss Gerald with him, but they would both return in the evening. Sadly the young man turned away, and it is to be feared that his horse had a hard time of it upon The Flats. The waste of sand was congenial with his mood, and so was the rapid motion.

But while he was riding about in an aimless way, Daireen and her father were driving along the lovely road that runs at the base of the low hills which form a mighty causeway across the isthmus between Table Bay and Simon's Bay. Colonel Gerald had received a message that the man-of-war which had been stationed at the chief of the Castaway group had called at Simon's Bay; he was anxious to know how the provisional government was progressing under the commodore of those waters whose green monotony is broken by the gentle cliff's of the Castaways, and Daireen had been allowed to accompany her father to the naval station.

The summer had not yet advanced sufficiently far to make tawny the dark green coarse herbage of the hillside, and the mass of rich colouring lent by the heaths and the prickly-pear hedges made Daireen almost jealous for the glories of the slopes of Glenmara. For some distance over the road the boughs of Australian oaks in heavy foilage were leaning; but when Constantia and its evenly set vineyards were passed some distance, Daireen heard the sound of breaking waves, and in an instant afterwards the road bore them down to the water's edge at Kalk Bay, a little rocky crescent enclosing green sparkling waves. Upon a pebbly beach a few fishing-boats were drawn up, and the outlying spaces were covered with drying nets, the flavour of which was much preferable to that of the drying fish that were near.

On still the road went until it lost itself upon the mighty beaches of False Bay. Down to the very brink of the great green waves that burst in white foam and clouds of mist upon the sand the team of the wagonette was driven, and on along the snowy curve for miles until Simon's Bay with its cliffs were reached, and the horses were pulled up at the hotel in the single street of Simon's Town at the base of the low ridge of the purple hill.

"You will not be lonely, Dolly," said Colonel Gerald as he left the hotel after lunch to meet the commander of the man-of-war of which the yellow-painted hull and long streaming pennon could be seen from the window, opposite the fort at the farthest arm of the bay.

"Lonely?" said the girl. "I hope I may, for I feel I would like a little loneliness for a change. I have not been lonely since I was at Glenmara listening to Murrough O'Brian playing a dirge. Run away now, papa, and you can tell me when we are driving home what the Castaways are really like."

"I'll make particular inquiries as to the possibilities of lawn-tennis," said her father, as he went down the steps to the red street.

Daireen saw a sergeant's party of soldiers carry arms to the colonel, though he wore no uniform and had not been at this place for years; but even less accustomed observers than the men would have known that he was a soldier. Tall, straight, and with bright gray eyes somewhat hollower than they had been twenty years before, he looked a soldier in every point — one who had served well and who had yet many years of service before him.

How noble he looked, Daireen thought, as he kissed his hand up to her. And then she thought how truly great his life had been. Instead of coming home after his time of service had expired, he had continued at his post in India, unflinching beneath the glare of the sun overhead or from the scorching of the plain underfoot; and here he was now, not going home to rest for the remainder of his life, but ready to face an arduous duty on behalf of his country. She knew that he had been striving through all these years to forget in the work he was accomplishing the one grief of his life. She had often seen him gazing at her face, and she knew why he had sighed as he turned away.

She had not meant to feel lonely in her father's absence, but her thoughts somehow were not of that companionable kind which, coming to one when alone, prevent one's feeling lonely.

She picked up the visitors' book and read all the remarks that had been written in English for the past years; but even the literature of an hotel visitor's book fails at some moments to relieve a reader's mind. She turned over the other volumes, one of which was the Commercial Code of Signals, and the other a Dutch dictionary. She read one of Mr. Harwood's letters in a back number of the *Dominant Trumpeter*, and she found that she could easily recall the circumstances under which, in various conversations, he had spoken to her every word of that column and a quarter. She wondered if special correspondents write out every night all the remarks that they have heard during the day. But even the attempt to solve this problem did not make her feel brisk.

What was the thought which was hovering about her, and which she was trying to avoid by all the means in her power? She could not have defined it. The boundaries of that thought were too vague to be outlined by words.

She glanced out of the window for a while, and then walked to the door and looked over the iron balcony at the head of the steps. Only a few people were about the street. Gazing out seawards, she saw a signal flying from the peak of the man-of-war, and in a few minutes she saw a boat put off and row steadily for the shore near the far-off fort at the headland. She knew the boat was to convey her father aboard the vessel. She stood there watching it until it had landed and was on its way back with her father in the stern.

Then she went along the road until she had left the limits of the town, and was standing between the hill and the sea. Very lovely the sea looked from where it was breaking about the rocks beneath her, out to the horizon which was undefined in the delicate mist that rose from the waters.

She stood for a long time tasting of the freshness of the breeze. She could see the man-of-war's boat making its way through the waves until it at last reached the ship, and then she seemed to have lost the object of her thoughts. She turned off the road and got upon the sloping beach along which she walked some distance.

She had met no one since she had left the hotel, and the coast of the Bay round to the farthest headland seemed deserted; but somehow her mood of loneliness had gone from her as she stood at the brink of those waters whose music was as the sound of a song of home heard in a strange land. What was there to hinder her from thinking that she was standing at the uttermost headland of Lough Suangorm, looking out once more upon the Atlantic?

She crossed a sandy hollow and got upon a ledge of rocks, up to which the sea was beating. Here she seated herself, and sent her eyes out seawards to where the war-ship was lying, and then that thought which had been near her all the day came upon her. It was not of the Irish shore that the glad waters were laving. It was only of some words that had been spoken to her. "For a month we will think of each other," were the words, and she reflected that now this month had passed. The month that she had promised to think of him had gone, but it had not taken with it her thoughts of the man who had uttered those words.

She looked out dreamily across the green waves, wondering if he had returned. Surely he would not let a day pass without coming to her side to ask her if she had thought of him during the month. And what answer would she give him? She smiled.

"Love, my love," she said, "when have I ceased to think of you? When shall I cease to think of you?"

The tears forced themselves into her eyes with the pure intensity of her passion. She sat there dreaming her dreams and thinking her thoughts until she seemed only to hear the sound of the waters of the distance; the sound of the breaking waves seemed to have passed away. It was this sudden consciousness that caused her to awake from her reverie. She turned and saw that the waves were breaking on the beach *behind her*—the rock where she was sitting was surrounded with water, and every plunge of the advancing tide sent a swirl of water through the gulf that separated the rocks from the beach.

In an instant she had started to her feet. She saw the death that was about her. She looked to the rock where she was standing. The highest, ledge contained a barnacle. She knew it was below the line of high water, and now not more than a couple of feet of the ledge were uncovered. A little cry of horror burst from her, and at the same instant the boom of a gun came across the water from the man-of-war; she looked and saw that the boat was on its way to the shore again. In another half-minute a second report sounded, and she knew that they were firing a salute to her father. They were doing this while his daughter was gazing at death in the face.

Could they see her from the boat? It seemed miles away, but she took off her white jacket and standing up waved it. Not the least sign was made from the boat. The report of the guns echoed along the shore mingling with her cries. But a sign was given from the water: a wave flung its spray clear over the rock. She knew what it meant.

She saw in a moment what chance she had of escape. The water between the rock and the shore was not yet very deep. If she could bear the brunt of the wild rush of the waves that swept into the hollow she could make her way ashore.

In an instant she had stepped down to the water, still holding on by the rocks. A moment of stillness came and she rushed through the waves, but that sand—it sank beneath her first step, and she fell backwards, then came another swirl of eddying waves that plunged through the gulf and swept her away with their force, out past the rock she had been on. One cry she gave as she felt herself lost.

The boom of the saluting gun doing honour to her father was the sound she heard as the cruel foam flashed into her face.

But at her cry there started up from behind a rock far ashore the figure of a man. He looked about him in a bewildered way. Then he made a rush for the beach, seeing the toy the waves were heaving about. He plunged in up to his waist.

"Damn the sand!" he cried, as he felt it yield. He bent himself against the current and took advantage of every relapse of the tide to rush a few steps onward. He caught the rock and swung himself round to the seaward side. Then he waited until the next wave brought that helpless form near him. He did not leave his hold of the rock, but before the backward sweep came he clutched the girl's dress. Then came a struggle between man and wave. The man conquered. He had the girl on one of his arms, and had placed her upon the rock for an instant. Then he swung himself to the shoreward side, caught her up again, and stumbling, and sinking, and battling with the current, he at last gained a sound footing.

Daireen was exhausted but not insensible. She sat upon the dry sand where the man had placed her, and she drew back the wet hair from her face. Then she saw the man stand by the edge of the water and shake his fist at it.

"It's not the first time I've licked you singlehanded," he said, "and it'll not be the last. Your bullying roar won't wash here." Then he seemed to catch sight of something on the top of a wave. "Hang me if you'll get even her hat," he said, and once more he plunged in. The hat was farther out than the girl had been, and he had more trouble in securing it. Daireen saw that his head was covered more than once, and she was in great distress. At last, however, he struggled to the beach with the hat in his hand. It was very terrible to the girl to see him turn, squeezing the water from his hair, and curse the sea and all that pertained to it.

Suddenly, however, he looked round and walked up to where she was now standing. He handed her the hat as though he had just picked it up from the sand. Then he looked at her.

"Miss," he said, "I believe I'm the politest man in this infernal colony; if I was rude to you just now I ask your pardon. I'm afraid I pulled you about."

"You saved me from drowning," said Daireen. "If you had not come to me I should be dead now."

"I didn't do it for your sake," said the man. "I did it because that's my enemy"—he pointed to the sea—"and I wouldn't lose a chance of having a shy at him. It's my impression he's only second best this time again. Never mind. How do you feel, miss?"

"Only a little tired," said Daireen. "I don't think I could walk back to the hotel."

"You won't need," said the man. "Here comes a Cape cart and two ancient swells in it. If they don't give you a seat, I'll smash the whole contrivance."

"Oh!" cried Daireen joyfully; "it is papa—papa himself."

"Not the party with the brass buttons?" said the man. "All right, I'll hail them."

Colonel Gerald sprang from the Cape cart in which he was driving with the commodore of the naval station.

"Good God, Daireen, what does this mean?" he cried, looking from the girl to the man beside her.

But Daireen, regardless of her dripping condition, threw herself into his arms, and the stranger turned away whistling. He reached the road and shook his head confidentially at the commodore, who was standing beside the Cape cart.

"Touching thing to be a father, eh, Admiral?" he said.

"Stop, sir," said the commodore. "You must wait till this is explained."

"Must I?" said the man. "Who is there here that will keep me?"

"What can I say to you, sir?" cried Colonel Gerald, coming up and holding out his hand to the stranger. "I have no words to thank you."

"Well, as to that, General," said the man, "it seems to me the less that's said the better. Take my advice and get the lady something to drink—anything that teetotallers won't allow is safe to be wholesome."

"Come to my house," said the commodore. "Miss Gerald will find everything there."

"You bet you'll find something in the spirituous way at the admiral's quarters, miss," remarked the stranger, as Daireen was helped into the vehicle. "No, thank you, General, I'll walk to the hotel where I put up."

"Pray let me call upon you before I leave," said Colonel Gerald.

"Delighted to see you, General; if you come within the next two hours, I'll slip the tinsel off a bottle of Moët with you. Now, don't wait here. If you had got a pearly stream of salt water running down your spine you wouldn't wait; would they, miss? Aw revaw."

CHAPTER XXXVI

I shall, first asking your pardon thereunto, recount the occasion of my sudden and more strange return.

O limèd soul, that, struggling to be free,
Art more engaged.

Lord, we know what we are, but know not what we may be. —*Hamlet.*

QUITE three hours had passed before Colonel Gerald was able to return to the hotel. The stranger was sitting in the coffee-room with a tumbler and a square bottle of cognac in front of him as the colonel entered.

"Ah, General," cried the stranger, "you are come. I was sorry I said two hours, you know, because, firstly, I might have known that at the admiral's quarters the young lady would get as many doses as would make her fancy something was the matter with her; and, secondly, because I didn't think that they would take three hours to dry a suit of tweed like this. You see it, General; this blooming suit is a proof of the low state of morality that exists in this colony. The man I bought it from took an oath that it wouldn't shrink, and yet, just look at it. It's a wicked world this we live in, General. I went to bed while the suit was being dried, and I believe they kept the fire low so that they may charge me with the bed. And how is the young lady?"

"I am happy to say that she has quite recovered from the effects of her exhaustion and her wetting," said Colonel Gerald. "Had you not been near, and had you not had that brave heart you showed, my daughter would have been lost. But I need not say anything to you—you know how I feel."

"We may take it for granted," said the man.

"Nothing that either of us could say would make it plainer, at any rate. You don't live in this city, General?"

"No, I live near Cape Town, where I am now returning with my daughter," said Colonel Gerald.

"That's queer," said the man. "Here am I too not living here and just waiting to get the post-cart to bring me to Cape Town."

"I need scarcely say that I should be delighted if you would accept a seat with me," remarked the colonel.

"Don't say that if there's not a seat to spare, General."

"But, my dear sir, we have two seats to spare. Can I tell my man to put your portmanteau in?"

"Yes, if he can find it," laughed the stranger. "Fact is, General, I haven't any property here except this tweed suit two sizes too small for me now. But these trousers have got pockets, and the pockets hold a good many sovereigns without bursting. I mean to set up a portmanteau in Cape Town. Yes, I'll take a seat with you so far."

The stranger was scarcely the sort of man Colonel Gerald would have chosen to accompany him under ordinary circumstances, but now he felt towards the rough man who had saved the life of his daughter as he would towards a brother.

The wagonette drove round to the commodore's house for Daireen, and the stranger expressed very frankly the happiness he felt at finding her nothing the worse for her accident.

And indeed she did not seem to have suffered greatly; she was a little paler, and the commodore's people insisted on wrapping her up elaborately.

"It was so very foolish of me," she said to the stranger, when they had passed out of Simon's Town and were going rapidly along the road to Wynberg. "It was so very foolish indeed to sit down upon that rock and forget all about the tide. I must have been there an hour."

"Ah, miss," said the man, "I'll take my oath it wasn't of your pa you were thinking all that time. Ah, these young fellows have a lot to answer for."

This was not very subtle humour, Colonel Gerald felt; he found himself wishing that his daughter had owed her life to a more refined man; but on the whole he was just as glad that a man of sensitiveness had not been in the place of this coarse stranger upon that beach a few hours before.

"I don't think I am wrong in believing that you have travelled a good deal," said Colonel Gerald, in some anxiety lest the stranger might pursue his course of humorous banter.

"Travelled?" said the stranger. "Perhaps I have. Yes, sir, I have travelled, not excursionised. I've knocked about God's footstool since I was a boy, and yet it seems to me that I'm only beginning my travels. I've been——"

And the stranger continued telling of where he had been until the oak avenue at Mowbray was reached. He talked very freshly and frankly of every place both in the Northern and Southern hemispheres. The account of his travels was very interesting, though perhaps to the colonel's servant it was the most entertaining.

"I have taken it for granted that you have no engagement in Cape Town," said Colonel Gerald as he turned the horses down the avenue. "We shall be dining in a short time, and I hope you will join us."

"I don't want to intrude, General," said the man. "But I allow that I could dine heartily without going much farther. As for having an appointment in Cape Town—I don't know a single soul in the colony—not a soul, sir—unless—why, hang it all, who's that standing on the walk in front of us?—I'm a liar, General; I do know one man in the colony; there he stands, for if that isn't Oswin Markham I'll eat him with relish."

"It is indeed Markham," said Colonel Gerald. "And you know him?"

"Know him?" the stranger laughed. "Know him?" Then as the wagonette pulled up beside where Markham was standing in front of the house, the stranger leapt down, saying, as he clapped Oswin on the shoulder, "The General asks me if I know you, old boy; answer for me, will you?"

But Oswin Markham was staring blankly from the man to Daireen and her father.

"You told me you were going to New York," he said at last.

"And so I was when you packed me aboard the *Virginia* brig so neatly at Natal, but the *Virginia* brig put into Simon's Bay and cut her cable one night, leaving me ashore. It's Providence, Oswin—Providence."

Oswin had allowed his hand to be taken by the man, who was the same that had spent the night with him in the hotel at Pietermaritzburg. Then he turned as if from a fit of abstraction, to Daireen and the colonel.

"I beg your pardon a thousand times," he said. "But this meeting with Mr. Despard has quite startled me."

"Mr. Despard," said the colonel, "I must ever look on as one of my best friends, though we met to-day for the first time. I owe him a debt that I can never repay—my daughter's life."

Oswin turned and grasped the hand of the man whom he had called Mr. Despard, before they entered the house together.

Daireen went in just before Markham; they had not yet exchanged a sentence, but when her father and Despard had entered one of the rooms, she turned, saying:

"A month—a month yesterday."

"More," he answered; "it must be more."

The girl laughed low as she went on to her room. But when she found herself apart from every one, she did not laugh. She had her own preservation from death to reflect upon, but it occupied her mind less than the thought that came to her shaping itself into the words, "He has returned."

The man of whom she was thinking was standing pale and silent in a room where much conversation was floating, for Mr. Harwood had driven out with Markham from Cape Town, and he had a good deal to say on the Zulu question, which was beginning to be no question. The Macnamara had also come to pass the evening with Colonel Gerald, and he was not silent. Oswin watched Despard and the hereditary monarch speaking together, and he saw them shake hands. Harwood was in close conversation with Colonel Gerald, but he was not so utterly absorbed in his subject but that he could notice how Markham's eyes were fixed upon the stranger. The terms of a new problem were suggesting themselves to Mr. Harwood.

Then Daireen entered the room, and greeted Mr. Harwood courteously— much too courteously for his heart's desire. He did not feel so happy as he should have done, when she laughed pleasantly and reminded him of her prophecy as to his safe return. He felt as he had done on that morning when he had said good-bye to her: his time had not yet come. But what was delaying that hour he yearned for? She was now standing beside Markham, looking up to his face as she spoke to him. She was not smiling at him. What could these things mean? Harwood asked himself—Lottie Vincent's spiteful remark with reference to Daireen at the lunch that had taken place on the hillside in his absence—Oswin's remark about not being strong enough to leave the associations of Cape Town—this quiet meeting without smiles or any of the conventionalities of ordinary acquaintance—what did all these mean? Mr. Harwood felt that he had at last got before him the terms of a question the working out of which was more interesting to him than any other that could be propounded. And he knew also that this man Despard was an important auxiliary to its satisfactory solution.

"Dove of Glenmara, let me look upon your sweet face again, and say that you are not hurt," cried The Macnamara, taking the girl by both her hands and looking into her face. "Thank God you are left to be the pride of the old country. We are not here to weep over this new sorrow. What would life be worth to us if anything had happened to the pulse of our hearts? Glenmara would be desolate and Slieve Docas would sit in ashes."

The Macnamara pressed his lips to the girl's forehead as a condescending monarch embraces a favoured subject.

"Bravo, King! you'd make a fortune with that sort of sentiment on the boards; you would, by heavens!" said Mr. Despard with an unmodulated laugh.

The Macnamara seemed to take this testimony as a compliment, for he smiled, though the remark did not appear to strike any one else as being imbued with humour. Harwood looked at the man curiously; but Markham was gazing in another direction without any expression upon his face.

In the course of the evening the Bishop of the Calapash Islands dropped in. His lordship had taken a house in the neighbourhood for so long as he would be remaining in the colony; and since he had had that interview with Mrs. Crawford, his visits to his old friend Colonel Gerald were numerous and unconventional. He, too, smiled upon Dairecn in his very pleasantest manner, and after hearing from the colonel—who felt perhaps that some little explanation of the stranger's presence might be necessary—of Daireen's accident, the bishop spoke a few words to Mr. Despard and shook hands with him—an honour which Mr. Despard sustained without emotion.

In spite of these civilities, however, this evening was unlike any that the colonel's friends had spent at the cottage. The bishop only remained for about an hour, and Harwood and Markham soon afterwards took their departure.

"I'll take a seat with you, Oswin, my boy," said Despard. "We'll be at the same hotel in Cape Town, and we may as well all go together."

And they did all go together.

"Fine fellow, the colonel, isn't he?" remarked Despard, before they had got well out of the avenue. "I called him general on chance when I saw him for the first time to-day—you're never astray in beginning at general and working your way down, with these military nobs. And the bishop is a fine old boy too—rather too much palm-oil and glycerine about him, though—too smooth and shiny for my taste. I expect he does a handsome trade amongst the Salamanders. A smart bishop could make a fortune there, I know. And then the king—the Irish king as he calls himself—well, maybe he's the best of the lot."

There did not seem to be anything in Mr. Despard's opening speech that required an answer. There was a considerable pause before Harwood remarked quietly: "By the way, Mr. Despard, I think I saw you some time ago. I have a good recollection for faces."

"Did you?" said Despard. "Where was it? At 'Frisco or Fiji? South Carolina or South Australia?"

"I am not recalling the possibilities of such faraway memories," said Harwood. "But if I don't mistake, you were the person in the audience at Pietermaritzburg who made some remark complimentary to Markham."

The man laughed. "You are right, mister. I only wonder I didn't shout out something before, for I never was so taken aback as when I saw him come out as that Prince. A shabby trick it was you played on me the next morning, Oswin—I say it was infernally shabby. You know what he did, mister: when I had got to the outside of more than one bottle of Moët, and so wasn't very clear-headed, he packed me into one of the carts, drove me to Durban before daylight, and sent me aboard the *Virginia* brig that I had meant to leave. That wasn't like friendship, was it?"

But upon this delicate question Mr. Harwood did not think it prudent to deliver an opinion. Markham himself was mute, yet this did not seem to have a depressing effect upon Mr. Despard. He gave a *résumé* of the most important events in the voyage of the *Virginia* brig, and described very graphically how he had unfortunately become insensible to the fact that the vessel was leaving Simon's Bay on the previous morning; so that when he awoke, the *Virginia* brig was on her way to New York city, while he was on a sofa in the hotel surrounded by empty bottles.

When Markham was alone with this man in a room at the hotel at Cape Town, Despard became even more talkative.

"By heavens, Oswin," he said, "you have changed your company a bit since you were amongst us; generals, bishops, and kings—kings, by Jingo— seem to be your chums here. Well, don't you think that I don't believe you to be right. You were never of our sort in Australia—we all felt you to be above us, and treated you so—making a pigeon of you now and again, but never looking on ourselves as your equal. By heavens, I think now that I have got in with these people and seem to get on so well with them, I'll turn over a new leaf."

"Do you mean to stay here longer than this week?" asked Oswin.

"This week? I'll not leave for another month—another six months, maybe. I've money, my boy, and—suppose we have something to drink— something that will sparkle?"

"I don't mean to drink anything," Oswin replied.

"You must have something," Despard insisted. "You must admit that though the colonel is a glorious old boy, he didn't do the hospitable in the liquid way. But I'll keep in with the lot of them. I'll go out to see the colonel and his pretty daughter now and again. Ah, by George, that pretty daughter seems to have played the mischief with some of the young fellows about here. 'Sir,' says the king of Ireland to me, 'I fale more than I can till ye: the swate girl ye saved is to be me sonn's broide.' This looked well enough for the king, and we got very great friends, as you saw. But then the bishop comes up to me and, says he, 'Sir, allow me to shake you by the hand. You do not know how I feel towards that young lady who owes her life to your bravery.' I looked at him seriously: 'Bishop,' said I, 'I can't encourage this sort of thing. You might be her father.' Well, my boy, you never saw anything so flustered as that bishop became; it was more than a minute before he could tell me that it was his son who had the tender heart about the girl. That bishop didn't ask me to dine with him; though the king did, and I'm going out to him to-morrow evening."

"You are going to him?" said Markham.

"To be sure I am. He agreed with me about the colonel's hospitality in the drink way. 'You'll find it different in my house,' said the king; and I think you know, Oswin, that the king and me have one point in common."

"Good-night," said Markham, going to the door. "No, I told you I did not mean to drink anything."

He left Mr. Despard on the sofa smoking the first of a box of cigars he had just ordered.

"He's changed—that boy is," said Despard. "He wouldn't have gone out in that fashion six months ago. But what the deuce has changed him? that's what I'd like to know. He wants to get me away from here—that's plain—plain? by George, it's ugly. But here I am settled for a few months at least if—hang that waiter, is he never going to bring me that bottle of old Irish?"

CHAPTER XXXVII

Why, look you now, how unworthy a thing you make of me! You would play upon me; you would seem to know my stops; you would pluck out the heart of my mystery; you would sound me from my lowest note to the top of my compass....'S blood, do you think I am easier to be played on than a pipe? Call me what instrument you will, though you can fret me, yet you cannot play upon me. — *Hamlet*.

OSWIN Markham sat in his own room in the hotel. The window was open, and through it from the street below came the usual sounds of Cape Town — terrible Dutch mingling with Malay and dashed with Kafir. It was not the intensity of a desire to listen to this polyglot mixture that caused Markham to go upon the balcony and stand looking out to the night.

He reflected upon what had passed since he had been in this place a month before. He had gone up to Natal, and in company of Harwood he had had a brief hunting expedition. He had followed the spoor of the gemsbok over veldt and through kloof, sleeping in the house of the hospitable boers when chance offered; but all the time he had been possessed of one supreme thought — one supreme hope that made his life seem a joyous thing — he had looked forward to this day — the day when he would have returned, when he would again be able to look into the face that moved like a phantom before him wherever he went. And he had returned — for this — this looking, not into her face, but into the street below him, while he thought if it would not be better for him to step out beyond the balcony — out into the blank that would follow his casting of himself down.

He came to the conclusion that it would not be better to step beyond the balcony. A thought seemed to strike him as he stood out there. He returned to his chamber and threw himself on his bed, but he did not remain passive for long; once more he stepped into the air, and now he had need to wipe his forehead with his handkerchief.

It was an hour afterwards that he undressed himself; but the bugle at the barracks had sounded a good many times before he fell asleep.

Mr. Harwood, too, had an hour of reflection when he went to his room; but his thoughts were hardly of the excitable type of Markham's; they had, however, a definite result, which caused him to seek out Mr. Despard in the morning.

Mr. Despard had just finished a light and salutary breakfast consisting of a glass of French brandy in a bottle of soda-water, and he was smoking another sample of that box of cigars on the balcony.

"Good-morning to you, mister," he said, nodding as Harwood came, as if by chance, beside him.

"Ah, how do you do?" said Harwood. "Enjoying your morning smoke, I see. Well, I hope you are nothing the worse for your plunge yesterday."

"No, sir, nothing; I only hope that Missy out there will be as sound. I don't think they insisted on her drinking enough afterwards."

"Ah, perhaps not. Your friend Markham has not come down yet, they tell me."

"He was never given to running ties with the sun," said Mr. Despard.

"He told me you were a particular friend of his in Australia?" continued Mr. Harwood.

"Yes, men very soon get to be friends out there; but Oswin and myself were closer than brothers in every row and every lark."

"Of which you had, no doubt, a good many?

"A good few, yes; a few that wouldn't do to be printed specially as prizes for young ladies' boarding-schools—not but what the young ladies would read them if they got the chance."

"Few fellows would care to write their autobiographies and go into the details of their life," said Harwood. "I suppose you got into trouble now and again?"

"Trouble? Well, yes, when the money ran short, and there was no balance at the bank; that's real trouble, let me tell you."

"It certainly is; but I mean, did you not sometimes need the friendly offices of a lawyer after a wild few days?"

"Sir," said Despard, throwing away the end of his cigar, "if your idea of a wild few days is housebreaking or manslaughter, it wasn't ours, I can tell you. No, my boy, we never took to bushranging; and though I've had my turn with Derringer's small cannons when I was at Chokeneck Gulch, it was only because it was the custom of the country. No, sir; Oswin, though he seems to have turned against me here, will still have my good word, for I swear to you he never did anything that made the place too hot for him, though I don't suppose that if he was in a competitive examination for a bishopric the true account of his life in Melbourne would help him greatly."

"There are none of us here who mean to be bishops," laughed Harwood. "But I understood from a few words Markham let fall that—well, never mind, he is a right good fellow, as I found when we went up country together a couple of weeks ago. By the way, do you mean to remain here long, Mr. Despard?"

"Life is short, mister, and I've learned never to make arrangements very far in advance. I've about eighty sovereigns with me, and I'll stay here till they're spent."

"Then your stay will be proportionate to your spending powers."

"In an inverse ratio, as they used to say at school," said Despard.

When Mr. Harwood went into the room he reflected that on the whole he had not gained much information from Mr. Despard; and Mr. Despard reflected that on the whole Mr. Harwood had not got much information by his system of leading questions.

About half an hour afterwards Markham came out upon the balcony, and gave a little unaccountable start on seeing its sole occupant.

"Hallo, my boy! have you turned up at last?" cried Despard. "Our good old Calapash friend will tell you that unless you get up with the lark you'll never do anything in the world. You should have been here a short time ago to witness the hydraulic experiments."

"The what?" said Markham.

"Hydraulic experiments. The patent pump of the *Dominant Trumpeter* was being tested upon me. Experiments failed, not through any incapacity of the pump, but through the contents of the reservoir worked upon not running free enough in the right direction."

"Was Mr. Harwood here?"

"He was, my boy. And he wanted to know all about how we lived in Melbourne."

"And you told him——"

"To get up a little earlier in the morning when he wants to try his pumping apparatus. But what made you give that start? Don't you know that all I could tell would be some of our old larks, and he wouldn't have thought anything the worse of you on account of them? Hang it all, you don't mean to say you're going into holy orders, that you mind having any of the old times brought back? If you do, I'm afraid that it will be awkward for you if I talk in my ordinary way. I won't bind myself not to tell as many of our larks as chime in with the general conversation. I only object on principle to be pumped."

"Talk away," said Oswin spasmodically. "Tell of all our larks. How could I be affected by anything you may tell of them?"

"Bravo! That's what I say. Larks are larks. There was no manslaughter nor murder. No, there was no murder."

"No, there was no murder," said Markham.

The other burst into a laugh that startled a Malay in the street below.

"By heavens, from the way you said that one would fancy there had been a murder," he cried.

Then there was a long pause, which was broken by Markham.

"You still intend to go out to dine with that man you met yesterday?" he said.

"Don't call him a man, Oswin; you wouldn't call a bishop a man, and why call a king one. Yes, I have ordered a horse that is said to know the way across those Flats without a pocket compass."

"Where did you say the house was?"

"It's near a place called Rondebosch. I remember the locality well, though it's ten years since I was there. The shortest way back is through a pine-wood at the far end of The Flats—you know that place, of course."

"I know The Flats. And you mean to come through the pine-wood?"

"I do mean it. It's a nasty place to ride through, but the horse always goes right in a case like that, and I'll give him his head."

"Take care that you have your own at that time," said Markham. "The house of the Irishman is not like Colonel Gerald's."

"I hope not, for a more thirsty evening I never spent than at your friend's cottage. The good society hardly made up for the want of drink. It put me in mind of the story of the man that found the pearls when he was starving in the desert. What are bishops and kings to a fellow if he is thirsty?"

"You will leave the house to return here between eleven and twelve, I suppose?" said Oswin.

"Well, I should say that about eleven will see me on my way."

"And you will go through the pine-wood?"

"I will, my boy, and across The Flats until I pass the little river—it's there still, I suppose. And now suppose I buy you a drink?"

But Oswin Markham declined to be the object of such a purchase. He went back to his own room, and threw himself on his bed, where he remained for more than an hour. Then he rose and wiped his forehead.

He pulled down some books that he had bought, and tried to read bits of one or two. He sat diligently down as if he meant to go through a day's reading, but he did not appear to be in the mood for applying himself to anything. He threw the books aside and turned over some newspapers; but these did not seem to engross him any more than the books had done. He lay back in his chair, and after a while his restlessness subsided: he had fallen asleep.

It was the afternoon before he awoke with a sudden start. He heard the sound of voices in the street below his window. He went forward, and, looking out, was just in time to see Harry Despard mounting his horse at the hotel door.

"I will be back about midnight," he said to the porter of the hotel, and then he trotted off.

Markham heard the sound of the horse's hoofs die away on the street, and he repeated the man's words: "About midnight."

CHAPTER XXXVIII

To desperation turn my trust and hope.

What if this cursed hand
Were thicker than itself with brother's blood,
Is there not rain enough in the sweet heavens
To wash it white as snow?

I'll have prepared him
A chalice for the nonce whereon but sipping
... he...
Chaunted snatches of old tunes,
As one incapable.

The drink—the drink—... the foul practice
Hath turned itself on me; lo, here I lie...
I can no more: the King—the King's to blame.—*Hamlet*.

OSWIN Markham dined at the hotel late in the evening, and when he was in the act Harwood came into the room dressed for a dinner-party at Greenpoint to which he had been invited.

"Your friend Mr. Despard is not here?" said Harwood, looking around the room. "I wanted to see him for a moment to give him a few words of advice that may be useful to him. I wish to goodness you would speak to him, Markham; he has been swaggering about in a senseless way, talking of having his pockets full of sovereigns, and in the hearing of every stranger that comes into the hotel. In the bar a few hours ago he repeated his boast to the Malay who brought him his horse. Now, for Heaven's sake, tell him that unless he wishes particularly to have a bullet in his head or a khris in his body some of these nights, he had better hold his tongue about his wealth— that is what I meant to say to him."

"And you are right," cried Oswin, starting up suddenly. "He has been talking in the hearing of men who would do anything for the sake of a few sovereigns. What more likely than that some of them should follow him and knock him down? That will be his end, Harwood."

"It need not be," replied Harwood. "If you caution him, he will most likely regard what you say to him."

"I will caution him—if I see him again," said Markham; then Harwood left the room, and Markham sat down again, but he did not continue his dinner. He sat there staring at his plate. "What more likely?" he muttered. "What more likely than that he should be followed and murdered by some of these men? If his body should be found with his pockets empty, no one could doubt it."

He sat there for a considerable time—until the streets had become dark; then he rose and went up to his own room for a while, and finally he put on his hat and left the hotel.

He looked at his watch as he walked to the railway station, and saw that he would be just in time to catch a train leaving for Wynberg. He took a ticket for the station on the Cape Town side of Mowbray, where he got out.

He walked from the station to the road and again looked at his watch: it was not yet nine o'clock; and then he strolled aside upon a little foot-track that led up the lower slopes of the Peak above Mowbray. The night was silent and moonless. Upon the road only at intervals came the rumbling of bullock wagons and the shouts of the Kafir drivers. The hill above him was sombre and untouched by any glance of light, and no breeze stirred up the scents of the heath. He walked on in the silence until he had come to the ravine of silver firs. He passed along the track at the edge and was soon at the spot where he had sat at the feet of Daireen a month before. He threw himself down on the short coarse grass just as he had done then, and every moment of the hour they had passed together came back to him. Every word that had been spoken, every thought that had expressed itself upon that lovely face which the delicate sunset light had touched—all returned to him.

What had he said to her? That the past life he had lived was blotted out from his mind? Yes, he had tried to make himself believe that; but now how Fate had mocked him! He had been bitterly forced to acknowledge that the past was a part of the present. His week so full of bitterest suffering had not formed a dividing line between the two lives he fancied might be his.

"Is this the justice of God?" he cried out now to the stars, clasping his hands in agony above his head. "It is unjust. My life would have been pure and good now, if I had been granted my right of forgetfulness. But I have been made the plaything of God." He stood with his hands clasped on his head for long. Then he gave a laugh. "Bah!" he said; "man is master of his fate. I shall do myself the justice that God has denied me."

He came down from that solemn mount, and crossed he road at a nearer point than the Mowbray avenue.

He soon found himself by the brink of that little river which flowed past Rondebosch and Mowbray. He got beneath the trees that bordered its banks, and stood for a long time in the dead silence of the night. The mighty dog-lilies were like pictures beneath him; and only now and again came some of those mysterious sounds of night—the rustling of certain leaves when all the remainder were motionless, the winnowing of the wings of some night creature whose form remained invisible, the sudden stirring of ripples upon the river without a cause being apparent—the man standing there heard all, and all appeared mysterious to him. He wondered how he could have so often been by night in places like this, without noticing how mysterious the silence was—how mysterious the strange sounds.

He walked along by the bank of the slow river, until he was just opposite Mowbray. A little bridge with rustic rails was, he knew, at hand, by which he would cross the stream—for he must cross it. But before he had reached it, he heard a sound. He paused. Could it be possible that it was the sound of a horse's hoofs? There he waited until something white passed from under the trees and reached the bridge, standing between him and the other side of the river—something that barred his way. He leant against the tree nearest to him, for he seemed to be falling to the ground, and then through the stillness of the night the voice of Daireen came singing a snatch of song—his song. She was on the little bridge and leaning upon the rail. In a few moments she stood upright, and listlessly walked under the trees where he was standing, though she could not see him.

"Daireen," he said gently, so that she might not be startled; and she was not startled, she only walked backwards a few steps until she was again at the bridge.

"Did any one speak?" she said almost in a whisper. And then he stood before her while she laughed with happiness.

"Why do you stand there?" he said in a tone of wonder. "What was it sent you to stand there between me and the other side of that river?"

"I said to papa that I would wait for him here. He went to see Major Crawford part of the way to the house where the Crawfords are staying; but what can be keeping him from returning I don't know. I promised not to go farther than the avenue, and I have just been here a minute."

He looked at her standing there before him. "Oh God! oh God!" he said, as he reflected upon what his own thoughts had been a moment before. "Daireen, you are an angel of God—that angel which stood between the living and the dead. Stay near me. Oh, child! what do I not owe to you? my life—the peace of my soul for ever and ever. And yet—must we speak no word of love together, Daireen?"

"Not one—here," she said. "Not one—only—ah, my love, my love, why should we speak of it? It is all my life—I breathe it—I think it—it is myself."

He looked at her and laughed. "This moment is ours," he said with tremulous passion. "God cannot pluck it from us. It is an immortal moment, if our souls are immortal. Child, can God take you away from me before I have kissed you on the mouth?" He held her face between his hands and kissed her. "Darling, I have taken your white soul into mine," he said.

Then they stood apart on that bridge.

"And now," she said, "you must never frighten me with your strange words again. I do not know what you mean sometimes, but then that is because I don't know very much. I feel that you are good and true, and I have trusted you."

"I will be true to you," he said gently. "I will die loving you better than any hope man has of heaven. Daireen, never dream, whatever may happen, that I shall not love you while my soul lives."

"I will believe you," she said; and then voices were heard coming down the lane of aloes at the other side of the river—voices and the sound of a horse's hoofs. Colonel Gerald and Major Crawford were coming along leading a horse, across whose saddle lay a black mass. Oswin Markham gave a start. Then Daireen's father hastened forward to where she was standing.

"Child," he said quickly, "go back—go back to the house. I will come to you in a few minutes."

"What is the matter, papa?" she asked. "No one is hurt?—Major Crawford is not hurt?"

"No, no, he is here; but go, Daireen—go at once."

She turned and went up the avenue without a word. But she saw that Oswin was not looking at her—that he was grasping the rail of the bridge while he gazed to where the horse with its burden stood a few yards away among the aloes.

"I am glad you chance to be here, Markham," said Colonel Gerald hurriedly. "Something has happened—that man Despard——"

"Not dead—not murdered!" gasped Oswin, clutching the rail with both hands.

"Murdered? no; how could he be murdered? he must have fallen from his horse among the trees."

"And he is dead—he is dead?"

"Calm yourself, Markham," said the colonel; "he is not dead."

"Not in that sense, my boy," laughed Major Crawford. "By gad, if we could leave the brute up to the neck in the river here for a few hours I fancy he would be treated properly. Hold him steady, Markham."

Oswin put his hand mechanically to the feet of the man who was lying helplessly across the saddle.

"Not dead, not dead," he whispered.

"Only dead drunk, unless his skull is fractured, my boy," laughed the major. "We'll take him to the stables, of course, George?"

"No, no, to the house," said Colonel Gerald.

"Run on and get the key of the stables, George," said the major authoritatively. "Don't you suppose in any way that your house is to be turned into an hospital for dipsomaniacs. Think of the child."

Colonel Gerald made a little pause, and then hastened forward to awaken the groom to get the key of the stables, which were some distance from the cottage.

"By gad, Markham, I'd like to spill the brute into that pond," whispered the major to Oswin, as they waited for the colonel's return.

"How did you find him? Did you see any accident?" asked Oswin.

"We met the horse trotting quietly along the avenue without a rider, and when we went on among the trees we found the fellow lying helpless. George said he was killed, but I knew better. Irish whisky, my boy, was what brought him down, and you will find that I am right."

They let the man slide from the saddle upon a heap of straw when the stable door was opened by the half-dressed groom.

"Not dead, Jack?" said Colonel Gerald as a lantern was held to the man's face. Only the major was looking at the man; Markham could not trust himself even to glance towards him.

"Dead?" said the major. "Why, since we have laid him down I have heard him frame three distinct oaths. Have you a bucket of water handy, my good man? No, it needn't be particularly clean. Ah, that will do. Now, if you don't hear a choice selection of colonial blasphemy, he's dead and, by gad, sir, so am I."

The major's extensive experience of the treatment of colonial complaints had, as the result proved, led him to form a correct if somewhat hasty diagnosis of the present case. Not more than a gallon of the water had been thrown upon the man before he recovered sufficient consciousness to allow of his expressing himself with freedom on the subject of his treatment.

"I told you so," chuckled the major. "Fill the bucket again, my man."

Colonel Gerald could only laugh now that his fears had been dispelled. He hastened to the house to tell Daireen that there was no cause for alarm.

By the time the second bucketful had been applied, in pursuance of the major's artless system of resuscitation, Despard was sitting up talking of the oppressions under which a certain nation was groaning. He was sympathetic and humorous in turn; weeping after particular broken sentences, and chuckling with laughter after other parts of his speech.

"The Irish eloquence and the Irish whisky have run neck and neck for the fellow's soul," said the major. "If we hadn't picked him up he would be in a different state now. Are you going back to Cape Town to-night, Markham?"

"I am," said Oswin.

"That's lucky. You mustn't let George have his way in this matter. This brute would stay in the cottage up there for a month."

"He must not do that," cried Markham eagerly.

"No, my boy; so you will drive with him in the Cape cart to the hotel. He will give you no trouble if you lay him across the floor and keep your feet well down upon his chest. Put one of the horses in, my man," continued the major, turning to the groom. "You will drive in with Mr. Markham, and bring the cart back."

Before Colonel Gerald had returned from the house a horse was harnessed to the Cape cart, Despard had been lifted up and placed in an easy attitude against one of the seats. And only a feeble protest was offered by the colonel.

"My dear Markham," he said, "it was very lucky you were passing where my daughter saw you. You know this man Despard—how could I have him in my house?"

"In your house!" cried Markham. "Thank God I was here to prevent that."

The Cape cart was already upon the avenue and the lamps were lighted. But a little qualm seemed to come to the colonel.

"Are you sure he is not injured—that he has quite recovered from any possible effects?" he said.

Then came the husky voice of the man.

"Go'night, king, go'night. I'm alright—horse know's way. We're tram'led on, king—'pressed people—but wormil turn—wormil turn—never mind—Go save Ireland—green flag litters o'er us—tread th' land that bore us—go'night."

The cart was in motion before the man's words had ceased.

CHAPTER XXXIX

Look you lay home to him:
Tell him his pranks have been too broad to bear with.

What to ourselves in passion we propose,
The passion ending, doth the purpose lose.

I must leave thee, love...
And thou shalt live in this fair world behind,
Honour'd, belov'd, and haply one as kind
For husband shalt thou—

Both here and hence pursue me lasting strife. —*Hamlet*.

OSWIN Markham lay awake nearly all that night after he had reached the hotel. His thoughts were not of that even nature whose proper sequence is sleep. He thought of all that had passed since he had left the room he was lying in now. What had been on his mind on leaving this room—what had his determination been?

"For her," he said; "for her. It would have been for her. God keep me— God pity me!"

The morning came with the sound of marching soldiers in the street below; with the cry of bullock-wagon-drivers and the rattle of the rude carts; with the morning and the sounds of life—the breaking of the deadly silence of the night—sleep came to the man.

It was almost midday before he awoke, and for some time after opening his eyes he was powerless to recollect anything that had happened during the night; his awakening now was as his return to consciousness on board the *Cardwell Castle,*—a great blank seemed to have taken place in his life— the time of unconsciousness was a gulf that all his efforts of memory could not at first bridge.

He looked around the room, and his first consciousness was the recollection of what his thoughts of the previous evening had been when he had slept in the chair before the window and had awakened to see Despard ride away. He failed at once to remember anything of the interval of night; only with that one recollection burning on his brain he looked at his right hand.

In a short time he remembered everything. He knew that Despard was in the hotel. He dressed himself and went downstairs, and found Harwood in the coffee-room, reading sundry documents with as anxious an expression of countenance as a special correspondent ever allows himself to assume.

"What is the news?" Markham asked, feeling certain that something unusual had either taken place or was seen by the prophetical vision of Harwood to be looming in the future.

"War," said Harwood, looking up. "War, Markham. I should never have left Natal. They have been working up to the point for the last few months, as I saw; but now there is no hope for a peaceful settlement."

"The Zulu chief is not likely to come to terms now?" said Markham.

"Impossible," replied the other. "Quite impossible. In a few days there will, no doubt, be a call for volunteers."

"For volunteers?" Markham repeated. "You will go up country at once, I suppose?" he added.

"Not quite as a volunteer, but as soon as I receive my letters by the mail that arrives in a few days, I shall be off to Durban, at any rate."

"And you will be glad of it, no doubt. You told me you liked doing war-correspondence."

"Did I?" said Harwood; and after a little pause he added slowly: "It's a tiring life this I have been leading for the past fifteen years, Markham. I seem to have cut myself off from the sympathies of life. I seem to have been only a looker-on in the great struggles—the great pleasures—of life. I am supposed to have no more sympathies than Babbage's calculator that records certain facts without emotion, and I fancied I had schooled myself into this cold apathy in looking at things; but I don't think I have succeeded in cutting myself off from all sympathies. No, I shall not be glad of this war. Never mind. By the way, are you going out to Dr. Glaston's to-night?"

"I have got a card for his dinner, but I cannot tell what I may do. I am not feeling myself, just now."

"You certainly don't look yourself, Markham. You are haggard, and as pale as if you had not got any sleep for nights. You want the constitution of your friend Mr. Despard, who is breakfasting in the bar."

"What, is it possible he is out of his room?" cried Markham, in surprise.

"Why, he was waiting here an hour ago when I came down, and in the meantime he had been buying a suit of garments, he said, that gallant check of his having come to grief through the night."

Harwood spoke the words at the door and then he left the room.

Oswin was not for long left in solitary occupation, however, for in a few moments the door was flung open, and Despard entered with a half-empty tumbler in his hand. He came forward with a little chuckling laugh and stood in front of Oswin without speaking. He looked with his blood-shot eyes into Oswin's cold pale face, and then burst into a laugh so hearty that he was compelled to leave the tumbler upon the table, not having sufficient confidence in his ability to grasp it under the influence of his excitement. Then he tapped Markham on the shoulder, crying:

"Well, old boy, have you got over that lark of last night? Like the old times, wasn't it? You did the fatherly by me, I believe, though hang me if I remember what happened after I had drunk the last glass of old Irish with our friend the king. How the deuce did I get in with the teetotal colonel who, the boots has been telling me, lent me his cart? That's what I should like to know. And where were you, my boy, all the night?"

"Despard," said Markham, "I have borne with your brutal insults long enough. I will not bear them any longer. When you have so disgraced both yourself and me as you did last night, it is time to bring matters to a climax. I cannot submit to have you thrust yourself upon my friends as you have done. You behaved like a brute."

Despard seated himself and wiped his eyes. "I did behave like a brute," he said. "I always do, I know—and you know too, Oswin. Never mind. Tell me what you want—what am I to do?"

"You must leave the colony," said Oswin quickly, almost eagerly. "I will give you money, and a ticket to England to-day. You must leave this place at once."

"And so I will—so I will," said the man from behind his handkerchief. "Yes, yes, Oswin, I'll leave the colony—I will—when I become a teetotaller." He took down his handkerchief, and put it into his pocket with a hoarse laugh. "Come, my boy," he said in his usual voice, "come; we've had quite enough of that sort of bullying. Don't think you're talking to a boy, Master Oswin. Who looks on a man as anything the worse for getting drunk now and again? You don't; you can't afford to. How often have I not helped you as you helped me? Tell me that."

"In the past—the accursed past," said Oswin, "I may have made myself a fool—yes, I did, but God knows that I have suffered for it. Now all is changed. I was willing to tolerate you near me since we met this time, hoping that you would think fit, when you were in a new place and amongst new people, to change your way of life. But last night showed me that I was mistaken. You can never be received at Colonel Gerald's again."

"Indeed?" said the man. "You should break the news gently to a fellow. You might have thrown me into a fit by coming down like that. Hark you here, Mr. Markham. I know jolly well that I will be received there and welcomed too. I'll be received everywhere as well as you, and hang me, if I don't go everywhere. These people are my friends as well as yours. I've done more for them than ever you did, and they know that."

"Fool, fool!" said Oswin bitterly.

"We'll see who's the fool, my boy. I know my advantage, don't you be afraid. The Irish king has a son, hasn't he? well, I was welcome with him last night. The Lord Bishop of Calapash has another blooming male offspring, and though he hasn't given me an invite to his dinner this evening, yet, hang me, if he wouldn't hug me if I went with the rest of you swells. Hang me, if I don't try it at any rate—it will be a lark at least. Dine with a bishop— by heaven, sir, it would be a joke—I'll go, oh, Lord, Lord!" Oswin stood motionless looking at him. "Yes," continued Despard, "I'll have a jolly hour with his lordship the bishop. I'll fill up my glass as I did last night, and we'll drink the same toast together—we'll drink to the health of the Snowdrop of Glenmara, as the king called her when he was very drunk; we'll drink to the fair Daireen. Hallo, keep your hands off!—Curse you, you're choking me! There!" Oswin, before the girl's name had more than passed the man's lips, had sprung forward and clutched him by the throat; only by a violent effort was he cast off, and now both men stood trembling with passion face to face.

"What the deuce do you mean by this sort of treatment?" cried Despard.

"Despard," said Oswin slowly, "you know me a little, I think. I tell you if you ever speak that name again in my presence you will repent it. You know me from past experience, and I have not utterly changed."

The man looked at him with an expression that amounted to wonderment upon his face. Then he threw himself back in his chair, and an uncontrollable fit of laughter seized him. He lay back and almost yelled with his insane laughter. When he had recovered himself and had wiped the tears from his eyes, he saw Oswin was gone. And this fact threw him into another convulsive fit. It was a long time before he was able to straighten his collar and go to the bar for a glass of French brandy.

The last half-hour had made Oswin Markham very pale. He had eaten no breakfast, and he was reminded of this by the servant to whom he had given directions to have his horse brought to the door.

"No," he said, "I have not eaten anything. Get the horse brought round quickly, like a good fellow."

He stood erect in the doorway until he heard the sound of hoofs. Then he went down the steps and mounted, turning his horse's head towards Wynberg. He galloped along the red road at the base of the hill, and only once he looked up, saying, "For the last time—the last."

He reached the avenue at Mowbray and dismounted, throwing the bridle over his arm as he walked slowly between the rows of giant aloes. In another moment he came in sight of the Dutch cottage. He paused under one of the Australian oaks, and looked towards the house. "Oh, God, God, pity me!" he cried in agony so intense that it could not relieve itself by any movement or the least motion.

He threw the bridle over a low branch and walked up to the house. His step was heard. She stood before him in the hall—white and flushed in turn as he went towards her. He was not flushed; he was still deadly white. He had startled her, he knew, for the hand she gave him was trembling like a dove's bosom.

"Papa is gone part of the way back to Simon's Town with the commodore who was with us this morning," she said. "But you will come in and wait, will you not?"

"I cannot," he said. "I cannot trust myself to go in—even to look at you, Daireen."

"Oh, God!" she said, "you are ill—your face—your voice— —"

"I am not ill, Daireen. I have an hour of strength—such strength as is given to men when they look at Death in the face and are not moved at all. I kissed you last night— —"

"And you will now," she said, clasping his arm tenderly. "Dearest, do not speak so terribly—do not look so terrible—so like—ah, that night when you looked up to me from the water."

"Daireen, why did I do that? Why did you pluck me from that death to give me this agony of life—to give yourself all the bitterness that can come to any soul? Daireen, I kissed you only once, and I can never kiss you again. I cannot be false to you any longer after having touched your pure spirit. I have been false to you—false, not by my will—but because to me God denied what He gave to others—others to whom His gift was an agony—

that divine power to begin life anew. My past still clings to me, Daireen—it is not past—it is about and around me still—it is the gulf that separates us, Daireen."

"Separates us?" she said blankly, looking at him.

"Separates us," he repeated, "as heaven and hell are separated. We have been the toys—the playthings, of Fate. If you had not looked out of your cabin that night, we should both be happy now. And then how was it we came to love each other and to know it to be love? I struggled against it, but I was as a feather upon the wind. Ah, God has given us this agony of love, for I am here to look on you for the last time—to beseech of you to hate me, and to go away knowing that you love me."

"No, no, not to go away—anything but that. Tell me all—I can forgive all."

"I cannot bring my lips to frame my curse," he said after a little pause. "But you shall hear it, and, Daireen, pity me as you pitied me when I looked to God for hope and found none. Child—give me your eyes for the last time."

She held him clasped with her white hands, and he saw that her passion made her incapable of understanding his words. She looked up to him whispering, "The last time—no, no—not the last time—not the last."

She was in his arms. He looked down upon her face, but he did not kiss it. He clenched his teeth as he unwound her arms from him.

"One word may undo the curse that I have bound about your life," he said. "Take the word, Daireen—the blessed word for you and me—*Forget*. Take it—it is my last blessing."

She was standing before him. She saw his face there, and she gave a cry, covering her own face with her hands, for the face she saw was that which had looked up to her from the black waters.

Was he gone?

From the river bank came the sounds of the native women, from the garden the hum of insects, and from the road the echo of a horse's hoofs passing gradually away.

Was it a dream—not only this scene of broad motionless leaves, and these sounds she heard, but all the past months of her life?

Hours went by leaving her motionless in that seat, and then came the sound of a horse—she sprang up. He was returning—it was a dream that had given her this agony of parting.

"Daireen, child, what is the matter?" asked her father, whose horse it was she had heard.

She looked up to his face.

"Papa," she said very gently, "it is over—all—all over—for ever—I have only you now."

"My dear little Dolly, tell me all that troubles you."

"Nothing troubles me now, papa. I have you near me, and I do not mind anything else."

"Tell me all, Daireen."

"I thought I loved some one else, papa—Oswin—Oswin Markham. But he is gone now, and I know you are with me. You will always be with me."

"My poor little Dolly," said Colonel Gerald, "did he tell you that he loved you?"

"He did, papa; but you must ask me no more. I shall never see him again!"

"Perfectly charming!" said Mrs. Crawford, standing at the door. "The prettiest picture I have seen for a long time—father and daughter in each other's arms. But, my dear George, are you not yet dressed for the bishop's dinner? Daireen, my child, did you not say you would be ready when I would call for you? I am quite disappointed, and I would be angry only you look perfectly lovely this evening—like a beautiful lily. The dear bishop will be so charmed, for you are one of his favourites. Now do make haste, and I entreat of you to be particular with your shades of gray."

CHAPTER XL

... A list of... resolutes
For food and diet, to some enterprise
That hath a stomach in't.

My news shall be the fruit to that great feast.

Why, let the stricken deer go weep,
The hart ungallèd play;
For some must watch, while some must sleep;
Thus runs the world away.—*Hamlet.*

THE Bishop of the Calapash Islands and Metropolitan of the Salamander Archipelago was smiling very tranquilly upon his guests as they arrived at his house, which was about two miles from Mowbray. But the son of the bishop was not smiling—he, in fact, seldom smiled; there was a certain breadth of expression associated with such a manifestation of feeling that was inconsistent with his ideas of subtlety of suggestion. He was now endeavouring to place his father's guests at ease by looking only slightly bored by their presence, giving them to understand that he would endure them around him for his father's sake, so that there should be no need for them to be at all anxious on his account. A dinnerparty in a colony was hardly that sort of social demonstration which Mr. Glaston would be inclined to look forward to with any intensity of feeling; but the bishop, having a number of friends at the Cape, including a lady who was capable of imparting some very excellent advice on many social matters, had felt it to be a necessity to give this little dinnerparty, and his son had only offered such a protest against it as satisfied his own conscience and prevented the possibility of his being consumed for days after with a gnawing remorse.

The bishop had his own ideas of entertaining his guests—a matter which his son brought under his consideration after the invitations had been issued.

"There is not such a thing as a rising tenor in the colony, I am sure," said Mr. Glaston, whose experience of perfect social entertainment was limited to that afforded by London drawing-rooms. "If we had a rising tenor, there would be no difficulty about these people."

"Ah, no, I suppose not," said the bishop. "But I was thinking, Algernon, that if you would allow your pictures to be hung for the evening, and explain them, you know, it would be interesting."

"What, by lamplight? They are not drop-scenes of a theatre, let me remind you."

"No, no; but you see your theories of explanation would be understood by our good friends as well by lamplight as by daylight, and I am sure every one would be greatly interested." Mr. Glaston promised his father to think over the matter, and his father expressed his gratitude for this concession. "And as for myself," continued the bishop, giving his hands the least little rub together, "I would suggest reading a few notes on a most important subject, to which I have devoted some attention lately. My notes I would propose heading 'Observations on Phenomena of Automatic Cerebration amongst some of the Cannibal Tribes of the Salamander Archipelago.' I have some excellent specimens of skulls illustrative of the subject."

Mr. Glaston looked at his father for a considerable time without speaking; at last he said quietly, "I think I had better show my pictures."

"And my paper—my notes?"

"Impossible," said the young man, rising. "Utterly Impossible;" and he left the room.

The bishop felt slightly hurt by his son's manner. He had treasured up his notes on the important observations he had made in an interesting part of his diocese, and he had looked forward with anxiety to a moment when he could reveal the result of his labours to the world, and yet his son had, when the opportunity presented itself, declared the revelation impossible. The bishop felt slightly hurt.

Now, however, he had got over his grievance, and he was able to smile as usual upon each of his guests.

The dinner-party was small and select. There were two judges present, one of whom brought his wife and a daughter. Then there were two members of the Legislative Council, one with a son, the other with a daughter; a clergyman who had attained to the dizzy ecclesiastical eminence of a colonial deanery, and his partner in the dignity of his office. The Macnamara and Standish were there, and Mr. Harwood, together with the Army Boot Commissioner and Mrs. Crawford, the last of whom arrived with Colonel Gerald and Daireen.

Mrs. Crawford had been right. The bishop was charmed with Daireen, and so expressed himself while he took her hand in his and gave her the benediction of a smile. Poor Standish, seeing her so lovely as she was standing there, felt his soul full of love and devotion. What was all the rest of the world compared with her, he thought; the aggregate beauty of the universe, including the loveliness of the Miss Van der Veldt who was in the drawing-room, was insignificant by the side of a single curl of Daireen's wonderful hair. Mr. Harwood looked towards her also, but his thoughts were somewhat more complicated than those of Standish.

"Is not Daireen perfection?" whispered Mrs. Crawford to Algernon Glaston.

The bishop's son glanced at the girl critically.

"I cannot understand that band of black velvet with a pearl in front of it," he said. "I feel it to be a mistake—yes, it is an error for which I am sorry; I begin to fear it was designed only as a bold contrast. It is sad—very sad."

Mrs. Crawford was chilled. She had never seen Daireen look so lovely. She felt for more than a moment that she was all unmeet for a wife, so child-like she seemed. And now the terrible thought suggested itself to Mrs. Crawford: what if Mr. Glaston's opinion was, after all, fallible? might it be possible that his judgment could be in error? The very suggestion of such a thought sent a cold thrill of fear through her. No, no: she would not admit such a possibility.

The dinner was proceeded with, after the fashion of most dinners, in a highly satisfactory manner. The guests were arranged with discrimination in accordance with a programme of Mrs. Crawford's, and the conversation was unlimited.

Much to the dissatisfaction of The Macnamara the men went to the drawing-room before they had remained more than ten minutes over their claret. One of the young ladies of the colony had been induced to sing with the judge's son a certain duet called "La ci darem la mano;" and this was felt to be extremely agreeable by every one except the bishop's son. The bishop thanked the young lady very much, and then resumed his explanation to a group of his guests of the uses of some implements of war and agriculture brought from the tribes of the Salamander Archipelago.

Three of the pictures of Mr. Glaston's collection were hung in the room, the most important being that marvellous Aholibah: it was placed upon a small easel at the farthest end of the room, a lamp being at each side. A group had gathered round the picture, and Mr. Glaston with the utmost goodnature repeated the story of its creation. Daireen had glanced towards the picture, and again that little shudder came over her.

She was sitting in the centre of the room upon an ottoman beside Mrs. Crawford and Mr. Harwood. Standish was in a group at the lower end, while his father was demonstrating how infinitely superior were the weapons found in the bogs of Ireland to the Salamander specimens. The bishop moved gently over to Daireen and explained to her the pleasure it would be giving every one in the room if she would consent to sing something.

At once Daireen rose and went to the piano. A song came to her lips as she laid her hand upon the keys of the instrument, and her pure earnest voice sang the words that came back to her:—

From my life the light has waned:
Every golden gleam that shone
Through the dimness now has gone:
Of all joys has one remained?
Stays one gladness I have known?
Day is past; I stand, alone,
Here beneath these darkened skies,
Asking—"Doth a star arise?"

She ended with a passion that touched every one who heard her, and then there was a silence for some moments, before the door of the room was pushed open to the wall, and a voice said, "Bravo, my dear, bravo!" in no weak tones.

All eyes turned towards the door. Mr. Despard entered, wearing an ill-made dress-suit, with an enormous display of shirt-front, big studs, and a large rose in his button-hole.

"I stayed outside till the song was over," he said. "Bless your souls, I've got a feeling for music, and hang me if I've heard anything that could lick that tune." Then he nodded confidentially to the bishop. "What do you say, Bishop? What do you say, King? am I right or wrong? Why, we're all here— all of our set—the colonel too—how are you, Colonel?—and the editor— how we all do manage to meet somehow! Birds of a feather—you know. Make yourselves at home, don't mind me."

He walked slowly up the room smiling rather more broadly than the bishop was in the habit of doing, on all sides. He did not stop until he was opposite the picture of Aholibah on the easel. Here he did stop. He seemed to be even more appreciative of pictorial art than of musical. He bent forward, gazing into that picture, regardless of the embarrassing silence there was in the room while every one looked towards him. He could not see how all eyes were turned upon him, so absorbed had he become before that picture.

The bishop was now certainly not smiling. He walked slowly to the man's side.

"Sir," said the bishop, "you have chosen an inopportune time for a visit. I must beg of you to retire."

Then the man seemed to be recalled to consciousness. He glanced up from the picture and looked into the bishop's face. He pointed with one hand to the picture, and then threw himself back in a chair with a roar of laughter.

"By heavens, this is a bigger surprise than seeing Oswin himself," he cried. "Where is Oswin?—not here?—he should be here—he must see it."

It was Harwood's voice that said, "What do you mean?"

"Mean, Mr. Editor?" said Despard. "Mean? Haven't I told you what I mean? By heavens, I forgot that I was at the Cape—I thought I was still in Melbourne! Good, by Jingo, and all through looking at that bit of paint!"

"Explain yourself, sir?" said Harwood.

"Explain?" said the man. "That there explains itself. Look at that picture. The woman in that picture is Oswin Markham's wife, the Italian he brought to Australia, where he left her. That's plain enough. A deucedly fine woman she is, though they never did get on together. Hallo! What's the matter with Missy there? My God! she's going to faint."

But Daireen Gerald did not faint. Her father had his arm about her.

"Papa," she whispered faintly,—"Papa, take me home."

"My darling," said Colonel Gerald. "Do not look like that. For God's sake, Daireen, don't look like that." They were standing outside waiting for the carriage to come up; for Daireen had walked from the room without faltering.

"Do not mind me," she said. "I am strong—yes—very—very strong."

He lifted her into the carriage, and was at the point of entering himself, when the figure of Mrs. Crawford appeared among the palm plants.

"Good heavens, George! what is the meaning of this?" she said in a whisper.

"Go back!" cried Colonel Gerald sternly. "Go back! This is some more of your work. You shall never see my child again!"

He stepped into the carriage. The major's wife was left standing in the porch thunderstruck at such a reproach coming from the colonel. Was this the reward of her labour—to stand among the palms, listening to the passing away of the carriage wheels?

It was not until the Dutch cottage had been reached that Daireen, in the darkness of the room, laid her head upon her father's shoulder.

"Papa," she whispered again, "take me home—let us go home together."

"My darling, you are at home now."

"No, papa, I don't mean that; I mean home—I home—Glenmara."

"I will, Daireen: we shall go away from here. We shall be happy together in the old house."

"Yes," she said. "Happy—happy."

"What do you mean, sir?" said the *maître d'hôtel*, referring to a question put to him by Despard, who had been brought away from the bishop's house by Harwood in a diplomatically friendly manner. "What do you mean? Didn't Mr. Markham tell you he was going?"

"Going—where?" said Harwood.

"To Natal, sir? I felt sure that he had told you, though he didn't speak to us. Yes, he left in the steamer for Natal two hours ago."

"Squaring everything?" asked Despard.

"Sir!" said the *maître*; "Mr. Markham was a gentleman."

"It was half a sovereign he gave you then," remarked Despard. Then turning to Harwood, he said: "Well, Mr. Editor, this is the end of all, I fancy. We can't expect much after this. He's gone now, and I'm infernally sorry for him, for Oswin was a good sort. By heavens, didn't I burst in on the bishop's party like a greased shrapnel? I had taken a little better than a glass of brandy before I went there, so I was in good form. Yes, Paulina is the name of his wife. He had picked her up in Italy or thereabouts. That's what made his friends send him off to Australia. He was punished for his sins, for that woman made his life a hell to him. Now we'll take the tinsel off a bottle of Moët together."

"No," said Harwood; "not to-night."

He left the room and went upstairs, for now indeed this psychological analyst had an intricate problem to work out. It was a long time before he was able to sleep.

CHAPTER XLI

CONCLUSION

What is it you would see?
If aught of woe or wonder, cease your search.

And let me speak to the yet unknowing world
How these things came about: so shall you hear
Of accidental judgments...
purposes mistook.

... let this same be presently performed
... lest more mischance
On plots and errors happen. —*Hamlet.*

LITTLE more remains to be told to complete the story of the few months of the lives of the people whose names have appeared in these pages in illustration of how hardly things go right.

Upon that night, after the bishop's little dinnerparty, every one, except Mr. Despard, seemed to have a bitter consciousness of how terribly astray things had gone. It seemed hopeless to think that anything could possibly be made right again. If Mrs. Crawford had not been a pious woman and a Christian, she would have been inclined to say that the Fates, which had busied themselves with the disarrangement of her own carefully constructed plans, had become inebriated with their success and were wantoning in the confusion of the mortals who had been their playthings. Should any one have ventured to interpret her thoughts after this fashion, however, Mrs. Crawford would have been indignant and would have assured her accuser that her only thought was how hardly things go right. And perhaps, indeed, the sum of her thoughts could not have been expressed by words of fuller meaning.

She had been careful beyond all her previous carefulness that her plans for the future of Daireen Gerald should be arranged so as to insure their success; and yet, what was the result of days of thoughtfulness and unwearying toil, she asked herself as she was driving homeward under the heavy oak branches amongst which a million fire-flies were flitting. This feeling of defeat—nay, even of shame, for the words Colonel Gerald had spoken to her in his bitterness of spirit were still in her mind—was this the result of her care, her watchfulness, her skill of organisation? Truly Mrs. Crawford felt that she had reason for thinking herself ill-treated.

"Major," she said solemnly to the Army Boot Commissioner as he partook of some simple refreshment in the way of brandy and water before retiring for the night—"Major, listen to me while I tell you that I wash my hands clear of these people. Daireen Gerald has disappointed me; she has made a fool both of herself and of me; and George Gerald grossly insulted me."

"Did he really now?" said the major compassionately, as he added another thimbleful of the contents of the bottle to his tumbler. "Upon my soul it was too bad of George—a devilish deal too bad of him." Here the major emptied his tumbler. He was feeling bitterly the wrong done to his wife as he yawned and searched in the dimness for a cheroot.

"I wash my hands clear of them all," continued the lady. "The bishop is a poor thing to allow himself to be led by that son of his, and the son is a——"

"For God's sake take care, Kate; a bishop, you know, is not like the rest of the people."

"He is a weak thing, I say," continued Mrs. Crawford firmly. "And his son is—a—puppy. But I have done with them."

"And *for* them," said the major, striking a light.

Thus it was that Mrs. Crawford relieved her pent-up feelings as she went to her bed; but in spite of the disappointment Daireen had caused her, and the gross insult she had received from Daireen's father, before she went to sleep she had asked herself if it might not be well to forgive George Gerald and to beg of him to show some additional attention to Mr. Harwood, who was, all things considered, a most deserving man, besides being a distinguished person and a clever. Yes, she thought that this would be a prudent step for Colonel Gerald to take at once. If Daireen had made a mistake, it was sad, to be sure, but there was no reason why it might not be retrieved, Mrs. Crawford felt; and she fell asleep without any wrath in her heart against her old friend George Gerald.

And Arthur Harwood, as he stood in his room at the hotel and looked out to the water of Table Bay, had the truth very strongly forced upon him that things had gone far wrong indeed, and with a facility of error that was terrifying. He felt that he alone could fully appreciate how terribly astray everything had gone. He saw in a single glance all of the past; and his scrupulously just conscience did not fail to give him credit for having at least surmised something of the truth that had just been brought to light. From the first—even before he had seen the man—he had suspected Oswin Markham; and, subsequently, had he not perceived—or at any rate fancied that he perceived—something of the feeling that existed between Markham and Daireen?

His conscience gave him ample credit for his perception; but after all, this was an unsatisfactory set-off against the weight of his reflections on the subject of the general error of affairs that concerned him closely, not the least of which was the unreasonable conduct of the Zulu monarch who had rejected the British ultimatum, and who thus necessitated the presence of a special correspondent in his dominions. Harwood, seeing the position of everything at a glance, had come to the conclusion that it would be impossible for him, until some months had passed, to tell Daireen all that he believed was in his heart. He knew that she had loved that man whom she had saved from death, and who had rewarded her by behaving as a ruffian towards her; still Mr. Harwood, like Mrs. Crawford, felt that her mistake was not irretrievable. But if he himself were now compelled by the conduct of this wretched savage to leave Cape Town for an indefinite period, how should he have an opportunity of pointing out to Daireen the direction in which her happiness lay? Mr. Harwood was not generously disposed towards the Zulu monarch.

Upon descending to the coffee-room in the morning, he found Mr. Despard sitting somewhat moodily at the table. Harwood was beginning to think, now that Mr. Despard's mission in life had been performed, there could be no reason why his companionship should be sought. But Mr. Despard was not at all disposed to allow his rapidly conceived friendship for Harwood to be cut short.

"Hallo, Mr. Editor, you're down at last, are you?" he cried. "The colonel didn't go up to, your room, you bet, though he did to me—fine old boy is he, by my soul—plenty of good work in him yet."

"The colonel? Was Colonel Gerald here?" asked Harwood.

"He was, Mr. Editor; he was here just to see me, and have a friendly morning chat. We've taken to each other, has the colonel and me."

"He heard that Markham had gone? You told him, no doubt?"

"Mr. Editor, sir," said Despard, rising to his feet and keeping himself comparatively steady by grasping the edge of the table,—"Mr. Editor, there are things too sacred to be divulged even to the Press. There are feelings—

emotions—chords of the human heart—you know all that sort of thing—the bond of friendship between the colonel and me is something like that. What I told him will never be divulged while I'm sober. Oswin had his faults, no doubt, but for that matter I have mine. Which of us is perfect, Mr. Editor? Why, here's this innocent-looking lad that's coming to me with another bottle of old Irish, hang me if he isn't a walking receptacle of bribery and corruption! What, are you off?"

Mr. Harwood was off, nor did he think if necessary to go through the formality of shaking hands with the moraliser at the table.

It was on the day following that Mrs. Crawford called at Colonel Gerald's cottage at Mowbray. She gave a start when she saw that the little hall was blocked up with packing-cases. One of them was an old military camp-box, and upon the end of it was painted in dimly white letters the name "Lieutenant George Gerald." Seeing it now as she had often seen it in the days at the Indian station, the poor old campaigner sat down on a tin uniform-case and burst into tears.

"Kate, dear good Kate," said Colonel Gerald, laying his hand on her shoulder. "What is the matter, my dear girl?"

"Oh, George, George!" sobbed the lady, "look at that case there—look at it, and think of the words you spoke to me two nights ago. Oh, George, George!"

"God forgive me, Kate, I was unjust—ungenerous. Oh, Kate, you do not know how I had lost myself as the bitter truth was forced upon me. You have forgiven me long ago, have you not?"

"I have, George," she said, putting her hand in his. "God knows I have forgiven you. But what is the meaning of this? You are not going away, surely?"

"We leave by the mail to-morrow, Kate," said the colonel.

"Good gracious, is it so bad as that?" asked the lady, alarmed.

"Bad? there is nothing bad now, my dear. We only feel—Dolly and myself—that we must have a few months together amongst our native Irish mountains before we set out for the distant Castaways."

Mrs. Crawford looked into his face earnestly for some moments. "Poor darling little Dolly," she said in a voice full of compassion; "she has met with a great grief, but I pray that all may yet be well. I will not see her now, but I will say farewell to her aboard the steamer to-morrow. Give her my love, George. God knows how dear she is to me."

Colonel Gerald put his arms about his old friend and kissed her silently.

Upon the afternoon of the next day the crowd about the stern of the mail steamer which was at the point of leaving for England was very large. But it is only necessary to refer to a few of the groups on the deck. Colonel Gerald and his old friend Major Crawford were side by side, while Daireen and the major's wife were standing apart looking together up to the curved slopes of the tawny Lion's Head that half hid the dark, flat face of Table Mountain. Daireen was pale almost to whiteness, and as her considerate friend said some agreeable words to her she smiled faintly, but the observant Standish felt that her smile was not real, it was only a phantom of the smiles of the past which had lived upon her face. Standish was beside his father, who had been so fortunate as to obtain the attention of Mr. Harwood for the story of the wrongs he had suffered through the sale of his property in Ireland.

"What is there left for me in the counthry of my sires that bled?" he inquired with an emphasis that almost amounted to passion. "The sthrangers that have torn the land away from us thrample us into the dust. No, sir, I'll never return to be thrampled upon; I'll go with my son to the land of our exile—the distant Castaway isles, where the flag of freedom may yet burn as a beacon above the thunderclouds of our enemies. Return to the land that has been torn from us? Never."

Standish, who could have given a very good guess as to the number of The Macnamara's creditors awaiting his return with anxiety, if not impatience, moved away quickly, and Daireen noticed his action. She whispered a word to Mrs. Crawford, and in another instant she and Standish were together. She gave him her hand, and each looked into the other's face speechlessly for a few moments. On her face there was a faint tender smile, but his was full of passionate entreaty, the force of which made his eyes tremulous.

"Standish, dear old Standish," she said; "you alone seem good and noble and true. You will not forget all the happy days we have had together."

"Forget them?" said Standish. "Oh, Daireen, if you could but know all— if you could but know how I think of every day we have passed together. What else is there in the world worth thinking about? Oh, Daireen, you know that I have always thought of you only—that I will always think of you."

"Not yet, Standish," she whispered. "Do not say anything to me—no, nothing—yet. But you will write every week, and tell me how the Castaway people are getting on, until we come out to you at the islands."

"Daireen, do all the days we have passed together at home—on the lough—on the mountain, go for nothing?" he cried almost sadly. "Oh, my darling, surely we cannot part in this way. Your life is not wrecked."

"No, no, not wrecked," she said with a start, and he knew she was struggling to be strong.

"You will be happy, Daireen, you will indeed, after a while. And you will give me a word of hope now—one little word to make me happy."

She looked at him—tearfully—lovingly. "Dear Standish, I can only give you one word. Will it comfort you at all if I say *Hope*, Standish?"

"My darling, my love! I knew it would come right in the end. The world I knew could not be so utterly forsaken by God but that everything should come right."

"It is only one word I have given you," she said.

"But what a word, Daireen! oh, the dearest and best word I ever heard breathed. God bless you, darling! God bless you!"

He did not make any attempt to kiss her: he only held her white hand tightly for an instant and looked into her pure, loving eyes.

"Now, my boy, good-bye," said Colonel Gerald, laying his hand upon Standish's shoulder. "You will leave next week for the Castaways, and you will, I know, be careful to obey to the letter the directions of those in command until I come out to you. You must write a complete diary, as I told you—ah, there goes the gun! Daireen, here is Mr. Harwood waiting to shake hands with you."

Mr. Harwood's hand was soon in the girl's.

"Good-bye, Miss Gerald. I trust you will sometimes give me a thought," he said quietly.

"I shall never forget you, Mr. Harwood," she said as she returned his grasp.

In another instant, as it seemed to the group on the shore, the good steamer passing out of the bay had dwindled down to that white piece of linen which a little hand waved over the stern.

"Mr. Harwood," said Mrs. Crawford, as the special correspondent brought the major's wife to a wagonette,—"Mr. Harwood, I fear we have been terribly wrong. But indeed all the wrong was not mine. You, I know, will not blame me."

"I blame you, Mrs. Crawford? Do not think of such a thing," said Harwood. "No; no one is to blame. Fate was too much for both of us, Mrs. Crawford. But all is over now. All the past days with her near us are now no more than pleasant memories. I go round to Natal in two days, and then to my work in the camp."

"Oh, Mr. Harwood, what ruffians there are in this world!" said the lady just before they parted. Mr. Harwood smiled his acquiescence. His own experience in the world had led him to arrive unassisted at a similar conclusion.

Arthur Harwood kept his work and left by the steamer for Natal two days afterwards; and in the same steamer Mr. Despard took passage also, declaring his intention to enlist on the side of the Zulus. Upon reaching Algoa Bay, however, he went ashore and did not put in an appearance at the departure of the steamer from the port; so that Mr. Harwood was deprived of his companionship, which had hitherto been pretty close, but which promised to become even more so. As there was in the harbour a small vessel about to proceed to Australia, the anxiety of the special correspondent regarding the future of the man never reached a point of embarrassment.

The next week Standish Macnamara, accompanied by his father, left for the Castaway Islands, where he was to take up his position as secretary to the new governor of the sunny group. Standish was full of eagerness to begin his career of hard and noble work in the world. He felt that there would be a large field for the exercise of his abilities in the Castaways, and with the word that Daireen had given him living in his heart to inspire all his actions, he felt that there was nothing too hard for him to accomplish, even to compelling his father to return to Ireland before six months should have passed.

It was on a cool afternoon towards the end of this week, that Mrs. Crawford was walking under the trees in the gardens opposite Government House, when she heard a pleasant little musical laugh behind her, accompanied by the pat of dainty little high-heeled shoes.

"Dear, good Mrs. Crawford, why will you walk so terribly fast? It quite took away the breath of poor little me to follow you," came the voice of Lottie Vincent Mrs. Crawford turned, and as she was with a friend, she could not avoid allowing her stout hand to be touched by one of Lottie's ten-buttoned gloves. "Ah, you are surprised to see me," continued the young lady. "I am surprised myself to find myself here, but papa would not hear of my remaining at Natal when he went on to the frontier with the regiment, so I am staying with a friend in Cape Town. Algernon is here, but the dear boy is distressed by the number of people. Poor Algy is so sensitive."

"Poor who?" cried Mrs. Crawford.

"Oh, good gracious, what have I said?" exclaimed the artless little thing, blushing very prettily, and appearing as tremulous as a fluttered dove. "Ah, my dear Mrs. Crawford, I never thought of concealing it from you for a moment. I meant to tell you the first of any one in the world—I did indeed."

"To tell me what?" asked the major's wife sternly.

"Surely you know that the dear good bishop has given his consent to—to—do help me out of my difficulty of explaining, Mrs. Crawford."

"To your becoming the wife of his son?"

"I knew you would not ask me to say it all so terribly plainly," said Lottie. "Ah yes, dear Algy was too importunate for poor little me to resist; I pitied him and promised to become his for ever. We are devoted to each other, for there is no bond so fast as that of artistic sympathy, Mrs. Crawford. I meant to write and thank you for your dear good-natured influence, which, I know, brought about his proposal. It was all due, I frankly acknowledge, to your kindness in bringing us together upon the day of that delightful lunch we had at the grove of silver leaves. How can I ever thank you? But there is darling Algy looking quite bored. I must rush to him," she continued, as she saw Mrs. Crawford about to speak. Lottie did not think it prudent to run the risk of hearing Mrs. Crawford refer to certain little Indian affairs connected with Lottie's residence at that agreeable station on the Himalayas; so she kissed the tips of her gloves, and tripped away to where Mr. Algernon Glaston was sitting on one of the garden seats.

"She is a wicked girl," said Mrs. Crawford to her companion. "She has at last succeeded in finding some one foolish enough to be entrapped by her. Never mind, she has conquered—I admit that. Oh, this world, this world!"

And there can hardly be a doubt that Miss Lottie Vincent, all things considered, might be said to have conquered. She was engaged to marry Algernon Glaston, the son of the Bishop of the Calapash Islands and Metropolitan of the Salamander Group, and this to Lottie meant conquest.

Of Oswin Markham only a few words need be spoken to close this story, such as it is. Oswin Markham was once more seen by Harwood. Two months after the outbreak of the war the special correspondent, in the exercise of his duty, was one night riding by the Tugela, where a fierce engagement had taken place between the Zulus and the British troops. The dead, black and white, were lying together—assagai and rifle intermixed. Harwood looked at the white upturned faces of the dead men that the moonlight made more ghastly, and amongst those faces he saw the stern clear-cut features of Oswin Markham. He was in the uniform of a Natal volunteer. Harwood gave a start, but only one; he stood above the dead man for a long time, lost in his own thoughts. Then the pioneers, who were burying the dead, came up.

"Poor wretch, poor wretch!" he said slowly, standing there in the moonlight. "Poor wretch!... If she had never seen him... if... Poor child!"